A WONDERFUL TEACHER

Stephen gazed down at Jubilee with his soft brown eyes, making her feel as if she were wrapped in an invisible warmth. "You're a wonderful teacher," he said meaningfully, then paused, and the air verily throbbed between them. "Thank you for all you've done for my son," he said, his voice deepening to a husky murmur. His gentle tone made her tremble, and when he touched her and moved his fingers in tantalizing circles over her shoulders, her heart felt as if it might burst from her rib cage.

The dim light of a gas streetlamp trickled through a window at the end of the hall and rain dripped from the eaves, increasing the sense of intimacy between them. *Go to your room,* she told herself, trying to fight the ever growing attraction. *Don't be a fool; twist away; run upstairs!* her brain advised her.

But even then, she knew she couldn't.

"You're so beautiful," he whispered. The desire in Stephen's eyes shocked and excited Jubilee at the same time; she felt hot blood sting her cheeks. She could detect the musky scent of bay rum wafting from his silk robe, and her limbs took on a languorous heaviness, rooting her where she stood. The overpowering sensual feeling was stronger than anything she'd ever experienced—strong enough to block out the good raising Granny had put in her, strong enough to steal every drop of caution from her soul and fear from her heart. She wanted him so very much.

LEISURE BOOKS   NEW YORK CITY

Kelly, Song of the Lark *was written just for you.
And only you know the thousand and one reasons why.
I love you more than ever.*

A LEISURE BOOK®

June 1998

Published by

Dorchester Publishing Co., Inc.
276 Fifth Avenue
New York, NY 10001

If you purchased this book without a cover you should be aware that this book is stolen property. It was reported as "unsold and destroyed" to the publisher and neither the author nor the publisher has received any payment for this "stripped book."

Copyright © 1998 by Sonya Birmingham

All rights reserved. No part of this book may be reproduced or transmitted in any form or by any electronic or mechanical means, including photocopying, recording or by any information storage and retrieval system, without the written permission of the Publisher, except where permitted by law.

ISBN 0-8439-4393-9

The name "Leisure Books" and the stylized "L" with design are trademarks of Dorchester Publishing Co., Inc.

Printed in the United States of America.

ACKNOWLEDGMENTS

Kudos to the very talented Matilda the cat, who lives with Tom and Janine in Fort Worth and was the inspiration for the fictional Matilda.

A heartfelt thanks to the following people and organizations who in some way have brightened my life while I was writing this book:

Davonia Leach, Rhonda and Teresa Rutledge and Mauna Kea Hughes of Faye's Books, Friends of the Burleson Public Library, Kyle Coleman, Kathyn Kelley, Gean Keller from Waldenbooks in Cleburne, Texas, Babe Thompson, Alline Franklin, Angela Pearson, and the friendly staff of the Burleson, Texas, Post Office, who believe in giving service with a smile.

A special message for my readers: *Cherish all living things.*

Chapter One

Asheville, North Carolina—May, 1875

"Hillbilly. Hillbilly. Go back to the mountains, you ignorant hillbilly!"

Jubilee Jones heard the jeering boys running after her, then felt a clod smash against her back as she rode down Asheville's main street on her white mule, General Sherman.

She tugged down her floppy hat and, turning in the saddle, studied her tormenters, whose eyes danced with mockery. There had been an afternoon shower earlier, filling the air with the scent of rain dust and speckling the children's britches and hands with mud.

Her anger quickly changed into pity. Poor little boys. They'd never known the joy of picking tangy blackberries bursting with juice for breakfast, or thrilled to the sound of bright-eyed hounds baying at a treed coon. They were just pasty-faced town boys in store-bought clothes and stiff shoes, already so bored with life that they'd rather taunt an outsider than accept one.

school!''

Jubilee smiled, enjoying their verbal sparring. "Sitting in a schoolhouse won't make you smart any more than sitting in a chicken house will make you a chicken."

The other boys roared and made squawking chicken sounds. One of them pranced about flapping his arms and crowing. "She's got you there," he hooted, holding his stomach with laughter.

The red-headed boy pelted his friends with the dirt clods he was holding, and the noisy gang scattered like a sack of spilled marbles, running to hide behind the wagons and carriages that lined the wide, unpaved street. Jubilee turned and rode on, a slight breeze riffling through her long hair. Since sunup the day before, she'd come all the way from Maple Leaf Hollow—all the way past Lookout Rock and Miller's Gap, sleeping on the ground, and she wasn't going to let a few rowdy boys stop her now.

It mattered little that they thought her a curiosity, for Granny Whitlow was ailing badly. All that mattered now was getting a job so that her grandmother could afford to see Doc Hall, the local physician. Jubilee had no choice. She could see the old woman's life slipping away like a morning vapor, and without the dollars a town job provided, her grandmother would soon die.

Carriages rattled past Jubilee in both directions, their occupants surveying her with contempt. Ignoring their derisive smiles, she proceeded straight ahead, the soft clop

Song of the Lark

of General Sherman's hoofs adding a rhythmic counterpoint to the creak of the saddle leather. At last she found what she was looking for—two neatly printed words above an office saying SERVANTS' REGISTRY.

Never in all of her life had Jubilee intended to become a servant, but Ella Spencer had gone to Asheville last winter and returned to the hills with enough hard cash to pay off her family's debt. If Ella could earn money, Jubilee knew she could certainly do the same. Why, from the way the girl had talked, it seemed that every man, woman, and child in Asheville had pockets just bursting with greenbacks.

By the time Jubilee had dismounted and slapped her reins around a hitching post, a cluster of well-dressed women stood in front of the office, tilting their fashionably coiffed heads with interest. A haughty-looking blonde gazed at Jubilee's mountain garb with disgust. With a toss of her head, the girl raised her nose and spat out, "Mountain trash! Why don't you stay in the hills where you belong?" Before Jubilee could fire off a reply, the blonde whirled and hurried away, the other women giggling and following in the wake of her swaying bustle.

Town folk, Jubilee thought with exasperation. Sometimes they didn't have any more manners than a dog on Sunday, mouthing off as they did—but she wasn't going to waste a drop of energy worrying about it now. Her buckskin boots sounded softly on the planked sidewalk as she walked to the office window.

There, lettered in gold, the words MRS. HAZEL RIFKIN, AGENCY OWNER gleamed brightly. Jubilee paused, a wave of apprehension breaking over her. What if Mrs. Rifkin didn't like her loose, unbound hair or her homemade clothing? What if she didn't present herself properly, or the woman couldn't understand some of her mountain slang?

For the hundredth time, Jubilee wished she could have healed Granny Whitlow herself. Folks in the hollow said

Jubilee was the best weed doctor in the hills, but she'd already tried dosing the old lady with her great pharmacy of mountain herbs with no success. Thank goodness Cousin Effie had agreed to move into the cabin and care for Granny until other arrangements could be made. Otherwise Jubilee couldn't have borne the thought of leaving her, and even now Jubilee would count the days until she could return home.

Jubilee pulled up her courage. She'd just have to deal with Mrs. Rifkin and the rest of these ornery town folk too, for she needed a job and she needed one badly. She twisted the knob and strode into the sparsely furnished office, her heart skipping a beat.

Mrs. Rifkin, a thin, birdlike woman, looked up from the littered desk with a start. A severe, dark-colored dress with a white collar garbed her scrawny body, and in her hand she clutched a note written on elegant crested stationery. The woman brushed back a strand of limp gray hair that had slipped from the bun atop her head. "Yes? Is there some way I may help you?" she asked in a thin, reedy voice.

Jubilee confidently stepped forward. "I've come to get a job as a maid," she began forthrightly. "I talked to Ella Spencer and she said you had one."

Mrs. Rifkin peered over the top of her wire-rimmed spectacles, apparently disliking Jubilee's homespun shirt and buckskin britches.

Jubilee didn't care a whit, she told herself. Why, she'd woven the material for this shirt on Granny's old loom and tanned the deer hide for the britches, before cutting out and sewing both garments herself. She doubted the woman could say as much for her uncomfortable-looking outfit.

The agency owner's thin lips curved with amusement. "Well, yes, I found a job for Ella. She worked during the winter social season when all the prominent Asheville ladies entertain—but we have no positions now." She arched her sketchy brows. "You've come at the wrong time of year. Everything is filled."

Jubilee mulled over the woman's words and decided she was telling the truth. Ella had possessed no special skill except the willingness to do hard, grubby work and she'd been hired. Besides that, Mrs. Rifkin wouldn't pass up the chance for a commission if a maid's position was available. But maybe she had something else. Anything would do.

Jubilee put her hands on the desk and leaned forward. "You must have *some* kind of job," she prodded. "I know how to cook, and scrub, and tend sick folks. And I'm a good hand with children, too."

Still holding the note, Mrs. Rifkin stood, light glinting from the watch pin decorating her flat bodice. She stared at Jubilee thoughtfully for a moment, then sighed and tossed the note on the desk. "No, I'm afraid we have nothing."

Jubilee felt her confidence trickling away like water from a cracked jug. If her brother Micah had only been at home, he'd have scraped up the money for Granny's doctor. The Lord knew they owed the old lady. She had taken care of them both after their parents had died, but now that Micah had been crippled in a logging accident, he was working at a place halfway to Raleigh as a clerk. Surely she couldn't depend on him for more than the small stipend he already sent home each month.

Jubilee looked the woman in the eye, knowing she'd have to go elsewhere. "I see," she replied finally, raising her chin and walking to the door. She'd just have to keep looking, she decided with fresh determination. Maybe she could get a job in a hotel washing dishes, or doing mending for a dressmaker. Lordamercy, she just *had* to find work—and today if possible. It was that or spend twenty-five cents to sleep in the local wagon yard with a passel of drifters and drunks. Jubilee's hand was on the doorknob when Mrs. Rifkin called out, "Wait a moment, miss. Perhaps I do have something, after all."

Jubilee turned. Her pulse fluttered wildly. *"Yes?"*

The woman walked around the desk, her skirt rustling. "You said you had experience with children?" she queried, looking as if she were trying to make a painful decision.

"That's right. I love children. We get along just fine." Jubilee moistened her lips. "What type of position is this?" she asked, eagerly moving back into the office.

"This morning I received a request for someone to take care of a little boy of five," Mrs. Rifkin informed her. She picked up the note and glanced at it. "The woman who had the job walked out just as the father was preparing to leave for a trip. The situation is something of an emergency, I'm afraid. Something must be done today."

"What about the boy's mother?"

"He has none."

Jubilee felt a flash of pity for the child. Then as she noted the scribbled-on folders littering the desk, her heart pumped with unease. Apparently Mrs. Rifkin had been searching her files, frantically looking for someone to fill the position. What made this job so difficult that no woman in Asheville would accept it?

"You'd be a nanny," the agency owner continued in an agitated voice. "You would live at the child's home, take care of him, and entertain him—read him stories and things like that." Her face tightened with worry. "You *can* read, can't you?"

Jubilee stiffened at the question. "Like most mountain people I learned to read from the Bible," she replied in strong, measured tones. "My father taught me."

The woman nervously smoothed back her hair. "Very well. The position wouldn't consist of much—just playing with the child and keeping him company."

Jubilee pondered the woman's words, amazed the boy's father was so rich. In the mountains, children worked—

Song of the Lark

chopping wood, feeding animals, and whatever needed to be done. How wealthy this man must be, wanting to hire a person to simply play with his son!

Mrs. Rifkin sat down again. "All right, then," she announced, a feeble smile settling on her lips. "The job is yours—but only for a week. On a temporary basis. By then I should be able to find someone more suitable."

Hot blood stung Jubilee's cheek's. There it was again—that insensitivity to a person's feelings it seemed most town folk had. The woman's face tightened, and Jubilee suddenly understood she was being offered the job because the agency owner was absolutely desperate. No doubt she was afraid of angering her wealthy client. She had to send someone to fill the position today, and Jubilee was that *someone*—just a warm body, hardly better than no one at all.

Well, at least she wouldn't have to sleep at the wagon yard tonight. And a week's grace would give her time to look around for something permanent. "Who is this family anyway?" she asked, her mind returning to the motherless child.

The woman was scribbling a note, and she glanced up with a serious expression. "The boy is named Tad—Tad Wentworth."

Jubilee went weak all over. "Are you talking about the family who owns Wentworth Enterprises?" she asked, her strained voice breaking.

"Yes—the same." The woman ducked her head and her pen scratched over the paper. "You can see why I was quite concerned that the position be filled."

Shock pierced Jubilee's bosom, quick and neat as a dagger. The Wentworths were the richest family in the western part of the state and ruled the lives of the mountaineers with an iron hand. When he was alive, old Hamish Wentworth was infamous for his lack of concern for the men who worked in his logging camps. Because of the shoddy rigging he provided, Micah had tumbled from a treetop and had his leg crushed. Lordamercy, how could she work for a family like that? How could she work for a family whose name was a curse word to every hillman in the Smokies, especially her own brother? "Hamish Wentworth is dead," she rushed out, hoping against hope that the woman had confused the Wentworth name with another.

Mrs. Rifkin kept writing. "Yes, but his son Stephen now manages Wentworth Enterprises. The boy is his."

Jubilee's mind worked faster than ever. She vaguely recalled that Hamish had several sons, but their exalted existence was so removed from her own that she knew nothing about them. She sighed. Could Stephen Wentworth be any better than his father? After all, the apple never fell far from the tree. The possibility of working for such a man filled her with dread.

The agency owner shoved the note into an envelope, then looked up with keen eyes. "What's wrong, miss? You look quite pale. I thought you wanted a job."

A dozen troubling emotions swept through Jubilee. A strange feeling possessed her and left her numb. As the woman blathered on, she swallowed hard and tried to reply, but her voice had abandoned her.

Mrs. Rifkin rose again. "Didn't you hear a word I was saying?" she asked irritably. She rounded the desk and clasped Jubilee's arms, pressing her fingers into them. "Well, speak up, girl. I need to know your decision right now. Mr. Wentworth's train will be leaving very shortly. *Do you want the job or not*?"

Jubilee ran General Sherman's reins through the loop on the iron hitching post, then stared at the Wentworth mansion, stunned that such an edifice could even exist. "What a place," she whispered to herself, marveling at its massive size and towering chimneys.

She'd done it, of course. She'd accepted the job. But the Lord knew she'd rather be back in the mountains—

Song of the Lark

or even working in a boardinghouse, slaving over a hot stove—than standing before this gray stone palace. However, things being what they were, she simply had no other choice. It would only be for a week, she advised herself, trying to bolster her flagging courage. Surely she could last out seven measly days.

She dragged her gaze over the mansion. Mrs. Rifkin had told her the place was the only one of its kind on Mulberry Street, an English-styled beauty, and she was certainly right. Covered in climbing ivy, it boasted three stories with tall turrets and diamond-paned windows that shone in the late afternoon light like beaten gold. Encompassed by a velvety lawn, neat hedges and stately trees, it was situated well back from the street and surrounded by a filigreed iron fence. Yellow daffodils and orange day lilies bordered the mansion, and all about Jubilee the light air was alive with the sounds of sweet-voiced mockingbirds and raucous jays, bickering for possession of the large oaks all around.

She neared the high, ornamental gate flanked by two stone lions guarding the graveled driveway to the mansion. Unwelcome tension built steadily within her, and she felt as if she were dreaming instead of standing there with sunlight warming her back. In the hills, fruit trees were bursting forth with a wild glory and the call of the mourning dove signaled corn planting time—a yearly ritual she was well acquainted with. But here, the immaculate rose beds and the forbidding mansion that to her resembled an ogre's lair reminded her that she was totally out of her element.

She returned to her mule, took off her hat, and searched the rolled pack that was lashed to her saddle and held her belongings. She produced a comb and tugged it through her curly mane of reddish hair, wishing she had a damp cloth to wash her face and hands. "Well, General, wish me luck," she murmured, pulling on her hat, then smoothing her clothes the best she could.

SONYA BIRMINGHAM

She pushed open the creaking gate and forced herself up the driveway, her boots crunching over the white gravel. No doubt Stephen Wentworth would look like his stern father and be given to bellowing rages, but then she'd probably only have to meet him once, she thought, fighting back her growing nervousness. At the door, she gripped the big brass knocker and her stomach churned with apprehension. She rapped the knocker solidly on the metal plate. There were brisk footsteps, and the door opened silently on perfectly-oiled hinges.

A nattily dressed butler glared down at her, granite-hard lines etched on each side of his bitter mouth. He was half bald, had puffy jowls, and beneath the tight dark suit there must have been rolls of flesh. But his legs were rather slim and he reminded her of a huge bird with a puffed-out chest and spindly legs. He carried himself like a prince—no, more like a king, she thought, trembling under his scorching appraisal.

"Didn't you see the sign?" he snapped, nodding at a brass plaque beside the door. A refined accent colored his clipped words. "No solicitors are allowed on the premises!"

Faced with such ferocity, Jubilee could scarcely speak. "I-I'm not a solicitor," she squeaked, guessing that the word was a fancy term for peddler.

"Well, who are you then," the man asked harshly.

"My name is Jubilee Jones," she managed, wondering what an Englishman was doing in Asheville. She added some strength to her quavering voice. "I'm here from the Servants' Registry."

The butler's eyes flashed imperiously and he began to shut the door.

"*No,*" Jubilee cried, her courage rushing back as she saw her chance for a job evaporating. "Mr. Wentworth wants a woman to take care of his son."

The butler paused and measured her with icy contempt. "I don't believe you're what he had in mind."

Song of the Lark

"But I am. The agency sent me." Jubilee vowed. She pulled Mrs. Rifkin's letter from her bosom and handed it to the stony-faced man.

"There must be some mistake," he growled, shoving it back at her. "Go away. I can assure you, Mr. Wentworth would never employ a woman who wears britches and boots."

"I have dresses in my pack," Jubilee declared, bravely inching forward. "But riding down from the hills on a mule"—she tilted her head in the direction of her mount—"and sleeping on the ground, I thought britches would be better."

The butler squinted at General Sherman, then swung an incredulous gaze over her. "Indeed, I'm sure they would. *Now, go away.*"

He started closing the door again and in her panic she clutched its edge. "Please . . . let me see Mr. Wentworth," she insisted in a louder voice. *"I want to see him."*

"No, he's a busy man!"

Jubilee clung tenaciously to the door, refusing to give up her one and only chance for a job.

Footsteps sounded beyond the door, and then a deep resonant voice boomed out, "What's going on, Chambers? What's all the commotion about?"

Suddenly there was no more resistance on the door, and Jubilee released it and moved back. In muffled tones, she heard the butler saying, "There's a mountain girl here claiming to be from the Servants' Registry, sir. I'm certain it's some mistake."

"It's no mistake. I sent a maid to the office with a note," the low, velvet-edged voice replied. A conversation followed, of which Jubilee could hear little except the butler punctuating it with phrases like, *"not suitable at all,"* *"white mule,"* and *"britches and boots."* "Sir, surely you cannot—" he began to add in disdain.

"That will be all," the voice cut him off with the ring of finality. "I want to talk to her."

Once again steps clicked over marble, and a great tide of relief surged through Jubilee. But as she realized that Stephen Wentworth himself would soon open the door, her heart jolted. She mentally braced herself, for she expected to see a younger likeness of Hamish, who had been noted for his wild white hair, stormy eyes, and fierce countenance.

When the door drew open, her breath caught in her throat. There before her stood the most breathtakingly handsome man she'd ever seen. Lordamercy, what a magnificent devil he was, she thought, quickly deciding that Stephen Wentworth must resemble his mother's side of the family.

Apparently in his thirties, he had an aristocratic nose and full mouth, and an abundance of crisp, wavy hair that glowed blue-black in the light. Laugh lines fanned from his strikingly gorgeous brown eyes. When those bold, wide-set eyes locked with hers, a delicious thrill ran through her, delighting and surprising her.

With a will of its own, her gaze traveled down Stephen Wentworth's tall body. His elegantly tailored garments complemented his muscular frame and bespoke wealth: an expensive tie set off his deep tan, a starched white shirt and a fine blue suit encased his torso, and sleekly cut trousers clung to his powerful legs. And he smelled so wonderful, she decided, picking up the fresh, clean scents of shaving soap and spicy bay rum as he stepped nearer.

His confident gaze played over her face in speculation. "And who might you be?" he inquired, the rich timbre of his voice raising a stream of goose pimples over her arms.

"I-I'm Jubilee—Jubilee Jones," she stammered, feeling her throat tighten with nervousness. She pulled the letter from her shirt and meekly offered it to him, praying

Song of the Lark

he wouldn't notice how rattled she was. "The agency sent me."

He slid an assessing gaze over her curves, making her blush hotly. And when he smiled beguilingly, showing animal-white teeth, what was left of her composure melted right there on the doorstep, leading her to think she might never speak again.

"Won't you come in?" he asked, standing back and ushering her into a grand foyer.

Jubilee gingerly stepped into the mansion. Here everything was luxury. There was a brass-trimmed chest, flanked with intricately carved chairs whose ball-and-claw feet made her blink in surprise. A huge mirror with a thick gold frame hung, on the wall above chest-level, and flashed back her disheveled appearance. A chandelier sparkled overhead, and a tall grandfather clock with a face illustrated with the four seasons towered in a corner.

She held her fragile composure in check as her prospective employer closed the door and began reading the letter she'd given him. Would he approve of her, or send her away in embarrassment—without the job she needed so badly?

Over the sound of her own thumping heart, she heard the noise of shuffling feet. Seconds later, a small, pale boy, all thin arms and legs, timidly edged into the foyer. Tad. This must be Tad, she thought, observing that he wore short pants and a silken shirt with a round collar. If she'd harbored any lingering doubts about working for the Wentworths, they vanished now, for, judging from the child's large, frightened eyes and tentative manner, he clearly needed a friend. Regardless of his last name. Forgetting that her own future hung in the balance, she immediately knelt, smiled, and extended her hand to him.

The boy ducked his curly head, then glanced up, meeting her gaze with soft brown eyes filled with pain.

How shy and delicate he was! she thought with sad wonder. Why, he reminded her of a timid fawn. "You're

Tad, aren't you?" she inquired in a friendly tone.

He stared at her and blinked thoughtfully.

She scanned him with bewilderment. Why didn't he reply? she wondered, determined to draw him out. "I'm Jubilee," she stated cheerfully. "I rode all the way from Maple Leaf Hollow on a mule. Have you ever seen a mule?"

He lowered his lids, displaying dark, heavy lashes. Slowly he glanced up, and the silence between them stretched to the breaking point.

Jubilee refused to give up. "Mrs. Rifkin said you're five years old. That's pretty old. Do you have any pets? Maybe a cat or a dog?"

Once again, Tad simply stared at her. His small lips quivered a bit.

Jubilee couldn't deny the evidence any longer. She was forced to admit that the child didn't speak at all, and the admission touched her profoundly. She instinctively looked at his father, and their gazes locked in mutual agreement that there was something amiss with the boy, not only physically but on a deeper level.

Lordamercy, she'd never imagined that the child might be mute. Completely baffled, she looked into the depths of Stephen Wentworth's glittering eyes, trying to puzzle out why his son didn't respond to her. Was the boy born this way or had some terrible event robbed him of his speech? What in God's name had happened to him? What had crushed his childish exuberance so totally?

Painful emotion centered in her bosom like a cold stone.

Chapter Two

Stephen read a host of unanswered questions in Jubilee's lovely green eyes and realized they all concerned Tad. He'd often seen that look of curiosity mingled with pity on the faces of his friends who had tried to communicate with the boy, but never had he noticed such an expression of gentle kindness. An inner voice told him he should explain everything to the stunned girl, but being so hard pressed for time, he simply said, "He doesn't speak."

Jubilee glanced at him in astonishment, then returned her attention to Tad. Stephen smiled inwardly when she palmed a nickel, then pulled it from the boy's right ear, making his mouth fall open in surprise.

"I'm magic," she murmured in a soft, lilting drawl. The boy's eyes widened when she palmed another coin, then placed both hands on his head and gently shook it. "I'll bet there's lots of change in your head. Let's see." She repeated the trick, pulling a dime from his left ear.

Stephen put away the letter as Jubilee stood. The willowy girl was garbed in boots, snug-fitting britches, and a soft, homespun shirt whose loose weave revealed the luscious swell of her bountiful breasts. Under a battered hat, the curliest auburn hair he'd ever seen brushed her finely sculpted cheeks and fell over her shapely shoulders. Her large, expressive emerald eyes danced with the fire of life itself, and her complexion was pure porcelain brushed with rosy highlights. But what was that around her neck? The homemade jewelry looked like nothing but dozens and dozens of mismatched buttons strung on a cord.

Lord, how like Hazel Rifkin to send an untrained mountain girl here with no regard for her feelings, just so she wouldn't miss her commission. It was too bad, he thought with regret, that the girl was so unsuitable and would have to be sent away. The least he could do was exchange a few pleasantries with her before he broke the bad news. "Where did you learn to palm coins?" he inquired, amused by her nimble dexterity.

Jubilee grinned, showing a flash of pearly teeth. "Well, my pa taught me. My twin brother Micah and I worked in his medicine show." Doffing her cap, she tossed back her cloud of glossy hair. "During the war, Pa soldiered with a corporal who'd once had a little medicine show and learned some magic tricks from him. When Pa came home, he started his own show and taught me how to palm coins and such," she went on, a touch of laughter in her voice. "The whole family used to make the rounds of the mountain villages selling his remedy."

Her face softened with memories. "Micah would play his fiddle and I'd do magic to bring the folks in. Then Pa would jump up on a stump and start sermonizing about the remedy. That's Pa's mule, General Sherman, tied out there at the hitching post." She laughed a little. "That old mule pulled that wagon all over the Smokies. We sold a heap of the remedy and had lots of fun"—her eyes took on a sad look—"then Pa up and died with pleurisy and that was the end of the medicine show."

Amazed, Stephen listened to her rattle on, wondering

Song of the Lark

what she would say next. He hadn't asked for her life story, but she was so animated he found himself caught up in what she was telling him. Yes, she was filled with life—such life when this house had seen so much sorrow lately.

She sighed deeply. "Mama died eighteen months after Pa, and Micah and me started living with Granny Whitlow when we were twelve. Gradually folks began coming to the cabin to get the remedy, and I started picking other herbs they might need." She fluttered her lashes, pausing thoughtfully. "That's how I got into herb doctoring, which is my true profession, although I still hold bed-cord strong to all things magical."

She paused to draw in a breath of air. "This winter Granny got sick and I couldn't cure her, so I had to come to Asheville so I could get a job, so she could see a regular town doctor." She blushed and gave him a half-smile. "And here I be, looking at you right now!" she finished, stepping back in embarrassment. "You talk now, I can't think of a thing to say."

Stephen felt his mouth quirk upward. Amazed with her story, he studied her open face, realizing there was something very decent and honorable about her despite her lack of education. What a blow it would be to her to be sent away without a job when she needed one so badly. After all, it wasn't her fault that Hazel had ignored her obvious unsuitability—but all that aside, could he trust her to keep his son company even for a few days?

She knelt by Tad again, and swiftly manipulating her slender fingers, gave the illusion of stretching her thumb, then let it snap back into place.

To Stephen's astonishment, Tad giggled, an action that pierced his heart to its core. Lord, how wonderful it was to hear that sound after months of nothing but silence from the boy.

Jubilee repeated the trick, and Tad actually laughed this time.

SONYA BIRMINGHAM

That does it, Stephen thought emphatically. This magical mountain herb doctor was going to stay the week, along with her white mule and button necklace. Estell would have a fit because the girl was so lovely, but he didn't give a damn. Just because he'd escorted the blonde to a few social functions—simply so that all of Asheville's giggling debutantes wouldn't pester him—didn't give her the right to dominate his life.

This mountain girl's courage and brave spirit were obvious, and her concern for Tad shone from her face like a light. After all, she'd only be a companion for the boy, someone to cheer him up, and Chambers could handle any real emergency. Perhaps by the time he returned from Knoxville, Hazel Rifkin would have come up with a real nanny.

Stephen helped Jubilee to her feet, feeling her silky hand tremble in his. "All right," he laughed, "you're hired to look after Tad while I'm gone." He noticed her eyes glisten with joy. "The pay is twenty dollars. Is that suitable?"

"Y-yes, that's fine," she stammered, her stunned face revealing that she was totally overcome with the sum.

Outside there was the sound of carriage wheels grinding sharply on the gravel, and a driver calling to his horses. Time to go, Stephen thought dully, dreading the vitally important business trip that was forcing him to leave Tad.

Jubilee stared at her new employer, surprised by the sweet fire that had raced up her arm when he'd taken her hand. She'd been so nervous answering his questions that she'd feared she'd blurted out far too much. The fact that she'd been hired in spite of her mistake made her feel as if a tightly coiled spring had been released somewhere deep within her. She experienced a sense of sublime happiness and felt like laughing and crying with relief at the same time.

Stephen walked to the rear of the foyer, and only then did she notice a fine hat resting on a mahogany console.

Lordamercy, he'd be gone soon, and she knew virtually nothing about the boy, she suddenly realized with a sense of panic.

"What does Tad like to eat . . . and what time does he go to bed?" she inquired, watching Stephen pick up the hat. She moved toward him, desperately wishing he had more time. "I have so many questions, I—"

"Chambers can help you with all your questions, and Delilah, too," he answered, his handsome face turning somber once more as he checked his pocket watch and put it away. "She comes at five to cook dinner, just like she has for years." He paced to the door and glanced over his broad shoulder, pain gathering in his eyes. "She knows all about Tad."

As if by magic, Chambers appeared carrying a piece of fine luggage, bearing the brass initials S. W. Obviously he'd been standing right outside the foyer, listening to everything that had been said.

The butler cleared his throat and inclined his bald head. "Your suitcase, sir," he intoned soberly.

"Yes, put it in the carriage, will you?" Stephen turned, hesitated for a moment, then fired a firm gaze at him, adding, "Carry on as usual while I'm gone. And see that Miss Jones is taken care of."

Chambers, his disapproval apparent, nodded stiffly, then opened the great door and walked toward the waiting carriage with the luggage.

Stephen knelt by Tad and hugged him close. "Miss Jubilee will be with you while I'm gone, and Chambers and Delilah, too," he explained to the boy, whose eyes welled with tears. Tad clung to him, but Stephen rose and, scanning Jubilee, sighed deeply. "I'm sorry. I really must go now," he told her, reluctance clouding his sad expression. With that, he left the mansion, leaving the door half open in his haste. As he walked toward a smart brougham with yellow wheels, he glanced over his shoulder at her in farewell and pasted a smile on his face. "Good-bye, Curly Top, and good luck."

The nickname he'd given Jubilee fell from his mouth like a smooth caress and made her feel warm and flustered inside. Alerted by the boy's sniffles, she sank to the floor and held him close as his father ducked into the waiting carriage. Once inside, he slammed the door, the driver snapped his reins, and the conveyance rattled away, passing the stone lions and turning onto the main street.

Tears trickled from Tad's eyes and Jubilee put her arms about his frail body, thinking that he was light as a little bird. "Hush now, baby, your daddy will be back soon," she advised in a consoling tone.

Chambers returned to the mansion and firmly closed the door. His eyes chips of cold blue ice, he stared at her as if she were a small animal beneath his notice. "The servants' quarters are in the attic. You will sleep there. Tad can show you to your room." He sniffed loftily. "You may put your mule"—he mouthed the word with distaste—"in the stables for the short time you'll be here." With regal silence, he pivoted and walked away, his heels tapping over the marble.

Jubilee released a deep breath, hoping Delilah, whoever she was, would be more friendly than Chambers. Deeply shaken, she stared into Tad's moist eyes. When she'd awakened this morning to the pleasant trill of birdsong, never in her wildest dreams had she thought that she'd be working in the Wentworth mansion. And never had she expected she'd be looking after the grandson of the man who, when all was said and done, was responsible for her brother's crippling accident.

She gnawed her bottom lip in thought. Surely she couldn't tell her family she was working for a Wentworth. She'd have to invent a fictional employer to write home about. She hated the deception, but the shocking truth might break Granny's already fragile heart.

She ran her fingers through the child's soft brown hair

Song of the Lark

and considered both him and his father. Stephen Wentworth looked so sad that she ached for him. It seemed that all his riches and handsome looks couldn't make up for a son who didn't speak. Gradually her pity turned to steely determination. She yearned desperately to break the chains about the child's heart—but the question was how. Yes, how in God's name could she reach the pale, silent boy?

After she and Tad had returned from the stables, Jubilee entered her room, where fresh air, redolent with the scent of green vegetation, flowed through an open dormer window. She dropped her pack of belongings on the floor and surveyed the snug little chamber, delighted with what she saw. "Oh my, Tad, this is nice!" she exclaimed with a rising sense of pleasure.

A plaited rug covered the polished floor, and beside a single bed, a nightstand supported a washbowl and a pitcher of water. A wardrobe stood in the corner, and on the other side of the bed, a table held a lamp whose beautiful globe was decorated with swirls of painted roses.

Imagine that! Jubilee thought with awe, tracing her fingers over the smooth globe—she'd have a real lamp to read by instead of a smoky kerosene lantern. No doubt Granny and Effie would be looking for a letter at Maple Leaf Hollow's tiny post office, and she could now report that she had work and a pretty room with a real china lamp. More important, by the end of the week, she'd be able to send them twenty dollars, a sizable sum in the mountains.

"I'm going to like sleeping here," she said to the boy, noticing how proud he was to be showing her the small room. A semblance of a smile rippled across his lips, and then he sprawled on the bed to show her the mattress was soft. Laughing, she went to him and tousled his hair. "Yes, this is going to be just fine." By now, she had realized that he was quite intelligent and understood everything she said, even though he had never yet said a word to her. "Now where do you sleep?" she inquired, sinking down beside him.

He scooted from the bed and motioned for her to follow.

She trailed him down the carpeted stairs to the second floor, wondering why her predecessor had left. Just because the child was mute was no reason to abandon him—no reason at all, she thought with growing indignation. She watched him turn right at the landing, pause to catch her eye, then walk into his room.

Jubilee cautiously entered, blinking in surprise. How could this grand chamber possibly be a little boy's room, she wondered, seeing dark furniture, a marble fireplace, and a huge canopied bed with a plumed crest. Such an enormous bed for such a little boy, she thought, imagining him propped against the silken pillows heaped at the base of the tall, elaborately carved headboard. "This room is beautiful, Tad, but it's *so big*. I can hardly believe you sleep here all by yourself."

He stood at the head of his bed, pale against the red velvet hangings. A small, lonely figure, he nodded soberly, indicating that he did.

She walked over the thick Oriental carpet, noting that despite the room's magnificence, it possessed a cold, intimidating look, more suited to a grown man than a young child. Surely this stiff, formal chamber wasn't appropriate for a five-year-old boy.

Then she told herself the Wentworths were so far above her, she could never begin to understand them. Still—where were the jars of captured bugs, and broken pocketknives and balls of twine and other clutter that all boys loved so much? Already she was beginning to see that Tad lived a much different life than most children his age.

"Let's go downstairs," she suggested, putting her hand on his back and moving to the door. "Will you show me the parlor?"

Song of the Lark

Quiet as a kitten on satin, he was off again, scooting down another flight of stairs.

On the steps, she met Chambers and a maid and nodded pleasantly, hoping to talk a bit, but they totally ignored her and proceeded up stairs, discussing some household business.

Jubilee's spirits plunged and she trailed her hand over the smooth, polished banister, deciding it was going to be a long week indeed. Once again the question resounded in her brain: Why couldn't Tad speak? Would she ever meet someone who would answer her questions about him?

Frail and small, he stood before the open parlor doors, a patient expression on his face.

Jubilee stepped into the sumptuous, high-ceilinged room and paused to catch her breath. Never in all of her nineteen years had she seen anything like this. The huge chamber smelled of freshly cut roses and with its petit point settees piled with frilly pillows, exquisite sideboards, and ornate mirrors, it completely overwhelmed her.

She strolled about, noticing that the creamy walls glowed with light and the mahogany furniture gleamed red, while the parquet surrounding the Oriental carpet glistened like glass. One side of the parlor was all windows, and with the heavy, moss green velvet drapes pulled back, sunbeams streamed through the sparkling panes and made bright spots on the floor. Crystal chandeliers shimmered at either end of the room, and there were immense portraits on the walls: one of old Hamish, glowering through his spectacles, one of Stephen and a young man, and one of a lovely lady with raven black hair.

Taken with the woman's striking beauty, she edged forward and studied the painted figure with awe. Dressed in a blue velvet riding habit with a froth of lace at her gently curved bosom, the lady looked over her left shoulder, a soft smile on her full pink lips. Mounds of shiny ringlets tumbled down her back and escaped from the jaunty plumed hat that crowned her head. Her cheekbones were high and noble, her complexion creamy white, and her almond eyes large and dark brown. The delicate lady seemed so fragile and ethereal, it was hard for Jubilee to believe the artist hadn't invented her, but as she gazed at Tad's face and saw a likeness, she realized the woman must be his mother.

Noting the emotion shining in his eyes, she knelt and put her arm about him. "Is this pretty lady your mother?"

The boy nodded sadly.

She scanned the portrait again, her mind swirling with questions about the exquisite creature—then she told herself she was being foolish. After all, she was here as a servant, and only for a few days at that. She was here to help Tad, not pry into the Wentworths' business.

Wanting to divert the boy from his melancholy, she rose and suggested they look at the rest of the room. At the end of the parlor two closed doors drew her attention and made her wonder what was behind them. She twisted the doors' levered handles, and to her alarm, Tad started to cry. With a panicked expression, he frantically yanked on her hands and tried to pull her away. She immediately stooped and held him in her arms until he stopped crying. "That's all right, baby. Don't worry. I won't open the doors."

Why was he so agitated? Even now she could feel his little heart thumping crazily against her breast. She brushed away the last of his tears and kissed the top of his head. Why did he want to move her away from the locked doors? she wondered, brimming with curiosity. What was in the closed chamber that disturbed him so violently?

She gave a seep sigh, then patted Tad's back. She was beginning to realize the mansion harbored many secrets,

Song of the Lark

and somehow she sensed they all concerned the tragedy that must have befallen this poor child.

Half an hour later, when Jubilee and Tad returned from a walk about the grounds, she heard the sounds of rattling pots and pans coming from the back of the mansion. Catching the scent of frying chicken, she realized someone was in the kitchen.

Tad's eyes brightened like a flash of sunlight, and he ran in that direction. *Good*, she thought, her own spirits rising. She'd finally get to meet Delilah. The boy, only a few steps ahead of her now, burst into the kitchen, which was filled with the comforting sounds of boiling water and crackling oil. He wrapped his arms around the legs of an immensely heavy black woman.

In her fifties, the woman had a snowy kerchief wound about her head and tied at the side, and gold hoops gleamed in her pierced ears. A clean but tattered calico dress clung to her ample body and a long white apron covered her large belly, which shook with laughter as she bent to hug the boy. "Lawsy, honey chile, you knows Delilah is gonna be here to cook your supper, don't you?" she asked, lovingly caressing Tad's face with her large, work-worn hand.

The boy kissed her cheek, then slipped away to idly trace his fingers over a table, which was dusted with flour and stacked with bowls.

The cook straightened up somewhat stiffly, her dark eyes glistening expectantly. "You must be Miz Jubilee," she said in a welcoming voice. "Chambers done told me you came today." Her tone was low and tender, her words filled with liquid vowels and soft, slurring inflections.

Jubilee was struck by the responsive warmth in her smile and the spontaneity in her broad face. "That's right . . . I am," she returned, liking the woman immediately.

The cook picked up a turning fork and indicated a table that held a tub of half-peeled potatoes and was surrounded by four cane-bottomed chairs. "Sit down and talk while I's cookin', chile. Let's visit a little." Her dark brows raised inquiringly. "Chambers say you be from the mountains."

"Yes, I just came down to get a job," Jubilee answered, moving to a basin and washing her hands. As she dried them, she noticed that the tidy room boasted countless cupboards, all gleaming white, and rows of shelves lined with canned fruit. Cheerful print curtains hung from windows facing the backyard. She pulled out a chair and, making herself comfortable, sat down to help Delilah peel potatoes, keeping an eye on Tad as she worked.

She and Delilah talked up a storm, and the kitchen floorboards groaned under the cook's weight as she dredged more chicken pieces in flour and dropped them into the bubbling skillet. There was a pause in the conversation, and without thinking Jubilee blurted out, "Lordamercy, who are you cooking all that chicken for?"

Delilah gave a crack of rich laughter that warmed Jubilee's heart. "Why, I's cookin' it for you and Tad." She stirred boiling carrots, rapping a large metal spoon on the edge of the pot. "Mist' Stephen have me cook for Tad whether he be here or not. He's always hopin' the boy will eat, and he tell me, "Delilah, you fix a bunch of what he like best.' " Then if Tad don't eat it, he tells me to take it." She shook her head in dismay. "Ninety-five percent of the time I carries most of it home with me." She shot Jubilee a conspiratorial look. "Sometimes I think Mist' Stephen havin' me cook for my own young'uns. That be just like him. He be a heap different than his daddy, you knows."

Jubilee recalled all the stories she'd heard about Hamish Wentworth's miserliness, then remembered the twenty dollars Stephen had agreed to pay her. Evidently, as she'd just been told, he *was* completely different from his father. She wondered why.

She realized that Delilah was good-natured and kind,

Song of the Lark

the direct opposite of Chambers, and for the first time since she'd arrived in Asheville she felt at ease. "Has Chambers been here long?" she ventured, realizing that if he'd had his way, she'd never have been hired.

Delilah rolled her eyes. "*Um-huum*. It be old Mist' Hamish that brung him here," she snorted. "He wrote one of them fancy agencies back east. He tells me he was gonna have a English butler to go with his English mansion." She beetled her brow in derision. "Well, he got him, and all his grouchy ways too!"

She took the bowl of potatoes from Jubilee's hands. "You sees, Mr. Hamish was all concerned what folks was gonna think about him," she muttered darkly. With a lumbering tread, she returned to the stove and poured the vegetables into simmering water. "He just knowed if he had the onliest English butler in the whole state of North Carolina he'd sure 'nuff impress everybody." She turned and nodded knowingly. "Mist' Stephen don't like Chambers much, but I reckon he let him stay for old times' sake."

"You must have worked for the Wentworths *forever*," Jubilee remarked, sensing that Delilah wouldn't mind the observation.

"Honey chile," she answered with a deep laugh, "I's been workin' for them since Mist' Stephen was just a tadpole. After Mist' Brandon born—that be Mist' Stephen's brother—Miz Wentworth just up and die on us. Mist' Hamish tells me, 'Delilah, you come here ever evenin' and cook for me and my boys'. And that what I's been doin'." She fixed a worried gaze on Jubilee. "I's got five young'uns and I's got to work all I can."

"Your husband must have passed away, then."

Delilah tilted her head in agreement. "Yes'um. He be killed workin' on the railroad right after my littlest one be born. Rosetta works for some white folks cleanin' house, and Leroy works in Mist' Stephen's lumber yard—but the rest of them be too little to earn money." She

35

shook her finger like she meant business. "I makes 'em go to school, 'cause I's raised in slave days when they weren't no school for black folks!"

She transferred her gaze to the screen door where a welcome draft wafted into the kitchen. "Cleo, you got them beans snapped?"

Seconds later a small black child entered the room carrying a bowl of green beans. His hair was cropped short and a plaid shirt and a pair of clean overalls clothed his slim body. Long curly lashes fringed his large eyes, and when he grinned his even teeth flashed white. With his smooth, chocolate brown skin and bright countenance, Jubilee thought she'd never seen such a sweet, appealing child in all her life.

"This be my littlest one," Delilah announced, motherly pride shining on her face. "I usually brings him to work with me. This be Miz Jubilee, Cleo. Say howdy."

A smile crinkled the corners of the boy's laughing eyes. "Howdy, ma'am."

Tad shyly glanced up from tracing patterns on the floury table top.

"Take Tad on outside and play with him some, so's us can talk," Delilah ordered her son. "He don't hardly get no fresh air a'tall."

Cleo placed the bowl on the table and widened his eyes at Tad. "*Come on*. Let's play hard. I's done snapped a jillion of them green beans!"

After the screen door had slammed behind the pair, Jubilee pulled the green beans toward her and began snapping them herself.

Delilah turned the browning chicken, then threw a relieved glance over her rounded shoulder. "Lawsy, I's sure 'nuff glad you's here. Sometimes I gets powerful worried 'bout that poor chile. He get awful lonesome when his daddy be gone, and lately he be gone a lot."

Jubilee felt there was a hidden meaning behind Delilah's words, but she couldn't decide what it might be.

Song of the Lark

Nevertheless, she sensed the moment was ripe to ask a question about Tad and she slowly pushed her bowl aside. "Has the boy never been able to talk?" she questioned softly, noticing a surprised frown flash over the cook's face.

"*Lawsy, no*. Till a while back he always talk up a blue streak. It was somethin' he saw that took his words away!"

Jubilee's heart turned over in her bosom, and she dreaded what she expected to hear next. "That's his mother in the portrait in the parlor, isn't it?" she ventured apprehensively.

"That's Miz Isabelle, all right." Sadness welled in Delilah's large, liquid eyes. "She be about the prettiest lady that ever walked the earth, and she be good too. That woman be plumb distracted about horses, and Mist' Stephen done bought her three of them. The last one be all hot-blooded and kind of wild, but Miz Isabelle say she'd take him in hand."

She drew in a ragged breath and forked the last of the chicken onto a serving plate. " 'Bout a year ago she took him to a path that go through the woods at the edge of town—and Tad be with her. Mist' Stephen buy him a little pony and his mama be teachin' him to ride."

She placed the skillet aside, then studied Jubilee with glassy eyes. "A rabbit done run in front of Miz Isabelle's new horse and spooked it. It throwed her off and broke her neck like a dry stick," she explained, her face a welter of emotion. She swallowed a sob, and Jubilee impulsively stood, wanting to comfort her, but not knowing exactly what to do.

Gradually, the cook managed to speak again. "That poor chile saw it all. Somebody finally come along and found them. Tad be holdin' his mama in his arms, cryin' and his face be white as paper. Startin' then and there, he done quit talkin' and almost quit eatin' too." A shiny tear raced down her full cheek. "He eat so little, I don't know how he keep on livin'. Mist' Stephen done carried him to a passel of doctors, but none of 'em ever done nothin' to help him."

With an inward shudder, Jubilee went to Delilah and, encircling her girth, caressed her back. "That's horrible," she whispered, searching for other words of comfort, but not finding any. "I-I don't know what to say."

The cook pulled a handkerchief from her apron pocket and dabbed at her eyes. "You don't have to say nothin', honey. I's gonna be all right," she muttered, her voice weak and breathy. "Sometimes I just gets all stirred up thinkin' 'bout it." She managed a tremulous smile and treaded across the kitchen, returning to her work.

Jubilee quietly observed her for a while to see if she'd recovered. She wanted to ask about the locked doors off of the parlor, but knowing it was the worst possible time to do so, she walked to the window, her bosom tight with suffocating emotion.

With a trembling hand, she pulled back the curtains, and as the horizon's red glow faded to pink behind the trees, she watched Cleo toss a ball, playing with a small dog while Tad stood by, strangely detached from the scene. A chill raced down her arms. No wonder the child wouldn't speak. He'd seen his mother killed before his very eyes.

She studied him in the twilight, considering how fragile he looked compared to Cleo, who brimmed with life and vitality. A shadowy dimness had settled over the yard, and like a silent little ghost, Tad moved about on thin legs, tagging behind the barking dog, now a soft blur in the dusk light.

The black child put the ball in Tad's hands and showed him how to throw it. Tad made a feeble attempt, then seemingly losing interest, ambled back to the mansion's high back steps and plopped down, his hollow eyes following the other boy.

Jubilee's heart nearly burst with compassion for Tad,

Song of the Lark

and she wanted to help him like she'd never wanted to help anyone in her life. But was there anything she could do to touch his broken spirit in such a short time? Then she recalled the way he'd responded to her magic tricks, and a germ of an idea blossomed in her mind.

Yes, that's it, she thought, turning about with a smile and crossing her arms—a magic garden might be just what he needed.

Chapter Three

Two days later, Stephen Wentworth sat on a hard bench in the lobby of a Knoxville bank, waiting for an appointment with one of its officers. The place was sparsely furnished and decorated with marble walls and floors, palms, and brass fittings about the tellers' cages. Its cold, impersonal ambience went hand in hand with Stephen's gloomy mood, for he was a man in serious trouble. He pulled a list from his pocket and ticked off the name of yet another financial institution. This afternoon he would be going to the State Bank, and the day after that to the Union Bank, and so on until he'd visited all the banks in Knoxville.

"Damn Brandon," he muttered under his breath, remembering the fierce look in his brother's eyes the last time he'd seen him. If it wasn't for his prodigal sibling he wouldn't be involved in this humiliating business in the first place. Then he told himself that after all was said and done, family was family and the most important thing in the world. He steeled his resolve, knowing he had to do everything possible to preserve the Wentworth empire. Neatly folding the paper, he put it back into his vest

Song of the Lark

pocket and felt responsibility settle onto his shoulders like a heavy cloak. His father's honor, his own honor, and Tad's future all rested on this trip and its outcome.

Stephen's mind drifted to Tad as it did dozens of times each day. He was a sweet child with a life-altering problem. After Isabelle had been killed, he'd taken him to several specialists, who all said the same thing: *There is nothing we can do for your son*. It was a classic case of hysterical trauma, they said ominously. *The boy might never speak again*. Refusing to give up, he'd worked daily with the child, trying to coax him to speak—but to no avail. To Stephen, the child's silence was the ultimate misfortune bequeathed to him by the bushwhacking hand of fate.

He considered the lovely girl who was looking after Tad. She claimed to be magic, and in the boy's case she was. He'd never seen him take to someone so quickly, or a stranger be so relaxed with the child. In all fairness to Hazel Rifkin, she'd sent a score of nannies to the mansion and they'd all walked out, including the last one, who'd said she simply couldn't stand the boy's silence a moment longer.

It surprised him somewhat that he'd left his son in the care of a mountain woman such as Jubilee but he'd liked her demeanor—and there was something about her angelic face that touched a part of him that had lain dormant for far too long. What wonderful eyes she had. Clear and green as a mountain pool, they were eyes a man could drown in if he looked at them too long.

The sound of a clanging grate being opened steered his attention to the present. A little man with a visor and a long green apron spun a clicking dial on a huge safe, and from the tellers' cages came the sound of coins spilling into cash boxes. Several people entered the bank, moved to the tellers' cages, and opened their wallets and purses. The day's business had begun.

A portly, distinguished-looking man emerged from a

private office with gold lettering on the door identifying him as the bank president. A young sandy-headed assistant whom Stephen had met the day before to set up the appointment accompanied him. The older man wore a starched white shirt with a high collar and an expensive brown suit which encased his well-padded body like a thick sausage skin. He took out a gold watch whose chain bisected his paunchy stomach, checked it, then nodded at his assistant.

Carrying a sheaf of folders under his arm, the young man approached Stephen with a professional smile, the warmest thing he'd encountered in the chilly, colorless bank this morning. "You may come in now," the assistant advised in polite, businesslike tones.

Stephen rose and strode over the cold marble, knowing what he had to do, but disliking it all the same.

The fleshy banker's eyes glinted with interest, and giving Stephen a smile, he thrust out his hand. "Hello, Mr. Wentworth. I understand you came all the way from Asheville. What may I do for you?"

Lord, Stephen thought, forcing down his rising emotions, if the man only knew.

Jubilee's big skirt pockets bulged with seed packets she'd bought in town that morning. They made a rattling sound as she picked up a hoe and started breaking up the earth and making trenches in the richly scented sod. As she worked she glanced at Tad, who sat on an apple crate near the freshly turned earth. He scanned the prospective garden with interest, and for the first time that afternoon, his eyes flickered with a bit of life.

Cleo tugged on her sleeve. "You sure this gonna be a real magic garden, Miz Jubilee?" he asked, his face splitting into a wide grin. "I ain't ever heard of nothin' like that before."

"Well, that doesn't mean we can't plant one," she answered, cupping his small face in her hand. "Magic is the

Song of the Lark

oldest thing on the earth and sometimes it's the most real, too." She pushed a tendril of hair from her damp face. "You can get a hoe and help me."

It was a gorgeous day, the fruit trees thick with blossoms and the air drenched with fragrance. She worked silently, listening to the twittering birds. Only now did she consider that Stephen Wentworth might not want a humble vegetable garden behind his great mansion, but she had a suspicion that he'd approve, if it helped Tad.

Noticing the boy slowly rise, she motioned him to her. After he'd timidly approached, she put the packets into his small hands. "Here," she suggested, "why don't you decide what we'll plant in each row?"

With a bright face, he shuffled through the colorful packets as if she'd given him a great treasure. A little breeze ruffling his hair, he stooped to place packets at the head of each row, selecting lettuce for the first, onions for the next, and finishing with spinach and okra.

For a good fifteen minutes there was the rhythmic sound of three chopping hoes scraping against small stones. Jubilee knew she'd be gone when the garden produced, but surely Delilah would help the boys tend the little plot. Tad needed someting to lure him into the fresh air, to make him believe life was worth living again.

Like a sweet scrap of music, Stephen's face kept returning to Jubilee's mind. How she'd love to entice the boy to speak before his father returned, she thought, bending to rip a stubborn weed from the ground. The idea twined itself about her heart. How wonderful it would be to know she'd given Stephen such a priceless gift.

After they'd finished the planting, Jubilee announced, "I have some magic growing powder I'll sprinkle on the seeds." She dipped into her pocket and produced a little vial of potassium nitrate, purchased at a local hardware store.

"Sure 'nuff?" Cleo chirped, his eyes becoming larger

than ever. "Lawsy, just wait till I tells Mama 'bout this. She's gonna think I's gone slap crazy."

Jubilee, crawling around on her hands and knees, lightly shook white powder over the seeds while the boys fell to the sod and trailed after her.

"I don't see anythin' happenin' yet," Cleo remarked. "Sure you ain't got some bad powder or somethin'? You see anythin'?" he added, gazing at Tad, who looked closely and shook his head.

"Oh, it takes about ten days to work," Jubilee casually explained, raising herself to a kneeling position. She surveyed the boys, whose faces were alight with curiosity. "If we come out here then, the vegetables will be poking their little green heads out of the ground, thick as fleas on a dog's back."

A faint smile rippled over Tad's lips and she knew her special brand of magic was, in fact, working right now. What did it matter that she'd called the chemical the clerk had recommended magic growing powder? Fertilizer could be just fertilizer or a magic powder—which was a lot more interesting any way you looked at it.

Jubilee let the boys use the rest of the chemical, then the trio dug their hands into the velvety earth and raked it over the seeds. "You boys remember to always stay right with the moon," she advised in a serious tone. "Plant everything that grows above ground during the increase of the moon, and everything that yields below ground during the moon's waning."

"Yes'm," Cleo piped up, "us will always stay right with that old moon!"

Jubilee rose and gave a start, for Chambers stood at the edge of the garden, his face lined with contempt. "Stay right with the moon?" he echoed with a fierce glower. "Why, I never heard such nonsense."

Splat! A handful of moist earth hit the butler's white starched shirt.

Jubilee gasped, and the boys, who were enthusiastically

covering up the last of the seeds, gazed up in alarm.

Chambers growled and brushed at his shirt, making the stain worse. "You've ruined my shirt!" he thundered at the frightened children.

Jubilee rushed to him and tried to brush the soil from his black suit. "I'm sorry, it was an accident, you see, and—"

"Oh, leave me alone," he stormed, knocking her hand away. "My clothes are a mess now." He drew his brows together in a ferocious scowl. "Be sure that Mr. Wentworth will hear of this. I'm going to report you as soon as he returns!"

Jubilee heard the back door slam and spotted Delilah on the high back steps, her face like a thundercloud. The cook descended the stairs and waddled toward them, her fists on her hips. If Jubilee wasn't mistaken, Chambers paled a shade lighter.

Delilah closed in and shook a finger in his face. "Don't you be interferin' with Miz Jubilee now. This be her business, not yours!"

The butler stiffened his back importantly. "Mr. Wentworth put *me* in charge while he was gone," he informed her in a haughty tone.

Delilah wagged her head. "Well, just 'cause you's got wings don't mean you can fly. Ever body know you's dead and just too dumb to fall over." She gave a deep laugh. " 'Sides that, with them little spindly legs, you's got to lean agin the fence just to gobble!"

The boys burst out giggling.

Delilah jabbed her finger at the mansion. "Now git on in the house and leave Miz Jubilee and them babies alone!"

Not waiting for a second helping of invective, the mortified butler stalked toward the mansion on his birdlike legs while the children smothered their laughter. Stunned, Jubilee gazed at the cook with admiration, not knowing how to thank her. Before she could compose a sentence,

Cleo ran to his mother, his eyes glistening like sun-dappled water.

"Mama, us just planted a garden and used magic growin' powder," he cried excitedly, throwing out his arms as he talked. "In about ten days them vegetables will start shootin' their little green heads out of the ground, just like that!" He snapped his fingers.

"Sure 'nuff?" Delilah laughed. "I sure wants to see them vegetables poppin' their heads up."

Still talking, the group walked toward the mansion, each carrying or dragging a shovel or a hoe. Tad couldn't express his thoughts like his friend, but Jubilee clasped his hand, noticing a new strength in his fingers that she hadn't felt before. He was so close to speaking, she thought, her heart aching for the event to actually happen. As excited as Cleo, he tugged on Delilah's long apron, then pointed back at the small garden. A thought sprang to his eyes, and for a moment it seemed he might speak, but then he hung his head.

Never mind, Jubilee promised herself, affectionately caressing the back of his neck—if she had anything to do with it, he would speak one day. Heaving a sigh, she realized he just needed some special event to penetrate the fear that had paralyzed his emotions for so long.

As soon as the boys had scrambled up the steps and entered the mansion, Delilah looked at Jubilee and laughed heartily. "I declare, chile," she exclaimed, scanning her with twinkling eyes, "*plantin' a magic garden. You's sure somethin' else!*"

A few days later Jubilee walked through the foyer and noticed that the doors at the end of the parlor stood slightly ajar. Her common sense advised her to proceed to Tad's room where he was resting, but with a prickle of excitement, she paced over the soft carpet and peeked inside the secret room. From the chamber's immaculate appearance and the lingering scent of lemon oil, she sur-

Song of the Lark

mised the maids must have been cleaning and forgotten to lock the doors after they'd finished.

Tall arched windows draped with the same moss green velvet as those in the parlor graced the half-moon-shaped room. A tall golden harp towered in the corner, and floor-to-ceiling shelves contained row upon row of colorfully bound books. There were white brocade chaises, rose velvet chairs, and a magnificent chandelier that hung over the largest piano Jubilee had ever seen. Why, this forbidden place that made Tad so nervous was only a music room, she realized with surprise. Why should this place affect him so strongly, and why had it been locked like some dungeon when it was so light and lovely?

Gingerly she approached the piano, wondering if Stephen played it. A bouquet of artificial flowers had been placed atop the gleaming instrument, and with golden light streaming through the tall windows, the blooms gave the room the feeling of a well-tended shrine.

The magnificent piano's keys were of pure mother of pearl, and in elegant gold script above them were the words STEINWAY AND SONS—NEW YORK CITY. *"New York City,"* Jubilee whispered with awe. The thought of the metropolis conjured up exotic images of tall buildings and beautiful shops. How wealthy the Wentworths were, she thought yet again, realizing how expensive it must have been to ship the beautiful instrument all the way from the East Coast.

Scarcely knowing what she was doing, she sank to the plush-covered bench, decorated with fringe. She noticed a piece of sheet music—"The Camptown Races" lay on the ornate rest above the shimmering keys. She couldn't read music, but she'd heard her brother play the piece many times on his fiddle, and lightly ran her fingers over the keys, thrilled by the Steinway's wonderful sound. After stumbling a bit, she was able to pick out something that resembled the tune she was trying to play. Soon a halting melody filled the air and floated into the parlor.

When she'd gone through the chorus three times, she heard soft footsteps and glanced up to see Tad walk into the room. He stood stock still, and astonishment touched his pale face. She thought he was only surprised she could play and continued plunking out the lively tune. Step by step, he neared the piano, his body trembling.

Alarmed, she stopped playing and, putting out her arms, pulled him to her. He wiggled away and, to her utter surprise, took her hands and replaced them on the keys, then nodded his head. She realized he wanted her to continue, so she did, seeing tears spill down his cheeks with every note. Lordamercy, what had she done? she wondered, thinking the boy was a constantly changing mystery. No doubt she'd touched something deep within him, but what consequences would her impulsive action bring?

The boy rubbed the piano's side with his small hand and, shaking with excitement, dragged his stunned gaze over to Jubilee. His eyes were full of pain and longing, but in their depths she noted a spark of unquenchable life. "M-Mama's p-piano," he stuttered, his childish voice breaking with emotion.

But her amazement was short-lived as Chambers strode into the music room, his thin mouth set in anger. "What do you think you're doing playing Miss Isabelle's piano! No one has touched it since the day she left us. Mr. Wentworth locked up this room in her memory."

Jubilee suddenly realized that she'd trespassed upon holy ground, and instantly took her fingers from the keys, feeling a hot surge of embarrassment.

Delilah entered the room, wiping her hands on a dish towel. Her dark eyes sparkled with awe. "Lawsy, what's goin' on in here?" she asked, approaching the instrument as if it were a religious relic. "You playin' Miz Isabelle's piano?"

"That's right," Jubilee piped up. "And Tad's talking. Listen to him."

Tad gazed at Jubilee and whispered, "Y-you played

Song of the Lark

Mama's piano.'' His lips quivered uncontrollably.

Happiness glowed through Jubilee like a scarlet sunrise. That special event she'd been yearning for had just happened, but in a very unexpected way. Her eyes flooded with tears and she swept him into her arms and held him tight. Never had she felt so alive, so blissfully happy and buoyant. "Yes, I played your mama's piano," she murmured, her words quavering with tender feeling.

She noticed that Chambers was still glowering at her, but decided to ignore him. She glanced back at Tad and flicked away his tears. "Do you want me to play some more?"

A luminous smile broke over his face, and he nodded with joy.

So excited that she could scarcely move her fingers, Jubilee continued picking out the song, profoundly grateful that she'd stumbled upon a way to reach the boy's heart. *Thank you, God,* she continuously repeated in her mind, a chant of thanksgiving.

"Mama's piano," Tad kept saying, looking both stunned and delighted that he could utter the words.

Delilah knelt and hugged him close. "Praise be, this baby done talked," she proclaimed throatily. Tears rolled unchecked down her face.

Chambers walked closer. Jubilee spied his lips trembling, but he quickly camouflaged his tender emotions with a frown. The butler regarded Tad quizzically. "Can you say anything else?" he inquired, his voice clipped and precise as always.

The boy pursed his lips. "I-I don't know," he stammered haltingly.

Everyone laughed, and grasping Tad under his arms, Jubilee rose and swung him around in a circle.

Delilah picked up the hem of her apron and wiped at her damp eyes. "Lord have mercy, Miz Jubilee, you done somethin' all them fancy doctors couldn't. Mist' Stephen will be so proud, he'll bust the buttons right off his jacket.''

Cleo walked into the room, holding a bowl of potatoes that he was peeling. "What's ya'll doin'? Somebody playin' Miz Isabelle's piano?"

His mother waved her large hand. "Hush, chile. Tad talked some!"

Cleo approached the boy with wondering eyes. "Talk some for me, boy. I wants to see if you can."

Tad blinked and pointed at the piano. "T-that's Mama's piano," he stuttered, squinting his eyes together with the effort.

Cleo laughed and danced around the room, spilling potatoes from his bowl.

"Watch what you's doin,' boy!" Delilah scolded.

Chambers gingerly picked up a potato and stared at it as if he'd never seen one before.

Cleo, the bowl of potatoes in the crook of his arm, grabbed Tad's hand and began larking around the room while Jubilee rushed back to the piano and awkwardly banged out the same tune until her fingers were stiff. Tad clasped Delilah's hand, and the trio pranced and laughed without restraint.

Chambers cleared his throat awkwardly. "Yes, no doubt Mr. Wentworth will be quite pleased with the young master's progress," he called loudly over the merrymaking, obviously distressed that he'd totally lost control of the situation. Looking as out of place as an undertaker at a square dance, he started meandering about the music room picking up the spilled potatoes.

Jubilee stopped playing and, provoked by a wild impulse she didn't understand, ran to Chambers and impulsively kissed him on the cheek, making him blush fiercely. "Yes, Chambers, isn't it wonderful?" she cried. "We're all quite pleased!"

Stephen closed the front door behind him, his heart beating faster. He'd only left a week ago, and now as he

Song of the Lark

stood in the foyer of his mansion, his hat in hand, he found the unbelievable had happened. Anger coursed through him like sheet lightning. Someone was playing the piano—Isabelle's piano!

A feeling of violation rose within him, fury that anyone would enter the room he'd personally locked the day his wife had been killed. Wordlessly, he tossed his hat on the console and strode through the parlor to the music room, his heart now at full gallop. Through the closed music room doors he heard someone trying to pick out a tune and the sound of Tad's laughter. Blood pounding in his temples, he opened the panels and fixed his gaze on his son, who ran to him with open arms.

"Papa, Papa!" the boy cried, his face aglow with gladness.

Stephen's anger transformed into surprise, and he knelt and swept the child against him, his chest tightening. "Thank God," he whispered against the boy's soft hair, as some of the anguish he'd carried for so long drained from his tense body.

He let his eyes drink in the magnificent sight of Jubilee, feeling a bubbly pleasure race through his veins. She rose from the piano bench, a mixture of delight and embarrassment wreathing her exquisite features. A simple homemade gown of rust-colored cotton clad her lithe body, and her loose auburn hair gleamed with copper highlights in the light that streamed through the windows. Flushed with excitement, her face looked especially young and fresh.

"I'm sorry ... I didn't know you would be returning so early in the afternoon," she murmured, nervously smoothing down her skirt. "I shouldn't have been in the room." She ran a noticeably shaky hand through her hair. "I-I didn't mean ..." she stammered, her apologetic words finally wobbling to a halt.

Stephen hoisted Tad in his arms and carried him across the sunny chamber. Near the piano, he placed the boy on his feet and ruffled his hair, feeling a warm glow steal though him that the seemingly impossible event of Tad uttering even one word had taken place.

Glorying in the magnificent moment, he studied Jubilee's pleased face. "He can speak," he announced, treasuring the first scrap of hope he'd experienced since Isabelle's death. He brimmed with satisfaction and noted that Jubilee's sparkling eyes reflected his own pride.

She smiled tenderly. "Yes. He has only said a few words, but it's a fine start," she answered, going on to describe what had happened at that very spot earlier in the week.

As her story rolled out, Stephen realized that the sound of Isabelle's piano had cut through the despair that had ensnared his son's mind. Why hadn't he thought of the instrument before, he wondered with nagging regret. He'd just been so hurt, he couldn't bear the thought of anyone touching the piano, so he'd closed the room, just as he'd closed his heart so it would never be broken again.

Jubilee glanced down in chagrin. "I'm sorry I ventured into this room in the first place," she apologized. "Chambers told me why . . . why it was locked. I didn't mean to be snooping. I—"

"*No,*" Stephen interrupted, raising her chin. He clasped her small hand in his. "I'm very glad you did." Their gazes locked, and as he studied her delicately curved face, a shudder of desire passed through him, stirring powerful, half-buried emotions. She colored prettily, and sensing her unease, he nodded at the piano bench. "Will you play something now?"

Stephen's husky voice set off a swirl of excitement in Jubilee's stomach. The touch of his hand rushed shivers up her arm, and she slipped it away with a hidden sigh of relief. "Yes, if you want, but I only play by ear," she answered, all weak and tingly inside.

She sat down, then patted the bench and signaled Tad to join her. When he was beside her, she took a deep

Song of the Lark

breath, and feeling as if her fingers would scarcely move, tried to pick out "The Camptown Races."

Stephen was standing so close behind her that she could feel his body warmth, and when he casually put his hand on her arm, her heart fluttered. A dizzying current raced up her shoulder from the pressure of his hand, and she fought the surge of poignant feelings his closeness aroused.

She made several mistakes and started again. She'd been at sixes and sevens all day, for she knew he was scheduled to return this afternoon. She could scarcely wait to see his face, and when she had, an unexpected tenderness had flooded through her. At the same time, she knew her time here was over. But it was all to be expected, she told herself philosophically, knowing that she'd only been promised one week's work.

After she'd stumbled through the tune, Stephen walked around the great instrument and, bracing his hands on it, gave her a smile of thanks that sent her pulses racing. Tad looked at his father and, fingering the piano keys, muttered, "M-Mama played that song."

Stephen came to his son's side and, squatting down, ran loving eyes over him. Jubilee noticed he seemed to be fighting back his emotions. "It's his favorite song," he explained, tracing his fingers over the boy's cheek. "Isabelle used to play it for him almost every day."

Muscles rippled under his finely tailored jacket as he helped the boy from the bench and embraced him. "Lord, if I had only known all that was in his mind," he said, letting out a long, audible breath. His dark eyes flooded over Jubilee. "Thank you for what you've done," he offered, his tone husky with gratitude.

She laughed gently. "Tad really did it on his own," she returned, embarrassed by the intimacy of the moment. She'd become quite attached to the boy, and sadness pierced her heart as she realized that in a day or so she'd never see him again. "I was just playing and he started talking."

"But you managed to reach him, something no one else has been able to do," Stephen answered, holding the child at arm's length.

"Yes . . . I did," she allowed, thinking Tad had shown his first interest in what was going on around him the day they'd planted the garden. Oh, what she'd give to stay. She had so many plans for that magic garden!

Several awkward coughs were heard from the area just outside the music room doors, and she saw Chambers usher in a large middle-aged woman wearing a plain felt hat pinned up at the back. Spectacles perched on the woman's long, thin nose, and silver streaked her tightly bound hair.

"This is Mrs. Henderson," the butler explained, respectfully bowing his head at Stephen. "She has recently arrived from Raleigh." He began to walk away, but paused at the threshold and added meaningfully, "She was sent here by Mrs. Rifkin to fill the nanny's position."

Jubilee's heart plummeted like a wounded bird. Her replacement wore a modest brown linsey dress, sensible shoes, and carried a large leather purse. One could tell she'd groomed herself with great care for this important interview, and as she stepped forward to shake hands with Stephen, she projected an aura of mature dignity.

The woman sent Tad a cold, brittle smile, then returned her attention to his father. She snapped open her purse and pulled out several stiff envelopes. "Here are several letters of reference," she intoned with an officious air. She raised her chin to a proud angle. "I think you will find my credentials in perfect order."

Stephen scanned the letters while Tad climbed back on the piano bench and scooted to Jubilee's side. She put her arm about him and noticed he was trembling.

Mrs. Henderson ran her sharp eyes over the room, then settled her gaze on Jubilee; glancing at the door, she si-

Song of the Lark

lently requested her to leave. A protective instinct flared within the girl, and she hugged Tad closer, refusing to abandon her charge to a woman he obviously disliked. When she held her ground, Mrs. Henderson looked haughtily away, signaling her displeasure.

Stephen returned the letters to their envelopes and handed them back to the woman, a frown creasing his brow.

"The lady at the registry informed me I was to start in the morning," she spoke up confidently. "If it's all the same to you, sir, I'll move in tonight and get settled."

His skeptical gaze drifted over her. "Your credentials are in order, but I'm afraid there has been a terrible mistake."

The woman paled. "Mistake?" she echoed in a choked voice. "What do you mean? Why, I was told—"

"I'm sorry if Mrs. Rifkin led you to believe you had employment here," he answered firmly, "but Miss Jones is working out quite well, and I'm afraid there is no position for you."

The woman glared at Jubilee. "Why, she's just a girl! And from what I've been told—"

"Yes, yes," Stephen briskly interrupted her. He pulled a bill from his pocket and put it in her hand. "I'm sure your driver is still waiting. This will more than pay for your fare."

Mrs. Henderson's eyes blazed fire. "Well, I never. To put a little nobody like her over me!"

Stephen took the woman's arm and ushered her to the music room doors, where she shoved the letters into her purse and allowed Chambers to lead her away.

Jubilee experienced a sweet rush of pleasure. Only a few minutes ago she'd thought her time at the mansion was nearly over, and now with breathtaking swiftness, she'd discovered she had a position—at least for the time being.

Tad didn't say a word, but his bright eyes and soft

smile spoke for him. She hugged him tightly, then watched him scamper past his father and leave the room, obviously bound for Delilah's kitchen.

An amused grin hung on the corner of Stephen's lips as his tall figure headed toward her. After the news she'd just heard, a warm tide of emotion overcame her, leaving her almost speechless. She rose at his approach, and when he folded his hand over her elbow, shivery pleasure trickled down her spine. He stood so close she could see the golden flecks in his pupils and noticed a happy smile playing at the corner of his mouth. "You sent her away," she whispered, a sudden shyness overcoming her.

"Yes, I have a feeling she was capable, but I need someone who is more than simply capable for Tad." His eyes held a dreamy look and he radiated an allure she almost found irresistible. "I need someone who the boy responds to. In that respect, I feel your credentials far outweigh hers."

A lock of raven hair draped appealingly over his forehead, and as she stared at his bronzed features, crinkles splayed from the corners of his eyes. He clutched both of her arms and ran his fingers up them, sending sizzling sparks over her skin. "As you say, Tad has made a fine start—but he has far to go. He's talking a bit, but before school starts he must be able to speak easily, and he must lose his shyness around people." He raised his dark brows. "That's where you come in, Curly Top."

He'd used that nickname again, and she felt herself blush to the roots of her hair. "But I have no special talent. I—"

"Don't underestimate yourself," he quickly interrupted. "You've managed to reach him and he obviously likes you." He paused meaningfully. "At this point, you can help him more than anyone else."

Jubilee's heart softened. "I'll do the best I can."

"Good. That's all I expect of you." A slow smile

Song of the Lark

curved his mouth upward. "You *will* stay the summer, won't you?"

His deep-timbred voice held a tinge of sensuality, and Jubilee found his nearness so arousing that a tormenting sexual hunger she'd never experienced before uncoiled within her. She reminded herself she wasn't acquainted with city customs, and once again told herself that the folks in Maple Leaf Hollow would be horrified to know she was working for a Wentworth.

On the other hand, with his mellow baritone echoing in her ears and his spellbinding eyes so near, there was only one way she could answer.

"Yes, of course, I'll stay," she murmured, her heart beating crazily.

Chapter Four

Three days later, Stephen looked up from paying bills as Jubilee entered his book-lined study. An oversized skirt and blouse, dyed muted hues of brown and lavender, hung on her slender frame. Her face held a shy, expectant expression, and she looked for all the world like an orphan.

"Chambers said you wanted me," she began, her eyes harboring a flicker of apprehension.

Stephen picked up an envelope from his cluttered desk. "That's right," he answered, handing it to her. "Here's your pay for last week and an advance on your wages for next month. I believe you wanted to send it back to the mountains."

Jubilee blushed, then gave it right back to him. "But I haven't earned all of this yet."

He rose and walked around his huge desk, a mahogany beauty which had been in his family for generations. "No, but you will." He forced the envelope into her hand, then turned his back and paced so she could put it away without further embarrassment. He turned and she stood there silently, her creamy complexion and shining hair painting a vivid picture against the dark paneling.

Song of the Lark

"If that's all," she said, nervously, "I'll be off now."

Stephen sat down on the corner of his desk. All morning his mind had been filled with Jubilee's strange mountain ways; some of them were charming, but others he simply didn't understand. "There's another matter," he announced not unkindly, but in a tone that brooked no reproach. "Tad said you were giving him *imagination lessons*."

"That's right," she answered with an open smile. "I just told him he could use his mind to be anywhere he wanted." A pleased expression claimed her face. "He thought he'd like to be in the mountains, so we imagined smelling the pines, and hearing the birds, and feeling the breeze."

"Yes, very nice, but he needs facts, not imagination lessons to get him through life."

She pointed to her temple. "Don't you know this is the most important muscle in the human body?"

"Your temple?"

"No," she laughed, "your imagination muscle! Anyone who doesn't have one isn't worth corn shucks. Even scientists need an imagination muscle. That's what Benjamin Franklin did when he put the key on the kite tail. I read about that in a book Pa gave me for Christmas one time."

Stephen coughed, knowing she'd caught him there. A swift change of subject was needed. "Very well. You may continue these imagination lessons—but superstition is another thing altogether. Chambers said that you advised Tad and Cleo to *stay right with the moon*."

Jubilee took in his frowning face, knowing Chambers had held fast to his promise of reporting her. "Yes, that's true. I *did* tell them to stay right with the moon. Why, staying right with the moon is important outside of gardening, too. You have to stay right with the moon to—"

"I'd prefer you not fill Tad's head with superstitious ideas," he cut in, his dark brows pulling together. "I don't believe in anything that's not a proven scientific fact, and I'd like my son to be brought up the same way."

She broke into an easy smile. "Well, you may not believe in staying right with the moon, but there's no harm in it."

"Actually there is. If I tell him one thing about life and you tell him another, it sets up a harmful conflict within him."

She smoldered, but remained silent.

"I want you to be realistic. I don't want him believing in myths and superstition. He's intelligent and wants to know the truth, and I want you to tell him the truth."

"I do tell him the truth."

He rose. "Your highly colored version of the truth. Parlor tricks can be amusing, but I have the uneasy feeling you actually believe there *is* a magical element to life."

Jubilee blinked in surprise. Had she completely misread him? She'd supposed he was not only warm and charming, but intelligent as well. "But life *is* filled with magic. It's all around us," she exclaimed passionately. "There's magic in the moon and sun and stars, and magic in the seeds that sprout from the earth and blossom into flowers."

"Don't confuse magic with the rhythm of nature," he scoffed.

Her mood shifted from cautious awareness to sharp interest. "How do birds know when to fly south, and salmon how to ford a stream?" she challenged, fiercely defending her position.

Stephen looked at her indulgently. "Natural instinct, nothing more."

A shudder passed through her that he was an unbeliever—an infidel, no less. Lordamercy, on this subject he was hard as a laurel burl. How did a person get through life without a little faith and belief? She moved toward him, step by slow step. "Just look around you," she continued, earnestly pleading her case. "There's magic all

Song of the Lark

around you, if you'd only see it. All miracles aren't huge like the parting of the Red Sea. Life is filled with little everyday miracles."

For a moment they stood silently, their gazes dueling.

Stephen noticed that Jubilee's eyes were bright as diamonds and excitement flushed her cheeks. He'd already observed how beautiful she was, and today he found out how single-minded she could be. On this topic, it seemed she wouldn't give an inch. "A charming philosophy," he drawled, "but I'm sure I can never believe in anything I can't see, taste, or touch. I believe in scientific fact and nothing more, certainly not magic, miracles, or *staying right with the moon*."

Jubilee clasped his arms and, seemingly forgetting herself, ran her fingers down them. "Life isn't simply scientific. It doesn't proceed in apple pie order. It's full of things we can't explain." Her green eyes pleaded with him. "What if there *is* something else?" she proposed with the zeal of a circuit-riding preacher. "What if there's something more than scientific fact? What if there's a whole world of something more, like faith, and hope, and miracles?" She paused dramatically, then closed with: "Promise me you'll think about that possibility."

Stephen chuckled, impressed with her tenacity. "All right, Curly Top, I'll think about it."

She ran her eyes over him. "Good. If I can't win you over today, there's still hope. I don't give up easily."

"You had better see what Tad's up to," he finished dismissively.

At the door, Jubilee paused and looked back over her shoulder. "Promise me you'll think about it, now."

When she'd left, Stephen sat down at his desk and laughed softly. He could easily see why Tad was drawn to her. She had not only fire and spirit, but unshakable faith. It seemed she'd charmed everyone in the house except Chambers, and he knew she was working on him feverishly.

He went back to his work but found his mind straying. Jubilee had a depth to her wit that challenged his time-honored beliefs. After a while, he pushed the papers aside and tapped his pencil on the desk, considering her proposition. For the first time in his life, Stephen Wentworth, who'd earned an engineering degree from a prestigious Ivy League university and graduated summa cum laude, considered the possibility that there might be something more than what could be proven by science. The thought floated by him like a bubble on the wind, teasing him with its magnificent potential.

Even as he told himself the idea was hogwash, the merest possibility of such a realm existing touched his heart more deeply than he'd ever thought possible.

A week passed and Stephen returned home from the lumber yard just as Delilah walked into the entry. A scowl marred her usually jovial face. Crossing her arms, she stood before him like a huge boulder in the middle of a stream. "I needs to talk to you, Mist' Stephen," she said ominously, not cracking a smile.

Stephen grinned, for he realized she'd been waiting for him to arrive. He knew an ambush when he saw one, but when Delilah had *that* tone in her voice, and *that* look in her eyes, he realized it was time to listen. From this loving woman he would take both counsel and rebuke. Delilah was family, and always would be family.

"You have my full attention," he replied, placing his hat aside. Amused, he noted the glint in her determined eyes. Undoubtedly she was going to ask for a set of cooking utensils or perhaps another stove. "Do you want something for the kitchen?" he asked, feeling especially generous that afternoon. "Just tell me what you need."

Delilah scowled. "I's not askin' for nothin' for myself," she retorted in a hurt tone. "I wants somethin' for Miz Jubilee."

Song of the Lark

Stephen glanced into the parlor and wondered where the beautiful nanny was.

"Don't worry none. She ain't gonna walk in," Delilah told him, seemingly reading his mind. "She be out in that magic garden of hers with Tad and Cleo, so us can talk all us want to." She drew in a tremulous breath. "That chile needs some new clothes—some real clothes," she exclaimed, pushing out her bottom lip. "I knows men folks don't think 'bout things like that, but women folks does, and they talks about it, just like they's talkin' now!"

That Jubilee might be the subject of nasty gossip irritated Stephen mightily. "And who's doing this talking?" he demanded, stripping off his gloves and tossing them on the console.

"When Miz Jubilee go into town with Tad, them club ladies that Miz Estell run with be talkin' like magpies 'bout her. Rosetta say the folks gossipin' 'bout her where she be cleanin' house, too." She shook her finger at him. "And I hears the old hens cacklin' with my own ears when I goes shoppin' for groceries. They say she look like a ragamuffin in them droopy mountain things she be wearin'." She waved a beckoning hand at him. "Come on. I wants to show you somethin'."

Curious, Stephen followed her into the kitchen where she swiped back the curtain on its rattling hooks. She nodded at Jubilee and the boys, who were laughing and having a good time as they worked in the garden. "The chile don't have nothin' to wear but rags. She done sent ever' dollar you give her back to that granny of hers." Delilah turned, her dark eyes flashing. "So's you's got to do somethin' and you's got to do it fast!"

Stephen assessed Jubilee's appearance and decided she did indeed look like a ragamuffin. Although she took great pride in those clothes that she'd made herself, they were frayed with constant use and much washing. Their dull colors did little to enhance her beauty, and their old-fashioned style betrayed her lack of sophistication. And that floppy hat she always wore—why, the battered head covering crowed that she was a child of the backwoods to all who saw it.

Stephen could just imagine what the club ladies were saying. *"Have you seen the new nursemaid Wentworth has dragged in for his son? Hamish is probably rolling in his grave. Why, the child is right out of the mountains and dresses like a ragpicker!"* Just the thought that some old biddies were laughing at Jubilee made gorge rise in his throat—especially when they had no idea what she'd done for Tad.

Delilah shook his arm. "Where's your mind, Mist' Stephen? You ain't listenin' to me a bit. I done told you, you's got to buy that chile some citified clothes."

He patted the cook's large, soft shoulder. "Thank you for telling me this. I'll do what I can, but you know how proud she is."

"I knows, I knows," Delilah sighed. She trod heavily to the stove, then turned and scanned him with her great, loving eyes. "You's gonna have to be cunnin' as a fox about this, Mist' Stephen, but somehow you's gonna have to do it."

Stephen studied Jubilee as she played with the boys. She was only his employee, but he'd become quite protective of her, he realized with a spurt of surprise. He chuckled to himself, thinking that in most respects she was perfectly able to protect herself. Yet, in her own way she was very vulnerable—open and sweet and honest—and she needed someone to look after her.

Lord, he had to stop thinking about her like this. He clenched his jaw and warned himself to regain some measure of his composure—put things into perspective. After Isabelle had died, he'd been crushed. When he'd lost her, something had died within him, and the burden of a love had become too much to carry. Physical release was one thing, but true love involved risking the heart and opening oneself up to all kinds of pain. Trying to protect his emo-

Song of the Lark

tions, he'd made a secret vow never to become emotionally involved with a woman again, to never remarry—and he intended to keep his vow.

Yes, he needed to get a rein on his emotions where Jubilee Jones was concerned. He had some responsibility to her as long as she was living in his home, but after school started, she would be gone and just a memory.

Jubilee stood in front of the huge foyer mirror and flushed with pleasure. She straightened the skirt of her plain blue dress, thinking it was the loveliest gown she'd ever seen. She now had a wardrobe of beautiful clothes—four new outfits, more than anyone could possibly want. Just this morning, one of the maids had accompanied her to town and helped her select clothing, undergarments, a corset that rubbed against her rib cage, and a new pair of shoes that pinched her toes. When they'd returned to the mansion, the maid had pinned Jubilee's hair atop her head, fashioning it into a stylish coiffure and showing her how to create the effect herself. Jubilee adjusted her button necklace. She felt . . . well, pretty!

She twirled about in happiness just as Tad and Cleo burst into the foyer giggling with delight. "My, Miz Jubilee," Cleo piped up, his dark eyes glistening with admiration, "you sure is fetchin' in them new clothes of yours. Why, I believes you be the prettiest lady I ever seed."

Tad grinned and shook his head in agreement. "Y-yes, you're p-pretty!"

"Thank you, boys," she replied, feeling a bit self-conscious. "This is the first store-bought dress I ever had."

"Well, I likes it," Cleo added with an emphatic shake of his head. "You's a real fancy lady now."

Jubilee turned sideways and glanced at her fashionable outline, provided by a modest bustle. Only Stephen's insistence that she must have the gowns had convinced her to go along with the plan. At first, she'd declined. It was only when he'd hinted that the townfolk would look down on *him* for not providing her with proper clothing that she'd agreed. When he put it that way, she knew she just had to accept his generous offer.

From the kitchen Delilah called out for her son, and Cleo glanced at Tad and rolled his eyes. "There goes that woman agin. I's got to go," he lamented with a long sigh. "A man can't have no pleasure a'tall with her around."

After the boy left, Jubilee heard Stephen close the study doors and walk toward the foyer. Excitement swirled in the pit of her stomach, for she'd supposed he was still at the lumber yard, working late as he did each evening.

The moment he spotted her, his eyes widened in astonishment. Dressed in a dark suit that fit his broad shoulders perfectly, he looked every bit the elegant gentleman. For a moment neither of them spoke; then to break the oppressive silence, she twirled about and asked, "Well, what do you think?"

He moved leisurely toward her and studied her openly. A look of pleased surprise shone in his eyes. "You look lovely," he replied in a deep, caressing voice. "Quite lovely indeed."

Lordamercy, he was handsome, Jubilee thought. And there was something sensual about his mouth that had a strange effect on her. To her embarrassment, her heart pounded erratically. "I'll go to my room now," she managed, thinking all her wits had flown right out of her head. She glanced down at Tad. "It'll be a real treat for the boy to eat with you tonight."

Tad surveyed her with pleading eyes. "I-I want you to e-eat with us, too," he struggled, pronouncing the words with great difficulty.

"Oh, I can't do that!" she said, flustered at the thought of spending a whole evening with Stephen.

Tad tightened his grip on her hand and tugged her in the direction of the dining room.

Song of the Lark

Something intense flared within Stephen. Clad in the simple blue gown, the girl who'd arrived at his mansion in breeches and a homespun shirt looked wonderfully feminine. The modest dress had a ruff of white lace at the throat that brought out the color of her eyes, and its cut made her slender waist look extremely small. With her soft auburn hair fashionably coiffed and spilling over her shoulders in glossy ringlets, she was absolutely gorgeous, and unlike the timid debutantes whom mothers pushed at him at every social gathering, she had an air of vitality and natural warmth.

He'd hoped the new clothes and coiffure would make her merely presentable to Asheville society, but he now found that she was far more than presentable. She was a beauty. Estell would be insanely jealous.

Stephen caught up with the pair at the dining room door and saw that despite Tad's insistence, Jubilee refused to enter.

He caught her eyes, knowing he shouldn't say the words that trembled on his lips, but spurred by a strange impulse, he said them anyway. "Yes, why don't you eat with us?" he suggested in a cordial tone.

"Oh, no. I don't suppose that would be proper!"

"I don't think we have to worry about what is proper tonight," Stephen laughed, realizing that she felt she was overstepping her position. "Delilah said Tad eats better when you're around, anyway."

"Well, I . . ." she faltered, looking very uncomfortable.

Settling the matter, he took her arm, noticing it trembled ever so slightly. His face aglow, Tad joined them as they entered the dining room, where Delilah was busily setting the table. "There will be three for dinner tonight," Stephen spoke up, pulling out a chair for Jubilee.

"I sees that, sir," the cook replied, quickly setting another place near the head of the gleaming mahogany table.

Jubilee sat down, but how ill at ease she was in her new corset and wobbly bustle that made her feel as if she had a basket of eggs attached to her behind! Tad took his accustomed seat and Stephen claimed a spot at the head of the table, then graced her with a smile that made her feel flushed and excited. She ate in this room every day, but somehow with Stephen home tonight everything seemed lovelier and brighter, more welcoming.

Delilah pushed in a serving cart filled with a pork roast, sweet potatoes swimming in butter, salad, fresh green beans, and golden biscuits, still smoking from the oven. "I hopes you likes pork roast, Miz Jubilee. I knows Mist' Stephen does," she commented, placing the already carved roast in front of him.

"Are we having magic vegetables tonight?" he asked the cook with a teasing grin.

Delilah placed a salad before him. "Why, yes sir, you all sure is. I just washed off this magic lettuce and onions a few minutes ago!"

When she'd left the room, Stephen rose, and from a sideboard fetched a crystal decanter full of dark wine and two glasses. "How about a glass of good blackberry wine?" he asked Jubilee, already filling the sparkling glasses.

She'd seen the wine before, but never dreamed of touching it, simply drinking water with her meals. "Very well," she replied, feeling more reckless by the minute.

After giving her the wineglass, Stephen served everyone's plate with vegetables and tender roast and soon they were all laughing and talking.

Jubilee was acutely conscious of her lower social status as compared with Stephen's, but she was soon swept away in the conversation and glow of the wine. "This tastes like Granny's wine," she observed, already sipping at her second glass. "She's the champion wine maker of the mountains. Blackberries, cherries, even dandelions, it doesn't matter to her. She can brew it up into something mighty tasty," she declared, feeling happy and warmly relaxed. "All homemade. That's the country way!"

Song of the Lark

Stephen glanced at her button necklace, and for a moment she regretted that she'd worn it. Did he disapprove of it, or was he simply curious?

"Tell me about that necklace of yours," he asked thoughtfully. "Is that homemade as well? I've been wondering about it since you came."

Jubilee lifted the long necklace away from her bodice. "Well, each button represents some happy event in my life," she began, fondly fingering the old buttons. "I added this button"—she indicated a blue one—"the morning Pa and me sold nineteen bottles of the remedy in three hours. We were selling it almost as fast as I could take the money. My magic tricks were going slick as butter, and Micah was playing his fiddle nine ways to Georgia. It was just an ordinary workday, but such a fine time I'll remember it all of my life."

"W-what's that big blue button f-for?" Tad asked, his eyes bright with curiosity.

"Why, this came from Delilah's sewing box. I put this button on the day you started talking. If a day ever deserved a button, it was that one!"

Tad laughed and pointed at a shiny button in the very center of her necklace. "I-I like that one. W-what's it for?"

She brushed her fingers over the old brass button. "This one? I strung on that button the day Pa came home from the war. It came from his Confederate uniform." She glanced at Stephen, who still looked a little puzzled.

"So the buttons are like souvenirs?" he asked, his voice wonderfully low and smooth.

"That's right. Lots of mountain women wear button necklaces. I found a sparkly button when I was a girl I'm saving for my wedding day." She hefted the homemade adornment in her palm. "Why, holding this is like having all my happy memories right in my hand," she added, feeling peaceful and satisfied just thinking about it.

Stephen caught her eyes and smiled. "How in the

world did you get the name of Jubilee? I've never known anyone named that before."

"Oh, that came from the Old Testament—from the Year of Jubilee." She laughed a little. "And Micah was named after the Book of Micah—that's right after Jonah. Mountain folks hold bed-cord strong to Bible names."

They talked about names a little longer, and when Stephen insisted she take a second piece of roast, she turned it over on her plate and playfully asked, "What kind of hog is this?"

He bit off a smile. "I wasn't aware that there was more than one kind."

She blinked at him, feigning amazement. "Why, there's all kinds. Lordamercy, didn't you know?" She held his amused gaze and settled into a story her father had often told her. "There's razorback hogs, and fish hogs, and chicken-footed hogs, and so many more I can't even name them all."

"Fish hogs?" he shot back with a grin. "Are you sure they exist?"

She plunked down her knife. "Of course! Fish hogs roam along creeks and they live on crawfish and things like that."

Stephen laughed at the mountain tale she was spinning to entertain Tad, who gazed at her with huge eyes.

"Chicken-footed hogs are mighty scarce, but they're not wild and always come home to roost," she continued in a serious tone.

"Why do they call them chicken-footed hogs?" Tad asked, speaking without the strain that usually marked his voice.

A smile shot across Jubilee's face. "Because they can root and scratch themselves like a hen."

"Can they lay eggs?" the boy chirped, his face shining with mischief.

Stephen threw back his head and laughed, while Tad went into a giggling fit. They went on this way for a good thirty minutes, laughing and talking as she spun more mountain tales.

Delilah entered the room carrying a tray with a steaming apple pie that scented the air with cinnamon and cloves. "Lawsy, I ain't heard such laughin' and goin' on in this old house in ages," she exclaimed, her eyes glinting with merriment. "I's mighty glad to see this. Mighty glad, indeed!" She widened her eyes at Tad. "And looky there, that boy done ate all his food!" She chuckled with pride as she served everyone large pieces of pie.

Stephen took a bite, then leaned back in his chair. "Lord, I haven't enjoyed a meal as much in ages."

Delilah sent her eyes to the nearly empty wine decanter. "Sure 'nuff? Well, it looks like you and Miz Jubilee nearly enjoyed that blackberry wine all up."

He forked into the flaky piecrust, then eyed Jubilee, whose face glowed with happiness. "Did you know this woman makes the best pies in North Carolina?"

"Oh, go on now, Mist' Stephen," Delilah chided, fanning herself with a towel. "You done ate my cookin' so long you don't know no difference."

"Yes, I do!" he corrected her with a smile.

Tad finished his pie, and with a hopeful expression held out a water glass for the last bit of blackberry wine.

Stephen shook his head. "I'm afraid you're a little young, son. We'll save your first taste of wine for a special occasion."

The boy looked at Jubilee, his eyes filled with adoration. "T-this is a special occasion, Papa."

Jubilee colored and instantly lowered her eyes.

"Yes, actually it is," Stephen said, catching her gaze as she glanced up, her eyes glistening with joy, "but I think it's already past your bedtime."

Jubilee placed her napkin aside, then rose and took Tad's hand. "I enjoyed the meal tonight," she told Stephen with honest simplicity. "I enjoyed the good food, good company, and good wine."

"Which all adds up to a good evening," Stephen finished for her, noticing she was still flustered from Tad's comment.

After Jubilee and Tad had left the room, he leaned back and lit a cigar, smiling to himself at some of the things she'd said. He'd never dined with a girl who wore a button necklace and believed in staying right with the moon, but he had to admit it had been a delightful experience. In fact, her highly colored version of the truth had been quite entertaining. Superstitious and ill-informed she might be, but she was as refreshing as a dip in a cool mountain pool.

"Does you want more pie?" Delilah asked, breaking in on his pleasant thoughts.

"No, go on and clear the table," he told her, stretching his legs before him. "I'm just going to sit here for a while and relax."

The cook placed the clattering dishes on a tray, chuckling to herself as she worked. "Lawsy, Mist' Stephen, I don't know when I's seen you acting so happy."

He blew a smoke ring into the air, silently agreeing with her. Since Isabelle's death, happiness had been a rare visitor, but for one glorious night he'd been able to forget everything and share a fine meal with his son, and the most amusing girl he'd ever met.

"Yes—it feels good to laugh again," he remarked thoughtfully, realizing how long it had been since he'd let himself go and really enjoyed life.

Delilah threw him a knowing glance. "I understands, sir," she returned with a soft smile that told him that she did indeed understand. "I understands real good."

Chapter Five

A clap of thunder jolted Jubilee from a sound sleep. Groggily, she sat up and gazed out her dormer window, seeing jagged lightning fork the sky. Instantly she thought of Tad and realized he would be afraid. Slipping from the covers, she opened a dresser drawer and retrieved a candle and holder. After lighting the wick, she threw on a shawl and walked down the shadowy stairs, moving as quickly as she dared.

The storm had settled directly over the mansion, and she heard Tad crying before she got to his door. "Don't be scared. I'm here," she announced in a soothing voice as she hurried into his room. The night air was damp and heavy, and rain droplets shone like tiny diamonds against the windows.

With frightened eyes, Tad sat in the middle of his huge bed, clutching the covers. She placed the candle aside and took him in her arms. "Don't cry, baby, it's only a little thunder and lightning. The old potato man just dumped a big load of potatoes from his wagon. That's what all the noise is about."

"W-what makes the lightning?" the boy asked, his face pale and stricken in the shadows.

Jubilee ran her fingers through his silky hair. "That's just the fairies waving their wands around. Sometimes they get carried away with those wands, trying to outdo each other." She rocked him back and forth in her arms. "Make a wish each time it thunders. If you can say it all before the noise stops, it might come true."

Thunder cracked overhead, and she watched him silently mouth a wish, wondering what he was saying. Was he wishing for the comfort of the mother he'd never see again? she asked herself, her heart going out to him.

A cough came from the darkness, and she twisted about and saw Stephen standing at the foot of the bed. A maroon silk dressing robe garbed his large frame and tousled hair hung over his brow, making him look younger than she'd ever seen him.

He smiled, and it triggered a small glow within her. "We must have had the same idea," he said easily.

"Yes," she whispered. Remembering she was in her nightgown, she pulled her shawl more tightly about her.

Tad held out his arms to his father, who sat down on the bed across from Jubilee. Stephen talked to his son quietly for a while, reassuring him, and in the simplest of terms explained what was going on outside.

When he'd finished, Tad sank back onto the lace-trimmed pillows, disappointment flooding his face. "It's e-electricity?" he stammered, turning his head to the window where lightning plunged out of the sky like a pitchfork and stabbed into the earth. He looked back at his father. "I liked the potato wagon and fairy wands a l-lot b-better."

Stephen frowned, and Jubilee glanced down, suppressing a smile.

They all talked comfortably for a while, and when the boy's eyelids drooped, Jubilee rose and pulled the covers over him. Soon he was fast asleep.

Song of the Lark

When she sat down again, Stephen caught her eyes. "Potato wagons and fairy wands?" he questioned accusingly, raising a brow.

She bit her tongue, wanting to remind him that Tad liked her story better.

"Don't fill his head with too much foolishness," Stephen continued, his expression serious. "If you'll remember, we talked about this subject once before."

"Haven't you heard those old tales?" she countered, somewhat hurt by the remark. "Pa always told me those stories when a spring storm came up. Spring is a real unpredictable season in the mountains. One day it'll be all soft and warm and sweet with the first lilacs in bloom, and the next day a fierce storm will tear through the hills and bring a bitter chill. Storms scared me to death when I was Tad's age," she confessed, vividly remembering her Smoky Mountains childhood.

Stephen's face softened. "You can recall all of that?"

"I sure can. Granny has a storm cellar behind the cabin and I remember racing to it, with rain pounding down on me and thunder shaking the earth." She smiled at her memories. "It was safe and cozy in that cellar and smelled of damp earth. We took the dogs too, and there was always a commotion before we got them settled down. Granny stored canned fruit there and Micah usually knocked a jar of peaches or green beans from the shelf." She laughed a little. "It always made Granny mad as fire!"

Stephen regarded her with smoky eyes. "You still long for the mountains, don't you?"

Jubilee gave a wistful sigh. "Yes—I do," she admitted. "I miss the sun pouring over the mountains like honey, and the mists rolling in at sundown making everything a hazy blue." She rose, walked to a velvety chair, and traced her fingers over the back of it. "I miss the persimmons turning gold after the first frost," she added, noticing he was listening to her every word, "and I miss the wild roses hanging over the fences, fairly bursting with a scent that made my head reel."

The quiet talk and sound of the steady rain had relaxed her, and forgetting to be nervous, she rattled on, letting her shawl slip to her elbows. "The woods are full of blue-winged teal, and on a frosty October morning the maples stand out orange and red like God had painted them with His own hand," she murmured, her gaze locked with his.

Stephen studied her and realized that for the first time, she was not only telling him about her past, but giving him a glimpse into her very heart. Gilded with candlelight, her tousled hair and scoop-necked nightgown edged in modest lace made her look extremely demure, and her heartfelt words stirred his imagination. He could see the mountains in his mind, and he found himself wanting to be there, far away from his troubles in Asheville.

He remembered how lovely she'd looked at dinner last week, and smiled to himself at how carefully she'd walked in her first pair of high-button shoes. Lord, her trials were just beginning, he thought a little sadly. If he knew anything about the Asheville sewing circles, she'd have to endure a lot more than a pair of tight shoes to appease them. Gossip was the club ladies' staff of life and they delighted in tearing apart every newcomer, especially the mountain folk. So much the pity, he thought, for Jubilee felt more deeply than all of them put together.

Jubilee saw Stephen rising and pulled up her shawl, realizing she'd been parading in front of him in her nightgown and running on like a ninny. No doubt her mountain memories were very dull to a sophisticated man like him who'd traveled all over the world. "I'm sorry," she offered, adjusting the shawl around her shoulders. "I didn't mean to bring all that up—to bore you."

He ran a heated gaze over her. "I don't think you could be boring if you tried."

His words made her feel all warm and tender inside. "Yes, I've talked too much," she insisted, thankful for the shadows that concealed her blush. She watched Stephen lovingly arrange the covers about his son.

"He's fast asleep and the storm has almost blown itself out. I believe we can go to our rooms now," he said quietly.

Jubilee nodded, distraught that she'd been keeping him from his rest with her prattle. "Yes, it's late. I should be going upstairs."

She was halfway to the door when he caught up with her. "There is something I've been wanting to tell you," he said, casually taking her arm. "Perhaps this isn't the best time, but it's been on my mind for days." He stood a little straighter as if he'd made an important decision. "I'm giving a party in two weeks, and I want you and Tad to attend."

She glanced at the boy's small form, outlined by the silken coverlet. "But he's still so frightened around people," she whispered roughly.

Stephen smoothed back his thick hair. "Yes, I know, but he can attend the party for a short while." A heavy sigh escaped his lips. "There's been so much sadness in this house, I think Tad and I should start living again. And he must lose some of his shyness by school time."

Jubilee bit her lip, believing the boy wasn't ready for such an ordeal yet. "But he's still so, so . . ." She looked into Stephen's eyes, searching for words.

"Fragile?"

"Yes, that's it," she replied with a rush of relief, hoping he'd understand.

Stephen clasped her shoulders, sending radiant pleasure through her. "You still have two weeks," he suggested reassuringly.

Two weeks? she thought, her mind whirling with the impossibility of it all. *Why, that was nothing where the shy, insecure boy was concerned.* Before she could reply, he gently moved her from the bedroom and shut the door behind them. "Two weeks isn't enough time," she implored, making a last attempt to plead her case.

Stephen gazed down at her with his soft brown eyes, making her feel as if she were wrapped in an invisible warmth. "Yes, but you're a wonderful teacher." He paused meaningfully and the air verily throbbed between them. "Thank you for all you've done for him," he said, his voice deepening to a husky murmur. His gentle tone made her tremble, and when he moved his fingers in tantalizing circles over her shoulders, her heart felt as if it might burst from her rib cage.

The dim light of a gas street lamp trickled though a window at the end of the hall and rain dripped from the eaves, increasing the sense of intimacy between them. *Go to your room*, she told herself, trying to fight the ever-growing attraction between them. *Don't be a fool; twist away; run upstairs!* her brain advised her.

But even then, she knew she couldn't.

"You're so beautiful," he whispered as the gentle rain drummed against the mansion's roof and enclosed them in a world of their own.

The desire in Stephen's eyes shocked and excited Jubilee at the same time. In all of her life no one had ever told her she was beautiful, and she felt hot blood sting her cheeks. She could detect the musky scent of bay rum wafting from his silk robe, and her limbs took on a languorous heaviness, rooting her where she stood. The overpowering sensual feeling was stronger than anything she'd ever experienced—strong enough to block out the good raising that Granny had given her, strong enough to steal every drop of caution from her soul and fear from her heart. She wanted him so much!

Stephen gazed at her loose, unbound hair shimmering like copper in the dim light and caught the sweet scent of her body on the moist air. He traced his fingers over her smooth cheek, and she stood very still, not moving a muscle, not frightened, but mentally reaching out for him. Her lips slightly parted, she gazed at him with large eyes blazing with need.

She was so delectable with the light washing over her delicate features, and there was something totally genuine and innocent about her that touched his deepest feelings. Unable to throttle his ever-building desire, he put his arms about her and pulled her close. Here in the stillness of the night, they were social equals and he wanted to hold her and make love to her. His conscience told him his behavior was shocking, but he felt his passion breaking free, taking on a willful life of its own.

Jubilee thrilled to the power of his steely embrace. He studied her a moment longer, his heart thudding against her bosom; then he lowered his head and brushed his lips over hers. With a sob of pleasure, she slipped her arms about his broad shoulders, her shawl slipping to the floor. When his mouth slanted over hers, warmth coursed through her in a golden flow. Never had such exquisite sensations surged through her trembling body.

He welded his mouth to hers, searing her lips with passion and making her moan in delight as she shuddered against him. The ache between her thighs swelled to bursting, compounding the curious heaviness that possessed her limbs; each kiss, each ravishing caress, made her blood roar like a mighty ocean. He covered her throat with kisses, his lips spreading liquid fire; he stroked her back, his hands so arousing that she thought she would die with delight. In that instant the great differences between them faded away and an all-consuming passion touched her soul.

As Stephen kissed and caressed her expertly, passion shot through her belly, consuming her with fire. She gasped in delight and pressed herself against him, rejoicing in the quick, hot surge of his manhood against her thighs. When he pulled her open-throated nightgown down and uncovered her full breasts, gently tracing his thumb over her erect pink nipples, his touch turned whispery soft, bringing hot tears to her eyes. She wanted to weep, to scream, to die with pleasure.

Then, gradually from deep within her, a warning voice rose, telling her she was making a grave mistake. Lordamercy, had she lost her mind? How could Stephen, who was at the very pinnacle of Asheville society, love someone like herself? True, he felt passion, but she wanted more than that—she wanted a coupling of the heart and soul as well as the body. As her blood cooled, fear and mortification stabbed through her. Surely he would think her a trollop if she stayed in his arms a moment longer. With a pounding heart, she pulled away from him and adjusted her nightgown with trembling fingers.

In the feeble light his face was tense and harsh and he looked as if he were carrying the burden of the world on his shoulders. A pulse throbbed in his temple and he gazed down at her with eyes full of pain and longing. Only a moment ago he was branding her lips with a kiss that left her weak; now his expression was flat and unreadable.

Too upset to speak, she picked up her shawl, her stomach churning with apprehension. With a leaden sense of loss, she hurried up the stairs to the attic, half stumbling in her humiliation. At last she reached the safety of her room and leaned against the closed door, so distraught she could scarcely breathe. Uncontrollable chills racked her body and she trembled like a dry leaf in the wind.

She couldn't let something like this happen again. Hot, salty tears pricked her eyes. She had to remember who she was—and who *he* was. Her father had been a peddler of herbal tonics, and his, one of the richest men in the South. What chance did she have of finding real happiness with someone like Stephen Wentworth?

But even as she spoke the words, she knew she already loved him with all her heart.

* * *

Song of the Lark

Jubilee sat on a stone bench, watching Tad and Cleo toss a ball across the great, velvety mansion lawn. Overhead, birds quibbled in the trees, and flowering freesia released their pungent vapor into the morning air, making the grounds seem almost magical.

In contrast, an emotional storm raged in Jubilee's mind, claiming all her thoughts and energy. The truth be told, her whole life had been transformed into a kaleidoscope of contrasts. In one sense her body glowed and tingled with life; on the other hand, she scarcely slept, thinking, trying to figure out what she should do. Should she go or stay? Fear and uncertainty lay like ice in the pit of her stomach and Stephen's face haunted her fleeting dreams. Would she be wise enough, and brave enough, to handle the situation the passionate scene outside of Tad's bedroom had started?

It all seemed like a dream, but every time she looked at Stephen she knew it was only too real. Since that evening they'd hardly spoken, but she dreamed of him every night, and to her embarrassment often woke up throbbing with desire. So this was what love was all about—this reckless longing that would make a person throw away the compass that had kept them straight and true for so long.

The ball bounced at her feet, and seeing Tad and Cleo run toward her, she stood and scooped it up. When they arrived, all smiles and shining faces, she put her arm about Tad's shoulder. "Who caught the most balls this morning?" she asked, her heart full to bursting with gratitude for the fine progress the child had made.

"I g-guess Cleo has."

"That's right," Cleo chimed in, hooking his thumbs under his suspenders, "I has—but Tad's gettin' better, Miz Jubilee."

Tad grinned. "That's r-right. I'm getting better!"

"Here you go," she laughed, tossing the ball over the grass and watching the children scramble for it. They burst into a gale of laughter, then Cleo snapped it up, and they raced around a shimmering fountain and started tossing it once more. Jubilee sat down again and looked at Tad, remembering the day she'd first seen him—the evening Cleo had tried to show him how to throw a ball and he'd failed miserably. He'd come so far since then. She'd considered leaving, but he still needed her so badly, and he had become the salt and savor of her life.

There was a slim chance that in time Stephen might even have some real feelings for her, too. Perhaps he'd develop a respect for her that would grow into true love. The wonder and pleasure of the thought filled her mind as the morning sun warmed her skin.

Her common sense warned against that hope, but she clung to it tenaciously. She'd made her decision. She would stay at the mansion and take her chances. If strength was what was called for, then she would be strong. She would be strong enough to carry each day as it came.

Jubilee straightened Tad's tie and brushed a speck of lint from his collar. "There—you look mighty handsome in that black suit and ruffled shirt—almost like a little prince." She rubbed his back reassuringly. "Let's go down to that party and let the folks see how good you look."

Tad gazed at her with pleading eyes. "M-my stomach feels funny—like it's sh-shaking or something."

Jubilee started to say that her stomach felt the same way, but knew it would do the boy no good. "Don't worry, it'll go away in a few minutes."

Tad slid a disappointed gaze over her. "Aren't you going to wear your button necklace?"

She smiled, touched that he liked it. "This is a mighty fancy party your father is having. My button necklace might not fit in."

"But it's all sparkly—and you look nice in it. Please wear it for me."

She considered his childish request. He had a hard evening ahead of him, and if wearing her button necklace would make him feel better, why shouldn't she? She could always let it hang under the high-necked bodice. No one would see it, but it would lift the child's spirits just when he needed it the most.

She put on the necklace, then took his small hand and left the room to be met with laughter floating up from the parlor below. Chatting with the boy to calm his fears, she walked down a flight of stairs, then paused on a landing for a last look in the big mirror.

Although her moss green gown with the white collar was plain and demure, it showed off her figure perfectly. With the help of one of the maids, she'd powdered her face, glossed her lips, and even put on a bit of rouge. With her upswept hair and bouncing ringlets, she felt presentable, but still terribly out of place.

She gave Tad's hand a reassuring squeeze and entered the parlor that was flooded with light from the great chandeliers. Her breath left her, for the cream of Asheville society was crowded into the huge room. The ladies were garbed in brightly colored gowns with low necklines and wore their hair piled high atop their heads with flowers or jeweled combs twined in their glossy locks. The men, with starched ruffles at their necks and wrists, sported dark frock coats, sumptuous silk vests, and glittering watch chains.

Tad looked pale and scared, and she knew it was all too much for him; he needed the comfort and security of his father. Quickly scanning the crowd, she saw Delilah serving champagne on a silver tray. Like a beacon of hope, the cook threw her an encouraging smile, then indicated Stephen with a tilt of her head.

Jubilee spotted his tall form at the far end of the parlor, but what she saw made her heart twist in her breast. He was talking to a distinguished-looking graying man while a stunning blonde held his arm possessively—the same blonde that had called her mountain trash the day she'd ridden into town! A purple gown with a fancy bustle skimmed over the girl's slender figure while rouge and lip color tinted her delicate features. With her fashionable dress, golden curls, and long gloves, she looked as if she were a princess. Who was this elegant girl, and what relationship did she have with Stephen? Jubilee wondered frantically. Fighting down her alarm, she tried to tell herself that they were probably just old friends.

Tad broke away and ran to his father, who picked him up and swung him around. Suddenly a hush fell over the room and all eyes riveted to Jubilee. Her pulse fluttering, she walked toward father and son, feeling as drab and insignificant as a little wren among a flock of beautiful peacocks.

The gown that only a few minutes ago had seemed lovely now seemed plain and dreary, only suited to the servant she was. She'd never realized how long the parlor was and she'd never felt so alone before. She held onto Stephen's gaze like a lifeline, and when he took Tad's hand and walked forward to meet her, she thought she would cry with gratitude.

"This is Tad's nanny," he said affably to the assembled guests. "I want all of you to meet her, for where the boy is concerned, she's a miracle worker." He picked up a glass of champagne from Delilah's tray and handed it to Jubilee, then urged the blonde forward. "This is Estell, Reverend Pennypacker's daughter," he said as if he'd known the girl all of her life.

She extended a slim hand, encased in white kid. "Why, I know you. You're the girl who rode into Asheville on a mule," she laughed, speaking loud enough for all to hear. "You seemed so lost, you reminded me of the Israelites who'd been wandering forty years in the wilderness." Several guests tittered at the comment, and the girl

Song of the Lark

ran a keen gaze over Jubilee as if she were searching for imperfections.

How shocked Jubilee was to discover that Estell was a preacher's daughter. Still stinging from the girl's latest jibe, she wanted to reply in kind, but mindful that she couldn't spoil Stephen's party, she simply inclined her head. As the socialite babbled on inanely, Jubilee noticed that her eyes had a dull, flat look like those of a painted china doll. Stephen introduced other guests, and Jubilee tried her best to respond, but often said the wrong thing, or was left tongue-tied by their questions.

At last a tall, thin man with a weak smile shook hands with her. With his pasty complexion, sunken chest, and emaciated form he reminded her of a cadaver. And if that wasn't a toupee he was wearing, Jubilee had never seen one, she decided, thinking it reminded her of a gnawed beaver pelt the hounds had dragged under Granny's cabin last winter.

"This is Reverend Pennypacker," Stephen explained sociably.

"My dear," the cleric gushed, pushing up his slipping spectacles with a bony finger, "let me invite you to my service this Sunday. My topic will be original sin."

Jubilee gazed at him, wondering what he was talking about. "Is there a new one? I-I thought they'd all been practiced," she replied softly.

Laughter rippled through the crowd again, making her realize she'd made yet another mistake.

A fat man with an oily smile and a gold tooth crowded in for an introduction. "And this is our banker, Winston Throg," Stephen continued, his voice marked by unmistakable distaste.

Throg's thinning hair was greased down and parted in the middle, and he'd evidently spent a great deal of time waxing his handlebar moustache so it would curl properly. A rosebud trembled from his lapel, its color matching the red veins in his nose.

He kissed Jubilee's fingers with moist lips, making her want to wash her hand. "How are you, Miss Jones? We are delighted to have you in our fair city. I would be happy to assist you with any financial matters you might have." As in the case of Estell, she felt as if she were being sized up rather than welcomed into their midst. She noticed the banker was attracted to the preacher's daughter, and decided it was because they had the same interests, namely money and society.

Everything went extremely fast from that point, and as more people crowded about, the champagne glass slipped from Jubilee's hand, its contents splashing over the front of her gown. With a stab of humiliation, she watched the empty glass bounce on the carpet, then roll under a chair.

She had no idea what polite society did in a case like this, but like a guardian angel, Delilah retrieved the glass and put it on a tray, then handed Jubilee a linen napkin to blot her gown. For a moment, their eyes locked, and with a sharp nod, the old woman willed her not to lose heart.

Jubilee's throat tightened with humiliation. She dabbed at the front of her moist gown and noticed sly grins creeping over the guests' faces. To make matters worse, she detected a flicker of disappointment in Stephen's eyes that tore at her heart.

Gradually, the cluster of amused spectators drifted away, and before she knew it, Stephen had taken Tad to meet some of his friends. Beset with awkwardness, she stood by herself for a while, and then with a prickle of dread she saw Estell approaching her. The debutante wore a satisfied expression which reminded her of a cat closing in on a mouse. Now only a few feet away, the blonde pasted a false smile on her face.

"So you're from the mountains?" she purred, making the statement sound like an accusation.

Jubilee collected her wits, determined to hold her own with the snippy woman. "That's right," she answered

Song of the Lark

evenly, "I am—a place called Maple Leaf Hollow."

"You speak very well for a mountain person."

"Yes," Jubilee came back, not missing a beat. "And I can read, too."

Estell widened her eyes, seemingly suddenly aware that she'd gotten more than she bargained for. She scanned Jubilee's sodden gown with distaste. "Is this the extent of your wardrobe? Surely Stephen has bought you more than this. I'll have to speak to him about it." She smiled tightly. "I have an idea. I have some old gowns I was going to give to charity. I'll give them to you, instead. They're too dressy for someone in your position, but you could remove the flounces."

Jubilee felt like telling her she'd rather wear a potato sack, but she nodded politely.

Estell raised her finely arched brows. "You seem to have a way with the boy. He's quite taken with you."

"And I care for him very much." Jubilee felt so uncomfortable she wanted to leave the room, but reminded herself that her first duty was to Tad. Circling her gaze, she found him standing nervously by his father, looking at her with longing eyes. "I should go now," she said, realizing he was emotionally exhausted. Without thinking, she took a few steps in that direction. "I need to take Tad to bed."

Estell grabbed her arm. "Wait a minute," she snapped, her eyes flaring. "I'm still talking to you."

Jubilee sent Stephen a silent message for help, and within seconds he was crossing the room with Tad in tow.

Estell brushed a speck of lint from Stephen's lapel, then clung to his arm with a proprietary air. She reached out to pat Tad's head, but he stepped back, and she instantly withdrew her hand. She smiled at Stephen, then held Jubilee's gaze, not releasing it. "The boy is shy now, but we shall get better acquainted this summer. Stephen has asked me to the June Cotillion, the Fourth of July picnic, and all the band concerts," she stated sweetly, obviously waiting for a reaction to her statement.

The words turned Jubilee's heart to ice. There it was. She finally had her answer, she thought, feeling as if she'd just received a stinging slap to the face. Estell wasn't simply a social acquaintance or an old friend. Stephen was courting her. Now she knew that all of his hours away from the mansion weren't spent at the lumber yard. She fought down a rush of anguish that left her weak and trembling. Why hadn't he mentioned the girl, spoken her name? With a fresh stab of pain, she knew that due to her position as a servant, he felt it wasn't necessary. She was just an amusing diversion to him, an object he could trifle with, then dispose of with no obligation to his social conscience!

Stephen threw Estell a dark look, and taking advantage of the tense moment, Tad rushed to Jubilee's side and clutched her hand.

"I should take him to bed now," she said quietly, her vision bleary with threatening tears.

"Yes," Stephen agreed, running a concerned gaze over his son. "He's had a long day."

Estell's eyes focused on Jubilee's neck, and she quickly pulled the button necklace from its hiding place. "What in heaven's name is this—some kind of mountain charm?" she asked, tugging down on the necklace too sharply. Suddenly the cord broke and dozens of buttons hit the carpet, some bouncing under chairs and others shooting against the guests' shoes and making them gasp in surprise.

Jubilee's cheeks burned like a hot brand, and she instantly sank to the floor to chase the scattering buttons. Tad helped her, and a bit later Delilah was on her hands and knees searching for buttons. The accident caused a great commotion, and when Jubilee rose, clutching a handful of buttons to her bosom, all conversation had stopped and every eye in the room was glued to her face.

Song of the Lark

Delilah spilled her buttons into a china bowl, then held it out so Jubilee and Tad could do the same. In the old woman's eyes Jubilee saw embarrassment, pity, and deep concern. On Estell's face, she caught a glimmer of amusement.

The room was deathly silent and Jubilee thought her legs might actually give way beneath her. Totally humiliated, she swallowed hard, then gazed at Stephen's stunned face. "Good night, then," she managed, thanking God above that her voice held steady.

She escorted Tad to the door with as much dignity as she could muster, determined that she wouldn't give Estell the satisfaction of knowing she was dying inside. As soon as she and the boy were on the stairs, her emotions gave way and tears spilled from her eyes.

Tad clutched her skirt, his eyes troubled. "Please—don't cry. E-Estell is mean."

Jubilee knelt on the stairs and hugged him close. "It's all right, baby. Don't worry."

On the landing she looked into the big mirror, flinging away her tears. "You little fool!" she whispered to her image, mortified that she'd been naive enough to think that Stephen might actually care for her.

Biting her lips to control her sobs, she hurried up the rest of the stairs with Tad, knowing she could no longer stay at the mansion.

Finished with her cry, Jubilee unrolled her old red blanket upon the bed—the same blanket she'd used to bring her meager belongings from Maple Leaf Hollow. As she did so, memories of the day she'd arrived in Asheville flooded her mind. How comical she must have looked astride General Sherman in her mountain garb. No wonder the town folk had stared at her and Mrs. Rifkin had been so condescending.

She smiled at the memory of the way Chambers had tried to run her off. On that day, Stephen had been the only one who'd taken her for what she was, looking into her heart and not judging her by her clothing or her speech. It was things like that made her fall in love with him. She hadn't planned on it, and the Lord knew she'd battled it all the way, but in the end she just couldn't help herself, she thought sadly.

She fought back fresh tears and threw her buckskin britches and homespun blouse on the blanket, folding them roughly. She would never fit in with Stephen's fancy friends, anyway. Hadn't the guests' amused stares demonstrated that in the parlor? Pa had said it a thousand times—you just didn't yoke a thoroughbred horse with a work mule. Besides that, Micah would have a conniption fit if she said she loved a Wentworth, and Granny would be mighty upset herself. The situation was just hopeless.

She went to the open wardrobe and stared at the clothes Stephen had bought her. Salty tears stung her eyes as she traced her fingers over the soft collars and silken skirts. "I won't need anything like this back home," she said, talking to her reflection in the mirror as she held a gown before her. "Folks would think I'd lost my mind wearing something so fancy in the mountains."

A knock sounded on the door and her heart jumped. For a moment she thought it might be Stephen, then the rap came softly again and she knew it wasn't. She tossed the gown down and tried to put on a cheerful face. When the door swung open, there stood Tad in his nightshirt, his eyes terrified. He entered without being invited and immediately scanned the clothes on the bed, his mouth forming a silent *no*. "I-I don't want you to go," he stammered, clenching her waist.

"I have to, baby," she explained, stooping down and taking him in her arms. She studied his anguished face, thinking he'd endured more pain than one child ever deserved. "I don't belong here," she gently added, smoothing back his mussed hair. "Look, honey, do you think an old mountain lion could live here in Asheville?" she questioned, laughing a bit to cheer him up.

"I-I don't know," he answered, hanging his head.

"Well, he couldn't. But you get that mountain lion up where he belongs and he'd do just fine. He'd know every foot of the hills—where the best food was and the caves that make the best dens."

She raised his chin, looking into his moist eyes. "I'm kind of like that mountain lion. I upset people down here in the flatlands and kind of scare them, too. They don't know how to take me, and I don't know how to take them."

"Y-you could learn to live here. I-I'd help you," he offered excitedly, his eyes flashing with hope.

She kissed his cheek, smiling inwardly. "I've tried to learn, but there isn't any help for it. Every critter, animal or human, has to live where he fits best—and I fit best in the mountains."

"B-but I want you here," he exclaimed, his voice breaking with anguish. He twisted away from her, then snatched up her britches and blouse and threw them back into the wardrobe. He closed its door and leaned against it, his chest heaving with emotion.

Jubilee blinked back tears. She knew leaving would be hard—but not this hard. At this moment she felt as if she held Tad's happiness, his very spirit, in her open hand, ready to cast them both aside. Why did things have to be so complicated, so difficult; why were people always saying good-bye and always getting hurt in this old world? she wondered, her heart squeezing with anguish. "Let me have my clothes, baby," she whispered, trying to steel her courage. "I have to roll them up in this blanket."

She could see Tad's fragile control crumbling, and he ran and fell on her bed and wept aloud, deep sobs racking his body.

Jubilee felt a flood of emotion released within her. At this moment her swell of pain was beyond tears. She sat down beside him and caressed his shoulders, wishing there was something she could do or say to ease his pain. "Hush, now. Don't cry," she murmured hoarsely. A heavy, sick feeling claimed her stomach.

Trying to obey, Tad took some deep breaths until he had the strength to raise his head. His face was blotched and bleak with sorrow. "E-everybody leaves me," he stammered, tears still clinging to his long lashes. "Nobody likes me well enough to stay. All the other nannies left, now y-you're leaving, too."

A suffocating sensation lodged in Jubilee's breast. She rocked his cold, trembling body back and forth, remembering how angry she'd been that her predecessor had left. In her heart of hearts she knew his confidence was low and suspected he just couldn't survive another farewell. If she left, he would keep on living, but he'd bear a wound to his spirit that would never heal properly. With a ripple of insight, she wondered if she was leaving because she didn't fit in, or simply because she'd been humiliated.

Tad clutched her desperately, pressing his small fingers into her flesh. "S-stay," he choked out, a shiny tear racing down his smooth cheek. "I like y-you best of all. I-I love you!"

A lump formed in Jubilee's throat that was too big to swallow. She asked herself if she'd taken on this child for money or out of a desire to help him. Some people might befriend folks, then cast them aside like an old rag when being friends wasn't convenient anymore—but that wasn't the way she'd been raised. To let a loved one down when they really needed you would leave a hole in your soul that a whole lifetime of church-going couldn't repair.

She eased Tad away and wiped his tears. "All right, baby," she sighed, knowing that she was walking into dangerous circumstances with her eyes wide open. "I'll stay until school starts," she promised in a consoling tone, her voice none to steady.

Tad gazed at her with adoration. "D-do you promise?"

Song of the Lark

Jubilee crossed her heart three times, knocked on her forehead twice, then blew through her cupped hands. "*I promise*," she answered with a big smile.

Tad tried to smile at the elaborate gesture, but he was so overcome with emotion, he could only lean against her and snuffle softly. Touched by his open gratitude, she caressed his hair and rocked him back and forth, hearing his snuffles finally subside and feeling warmth return to his trembling limbs.

Looking over the top of his head, she peered at her reflection in the mirror. "You're a fool for sure now, Jubilee Jones," she whispered to herself.

Chapter Six

Jubilee walked into Stephen's study, looking for a book to read. Although he wasn't there, the room held the scent of his bay rum cologne and fine cigars, and a chill raced over her arms as she pulled out a handsome volume of Scott and started examining it. A whole week had passed since her disgrace, but she flipped through the book's pages still unable to concentrate.

She couldn't shake her sense of humiliation and remorse that she'd once thought Stephen might be in love with her. How foolish she felt—mooning over him when he was courting a beautiful Asheville socialite. Several times he'd looked as if he wanted to speak with her, but she hadn't given him a chance. Why should she be humiliated yet again? Determined to pull herself together, she tucked the book under her arm and started to leave just as he walked into the room.

"I-I thought you were at the lumber yard," she stammered, her heart thumping in surprise. She stared at his handsome face, but saw no rebuke there. "I was looking for a book," she added to justify her presence in the study.

Song of the Lark

Stephen's dark suit strained against his body, emphasizing his powerful shoulders and thighs as he went to his desk and opened its drawer. "I forgot these," he explained, pulling out a sheaf of documents and riffling through them. He glanced at the gold-stamped volume she held. "You're welcome to read what you might find," he offered amiably, his expression reflecting interest in her choice. He studied her with speculation. "You have a hunger, don't you?"

"A hunger?"

"A hunger for knowledge."

"I never thought of it that way," she answered, feeling as if he'd caught her trespassing on his personal domain. "But I like to learn. It's fun to learn things."

Stephen smiled. "Yes, it is. But you'd be surprised how few people share your opinion." His face softened and she read approval in his eyes.

He walked toward the door and she gave a secret sigh of relief. She'd been anxious about speaking with him ever since the party, and now it was behind her. He didn't seem upset with her, but she sensed a deep tension still hovering between them.

At the threshold, he stopped and turned, his face thoughtful. "Tad said you'd considered leaving."

"Yes," she answered, nervously fingering the book, "but I changed my mind. I decided Tad needed me too much."

He studied her as if he was seeing her for the first time, and her heart turned over in her breast. "Yes, he does need you, and I'm glad he talked you into staying. He hesitated for a moment, then walked over and lifted her chin. "I hope Estell didn't hurt you the night of the party," he said in a soft tone. "She can be ... umm ... difficult at times."

Jubilee flushed. "No," she lied, her face turning hot. "Of course not." Horrified, she wondered if she'd been so transparent that everyone there had witnessed her shame.

"Estell has a way of coloring the truth, presenting things in a way that make them seem more than they are," he continued, measuring his words as if he'd given them some thought.

Her knees went weak beneath her. What was he saying? What was he trying to tell her? She ached to ask, but knew she couldn't risk her pride again, not when it was already so battered and bruised. "No," she repeated, becoming more uncomfortable by the minute. "Why should something one of your guests said bother me? After all, I have no part in your life here."

A moment of charged silence filled the air, then he said, "Actually, you do." His eyes suddenly darkened and a muscle twitched in his jaw. "You're becoming more important to Tad and me every day."

A thrill of excitement ran through Jubilee and she stood rooted to the floor, wondering how she should respond. Her natural instincts told her to smile, to reply, but her pride held her back, so she said nothing.

Stephen paused, then reached into his deep jacket pocket and pulled out a slim jewelry box. "Here, this is for you," he announced, placing the box in her hand. "I was going to give it to you tonight, but I'll give it to you now instead. Go ahead, open it."

Jubilee's pulse fluttered wildly. Scarcely knowing what she was doing, she opened the box and found a lovely strand of pearls. She let out an audible breath, then took out the necklace and laid the box aside. "They're beautiful," she whispered, meeting his pleased eyes. "Why, I've never had anything so nice!"

"The pearls don't have the same sentimental value, but perhaps they can replace your button necklace."

"Th-That's all right. I restrung them."

"Well, now you'll have two necklaces," he laughed.

She sensed he wanted to say something else about the

pearls, about the terrible night of the party, but he just looked at her silently. Then, something flickered deep in his eyes and his face slowly set in cold resolve, like a pond freezing over.

"Well, I must go. I have work waiting," he finally offered, placing the portfolio under his arm. With that, he left the study.

Jubilee realized that she hadn't properly thanked him and her bosom burned with regret. Why hadn't she said something, just anything, instead of standing there like a hapless mute? She traced her fingers over the cool pearls resting in her palm, amazed by the costly gift—then she warned herself not to become too excited. She wasn't anyone special to him. He was just offering her the gift out of common decency. He probably felt sorry for her.

Had she made the right decision in staying, knowing what lay ahead of her? It would only be for a few months, she thought, getting up her strength. Surely she could last until school started. She just had to focus her life on sending her wages back to Granny and helping Tad all she could. Still, the gift of the pearls touched her deeply, and just thinking about becoming more important to Stephen every day made her glow with happiness. Brimming with unanswered questions, she rushed to the study window and parted the drapes to catch a glimpse of him getting into his carriage. She watched the smart brougham until it was gone, and then she leaned her forehead against the smooth windowpane, her good sense finally smothering her blossoming hope.

The pearls meant nothing. They were only a thoughtful gift from a generous employer. She might have had a chance of winning his love without Estell in the picture, but how could someone like herself compete with a gorgeous blonde so well versed in the social graces?

She'd made a fool of herself once. She wouldn't make the same mistake twice.

* * *

The next afternoon as Jubilee sat in the kitchen with Delilah, helping her peel turnips, she studied the old woman's wise face, realizing she was fiercely loyal to the Wentworths and knew all their secrets. She was so attached to the family that every detail of their life was important to her. The pair worked in silence for a while, and then thinking that she just had to mention it, Jubilee suddenly piped up, "Delilah, would you tell me about Brandon? Why does no one even speak of him? Why is there so much secrecy in this house where he's concerned?"

Distress clouded the cook's eyes. "Oh, Miz Jubilee, that's a long old story," she answered, continuing with her work. "You don't wants to hear that."

Jubilee held her ground. "Yes, I do. I truly care. Where in the world is he?"

Delilah wagged her head with disapproval. "I thinks he's back with those New York folks where he went to school. But only the Lord knows for sure."

"New York? Why did he leave here?"

The cook sighed with distress. "Oh, chile, you's sure full of questions."

"Well, it just seems strange that he doesn't live here in this fine mansion when the Wentworths have so much money."

"You only knows the half of it," Delilah said, flicking a turnip peeling aside. "Mist' Stephen don't have much money a'tall. He be in debt real bad."

Jubilee searched the old woman's face to make sure she'd heard her right. How could the richest man in Asheville not have money? Why, everyone knew the Wentworths were rolling in money. "I-I don't understand," she murmured in disbelief. "How can that be?"

Delilah frowned and shoved the vegetables aside. "Does you remember the day you came here—the day Mist' Stephen was leaving on a trip?"

Song of the Lark

Jubilee nodded, remembering the dark look on his face as he'd walked from the mansion.

"Well," Delilah said in a hushed tone, "he was goin' to mortgage his lumber yard so's he'd have money to keep goin'. Mist' Stephen go all the way to Knoxville 'cause he don't like borrowin' from that banker Throg one bit. That man be awful stingy and ill as a old mare, too!"

Jubilee let out a sharp breath. "Why, I thought Stephen had tons of money," she exclaimed, slumping back in her chair.

"No, he be tryin' to keep the lumber yard goin' so folks around here will have work—and the folks in the mountains, too. Everybody 'round here is gonna be in big trouble if Wentworth Enterprises fails."

"Fails?" Jubilee echoed, her body stiffening. "Why, that's impossible. How did he get in such a fix?"

Delilah heaved a weary sigh. "Since you be livin' under this roof, I reckon I's gonna tell you." Her eyes flashed. "But you's got to promise to keep this quiet as quiet can be."

Jubilee nodded, only imagining what she might hear.

"When old man Hamish died," Delilah began, picking up her knife once more, "Mist' Brandon jump up and say he want his half of his daddy's money—and he say he want it right then, too. Mist' Stephen couldn't sell the lumber yard, so he had to go into the bank savin's." She shook a peeling aside. "Fact of it bein', he had to give Mist' Brandon 'bout all of it, and it near broke him." She wagged her head sorrowfully. "Mist' Stephen thought the business would save him, but lately other lumber companies been underbiddin' him for big jobs. And he spent a heap of money carryin' poor lil' Tad to doctors."

Jubilee recalled the flicker of pain she sometimes caught in Stephen's eyes and suspected it had to do with his brother, but she'd never imagined this. Feeling sick inside, she wondered what kind of person Brandon was and how he could be so selfish. For long moments she sat there trying to digest the horrible news. At last she whispered, "Well, what is Brandon doing with all his money?"

Delilah jerked her brows together. "I reckon he be havin' a good time like he say he was gonna do." She leaned forward and in a confidential tone added, "It hurt Mist' Stephen real bad when his brother jump up and run off leavin' him sittin' here high and dry."

Jubilee mulled everything over. No wonder Stephen didn't want to talk about Brandon. How heartbreaking it must have been for his own brother to desert him. What a strain he'd been living under.

"What make it bad," Delilah went on in a sympathetic tone, "is when them boys was little they was close as two peas in a pod. Now they's hard feelin's 'tween them—that what hurt Mist' Stephen worst of all."

Shock ran through Jubilee as she considered Tad's future. By the time he was grown there might not be anything for him to inherit. "Does anyone know how to reach Brandon?"

A thoughtful expression moved over Delilah's face. "I reckon not, 'cept maybe Alice Tallant." She picked up a potato and brushed it off. "He used to be sweet on that gal. Maybe he wrote her a letter or somethin'. He sure never wrote Mist' Stephen nothin' though."

Jubilee pressed her lips together. How could one brother treat another in such a fashion? she wondered, feeling herself go cold inside. True, sometimes money made folks lose all their sense, but she'd never heard of *anything* like this. Her mind awhirl, she sat there silently, wondering if anything could be done.

Jubilee finished the letter she'd been writing and inserted it in an envelope, feeling only a little guilty for interfering in her employer's affairs. She pushed back from Stephen's desk. "There—that's that!" she said under her breath, imagining all the good work the letter would do.

After a few nights of tossing and turning, she'd finally decided to visit Alice and found that the lovesick girl had received only one letter from Brandon, and that was months ago. The tattered envelope bore the address of a New York City hotel. Jubilee could only hope the younger Wentworth still lived there, or if he'd moved that the letter would be forwarded to him. She suspected that Stephen would be upset about her writing to his brother, but there was no reason he should know about it—not right away anyway. In the letter, she'd mentioned Isabelle's untimely death and also added that Stephen was in deep financial trouble and needed Brandon's help. She was certain Stephen would be too proud to admit this, so she'd do it for him.

She closed the envelope and put a stamp on it. She was so lost in thought that she didn't hear Chambers until he'd entered the room and was halfway to the desk. "Chambers!" she said, her stomach lurching as she looked up and met his questioning eyes.

"I see you've just finished a letter," he stated in his usual chilly tone. He walked to the desk and put out his hand. "Give it to me and I shall post it."

Jubilee inched her fingers over the address, not wanting him to see it. "Oh, that's all right," she replied, wondering how she could get out of this sticky situation. "I'll do it later."

"Don't be silly," Chambers snapped, hard lines settling about his mouth. "The carrier will be here soon and it's my job to collect the mail." Before she could protest, he snatched up the envelope and slid his gaze over the address. His face went milk white. "You're writing Mister Brandon?" he remarked in harsh astonishment. His condemning eyes bored into her. "Where did you get the address?"

Jubilee stood, deciding she'd have to confide in him

whether she wanted to or not. Thank the Lord the letter was sealed. Even Chambers wouldn't be bold enough to open someone else's mail. "From Alice Tallant," she answered, lifting her chin a notch higher. "I'm surprised no one has spoken to her before this."

"You're meddling into things that don't concern you," he warned, his jowls quivering with outrage. "Where Mister Brandon is concerned, the subject is closed!"

She paced the study, crossed her arms, and decided she wouldn't be bullied. "If you aren't aware of it, your employer needs some help. So, maybe you should stop being so stubborn and start worrying about helping him."

Chamber's brows shot up. "I'm *aware* of all that goes on in this house," he intoned as if she were foolish to think that he wasn't. "He'll get no help from Mister Brandon, you can bank on that." Glancing at the envelope again, he studied the address. "New York," he murmured thoughtfully. "Yes, that would be like him."

"What do you mean by that?" Jubilee questioned, sensing he might reveal another piece of the puzzle.

The butler sighed heavily, then took some letters Stephen had written from his bronze mail rack. "Mister Brandon always pined for the bright lights—the fast life, if you will. He found living here in Asheville frightfully dull, even as a boy. His father sent him to a preparatory school in the East. That and a few trips to Europe made him quite dissatisfied with life in North Carolina."

Jubilee walked back to the desk. "But this is his home. He needs to know what's going on here. After all, he's still a member of the family."

The butler's face hardened. "That means absolutely nothing to him." He swept a disparaging gaze over her. "And I can assure you that Mister Stephen would be furious if he knew you were sending such a letter." He straightened his back. "As his butler, it's my duty to look after his best interest, so I must confiscate this correspondence."

Song of the Lark

Jubilee's heart dipped. Chambers was right, Stephen would be furious, but more importantly, all her work would be in vain. "But that's just it—it would be in his best interest to mail the letter," she explained in a pleading voice, "but to keep it a secret." She clutched his arm, not above begging if it would help. "Don't you see that something good might come of it? If nothing happens, we've only lost a stamp and a little time."

Stoically silent, the butler left the study with the mail. Frantic that he had the letter, she followed at his heels. "Have some faith in Brandon," she advised, moving in front of him so that she could hold his hard gaze. "Perhaps he *does* care about his family," she added, hoping Chambers's great loyalty for his master's well being would make him do the right thing.

In the foyer, Chambers stopped, then slapped her letter atop the others. "Very well. I shall post the letter as you've requested, but it will do you no good. It will come back unopened, so it makes little difference if it is posted or not. You will see. Your good intentions are quite misguided."

"And this will be our little secret?" Jubilee asked, weak with relief.

He stiffly nodded his head. "As you wish."

Flushed with joy, she snapped off a rosebud from the bouquet that sat on the console and slipped it through his buttonhole. "There," she said, thinking the red bloom gave him a bit of color. "You look fetching—like you're ready for a party." She gave him her best smile, so happy the letter would be mailed she couldn't be angry with him.

Chambers gazed at her as if she'd lost her mind, then pulled the rosebud from his buttonhole and tossed it on the console. "For me to wear a boutonniere would be quite improper, miss—very bad form. I'm a *butler*, not a gentleman of leisure."

"But you must have some private life. Some home in England."

Chambers face took on a faraway look. "Yes, indeed. But that was all long ago."

She watched him as he ran a white glove over a piece of furniture, checking for dust. "Tell me about it. What was it like there?"

He paused for a moment. "I was born in the Cotswolds. Lots of lovely limestone cottages there, and thousands of sheep with the finest wool in the world."

Jubilee saw a crack in his armor and tried desperately to prize it open. "And?"

His eyes cleared as if he were forcefully bringing his mind under control. "And that is all," he said woodenly. "I shall never see England again and do not choose to talk about it."

Jubilee put her hand on his arm, sorry for him that he was so emotionally constricted. "You must have drunk tea there. All Englishmen drink tea, don't they?"

His eyes brightened and she knew she'd stumbled upon a subject that he felt passionate about. "Yes, but not just any tea, miss. Earl Grey is preferred." His face darkened. "But it isn't obtainable in this backwater." He gave a heartfelt sigh. "What I would give for a good cup of Earl Grey. In many ways this country is scarcely civilized," he proclaimed dourly. With that, he opened the door and left the mansion to carry the letters to the mailbox at the end of the driveway.

Jubilee watched him walking away, then closed the heavy panel and leaned against it, wondering if he'd ever had a good time in his life. She'd tried so long to break down Chambers's wall of reserve and he always rebuffed her friendly overtures. When he'd spoken of home, his stern visage had slipped only for a second, but in that moment she suddenly understood he was really quite a lonely man who used stiff formality to hide the fact.

She let out a long breath and vowed then and there that before she left this household she would get him to smile and even laugh. The man had to be human, even if he didn't act like it.

An hour later she walked into Tad's room, finding him sitting on the floor playing with some tiny toy wagons. "Hello, young man," she greeted him, easing down beside him and picking up one of the little wagons. "You look like you could use some company."

He smiled, obviously glad to see her. "Y-you want to play?"

She lined up three wagons, then moved the first one several feet. "You know, it's wonderful outside today," she commented, crawling over the rug on her hands and knees as she moved her wagon parallel to his. "All clear and cool, and the clouds look like big cotton balls. Why don't we go outside and take a little ride?" She glanced at Tad and noticed a glint of fear in his eyes.

"N-no. I don't want to," he answered slowly, his voice stiff and hesitant.

"You could ride General Sherman," she offered lightly, hoping to entice him with his fascination in the mule.

Interest flickered across his face, but then his expression clouded up once more. He shook his head and went back to playing with the wagons.

Jubilee knew she'd have to go slowly with Tad to get him over his fear of riding. She'd asked him to ride many times and he'd always refused. Just getting him to the stables would be a huge victory. "I'll tell you what," she suggested, sitting up and clasping her arms about her legs. "Let's go to the window. It's so pretty I just want you to look out."

Just to please her, Tad slowly got up, and she guided him to the window. The mansion's summer grounds were in all their glory. The beds were ablaze with scarlet azaleas, and buttercups peeked shyly out from among the moss under the leafy trees. From the bedroom window they could see the stables, where one of the grooms was leading a glossy mare about under the shady trees as he prepared to curry her.

"Why don't we go on down?" Jubilee suggested, knowing Tad hadn't been outside all day. "I'll groom General Sherman, and you can brush and curry your pony. I'll bet he's getting real lonesome for you."

Tad looked at her with trusting eyes. "We'd just brush him?"

Jubilee sent him an encouraging smile, her heart aching for him. "Sure, if that's what you want." She gave him her fancy promising gesture that always made him smile.

They left the room and went down the stairs, and all the while Jubilee kept up a cheery line of chatter to boost Tad's mood. Outside, she felt a breeze stirring the fine curls on her forehead and dancing across her cheeks. When they arrived at the stables, the groom greeted her respectfully, doffed his hat, and smiled at Tad. In the dim stables the mingled scents of hay and leather and horses hung on the heavy air, all aromas with which Jubilee was well acquainted.

First they curried General Sherman's coarse coat, and Jubilee got Tad to smile with tales of her medicine-show days. At last they brought his pony, a beautiful Shetland with a golden mane and tail, from his box. The pony whickered and nuzzled Tad, and the boy ran his hand over the animal's withers affectionately.

While they worked on the pony, brushing its coat until it shone like satin, Tad looked at Jubilee and started talking. "D-do you know a-about my mother?" he asked, his tone announcing he was hungry to talk. "Do you know how she died?"

Jubilee was instantly alert. This was the first time Tad had ever mentioned his mother's death, and she sensed that what he was going to say was important. "Yes," she said kindly, talking in a relaxed manner as they curried the pony. "Delilah told me about it. She also told me she was the prettiest lady in the world, and the nicest too."

Tad shook his head, working silently. A few minutes later, he put the curry comb aside and said, "You're magic, aren't you?"

Jubilee laughed. "I can do some magic tricks, but we can all be magic if we want to. It's all how you look at things."

His eyes soft and luminous, he held her gaze. "Can you see people in heaven?"

Jubilee's heart pitched. Seeing the direction the boy was going, she stopped currying the pony and knelt beside him. "No," she replied, gently taking his shoulders. "No one can do that."

"No one?"

"No one in the whole world. That's what pictures are for, and memories, and sometimes dreams."

Tad looked at her as if he didn't understand.

She cupped his face, wondering if she'd done him a disservice. Had Stephen been right about his advice to teach the boy to only believe in what he could see, taste, and feel? No, there had to be something more. Still, she couldn't give him false hope.

"When I was about twelve my father was sick for a long, long time," she said softly. "Then one day he died. But I still talk to him here"—she touched her head—"and here"—she laid her hand over her heart. "When you love someone very much, they never leave you, for they become a part of you." She drew him closer. "If you want, you can always have them near you. All you have to do is think of a happy time you had with them—or imagine what they would say when something funny happens. You can still share your life with them."

Tad smiled softly. "I-I like that idea—but I really wanted it to be magic."

Tears pricked Jubilee's eyes. "If you want, you can think of that as magic, for in a way it really is."

They continued talking, and for the first time Tad

opened his heart about his mother, bringing up dozens of memories of her. He told Jubilee about the times he'd ridden with his mother, and how he remembered the scent of her perfume, and the sound of her laughter. She'd never heard him talk so much at one time and noticed that he was so caught up in his memories that he wasn't stuttering as much as usual.

Tad gazed at her with big eyes. "Mama was always so good. She was kind to everyone."

"And that's just how she'd want you be with everyone, too. When you do that, you show her honor."

He tilted his head to the side. "H-how is that?"

"Well," Jubilee began, trying to put the idea into words that he could understand. If you see someone who needs help, you can help them. That would make your mother happy."

"She would kn-know about it?"

"I like to think so."

A mewing sound floated from the dim shadows, and Jubilee saw a large cat round a bale of hay and look their way. Hay covered the animal's scruffy fur, one of her ears was tattered and torn, and her plume-like tail was so big it seemed that her body was attached to it, rather than the other way around. Obviously the survivor of many scraps, the battle-scarred cat approached them, step by cautious step. She gazed directly at Tad, blinking great green eyes that glittered in the gloom.

The boy's face brightened and he crouched forward, holding out welcoming arms. Jubilee started to tell the boy that the animal might scratch him, but she noticed the cat seemed exceptionally tame. In a matter of seconds, the animal started purring and rubbing against Tad's welcoming hands.

The boy cradled the bedraggled cat in his arms, his face suffused with hope. "C-can I keep it and take care of it? Mama would like that, wouldn't she?"

Jubilee knew she'd been caught by her own words, and

had to admit that her lesson on kindness applied to stray, starving cats as well as humans. She had no idea what Stephen would think about Tad keeping the bedraggled feline, but she knew she'd make it right with him somehow. The flash of hope in the boy's eyes couldn't be denied. She smoothed her hand over the stray, its deep purr vibrating against her palm. "Yes," she answered, her throat tightening a bit, "I think that would make her very happy."

"Wh-what will we call her?" Tad asked excitedly.

Jubilee eyed the animal's striped coat, which looked like butter and dark molasses mixed together. Remembering a cat she'd had with the same coloring, she suggested, "Why don't we call her Matilda? I used to have a fine cat named that."

Joy animated Tad's face. "Y-yes, I like that." He smiled and hugged the cat close, and Jubilee felt warm and grateful.

Watching the boy, she considered his father and how he'd been hurt—hurt so badly that he'd lost his hope and faith. How lonely he must be inside, she thought. How he needed someone to help him believe that life was worth living once more. It was funny how people could easily see a person's maimed body, but not a wounded spirit like Stephen's. She knew how to cure many illnesses with herbs, but this malady of the heart and soul was something else again.

Thank the Lord, the boy had made another precious step forward. If only she could help Stephen to do the same.

Chambers handed Jubilee a letter as he passed her in the foyer, then briskly went on his way. Interest perked her up when she noticed Effie's handwriting on the envelope. She ripped into it then and there and started reading. Afternoon light streamed over her cousin's crude sentences that stood out bold and clear. Jubilee's heart constricted with pain, for Granny had taken a turn for the worse. Jubilee was being asked to return to Maple Leaf Hollow.

She read the letter again and her hands trembled. As the startling news sank in, her stomach drew up in a knot. How could she prepare Tad for school when she must return to the mountains? How could he do without her when he'd come to depend on her so much? On the other hand, her first duty was to her family, especially the grandmother she loved so much. Would she be forced to choose between two people who both needed her dearly?

She walked into the parlor and sank onto a chair. She couldn't leave Tad when he was doing so well. It would destroy all the progress he'd made, and, justified or not, he'd feel abandoned yet again. She rose, emotions warring within her. There was a solution to the problem: she just had to be clever enough to find it. She paced about and pulled her confused thoughts together, and then something clicked in her mind. Yes, that was it, she decided with a glow of hope. It was dead simple. She'd just take Tad with her. How she'd convince his father to agree to the plan, she had no idea.

After a few moments of confidence building, she strode into Stephen's study, the letter clenched in her hand. He sat behind his desk and looked up with a smile. "Have a seat," he said in a pleasant tone that still made her tremulous even after all the time she'd known him.

She gingerly sat down and stole a glance at him as he shuffled through the papers on his desk. Just the sight of him melted her heart. Despite her efforts to keep her heart in check, she was more besotted with him than ever, and found it increasingly difficult to hide her feelings from him.

He pushed his papers aside and gave her his full attention. "You wanted to speak to me?"

"Yes, I just got a letter from Cousin Effie." She showed him the letter and prayed silently. "It's about

Song of the Lark

Granny. She's feeling poorly and wants to see me. I have a feeling I may be gone for quite a spell."

A deep frown furrowed Stephen's brow. "This is a bad time for a trip. Tad is just beginning to improve. I was hoping you'd stay until school started." He looked at her with genuine concern. "How long would you be gone?"

"The rest of the summer," she admitted, her voice quavering with nervousness. Was she ruining her chances for a long-term position with her request? Whether he would ask her to return if she left, she had no idea.

His face clouded with uneasiness. "What happens to Tad while you're gone? Must you leave?"

Her throat tightened with emotion. Somehow she had to make him understand just how important her presence was at her old home. "Granny is all the close kin I have. When I left the mountains I promised her I'd come back right away if she really needed me."

Stephen stood and walked around his desk. "I understand," he said with some warmth, "but I'm afraid we'll lose all the ground we've made with Tad."

She rose, her legs trembling. "There *is* a solution to the problem," she proposed softly, noticing his eyes spark with interest.

"And what's that?"

Jubilee moistened her lips and hoped her next words would come out just right. "I-I could take Tad with me."

Surprise flashed on Stephen's face. "No. I don't think that would be a good idea," he returned with a disapproving frown.

"*But why?*" she shot back, her voice rough with disappointment.

Stephen crossed the room, then paused and surveyed her with knitted brows. "Because Tad's never been away from this mansion. He's a delicate child, and at this point emotionally very fragile." He sighed as if facing up to a fact. "Besides that, he's always had the best and been cared for by servants. He has no idea how to fend for himself or make do when the situation requires." His eyes clung to hers, analyzing her reactions. "Are those enough reasons?"

"But the mountains would be a good place for him to start doing that," she insisted, taking a brave step forward. "And the fresh air would be a real tonic for him."

Stephen regarded her evenly. "What if he fell—hurt himself in some way?"

"Old Doc Hall could take care of him." She laughed, trying to ease the tension of the situation. "He's no fancy city doctor, but he's tended hundreds of mountain young'uns."

Stephen's scowl told her it would be impossible to change his mind, and all the self-doubt she'd ever experienced rushed over her. Then, from somewhere deep within her, she drew courage. She had to make him agree to the plan. It was either that or crush a tender heart. "Change is just what he needs," she contended, pursuing her argument with renewed vigor. "It's time for him to learn about the real world. It's time he wasn't carried on a feather pillow." She spoke in a softer voice. "He hasn't been away from this house since his mother was killed. The change would let some of the bad memories fade from his mind." She inched closer yet. "I know what he eats and I'll cook for him," she promised, searching for any hopeful sign on Stephen's expressive face. "The mountain folk love children and he would love them. A few months in the hills would whet his appetite and put the weight on him. Oh, don't you see this is a real blessing in disguise? It's just what Tad needs!"

Stephen's mouth softened a bit, but he remained silent.

Jubilee was now close enough to touch him. "I know how precious he is to you," she conceded, gazing into his dark eyes. "He's precious to me too. I won't let anyone or anything hurt him. I bind my word to it." He seemed half convinced and so she pushed her case farther. "As you said, he's hardly been out of this mansion since

Song of the Lark

he was born. The trip will make him believe in himself and put a little gravel in his craw if the big boys try to push him around this September." She put her hand on his arm. "What's your answer?" she asked, her heart overflowing. "Won't you say yes? It would be the best thing you could ever do."

Stephen looked at her young face, shining with hope, her direct green eyes, and the cloud of glossy auburn hair tied back at the nape of her neck. In truth, he knew that she would look after him and give him the best of everything she had. Actually, it seemed that children needed little as long as they had love and attention, and those were things she'd give in abundance. As far as his son becoming homesick, he realized that the boy was so emotionally attached to Jubilee that she could easily divert his mind. But it was her statement about the mansion being filled with bad memories that convinced him. Truly, it would be a blessing if Tad could get away for the summer and start the school year with a fresh outlook on life.

A moment of charged silence filled the air, and then he replied, "Very well, Curly Top, you win. I agree, but only under one condition."

Jubilee's eyes swam with glistening tears and shone as brightly as the lustrous pearls she wore about her neck. "Yes," she answered quietly, "and what might it be?"

"I suppose you know there's a Wentworth logging camp near the hollow."

"Yes, that's where Micah used to work."

"If anything comes up, anything at all," he commanded, "you must contact the manager of that camp. He'll send a rider for me immediately."

"Of course," she replied, her expression marked with deep relief.

"Another thing—I insist my yard foreman escort you to the hollow. He can spend the night at the logging camp, then return and give me a report on your trip."

A smile blossomed on her face and made her prettier than ever. "All right, if that's what you want. And I'll work with Tad all summer. Why, by the time he gets back, he'll be talking just fine."

Stephen walked to the window and stared at the vast green lawn. Had he been a fool for agreeing to her proposition? The mountains could be a formidable place, full of beauty and mystery, but also danger. And how much did he know about the people in Maple Leaf Hollow? Then, in a calmer frame of mind, he considered Jubilee. She'd accomplished miracles since she'd arrived. Surely he could trust this miracle worker to look after Tad for a few months. He turned about and met her sympathetic gaze. "This is a new experience for me," he admitted awkwardly. "I've never been away from him for more than a week at a time."

She came to the window. "I'll take care of him," she vowed in a soft voice alive with love. She clutched his arms and a gentle, wistful look misted her eyes. "I promise you that with everything I hold dear."

The tender moment penetrated his heart. What a striking effect she had on him, filling him with forbidden desire. He forgot himself and caressed her shoulders, moving his thumbs in gentle circles. Lonely to the core of his being, he was seized with a strong urge to take her in his arms and brush his lips over hers.

He violently suppressed the aberrant notion, warning himself that he couldn't become personally involved with her. He'd let his emotions run free once before and that was enough. She was a girl who was helping his son, and could be nothing more. She knew it, too. She could be no more than an employee. If she were more, it would bring disaster on both their heads. At that moment all he could think of was sending her away so he wouldn't be tempted by her exquisite face and tender curves. "You'd better tell Tad," he said lightly, silently cursing his body for betraying him. "I'm sure he'll be excited."

Her eyes danced with happiness. "Yes. We have a lot to do before we leave." A gentle smile lit her face. "Thank you. Thank you so much." She stepped backward, then hesitated, an expectant look on her face.

"Yes, is there something else?"

"Do you think—I mean would it be all right," she stammered, "if Cleo ate dinner with Tad in the dining room tonight?"

Stephen considered her hopeful face, staggered by the question. Never in a million years would his father have permitted such a familiarity with colored folk, and he'd never thought of the possibility himself, but when all was said and done, he could find no fault with the request. Tad and Cleo were best friends, period. "Yes, tell Delilah to set another plate for dinner tonight. I think they'd enjoy eating together."

"Yes, of course," she rushed out, her bosom heaving with pleasure as she walked to the door.

Stephen smiled to himself, knowing what to expect, and seconds later Delilah came into the room, a white cup towel thrown over her shoulder. She sent him a measured glance. "Are you sure you wants Cleo to eat with Tad tonight?" she asked doubtfully. "Miz Jubilee say you are, but I ain't ever heard of nothin' like that in all my born days!"

"I'm sure as I can be," he replied lightly.

"Mist' Hamish shore wouldn't like that."

"My father was a bigot. He's gone now and his ways with him."

A slow smile crept over the cook's face. "You's never done nothin' like that. You's changin' right 'fore these old eyes, Mist' Stephen." She regarded him again, then shook her head and left the study, chuckling to herself.

Stephen considered her words. The old woman was

right. He'd never done anything like this, but he saw it as an opportunity of sorts. He'd been carried along by Jubilee's thoughtfulness and made the right choice. Slowly but surely something was coming to life in him once more and it felt wonderful.

Chapter Seven

"See all those big trees?" Jubilee asked Tad as her mule pulled their buggy down the mountain road. "Those are what your father cuts and takes to his lumber mill so people can build houses."

With an expression of awe, the boy surveyed the misty blue mountains and the tall pines that stood out like sentinels against the glowing sunset. He said nothing, seemingly mesmerized by the gorgeous scenery around him.

Jubilee pointed to the sky, streaked with orange and gold. "Look, there's an eagle!"

Tad peered at the bird that was silhouetted in graceful flight against the ruddy heavens. "I-I've never seen a bird that b-big," he stuttered, idly stroking Matilda's silky coat as she nestled in his lap.

"You're going to see a lot of new things up here in the mountains," Jubilee explained, noticing that there was already a new light in his eyes. Hope glowed within her, for she was sure that he'd be loved here and that it would be the best medicine he could ever get.

How different this trip had been from her last. Funded

with Stephen's money, she and Tad had slept in an inn and enjoyed a relatively easy journey. Their escort from the lumber yard had taken the cutoff to the logging camp fifteen minutes ago and they were now on their own, excitement building within them by the second.

The road was becoming steeper, and boulders jutted from the land, sweeping upward toward the trees. The pines towered taller and greener and the moist air was pungent with their tangy scent. They'd already passed several rocky farms, and Jubilee knew the people who lived in all of them. "If we hurry," she told Tad, "we can make it to the cabin for supper. Effie is sure to have something good cooked. She always does."

By now General Sherman seemed to know he was going home, and his pace picked up. Jubilee's heart lurched as they came around a bend and she saw Granny's cabin snuggled against a rocky mountain covered with pines and flanked by a small peach orchard.

The log cabin had been added on to years ago, forming a T-shape, and its precious glass windowpanes glimmered gold, setting it apart from most of the cabins that only had shuttered windows. In contrast, its roof was patched and some of the chinking had crumbled out between the logs, giving the structure a dilapidated appearance. A great stone chimney towered at one end and blue smoke drifted upward, its homy, woodsy scent already reaching her nostrils. "There it is. There's home," she said excitedly.

Infected with her enthusiasm, Tad laughed and hugged Matilda close.

When they were fifty yards from the homestead, three hounds bounded from their place on the cabin porch and loped toward the buggy, barking joyously. Jubilee eased General Sherman to a halt, then called out, "Tray ... Blue ... Smoky!" soliciting an excited yapping and a furious wagging of tails.

Cousin Effie emerged from the cabin, wiping her hands

Song of the Lark

on the bottom of her long white apron that stood out in the gathering shadows. Garbed in a faded print dress, the heavy woman squinted at the buggy for a moment, then smiled and ran toward it, calling Jubilee's name. "Well, I declare, if you ain't a sight for sore eyes!" she exclaimed, reaching into the buggy and hugging her long lost cousin. "Praise the Lord, you're finally here!"

Brown hair, streaked with gray, slipped from the bun atop her head and her broad face flushed with excitement. Her ample body, free of a restricting corset, jiggled under her cotton dress as she rushed to the other side of the buggy to welcome Tad, who watched the proceedings with big eyes. "Well, bless my soul, who's this fine-lookin' young man?" She hugged the boy against her large bosom and embraced both him and Matilda at the same time.

Overwhelmed at her effusive welcome, Tad stared at her silently.

Jubilee laughed. "This is Tad. He's the boy I'm taking care of in Asheville." She patted his shoulder. "He's not much for talking to strangers unless he's in the right mood, but once he gets warmed up, he'll talk aplenty."

Cousin Effie eased back and ran a kind gaze over the travelers. "Well, don't just sit there like knots on a log. Y'all climb out of that buggy. I just made a stack cake, and I'll bet this boy would like to have a big hunk of it while it's still warm."

Relieved that she was finally home, Jubilee got out of the buggy and helped the boy down. Still unsure of himself, Tad took in his surroundings with wondering eyes. Jubilee watched Effie entertain him with questions about his cat, and when he'd lost his shyness, she removed some of her things from the buggy. Jubilee had left her new clothes in Asheville, but had brought a satchel of books she'd borrowed from Stephen's study, and eager to see Granny, she toted the heavy leather bag across the clearing.

Once inside the cabin, Jubilee dropped the satchel to the floor. Everything seemed right and familiar, and deep feelings swirled within her. Yes, it was all here just as she'd left it: the rough puncheon tables and chairs, the cupboards, the iron kettle and pewter dishes, the gun rack above the smoky fireplace, the braided rugs. The place even held the same warm reassuring scents of wood and kerosene, onions and potatoes, feather ticking and bacon grease. She was home at last.

Her heart beating with anticipation, she quietly walked into Granny's bedroom. There, asleep on a big feather bed, covered by a bright patchwork quilt and propped against several pillows, was a small, wizened mountain woman with snowy white hair twisted in a knot atop her head. Lines seamed the old woman's face, but delicate bones lay beneath the pale skin, bearing evidence of the beauty she'd once been.

Garbed in a mended nightgown, she lay on her back with one hand resting on top of the quilt. Jubilee looked at her gnarled, blue-veined hand with love and thought of all the clothes the woman had washed and meals she'd cooked during her long, hard life. With a rush of nostalgia, she sat on the side of the bed and clasped her grandmother's arm. "Granny, it's me," she murmured, her throat tightening.

The old woman's eyelids flickered open and revealed irises that were still a surprising cornflower blue. Then, in a voice as soft and delicate as thistle down, she whispered, *"Jubilee,"* the name filled with tenderness. Joy stole over Granny's weathered features and made her look strong and vital for a moment. "I been a-lookin' for you ever' day—a lookin' for my pretty Jubilee girl."

Jubilee smiled down at the blotchy, wrinkled face she loved so well and gently gathered the old's woman's slight frame close against her. How small and frail she was, she thought, wondering how long it would be before she went to her well-deserved reward. She laid her head

Song of the Lark

against her grandmother's bosom and felt the woman lightly stroke her hair just as she'd done after Jubilee's mother had passed away. Memories poured through her: Granny's voice waking her every morning, the sound of warbling birds as the pair picked herbs, the scent of flour and spice that the old woman's clothes emitted as she tucked Jubilee into bed as a child. It was all too much, and she brushed tears from her eyes.

They clung to each other for long moments, sharing unspoken messages of love. At last Jubilee eased her grandmother against the pillows, and the old woman took her face between smooth, work-worn hands. "I'm so glad you're here, girl. So glad you're here," she whispered, her eyes swimming in tears.

Being away from the hills had given Jubilee a new perspective, and in that moment it was as if she were seeing Granny anew, seeing her tender face whose beauty had been dimmed by years of work, but whose eyes still held the flame of life.

"I knew you was a-comin' today," Granny announced matter-of-factly. "A lark commenced a-callin' right outside my winder this mornin'. There ain't no better sign than that. A person always gets their heart's desire when they hear a lark a-singin' like that."

Jubilee smiled, remembering some of the old mountain omens Granny had taught her. She still half-believed in them, believed in them because they gave a person hope when they had nothing else.

Effie's warm laughter filtered into the bedroom and seconds later she walked in, carrying Tad on her broad hip. Matilda peeked from behind her tattered skirts, staring at the old woman with an unflinching gaze.

"Granny, this is Tad," Jubilee calmly explained. "He's the little boy I keep in Asheville—and that's his cat. I thought if it was all right, they'd visit with you a spell too. The way things worked out, we all kind of need to be together."

The old woman smiled and peered at the boy with open curiosity. "Well, ain't he a pretty little thing?" she remarked, showing the immediate acceptance and joy most mountain folk took in children. "He's so soft and tender lookin', he puts me in mind of a little chickadee-bird." Her eyes registered delight as they ran over his innocent face. "Howdy, boy. Make yourself t'home," she called in a quavering voice.

Silent, Tad shyly raised his hand in greeting.

"He doesn't talk much," Jubilee explained, slowly arranging the covers about the old woman's thin shoulders. She made her voice even softer. "His mama died and he's had a lot of bad luck."

Gentle compassion flooded Granny's face. "Well, ain't that a shame." Her head trembled slightly and she caught Effie's eye. "Fix that young'un a good supper with lots of white-sop gravy and biscuit-bread. We need to put some meat on them little bones."

Effie carried Tad from the room, regaling him with a steady string of cheerful chatter. Afterwards, Jubilee had a good talk with Granny, making her laugh as she described some of the things she'd seen in Asheville. When they'd caught up on all the news about the mountain folks, the old woman's eyes took on a happy glint and for a moment she looked twenty years younger.

"I've got somethin' special to tell you, girl," she drawled in her cracking voice. "Somethin' that will make you feel like a-dancin'."

Jubilee laughed. "Well, tell me. I haven't danced in a long time."

Granny's eyes snapped. "Micah's a-comin' home— and real soon too. Your brother's a-comin' home, honey."

Jubilee's heart skipped a beat. Lordamercy, she hadn't expected this when she'd decided to bring Tad to the mountains. How could she tell Micah she'd been living in the Wentworth mansion since she'd left the hollow?

Song of the Lark

With his pride and downright hatred for the Wentworths, it was something he'd never understand or accept. To Micah, the Wentworths represented only one thing: a family who'd maimed him, who as far as he was concerned had made him half a man. Her mind frantically grappled with the problem, but she found no answer.

"Why, that's wonderful, Granny," she commented softly, knowing she couldn't spoil her grandmother's happiness. She impulsively kissed the old woman's cheek as if the show of affection might offer protection from the terrible secret she carried. Sick with worry, she forced her trembling lips into a smile and tried to reflect her grandmother's enthusiasm. "With us all together again everything will be mighty fine," she said, praying she spoke the truth.

That night after Tad and Granny were asleep, Jubilee and Effie sat up talking and drinking coffee out of battered tin cups. Jubilee lounged at the table, feeling more relaxed than she had in a long time. Here in the mountains where she felt most secure, she didn't have to impress anyone or remember a senseless list of rules. Here she could simply be herself. She searched Effie's broad, flat face, bathed in the glow of a kerosene lamp. "How is Granny? She seems so frail. How is she really doing?" she asked, worrying about the weight the old woman had lost since she'd last seen her.

"She's not doin' good. She keeps gettin' weaker and weaker, and doesn't have any more strength than a newborn kitten."

"Does Doc Hall really know what's wrong with her?"

Effie gave a resigned sigh. "He knows somethin' is wrong with her heart, but he don't know exactly what. He's givin' her a tonic with laudanum, but it don't seem to have helped her much. She got real bad week before last. Her heart was beatin' so slow and faint, Doc Hall said he didn't know how she could make it. That's when I wrote you."

Jubilee considered the old doctor who'd served in the Confederate Army. She'd thought of him as ancient when she was a girl; perhaps he was now verging on senility. She yearned to take Granny to a modern city doctor, but realized the woman would never survive a visit to the flatlands. Like it or not, Granny would have to be tended by Doc Hall, and Jubilee would have to pray for a miracle.

They talked of Granny and drank more coffee, and then Effie scanned her with curious eyes. "Do you do any doctorin' in Ashville?"

Jubilee laughed. "Not really. Town folks don't hold strong to weed doctors."

They continued chatting about the kinfolks, and Effie mentioned that the mountain men were thinking of building a mill.

Jubilee put down her coffee cup. "A mill?" she echoed, becoming really interested. "Well, it's about time. We've needed one for years," she added, remembering how her father had been forced to travel all day to Skinner's Crossing to get corn and wheat ground at exorbitant prices. "Where will they build this mill?"

"On Sadlow Creek, near where it joins the French River. They's talk of havin' two sets of stones, and folks say Jordan McCoy will be gatherin' up the men to build it all."

Jubilee frowned, remembering the sour mountaineer who'd always challenged her father, and wondered why the hillmen couldn't find a better man to be in charge of things. But then McCoy had always been a bully, and he'd probably connived and harassed his way into the position.

They sat silent for a while, and then Effie suddenly blurted out, "I've got somethin' to tell you. When Micah comes, I'm goin' to move back to my old place for a while."

Jubilee looked at the woman who'd done so much for

her and Granny. Effie's brown hair was now streaked with gray and a web of wrinkles had settled around her eyes, across her forehead and her once smooth throat. She'd nursed everyone in the hollow since she was a girl, always giving, never taking. Sadly, the mountain men were blind to her inner beauty and only saw her plain face. What a shame that at thirty-five Effie was condemned to a lonely future without the comfort of a family to look forward to Jubilee thought, picturing the woman alone in her small cabin. "Why don't you just stay here with us?" she offered with real affection. "We could make the room. It wouldn't be any trouble."

Effie's forehead wrinkled in an unaccustomed frown. "No, with the boy, it would be too crowded. " 'Sides, I've been wantin' to go back and see my place—see how things are doin' there. With summer comin' in, the brambles will be takin' over everthin' 'less I yank 'em out. If you ever have to leave, I'll come back and stay with Granny then."

The statement made Jubilee wonder if she'd be invited back to Asheville at all. Stephen hadn't been that happy about her taking Tad to the hills for the summer. Would he find someone else to take care of the boy when she returned? All these things she mulled over in her mind, but to Effie she said nothing.

The woman reached across the table and patted Jubilee's arm with her rough, cracked hand. "You and Micah and Granny need to be a family again—like the old days," she said tenderly with a smile that softened her homely features.

Jubilee stiffened at the mention of Micah, for she knew that once he found out about Stephen, things would never be the same between them. Oh, if there were just some way she could tie up all the loose ends of her life, some way she could make all the jagged pieces fit properly.

After they'd finished their coffee, Effie rose and picked up Tad's jacket and carefully hung it on a peg. "What pretty little clothes he has," she remarked, her voice rising in wonderment. "The finest I ever saw a child wear. I noticed that fancy buggy you come in, too," she continued, her tone shot through with curious admiration. "His daddy must be powerful rich. I think you mentioned in a letter his name was Mr. Adams."

Jubilee's cheeks burned hot. Twisting the truth in her letters and lying to Effie face to face were two different things, and she moistened her lips and wondered if she could even speak the words. "Yes, his name is Adams," she said, thankful she'd been spared the shame of repeating the falsehood to Granny.

Lying to Effie was extremely painful and Jubilee felt sick inside, but she could see that her cousin took the words at face value. She'd have to lie to Micah too, she thought miserably, feeling her face flush with embarrassment. She only hoped no one would repeat the name Adams in front of Tad, who was sure to pipe up that he was a Wentworth. Heartsick, she thought about the lie she'd spun and the web she was now tangled in. Yes, she'd managed to deceive sweet, innocent Effie. The question was, would Micah believe her so easily?

Jubilee slipped back into the mountain life with ease. She always awoke early and walked outside to drink in the old, consoling sights and sounds she'd known as a child. She experienced pangs of loneliness for Stephen, but there was the scent of freshly turned earth, the tang of the pines, and the gentle low of Granny's milk cow to comfort and sustain her.

A fortnight after she returned, she watched the dawn blush turn into a vivid blue behind the tall trees and decided it would be a good day to wash the clothes. When breakfast was over, she found several cakes of lye soap and gathered wood chips to kindle a fire under the washpot. Soon she and Effie were hard at work.

Her cousin pushed back a strand of loose hair from her

flushed face. "I declare, I do believe washin' and beatin' clothes all these years is what caused me to grow so big at the top," she proclaimed good-naturedly, whacking a paddle at one of Granny's nightgowns that was flung over a battling bench.

Jubilee sat on a stool, shaving curls of soap with a big knife. "You might be right," she laughed, letting the soap chips drop into a large can. "Do you know the town folks have a thing called a rub board? It's rough, and women just rub their clothes against the boards instead of beating them."

"Well, I declare. What will they think of next? Did you ever use one of them washboard things?"

"No, not myself. Tad's daddy has several women who come once a week just to wash clothes. And he has a lady named Delilah that cooks supper for him every evening and Sunday dinner."

She walked to the black washpot filled with boiling water and dumped in the pieces of soap. The fire around the base of the large pot crackled and popped, and she picked up a long paddle and stirred the water vigorously. At the battling board, she used her paddle to whack at an apron as if she were trying to beat away her lingering worries about Micah.

With a burst of laughter, Tad suddenly rounded the cabin and ran past the battling board. He waved a long rag at a floppy-eared pup who snatched on to it with his teeth, then growled playfully and backed up, trying to pull the material from Tad's hands. Matilda trotted behind the pup, obviously miffed that the dog had even temporarily replaced her in the boy's affections.

"Having a good time?" Jubilee asked the youngster.

Tad laughed harder than she'd ever heard him. Two weeks in the mountains had done wonders for the boy, putting weight on him and bringing new color to his cheeks. Besides eating better, he was relating to people better, talking without strain to Effie and Granny and the mountaineers who came to visit the "poor little boy from the flatlands." Determined to restore the boy's health, everyone in the hollow had outdone themselves, showering him with attention and love that he sopped up like a dry sponge. Pride warmed Jubilee's heart, and she made a mental note that she'd have to relate these facts to Stephen in one of her frequent letters.

"Don't go off in the woods, baby," she warned the boy. "We'll be finished washing pretty soon."

He glanced her way, then disappeared around the side of the cabin, Matilda and the pup racing after him.

Effie chuckled fondly at the scene, then whacked at the battling board a little harder. "What does them rich women have to do?" she asked Jubilee, continuing their interrupted discussion about life in the flatlands. "They's got other women to wash their clothes for them, and they don't have to fetch water or cook or nothin'."

Jubilee fished another piece of laundry from the steamy washtub. "They dress up and go to parties to pass the time," she answered, wringing the garment dry and throwing it into another tub. "They have women who sew their fancy gowns and even women to fix their hair."

Effie laughed heartily. "I reckon they hire women to have babies for them, too."

Jubilee chuckled. "No, but they would if they could!"

She continued working, boiling Granny's gowns and beating them until they were a snowy white. Jubilee's arms hurt and a fierce, hot ache asserted itself between her shoulders, but she took pleasure in the clean scent of the bubbling laundry, the light breeze on her hot face, and the sounds of the chirping birds flitting through the trees. Tired to the bone, but pleased with the clean wash, she wrung the last bit of water from the heavy, sodden garments, then draped them upon a line stretched between two tree limbs.

It was almost midday when she and her cousin finished washing. Wisps of damp hair hung in Effie's face, and when she placed her reddened hands upon her hips, dark perspiration stains were visible under her arms. "I'm gettin' mighty hungry, and Granny and Tad will be needin' somethin' to eat," she announced, wiping her glistening forehead with the back of her hand. She glanced at the cabin, whose patched roof gleamed bright in the midday sun. "I'll go on and start noon vittles."

After she'd walked away, Jubilee dumped the water from the washpot and rinsing tubs, creating a great sizzling sound as the fire flickered out. She put the pot and tubs in a shed behind the cabin, then walked back to the clearing, straightened her aching back, and wiped her damp forehead with the edge of her apron.

Resting, she scanned the mountains that stretched ridge after ridge as far as the eye could see. How much of her soul was tied to these hills, she thought with awe, recalling her childhood. She remembered the clicking sound of her grandmother's knitting needles and the feel of the icy floor against her bare feet as she got up on February mornings to make biscuits. Most of all, she remembered sitting by the hearth in winter and listening to her father's low, soft voice as he spun tales about life in the flatlands where everyone was rich and kings and queens.

So many sweet, tender memories.

But now that she'd lived in Asheville she had mixed emotions about life in the Smokies. There was washing, ironing, mending, cooking, splitting kindling, all under the most primitive conditions. She thought of Effie. Day after day of mindless drudgery with no hope in sight had put the lines on her once youthful face. Existence here was so hard, especially for women. A veil had been taken from her eyes, and she could see everything in a new light. It was like being reborn, like seeing the world for the first time.

A flock of jays in the garden cried shrilly and flew away, jarring her out of her thoughtful trance. After they'd disappeared with a whir of wings, the woods lay still in the high sun. Then gradually like the sound of a rhythmic drumbeat becoming more distinct by the second, she heard the thud of a horse's hooves against the dirt road that joined the mountain hollows. Someone was coming down the road to the cabin. Perhaps it was one of the neighbors who often came to visit, she decided, pleased at the idea of having company for the noon meal. Brimming with anticipation, she walked to the edge of the clearing to get a better look.

At first all she could see was a horse and rider lost in the dust of the trail. Yard by yard they came closer, veiled by a rosy haze. At last, light from the sun shone through the trees and flickered over them, revealing the rider's face plain and clear. Jubilee's heart leapt to her throat.

It was Micah.

That same day at dusk Jubilee and Micah took a long walk in the woods. Garbed in his old clothes that he'd changed into as soon as he arrived at the cabin, Micah limped along on his lame leg telling his sister about his troubled life in the flatlands.

The pair stopped to look at a tiny waterfall spouting down a mountainside like a gauzy white ribbon, threading between the tall green trees. Jubilee observed her brother with alarm, noticing that his mouth was drawn in a thin gash and the flesh was tight across his high cheekbones. She remembered his tall, raw-boned frame and shock of auburn hair, his rough complexion, but his face now bore deep, bitter lines she'd never seen before. His face was that of a sad stranger.

"Remember all those good times we had running through these woods?" she asked, trying to cheer him up. She recalled fishing and hunting with him through a score of lazy, leafy summers and snowy, breathtakingly beautiful winters. She knew that they were now steadily marching in different directions, but she prayed the mem-

Song of the Lark

ories of light-hearted seasons past would bind them together again, if only for a while.

Micah shook his head. "Yeah, I remember," he answered with a disgusted sigh, "but my runnin' days are over."

Jubilee searched for words of comfort, words to ease his deep abiding pain, but found none. They walked on in silence, dry pine needles crunching under their boots. The breeze brought the scent of lush vegetation, and in the distance Jubilee heard a creek babbling over rough stones. Soon she saw that the stream rippled through a little ravine, hills crowding in on either side, with trees surrounding and shading it. When the pair reached the water, they rested upon a grassy bank and simply sat in silence for a while, enjoying the birdsong and companionship of being together again. A big fish jumped out of the creek, and Micah idly threw a pebble in that direction.

Jubilee laid her hand on his arm. "Does your leg pain you anymore?" she asked softly, moving closer to his side.

He stared sullenly at the glinting water. "Nope, but I ain't a whole man no more. I have to do women's work in a store, clerkin' and measurin' cloth, sellin' buttons to old ladies. Sayin' yes'um this and yes'um that." He surveyed her, bitterness gathering in eyes that were once soft and playful but were now as hard as mountain granite. "It ain't proper work for a man, but I reckon that's all I'm good for now."

"That's not true," Jubilee shot back, cut to the quick with his air of self-defeat. "You're a fine musician. You make the best dulcimers and fiddles in the hills. You could open a shop and sell instruments. Folks in the flatlands would buy them for sure."

He smiled and patted her hand condescendingly, as if he appreciated her interest but thought the idea a farfetched dream. "Somethin' like that takes money, girl, and that's somethin' I ain't got."

Not knowing what to say, she held her tongue, and he surprised her by suddenly remarking, "We're losin' Granny, ain't we? I can see her slippin' away like a mornin' haze every time I come."

Jubilee saw his grief, but decided that he should know the truth. "Yes, I'm afraid we are. I don't know how long we'll have her with us." Her throat tightened painfully. "It would do Granny good to know you'd found your way before she left, Micah." She gathered up her courage. "Don't hate so. It's making you sick, eating you up inside. I can see it in your face. You have to let the past go."

Fire flashed in his eyes. "How can I forget when I got this to remind me every blessed day?" he rasped, slapping at his lame leg. "I got this 'cause old Hamish Wentworth didn't think nothin' of the men who was workin' for him."

"Are you going to waste the rest of your life hating a dead man?"

"He may be dead but I heard he's got two sons. I reckon gettin' a little revenge on them would ease my mind some."

Jubilee fought down a sharp, sick feeling. "They can't help what their father did, any more than we can help what Pa did. You know that," she countered hotly.

"They's all Wentworths and they's all alike!"

Jubilee bit her tongue, wanting to tell him that Stephen was nothing like his father.

"You tell me to forget," Micah went on in a softer voice, "but I don't know how to forget. Where do I begin forgettin' bein' crippled the rest of my life?"

Jubilee took his big, callused hand. "Make your life count for something—that's how. You've got years and years ahead of you, just waiting to be filled with good things."

Micah flushed, then gazed down and murmured, "You and Pa were always good at spinnin' big dreams out of a

Song of the Lark

little piece of hope—but I just don't know how to start."

Jubilee's heart ached for him. He was struggling with life so hard and failing, floundering in a net of hate that he'd spun himself. "Start thinking about other people, about how you can help them. You'll see—your hate will fade away a little bit at a time."

He released her hand, then studied her long and hard as if he wanted to believe her, but something was pulling him back.

"Promise me you'll try," she urged, knowing he was on the verge of making a commitment.

He sat forward and sighed. "All right," he promised, raking back his windblown hair. "I'll try, 'cause I'm tired of livin' this way."

Tears flooded her eyes. The statement was filled with grief for his loss and unfulfilled hopes, and deep pity squeezed her heart. "Good," she whispered, looping her arms about his broad shoulders. Trying to encourage him and give him a place to start living, she added, "You like the boy, don't you?"

Micah grinned, his face looking softer than it had since he'd arrived. "Tadpole? Yeah, I sure do. He's a quiet little mite, but he has a way of kinda gettin' next to your heart."

"Yes, I know." She searched her brother's pain-filled eyes. "Try doing something for him. He's been hurt bad and needs all the love he can get."

Micah nodded as if he was already thinking of something he might do for the boy.

Jubilee leaned against her brother's shoulder. She prayed the Lord would forgive her for not telling him who Tad's father was, but at this point her brother's spirit was just too weak. Perhaps when he'd released some of the hate he'd carried so long, she could tell him that the little boy that had stolen his heart was Hamish Wentworth's grandson.

* * *

That night at nine o'clock Stephen sat at his desk working; the only sound to be heard was a ticking grandfather clock. Depressed by the silence, he tossed down his pen and pushed back in his chair, experiencing a pang of loneliness for his son and the saucy mountain girl who'd turned his life upside down. "Work—that's all I do," he murmured to himself in a disgusted tone.

He picked up Jubilee's latest letter that reported Tad was growing like a ragweed in the wet season and read it for the tenth time. He toyed with the idea of visiting them, then dismissed the fantasy as irresponsible. He'd mortgaged his holdings to keep afloat and he needed to do everything possible to see that his business was a success, not traipse off like a moonstruck lad following some tempting maiden.

He sat there thinking of the picture Jubilee and Tad had made as they left for the mountains. Excitement had flamed in the girl's eyes and Tad had displayed more enthusiasm than he'd shown in months. How he missed the boy's soft smiles and quiet ways, missed them more than he'd ever thought possible. And how silent and empty the mansion seemed, almost like a tomb.

He rose and paced about his study, reviewing how dull his life was since the pair had left. One could hardly call Chambers company, and he only saw Delilah a few minutes a day. Estell was always pestering him to take her to some social function, but he grew more disgusted with her snobbery and materialism every day. Of course he talked to numerous people at work, but his heart longed for a companionship these casual acquaintances couldn't provide. It seemed that Jubilee and the boy were the very sap of life itself.

He walked to the window and pulled back the heavy velvet drapes. Twinkling stars blinked in the dark sky like diamonds on velvet, making him feel lonelier yet. He recalled the day he'd returned from Knoxville and found Jubilee and Tad in the music room; he thought of that thrilling afternoon his son had called to him after months of silence. "Papa, Papa!" It seemed he could almost hear the boy calling him now.

He walked about the study and tried to get a grip on his emotions. All at once his foot crunched on something hard on the carpet, and he bent on one knee to pick up the object. With a dart of feeling, he saw it was one of Tad's tiny toy wagons. A rush of affection overtook him. He stood and examined the toy, thinking of the many times he'd played with Tad reenacting something the boy had seen in town.

He traced over the toy with his long fingers, hearing the child's laughter in his mind. To intensify his loneliness he remembered Jubilee's dazzling smile and her soft Appalachian drawl that fell so sweetly on his ears. Just being with her felt like basking his soul in sunlight.

He surveyed his littered desk once more, then pitched the toy wagon upon it. The work would wait. It would always be there, he advised himself, surrendering to his emotions. Somehow he'd steal nine days away from his work—two days up, five days there, and two days back. He had to see his son, and he had to see Jubilee, too, and damn the consequences.

More cheerful than he'd been since they'd left, he strode from the study to tell Chambers to prepare his things. Lord, how surprised they'd be to see him, he thought with a rush of happiness. How surprised they'd both be.

Chapter Eight

From her perch atop a rickety ladder Jubilee looked downward, watching Micah and Tad scoop ripe peaches from the ground and toss them into an old gunnysack.

"There's a big one, Tadpole. Get that one," Micah called out, his voice floating upward on the light summer air.

It was a wonderful day, warm, but not so hot that work was exhausting. Effie had come over to help and stood on another ladder, plucking fruit from a nearby tree. The group had enjoyed a fine lunch of corn bread and butter beans, and a companionable feeling flowed between them, making the fruit picking more play than work.

Jubilee glanced at her brother and smiled to herself. In the four days he'd been here, he and Tad had forged a close friendship just as she'd expected. Hungry for male companionship, Tad followed Micah about, and Micah always took time to answer the boy's many questions, which boosted the self-confidence of both parties. The boy who needed love and the man who needed to learn to forget had been wonderful medicine for each other.

Song of the Lark

Jubilee returned to her work, thankful for the trees' abundance. So far it had been a good summer, but there was always work to do. The hogs were growing fat and the chickens were laying well. She'd already put up blackberries and green beans, and there would soon be luscious melons and ripe tomatoes. She'd worked hard while she was here, weeding the garden, carrying water, cleaning out the pig pen, and canning every vegetable and fruit in sight. She rose at dawn and fell in bed dead tired every night, for she'd promised herself that before the winter snows flew, Granny would have hay in the stable, meat in the smokehouse, and corn in the crib.

Surrounded by the scent of ripe peaches and the sound of rustling leaves, Jubilee worked until mid-afternoon. By then, her arms ached and for the first time that day, she realized how exhausted she really was. Needing a rest, she decided to check on Granny and drink a dipper of cool water.

She found Granny sound asleep, and she'd just finished her water when she heard Tad let out a shrill cry. She thought he'd hurt himself and rushed to the window and peered out, her stomach turning over in fright. She saw the boy run across the clearing and heard him crying, "Papa!" She swept her gaze in that direction and her heart lurched. Lordamercy, it was Stephen, sitting astride a handsome black stallion.

Joy shot through her, for she'd longed to see him since the day she'd left Asheville, but then as he swung from the saddle and scooped Tad into his arms, it hit her that she was in serious trouble. Never had she prepared for the possibility that he might come to visit them. Micah slowly walked toward him, and her mind spun wildly trying to come up with a plan. Her brother stared at Stephen not unkindly, but with open curiosity, obviously assuming he must be the Mr. Adams she'd invented out of desperation.

With a thumping heart she ran from the cabin, still not

sure what she should do. Stephen set Tad on his feet, then locked eyes with her, and she trembled with fear and excitement. Never had she experienced such mixed emotions. Had he come to see his son or had he missed her, too? Just the thought of that possibility filled her with incredible pleasure, yet at the same time she quaked at the conflict in the making.

With escalating panic, she started across the clearing. She remembered her brother's great strength and fiery temper when he was provoked, his twisted sense of justice. If she could only reach Stephen first and warn him off. Then it happened. For the first time in his life, her quiet, timid brother strode forward and stuck out his hand in greeting, introducing himself.

Panic spurted through her. She ran to the pair, and just as she arrived, Stephen shook Micah's hand and announced, "My name is Wentworth—Stephen Wentworth. I'm Tad's father."

Micah's hand dropped like a rock. His shocked, confused expression hardened into sudden fury. Jubilee groaned inwardly, dreading the next words out of his mouth.

"Wentworth?" he mumbled, his face red with anger. "Do you mean the Wentworth that owns Wentworth Enterprises—Hamish's son?" he asked in a sharp voice.

Stephen gave him a puzzled look, obviously taken back by his sudden change of personality. "Yes, Hamish was my father."

With blazing eyes, Micah surveyed Jubilee, his face twisted with outrage. "You lied to me," he accused in a thunderous voice, his hands clenching into fists. "You said the boy's name was Adams!"

Tad stared at him with a stricken face, and tears welled in his eyes.

"Be quiet!" Jubilee ordered her brother, thinking he'd lost his wits to speak in such a fashion before a child who looked up to him. "Don't you see, I *had* to lie to you. I wanted to tell you. I really did, but I knew it would crush you. I lied to protect you."

Micah flicked a hot gaze over her. "I think you've done forgotten who you are. Who your family is. You've done taken up town ways!"

Overwhelmed, Tad ran to Jubilee, buried his face in her apron and started crying. She stooped down and folded her arms about him, feeling his wet tears against her bosom. How foolish she'd been. She'd lied, but Tad was now paying the price for that lie, and regret settled in her stomach like a chunk of ice.

Stephen neared Micah, his face hard and implacable. "Now wait a minute," Stephen ordered, his mouth tightening with rage. "I think it's *you* who have forgotten—forgotten that you're talking to your sister." His eyes glittered like flint.

Micah jabbed a finger at him. "Keep out of this, Wentworth," he lashed out, smacking his fist into his open palm. "I don't need any advice from the likes of you."

Jubilee rose and grabbed her brother's arm. "He's not like his daddy. He's different," she cried in desperation.

He threw off her hand. "Oh, he ain't no different. He may have you fooled with his good looks and silvery tongue, but he ain't got me fooled!"

Effie had finally made her way down the ladder and now approached, her face pale with concern.

"Thank God you're here," Jubilee exclaimed, gently pushing Tad into her welcoming arms. "Take him into the house. He doesn't need to hear this."

Speechless with shock, Effie nodded, but before she hoisted the boy to her hip and carried him away, Jubilee saw fresh tears spill from his eyes and streak his grimy face. Soothing his sobs, the older woman put his head against her shoulder and hurried into the cabin.

Micah glared at Stephen, then turned on his sister. "Now I know how you been makin' all that money back in Asheville, and it weren't from taking care of no young'un. There's only one thing a Wentworth would want from you, and I know what it is!"

Stephen stepped forward and straightened his back. "You owe your sister an apology," he growled, hard lines darting across his brow.

"The truth's the truth," Micha snarled. "She ain't gonna get one and neither are you."

"Wait a minute, Micah," Jubilee said in a softer voice, trying to calm him down. "Be reasonable. Let me explain."

"There ain't no need jawin'. You been sleepin' with him, ain't you?"

"No!" she answered, trying to think of a way to cool his temper. "If you'd just listen to—"

Before she could finish her sentence, Micah swung wildly at Stephen, but her brother was so enraged his fist missed its target. A wild light flickered in his eyes and she knew he was capable of doing anything at this point. Sick with fear, she ran to him and grabbed his arms. She trembled as she struggled with him, crying, "Get a hold of yourself!"

Micah broke away and picked up a long stick. Jubilee's heart lurched, for she thought he might strike her. Instead he threw it toward the woods as hard as he could, then whirled on her and Stephen. He stood there half-crazed, his chest heaving, his eyes glittering. "Both of you make me sick," he shouted, before stumbling backward and wiping an arm over his face.

Jubilee felt a gush of pity for him. Never had she been so hurt and so embarrassed, ashamed that the brother she loved could act this way. *"Micah!"* she called wildly. The name was a choked plea.

For a moment she thought he might speak, but anger flushed his face and he turned and stalked into the woods like a wounded animal. Her heart aching, she watched him go. Stephen put his hands on her shoulders, and she met his questioning gaze and tired to mouth the words "I'm sorry" but found she couldn't speak. He held her tight and she bit back her turbulent emotions, having no idea how she'd untangle the problem her lie had prompted.

Stephen glanced at the spot where Micah had entered the woods, then slowly looked back at her, his eyes hurt and confused. "Jubilee—what in God's name is going on here?"

That night after supper, Jubilee stood in front of a piece of mirror hanging on the cabin wall. Granny and Tad were asleep, and now that she and Stephen were finally alone, they could talk. What would he think of her? She looked at her tangled hair and ripped gown stained with peach juice and thought of him sitting on the front porch, waiting for her to emerge.

Lordamercy, she'd never seen herself looking worse. She hadn't realized how she'd neglected her appearance since she'd returned to the mountains. Her skin was sunburned and there were streaks and scratches on her arms from working in the fields and the garden. She quickly changed her gown, then washed her face and dried it on the big homespun towel that hung on a nail beside the washpan and gourd dipper. She tugged a brush through her tangled hair, thinking that her hasty grooming would have to do.

By the time she stepped onto the porch, the light had faded, and the scent of Carolina jasmine, climbing over the end of the cabin, hung on the humid air. The stars were out, and the katydids' lulling chirp rose and fell in the shadows. After her eyes had become adjusted to the darkness, she saw Stephen sitting in an old cane-bottomed chair, gazing at the star-sprinkled sky.

She sat down beside him and the soft night air washed against her face. This afternoon, after they'd gone into the cabin, she'd told him her brother's story, but a stiffness still hung between them, cramping conversation. She had been sure he'd bring up the incident now, but instead he idly remarked, "There must be a million stars up there."

Jubilee gazed at the starry sky and the golden moon that had just risen behind the inky blue mountains. "Yes, I love to look at the sky in the summer. Sometimes the stars are so bright and clear, it looks like a person could reach up and grab them right out of the heavens."

He smiled at her, and the pleasure of his company filled her mind, even as the stars filled the summer sky. On the other hand, she was now thrown together with Stephen in an all too intimate setting. It seemed strange to have him here in the mountains, and that definitely changed things between them. The protective formality that had existed in Asheville was gone and left her feeling vulnerable and exposed. She ached to ask him why he'd come. Was it only to see Tad, or to see her as well? She tried to mouth the question, but the words stuck in her throat.

Stephen looked at Jubilee, confusion still filling his heart. Why hadn't she told him her brother's story in Asheville? He'd wanted to knock Micah to the ground today when he'd insulted her, and the intensity of his protective feelings for her had surprised him a bit. Why had he come to the mountains anyway? Of course he could always tally up his trip to fatherly concern for Tad—but deep in his heart he knew there was more to it.

"Supper was good," he said quietly, thinking of how she'd cooked corn bread, vegetables, and ham, trying to pretend that nothing had happened, that everything was all right. But he'd seen her trembling hands that she'd tried to hide, and his heart went out to her.

Jubilee smiled shyly. "What did you think of Granny?"

Stephen laughed, surprised that the old woman had insisted on getting up and dressing to have supper with him. "She's amazing. I've never met anyone like her. Now I know where you get your fire." Privately he thought the old woman had handled a difficult social situation with amazing grace and humor.

Song of the Lark

They fell silent for a moment, and he considered the young woman sitting next to him. He had set a course for the rest of his life, and had planned to stick to it, but Jubilee was changing all that. Surely this couldn't be love he felt. It was more like madness, a madness he was succumbing to more each passing day. Madness or not, all he knew right now was that he wanted to kiss her more than anything in the world.

Jubilee's mind went to Tad. When she thought of him witnessing the terrible scene this afternoon, she had to swallow back her tears. "How's Tad?" she ventured, remembering the tired, drained look on his face when his father had carried him to bed.

For a moment it seemed the shadows deepened under Stephen's eyes, and then he replied, "He's fine. He was hurt, but I explained that Micah's anger had taken over his good feelings and made him act that way."

She nodded. "Yes, Micah was bursting with anger. You see, to a mountain person their word is sacred," she explained. "That was the reason he was so angry when he found out I lied to him about working for you. He felt I'd betrayed him in the worst way."

Light flickered from the cabin windows and dappled over Stephen's face. "I see," he replied softly. He sat silent for a moment, then asked, "Where do you think he went?"

"He has a friend he used to hunt with before he left the mountains. He probably went there."

His eyes played over her. "You two are very close, aren't you?"

"We were at one time. When Ma and Pa died we sort of depended on each other."

Stephen leaned back in his chair and studied her thoughtfully. "Why didn't you tell me about all this in Asheville?"

She looked at her clasped hands. "I'm not sure," she answered, feeling very foolish. "Perhaps I thought it would offend you—maybe I thought you just wouldn't understand." She met his inquiring eyes. "I supposed you would never meet Micah. You have to be in his place to know how he feels." She nervously smoothed back her hair. "He used to be warm and fun to be with. When he got hurt it seemed to kill something inside him—in a way, the best part of him." She studied Stephen, hoping he'd understand. "I've tried talking to him, making him realize he has to forgive before he can start living again. I thought he was beginning to understand. I—"

He put his warm hand over hers. "You don't have to explain. Tad is very fond of him, you know."

She nodded her head. "And the boy had started to melt his hate." She bit her lip. "If he'd just had a little more time." She put her hand on Stephen's arm. "I'm sorry. I wish there was some way I could change things—go back and fix it where this afternoon never happened."

Stephen stood and pulled her up beside him. "Don't apologize for life," he said, a flicker of a weary smile playing over his lips. He took her hand, opened it, and branded her palm with a kiss that rushed pleasure all the way up her arm. In one smooth move, he took her shoulders and pulled her to him. She knew that he was stepping over the bounds as her employer, and she knew she should stop him, but she didn't. His strong, thickly muscled body pressed against her and stirred the embers of desire that she'd so carefully buried in her heart. With a tender hand, he reached under her hair and caressed the back of her neck, and warmth flushed though her and made her weak.

She laid her head against his shoulder and she could smell the masculine scent of his trail-stained chambray shirt against her face. She wanted to ask him how many days he could spare away from Asheville, but she held back the words, thinking they might seem presumptuous. "Where will you stay?" she whispered, knowing she had nothing to offer him but the cabin floor.

"At the logging camp," he murmured against her hair.

Song of the Lark

"It couldn't be more than three miles from here and it'll give me time to look at this end of the operation." He cupped her chin and looked at her with hot eyes. A quiet fell about them. Moonlight gleamed in his hair and accentuated the strong planes of his face. His masculinity would tempt any woman, and at this moment she felt extremely feminine. She could hear the soft call of a mockingbird, and she felt herself giving in, losing her resistance to fight him.

"I've missed you," he whispered huskily. "You have the very flame of life in you, girl. I've found the mansion lonely without you." He moved his hand in wonderful circles upon her back. "I kept thinking about you, remembering everything you did, everything you'd said."

A mixture of pleasure and regret knotted itself about her heart as his lips brushed hers. A groan echoed from his chest as he pulled her closer, and what started as a slow, languid kiss erupted into a tempest of desire. Scarcely knowing it, she encircled her arms about his neck and returned his kiss. When he skillfully slipped his tongue into her mouth, fire erupted in the pit of her belly and spread rapidly through her veins. With a prickle of alarm, Jubilee realized the fiery kiss was turning into something she couldn't control, and with what was left of her rational mind, she tried to sort out her jumbled emotions. Did she really love Stephen or was the attraction she felt only a physical longing? Perhaps he'd simply awakened some primitive need within her that had been lying dormant, ready to explode. Perhaps another man would affect her just as strongly.

With great effort, her rational mind gradually reined in her runaway emotions and she gently eased herself away from him, stealing a glance at his puzzled face. Embarrassed that she'd let her good intentions slip, she traced her fingers over her burning cheeks and turned about, pulling in a deep breath of night air.

He clasped her shoulders and murmured her name, but

she stubbornly fought down her desire and whispered, "It's getting late. I should go in." Part of her desperately yearned to face him and declare her love, but a sober, sane part told her to remove herself from his presence and give herself some time before she spoke. Afraid she might lose her courage if she delayed, she hurried into the cabin and closed the door, leaning against it for a few seconds until she regained her strength.

With a pounding heart, she blew out the kerosene lanterns and moved to her bed, undoing her gown with fumbling fingers as she went. There were creaking footsteps on the porch; then a moment later she heard Stephen ride away.

After she'd slipped on a soft nightgown and lain upon her mattress, the horrible scene from this afternoon kept dancing across her closed lids. Hours later, the memory finally faded away, only to be replaced with the feeling of Stephen's hands caressing her body, setting her blood afire.

Although her body ached with weariness, her mind raced and would not calm itself. She knew she'd toss and turn all night.

The next afternoon Stephen, Jubilee, and Tad strolled through the woods and she told both father and son about all the trees, herbs, and flowers, naming each one. Besides the tall pines, sturdy oaks, and graceful cedars, she showed them redbuds, sugar maples, pawpaws, leatherwood, and wahoo trees. As for flowers there were several varieties of goldenrod, early asters, pennyroyal, evening primrose, and in the glades, clusters of wild sunflowers, turning their faces to the warm sun.

True to her prediction, she'd tossed all night, worrying not only about Micah but herself. Stephen was drawing her closer and closer to him, and she was finding it more difficult to resist him. Could she control her own future as she'd always hoped, or was she already destined to love

Song of the Lark

a man who might never return her love? Over and over, a voice deep within her kept warning, *Guard your heart well.*

The trio rested for a while on a log and she pulled a bearberry plant from the fragrant earth and tapped its small red blossoms with her fingertips. "This herb is good for all kinds of aches and pains, especially if they're in your back." Tad observed her with big eyes, absorbing everything she said, but she could tell that Stephen took her words lightly.

"All right," he ventured, an irritating grin twisting his lips, "what would you do if I had a headache?"

She arched a brow. "I'd give you chamomile tea, and if you had sinus trouble I'd give you mullein. For a bad heart I'd dose you with goldenseal root." She pulled up another herb from the soft forest floor and shook off the moist earth that clung to its roots. "This is chickweed. Delilah could lose some weight if she took this, and Reverend Pennypacker could see better if he took eyebright."

Tad tugged on her hand. "What would you give me if I'd eaten a whole pie and had a stomachache?" he asked with an impish grin that reminded her of Stephen's.

"I'd give you fenugreek seed and see that you never ate a whole pie again!"

"Fenugreek seeds?" he echoed with a bubbling laugh. "That's a funny medicine." His expression stilled and grew serious. "Do you have any weed to give Chambers so he won't be so grouchy?"

She and Stephen both laughed.

She clasped Tad's head and shook it playfully. "Yes—a good dose of valerian root each day would soothe his nerves considerably."

They continued talking, and after they'd eaten a few jelly-smeared biscuits she'd brought with her, they walked on toward their destination, Miller's Meadow, which was a riot of color at this time of year.

The summer woods were alive with activity. To Tad's

delight, they saw some young cottontails playing tag along the trail and found a pair of bobwhites taking a dust bath near a blackberry thicket. Farther along the trail, they watched a litter of fox babies frolicking before their den and spied a doe and her fawn race through the tall grass like two streaks of russet-colored lightning.

Deep in the woods, Jubilee pointed at a huge oak. "Oh, look, there's a spirit tree!"

"A spirit tree?" Stephen echoed, gazing at the oak whose thick bark seemed to bear slashes near the bottom of the trunk.

"That's right," Jubilee answered, walking to the tree to trace her fingers over the ancient markings. "You don't find many of these. The Cherokees who lived here believed that everything has its own spirit—even the trees—and they often marked those they thought were strong medicine."

Stephen and Tad now stood by her side and the boy traced his hands over the markings, his face alight with fascination.

Jubilee caught Stephen's gaze. "In fact, the Indians believed that we're all brothers and sisters with every living thing. That's a nice thought, isn't it?"

A grin spread over his face. "Umm, I suppose so, but the idea of being related to Winston Throg and every garden variety skunk in the woods will take a little getting used to."

At last they reached Miller's Meadow and, standing on some high ground at the edge of the woods, surveyed a depression filled with pink roses and purple periwinkles that nodded their colorful heads in the gentle breeze.

"This is a beautiful view," Stephen remarked, thoughtfully scanning the undulating sea of color. "I've lived in Carolina all my life and never knew this place existed."

A smile ruffled Tad's pink lips. "Look at all the flowers," he exclaimed, blinking in amazement. "I've never seen so many! Can I pick some?"

Song of the Lark

Jubilee nodded and the boy raced down the grassy slope and waded into the sea of blossoms, looking back to see if she was watching him. He walked among the flowers, stooping here and there to choose a special bloom and hold it up so she could see it.

Stephen laughed, his eyes warm. "You were right about him coming to the mountains. He's put on weight and hardly stutters anymore. I've never seen him looking better."

Jubilee stooped to pick a little bunch of lily of the valley, then rose and gazed at him through her lashes. "Yes, he's growing like—"

"Like a ragweed in the wet season!" he finished for her as they laughed together.

Jubilee watched Tad for a while, but the boy finally became so absorbed in picking flowers, that he scarcely noticed her or his father, and focused his attention on gathering the biggest bouquet possible. She dared not look at Stephen for her heart burst with questions she was afraid to ask. She twirled the frothy lily of the valley between her fingertips, then inhaled its sweet, pure fragrance that reminded her of a marriage of honeysuckle and jasmine. She felt Stephen's eyes upon her and, flustered, glanced down and started to stroll away, thinking she'd join Tad.

Stephen caught her arm, then gently turned her about. He slipped his hands into her hair and cupped her face, tilting it up so he could meet her eyes. "No, don't move—let's talk awhile," he suggested, the expression on his rugged features promising more than simple conversation. His breath whispered over her face, and when she gazed into his spellbinding eyes, she didn't have to analyze his emotions. "I don't know what to say," she murmured, surrendering to the multitude of sensations clamoring within her.

"Why don't you ask me all those questions I see spinning in your head?" he urged her, his fingers delicately tracing over her cheek and collarbone.

Familiar sensations unfurled deep within her, blossoming and growing until they consumed all reason, all good judgment. She pushed down that nagging voice that kept holding her back and telling her he would think her a fool. Perhaps this was the time to ask the question she'd wrestled with all night. Would there be a better time? "Why did you come here?" she softly asked, wondering if she even had a right to pose the question. "To see Tad?"

A spark flared in Stephen's eyes. "Yes—but I came to see you, too. I would have come if Tad were nowhere about. I wanted to see you"—he paused for a moment, then continued, putting a special emphasis on each word—"and I needed to see you." He walked her to a secluded spot behind a thicket of huge trees, out of Tad's view but still close by so they could hear the child if he called.

Jubilee's heart thumped and she started to turn her head, but he caught her chin. "No," he said, his voice a velvet murmur. "Turnabout is fair play. I have a question for you. Why did you go into the cabin last night?

Lost in a haze of emotion, she met his questioning eyes. "I-I thought it was best," she stammered, frightened by the idea of emptying her heart to him. Then feeling he deserved an answer, she murmured, "Why should we continue something that will only bring us heartache?"

For a moment Stephen was content to gaze into her eyes and remember the exquisite magic between them. Jubilee was like an uncontrollable addiction, an incessant craving that wouldn't go away. Each time he kissed her he wanted to kiss her again. He could tamp down his desire for a while, but the need kept building within him into an all-consuming craving. He traced his fingers over her lips. "But are you sure it will?" he asked, surprising himself with the words.

She looked away, but not before he saw a mist cloud her eyes.

Song of the Lark

He turned her face back toward him, then pulled her close and ran his hands lovingly over her back. He was losing his battle with his good sense, his actions had careened out of control, but at this moment he just couldn't help himself. He realized he must analyze this overpowering feeling, but his understanding would surely come in stages, and he wanted to enjoy each day as it came. "Jubilee, I don't understand this attraction between us, but it's there, and try as I might, I can't deny it and neither can you. Maybe we don't need to understand it but just accept it."

Jubilee started to say she could never accept such a situation, when he slanted his mouth over hers, making her heart skip several beats. A sigh caught in her throat. Lordamercy, it was happening again! Just like last night when he'd kissed her on the porch, and when he'd first kissed her on the night of the storm. That deep wonderful, luscious feeling was welling up within her, and it seemed that twinkling starlight was streaking through her bloodstream. His tongue flicked over her lips and she shivered with desire. Already her alliance with Stephen had torn her family apart and she had no assurance that their relationship would be permanent. Everything within her told her she was plunging headlong into folly, yet still she could not help herself.

She felt him ease down her low-cut gown, and then his hand was on her breast and hot blood stung her cheeks. Filled with shock, she stiffened and warned herself she should move away, but he teased and pleasured her until she whimpered with joy. Once she was over her first shyness, he rolled her nipple between his lean fingers and a sharp, sweet pulse throbbed between her legs, making her think she might swoon with delight.

Jubilee was so lost in the kiss, she scarcely heard the sound of footsteps breaking over dry twigs, then with a shaft of sickness, that nagging inner voice told her who it was. She jerked from Stephen's arms, and ony a few yards away saw Micah watching them, his face twisted with hatred. She clutched at her drooping bodice, but he continued staring at her, his face dark with accusation. How could she tell him that Stephen had only kissed her twice before? How could she explain that what he'd just witnessed wasn't her usual pattern of behavior? Stephen, his face watchful, stepped partially in front of her in a protective gesture as she finished arranging her clothing.

"I-I didn't know you were here," she said to her brother as she smoothed her clothes into place and raked her fingers through her tousled hair. She realized immediately that the words made her sound foolish and guilty, but she knew no remedy for it.

"Yeah, I can see that," Micah sneered, glaring at Stephen as if he wanted to cut his throat. He swung a murderous gaze back to his sister. "I thought about what you said about me bein' wrong, about not understandin'. I thought about it all night till my head nearly burst. Fool that I was, I trailed you two through the woods to work things out, and this is what I find."

"You still don't understand," Stephen said, walking to his accuser to confront him. "Let me tell you how I feel about your sister. Let me explain."

Micah gave a crack of bitter laughter. "I know how you feel. You gulled me once, but you ain't gonna do it again, Wentworth. I ain't no green corn young'un. I can see for myself what's going on without you *explainin'* anything. I ain't blind!"

Jubilee hurried forward and tried to catch his arm. "That's no way to talk."

His eyes wild as a stag's, her brother backed away. "I'm leavin'," he snarled, his lips curling with disgust. "I wish I'd never come home." Anger and pain contorted his face. "You make me sick—the pair of you." He gazed at Jubilee, his eyes dead and empty. "I never thought I'd see my own sister turned into a liar and a Wentworth whore to boot."

Song of the Lark

Jubilee let out a sob, but he turned on his heel and disappeared into the woods. The fading sound of his legs crashing through the brush told her it would be fuitless to try to call him back. Shaking, she turned to Stephen, who took her in his arms. He clutched her to him and, caressing her shoulders, murmured, "Don't worry, I'll make him understand."

He started to move away, but she grabbed his arm. "No. Let him be," she pleaded, her eyes burning with unshed tears. "If he sees you it will only make him angrier. Bring Tad back to the cabin after I've had time to talk to Micah." Stephen pulled against her grip, so she cried out again, "Let him be!"

He stared at her, apparently seeing that she was dead serious.

"Go find Tad. I'll be all right," she said in a softer tone. "Don't forget, he's still my brother."

Half an hour later Jubilee leaned against a towering oak, her breath coming in sharp gasps. A catch throbbed in her side and scratches streaked her hands and arms from rushing through the woods. The bitterness she'd seen on her brother's face chilled her blood, but she couldn't let him ride away without trying to reason with him. She had to make Micah understand. Damp hair fell in her eyes as she stumbled through the woods again, torn between her love for Stephen and for her brother. When her hem caught on a bramble, she jerked it loose, impatient to move on. She knew Micah would be headed for the cabin. There he'd bundle up his clothes and ride away, breaking Granny's heart.

When she finally reached the clearing, she saw him stride into the cabin, leaving the door standing open in his haste. With a pounding heart, she hurried across the clearing and entered the dwelling herself. He stood at the table, throwing his clothes into a battered satchel. "Micah, don't go. Let's talk," she rasped, taking a few steps in his direction.

He whirled on her with fiery eyes. "Talk about what?" he echoed loudly. "There is nothing to talk about. "You've taken up with my enemy!"

"Hush," she ordered. "You'll upset Granny!"

She ran to her grandmother's bedroom and saw the woman sleeping, the laudanum Doc Hall had given her sitting on her nightstand. Jubilee went weak with relief. Thank goodness the old woman was lost in a drugged sleep and would be spared a scene that might kill her.

She hurried back to the front room, and Micah strode to her, the light in his eyes wavering like flame. "You know the code of the mountains. When you're for someone you're for them—right or wrong. I always thought you were for me."

"I am for you. You're not being fair."

"Fair, hell. You think Wentworth Enterprises was fair to me when they sent me up that tree with a rotten riggin'?" He raised his voice. "My leg is ruined for the rest of my life because of them, and they never gave me a nickel!"

Jubilee clasped his arms. *"Please*—be quiet," she pleaded, her voice like a sob. "Don't disturb Granny. Her heart won't take it."

He jerked away, but in concern for his grandmother, he lowered his voice to add, "I never thought I'd see the day when you'd take *their* side."

He snatched up his satchel and strode from the cabin without looking back. Determined to not give up, Jubilee followed him to the stable, holding her aching side. She saw him take his mare from a stall and, walking into the dim, murky light, rushed to him. "Micah, I just happened to go to work for Stephen. I didn't plan it. I wanted to get some money to have Granny doctored!"

Silent, her brother flung a saddle on his horse and girt it up. When he'd finished, he stared at her, his expression piercing her tender feelings like a thorn. "If I hadn't got hurt workin' for that skinflint Wentworth, I'd have been man enough to take care of all of us."

"I don't mind working," she cried, trying to soothe his bruised pride.

He hung his satchel over the saddle horn, then glared at her with flinty eyes. "I'll bet you don't," he retorted, leading the nickering mare from the stable.

It tore Jubilee's heart in half that her brother would talk to her that way, but she brushed the pain aside and ran after him, knowing she only had a little time to reason with him.

Micah put his good foot into the stirrup and swung his tall body onto the animal. He stared down at her, contempt and revulsion shining in his fiery eyes. "Tell Granny good-bye," he ordered gruffly. He swallowed hard. "Tell her I love her—but I won't be back."

Scarcely knowing what she was doing, she grabbed his leg. "And I love you, Micah. Don't go!"

He regarded her momentarily, his face never softening. "You have to choose, little sister. The city way or the mountain way—it's me or him."

Tears stung her eyes. "No, don't make me choose," she choked out, tightening her grip on his leg. "I can't!"

His face became even harder. "Then I'll choose for you. You ain't my sister no more," he spat out with icy contempt. His words had the effect of booming thunder, and the silence that rolled after them was totally crushing. He dug his heels into the animal's flanks and it moved away, tearing his leg from her hands.

Jubilee watched him gallop across the clearing. She shook with sobs as he melted into the dusky shadows, for it seemed she was losing a part of herself. For a moment an otherworldly feeling possessed her and she felt as if she were viewing the scene from afar. She stood numb with shock, hearing her brother call her a Wentworth whore, hearing his voice slice into her heart as he told her she was no longer his sister.

She put her hands over her face and cried for them both.

Chapter Nine

The afternoon Micah rode away, Jubilee cried in Stephen's arms, but then she told herself she'd cry no more. She had to be strong for her family and Tad, who depended on her for emotional support. She bore her sorrow by herself, and as if reading her silent message, Granny and Effie scarcely mentioned the incident, showing their concern with soft, tender eyes.

Now, two days later, Stephen had taken her for a buggy ride, no doubt, she thought, to raise her spirits for she'd felt half-numb for days. She gazed at the bursts of rose pinks bordering the road and the pastel blur of lavenders, mauves, and plums that were the Smoky Mountains. How wonderful that there were some things in life she didn't have to worry about: the mountains, the tender green leaves of summer, the deeply fragrant woods. People changed—even those closest to you, it seemed—but the earth remained constant.

At the top of a rise, the buggy gently rolled to a halt. Jubilee watched Stephen scan Bitter Plum Meadow where Sadlow Creek joined the French River and snaked through the green valley like a silver ribbon glinting in the afternoon light. There, clustered about the half-built mill that nestled near the rushing water, a dozen mountain men dragged logs with mules, measured and plastered, sawed and hammered. The laborers had already built a dam at the mouth of the creek in an attempt to get a head of water, and, from her high perspective, she saw one group digging foundation trenches for the mill itself while another peeled logs to be used for flooring.

Stephen's handsome face tightened as he pointed at the laborers. "They're going about this in all the wrong way," he remarked, almost as if he were making a mental note to himself.

To Jubilee's amazement, he'd paid close attention when she'd told him about the mill. Keen interest now flickered in the depths of his dark eyes.

She glanced at his clear-cut profile. "What do you know about building mills?" she asked teasingly, slightly amused at his concentration. "What tells you they're doing it wrong?"

He lit a cheroot and snapped out the match. "Several university classes in engineering and some plain old common sense," he returned, searching her face through the smoke. "They'll need a better dam if they're going to use two sets of stones." A grin played over his mouth. "What do you say we go on down?"

Jubilee felt her cheeks heat with embarrassment. Lord-amercy, all the loggers for miles around despised the Wentworth name almost as much as Micah. Stephen's presence would be most unwelcome, but how could she tell him that? "I don't think that would be a good idea," she hesitantly advised, hoping he'd take the hint. "Mountain men don't cotton much to advice from outsiders."

"Let's do it anyway," Stephen said, a ripple of mirth in his voice. "Surely they won't mind if we just watch."

Before she could protest, he snapped the reins and the creaking buggy moved down the hill, bouncing over ruts and stirring up clouds of dust. After a half dozen jarring jolts, they rounded the last curve and rolled into the mill site.

"Whoa!" Stephen halted their buggy about fifteen yards from the half-built structure and wrapped his reins about the brake lever.

Wearing old hats and frayed overalls, the hillmen were loose-jointed and sported long, greasy hair. If any of them saw they had company they gave no sign and continued with their work, filling the air with the sound of ringing hammers and rasping saws.

"Howdy," Stephen called out, nodding in a friendly gesture. "Need any help?" He gazed at the dam. "Seems like you might think of enlarging that dam a bit."

Jubilee knew most of the men, including the best of the lot, a slow-speaking giant of a man named Dub Calahan, a bachelor of forty who had never courted a woman to Jubilee's knowledge. Dub had a decent heart and the potential to become more than he was. After Stephen had spoken, Dub put down his work and looked up, and seeing him do this, several of the other men followed suit. When Dub ambled toward Stephen with an interested look on his face, a handful of workers trailed his steps.

She was about to greet Dub when she spotted Jordan McCoy. Tall and lanky, his face was creased by wind and weather, his eyes set deep in their sockets, and his brows wild and bushy. When their gazes locked, he shoved his hammer into the loop on his pant leg and stalked toward the buggy where he focused flinty eyes on Stephen. "I know who you are, Wentworth," he hollered, "and we don't need no advice from the likes of you!" He waved back Dub and the others.

McCoy wore a permanent snarl on his bearded face, and Jubilee knew that he detested outsiders. True, the hillmen considered him a leader, and a leader he might well be, but only in the roughest, most elemental way. McCoy held his position with an aggressive assertiveness that had gone unchecked since Jubilee's father had died seven years ago. Of all the men in the group, only Dub had the makings to stand up to him, but he still lacked the confidence needed to challenge the bitter-faced bully. "Seems you're mighty ill-natured today, Jordan McCoy," Jubilee called out boldly. "What has this man ever done to you?"

The mountaineer yanked down his floppy hat. "His family's been a-puttin' down all us hill folk for years. Iffin you don't know that, you *should*. They done made your brother a cripple fer life!"

The words gouged into Jubilee's heart. She'd been away too long and forgotten how downright rude the hill people could be to anyone they considered an enemy.

Stephen took a draw from his cheroot. "Don't you work at the logging camp?" he inquired of the man in a voice that never wavered.

McCoy walked to the buggy, and the broken blood vessels in his nose and across his cheeks told her that he was a drinker. The hammer dangled from the loop on his overalls like a weapon. He put his hand on the horse's bridle, making the simple action seem threatening. "I used to," he replied, an angry flush moving over his pitted skin, "but I got tired of slavin' fer somebody who was only interested in workin' me like a mule and I quit." His bottom lip curled down like an angry slash. "Like I said, we don't need no help from you!"

Dub Calahan listened silently. He analyzed the situation with a frown, but lacked the courage to intervene.

McCoy dragged a hard gaze over Jubilee, his eyes smouldering in his dark face. "Us mountain folk don't break loyalty to each other. You know that—or you used to. Looks like you got above your raisin' and took up fancy ways yourself"—he glared at Stephen—"consortin' with the likes of him."

"That'll be enough," Stephen warned, his voice icy cold.

McCoy's mouth twisted in a sour grin that showed rotten teeth. "Yeah, you're damn right it's enough," he snorted. He moved his flinty eyes to Jubilee again. "I always thought the Jones family was decent folks, but reckon I was wrong."

Stephen half rose, starting to climb from the buggy.

McCoy's eyes flared with surprise and he moved away. He swept a questioning gaze over the other men, looking for reinforcements, but one by one, including Dub, they returned to their work.

Jubilee grabbed Stephen's arm. "No, don't pay any attention to him," she pleaded, going cold about her heart.

He stared back at her, his eyes snapping. "I won't let him talk to you like that."

She laughed off the matter lightly. "It doesn't make any difference what Jordan McCoy says and it never did," she asserted, feeling the resistance of his arm as he pulled against her. "No one listens to him but someone more foolish than himself." In her heart she knew it wasn't true, but she dared not let Stephen face a dozen men who all had personal grudges with his family.

"Please," she whispered, forcing an intimate plea into her voice, "let's go on and finish the buggy drive."

Stephen assessed Jubilee's anguished face and slowly reined in his anger. He reclaimed his seat, realizing that for the time being she was right.

By now McCoy was at work again, but he looked up with a glare and jabbed his finger at Stephen. "You better watch yourself, Wentworth—this ain't over yet!"

Stephen angrily tossed his cheroot to the ground, refusing to dignify the man's comment with an answer. His days visiting Jubilee had taught him that below their seemingly relaxed way of life the hill people had a whole network of allegiances, taboos, and suspicions he knew almost nothing about.

He considered the way Micah held him responsible for his father's actions, how that here in the hills a man's whole future was bound up in his family's name. This afternoon had brought the facts home like a punch in the gut. No wonder the foremen in his logging camps always reported constant complaining from the workers and had trouble keeping them in line.

The loggers were boiling with malice and pent-up rage. Even now he could see that Jubilee trembled and breathed a silent prayer of thanks that they were leaving. He unwound the reins and slapped them on the mare's rump, yelling, "Move on!" He turned on the seat and locked gazes with McCoy, who stared back boldly.

As the buggy bounced away from the mill, the drooping lines of Jubilee's body amply expressed her emotions. "Most of the hill people aren't like that," she began with sad eyes. "It's just that Jordan McCoy—"

"It wasn't your fault," Stephen interrupted, concentrating on the twisting road. He didn't want to talk about the situation now, or even think about it.

She gave him a feeble smile that spoke volumes.

Stephen heaved an inward groan. She'd tried to warn him, but he wouldn't listen. Right about now he felt as if he'd gone back a hundred years in time. He thought of the mountaineers' wildness and poverty, of their weather-beaten shacks perching on the hillsides, of their gully-streaked hard-scrabble farms, hardly producing enough for their own families. He thought of their rudeness and lack of manners.

It seemed that when he'd left Asheville he'd returned to frontier days and left all vestiges of social conventions behind. For all practical purposes, the men who worked for him in these mountains were still living in the 1700s.

He'd always considered the loggers simply as "those men in the mountains who cut trees," having no idea what they thought or felt. Now he knew. To them he was a hated feudal lord. It all seemed like something out of a novel. But this was no novel—this was real. He realized he had an enormous problem to overcome if Wentworth Enterprises was going to succeed.

Song of the Lark

* * *

It was about ten at night and the cabin was quiet, Tad having gone to sleep. Jubilee sat by Granny's bed and, seeing her grandmother close her eyes, she put the book aside that she'd been reading aloud, assuming the old lady had drifted off.

The room held a melange of wonderful aromas: kerosene, freshly washed linen, lemon oil, and the ambery, musky scent of spicewood tea floating from a cup on Granny's bedside table. The scents brought back Jubilee's childhood memories in gushing detail and she recalled evenings when she and Micah had talked to Granny as the old woman sat on the side of the bed, unbraiding her long silver hair.

Micah—Jubilee thought with a long weary sigh. How would she ever bridge the terrible rift between them now?

"Jubilee?" Granny whispered, her eyes slowly fluttering open once more.

"I thought you were asleep," Jubilee murmured, taking her grandmother's slim hand in her own. Light from the kerosene lamp wavered over the old lady's face and Jubilee marveled at the spirit she saw there, the stubborn spirit that refused to submit to death. "You *should* be asleep, you know," she commented with mock sternness. "You need your rest."

Granny laughed low in her throat. "It won't be long till I get all the rest a person could ever want. I'd rather talk to you than rest, child." Her eyes gleamed. "Now, what were you a-doin' all that sighin' about?"

Jubilee pasted a smile on her face. "Nothing," she answered affectionately. "You were just cat-napping and dreamed that."

Granny ran a soft gaze over her. "Don't think my mind's gone just 'cause I'm old, honey," she chuckled. "You was a-thinkin' of your brother, wasn't you?"

Jubilee started to fib, then remembered she'd never

been able to fool Granny. "Guess I was," she admitted feebly.

The old woman's eyes caught and held hers. "Micah loves you too much to hold a grudge. He'll come to his senses soon enough."

Astonished, Jubilee stared at her, wondering if she could actually be suggesting that she approved of her relationship with Stephen. "What do you mean by that?" she inquired in an incredulous tone.

Granny's face took on a mellow look. "Oh, nothin' much—just that folks always bend when they have to."

Jubilee smoothed back her grandmother's soft white hair, remembering the energetic little lady of years gone by whose laughter rang through the cabin. "You're talking in riddles, Granny," she said kindly.

The old woman's eyes drifted for a moment. "When Clem started a-courtin' me, my pa didn't like his family, and his family didn't like Pa. None of the folks would budge an inch on us a-gettin' together. Why, I thought our folks was a-goin' to split us up in spite of all we could do."

Jubilee laughed in surprise, recalling how her grandpa had worshiped his *blue-eyed darlin'* as he'd called her. "Why, I never heard anything about this!"

Granny nodded knowingly. "Well, it happened. It went on for a whole year," she continued, staring straight ahead as if she were seeing the scene that very moment. "Clem's folks and mine was a-threatenin' to shoot each other dead like some river trash. Clem finally told me he was a-goin' to steal me away and move out of the country." She stared at Jubilee, her eyes flaring. "In the end we had to slip off to get married."

Speechless, Jubilee eyed her granny's face. She'd never heard the colorful story before, but it rang true, for Granny had always listened to her heart rather than her head. "Well, don't leave me wondering what happened," she teased with a laugh. "Tell me the rest of the story."

Song of the Lark

Granny chuckled softly. "It was in December and everythin' was covered smooth with snow, a-glistenin' like silver. We went to the Baptist preacher-man over in Sugar Loaf and got him to marry us up." Her old face softened. "Clem wanted to give me flowers that day, 'course it was cold enough to freeze water in the teakettle and there weren't a flower blossom in sight." Moist emotion flooded her eyes. "He found some bright red holly berries in the woods and broke off a bunch for me to hold while the preacher-man was a-marryin' us." Her face became young and vital for a moment. "I've been partial to holly berries ever since."

Still amazed, Jubilee listened silently, taking in every word she said.

"My pa nearly had a conniption fit," Granny went on in a soft, raspy voice that belied the emotion in her eyes. "He got down his rifle-gun and said he was a-goin' to shoot Clem through the heart. Ma had more sense than the rest of the folks and fetched that Baptist preacher-man from Sugar Loaf." Laugh lines flared from her cornflower blue eyes. "He gave Pa a good talkin' to and told him Clem and me was married up forever and he'd just have to live with it." She laughed a little. "From what Ma said, that preacher-man put the fear of the Lord into Pa."

She smoothed her frail, blue-veined hands over the soft quilt. "Pa was swelled up like a toad for more than a year and wouldn't sit in the same room with Clem." She grinned like a young girl. "But there weren't no more shootin' talk. Your granddaddy always made me a good livin' and he treated me real fine, too."

She picked up a faded daguerreotype of Clem that sat by the cup of spicewood tea and traced her fingers over it. Tears sparkled in her eyes. "Lordamercy, how foolish I was about that man. Sometimes my old heart still aches fit to bust just a-thinkin' about him a-bein' gone—and he's been buried nigh onto fifteen years now."

Jubilee ached for her sorrow. All these years her grandmother had endured a terrible loneliness, but in the mountain tradition had kept it to herself, not wanting to inflict it on another soul. "Why didn't anyone in the family ever tell me about this?" Jubilee whispered, still amazed at what she'd heard.

Something that looked suspiciously like a blush tinted Granny's lined cheeks. "To tell you the truth, child, I reckon they was all ashamed of themselves. When the young'uns started a-comin' it kind of bound everybody together, both families' blood bein' poured into the same pot, so to speak. Folks had a hard time a-rememberin' that they'd been ready to kill each other a few years back."

A wry smile touched her lips. "Clem and me never brung it up, either. We thought there weren't no need a-resufrectin' hard feelin's when everybody was sort of ashamed of the way they'd acted." She was silent for a moment, then patted Jubilee's hand. "Honey, while we're a-talkin' I just wanted to tell you I like your Mr. Wentworth."

Jubilee's heart swelled with feeling. "*You do?*" she returned, remembering all the nights she'd tossed and turned back in Asheville wondering what Granny would say about her working for the man.

"Yes, I do. He's fine as frog hair split up the middle. I thought I could never like a Wentworth, but I do. I plumb surprised myself. Just goes to show a person should keep an open mind 'bout folks they ain't met yet. I like your feller just fine."

Jubilee's throat tightened with emotion. "He's not my *feller*, he's my employer," she responded, trying to control her voice. "There's a whole world standing between us. He's a high, refined gentleman used to the best things in life—and I'm"—she sighed heavily—"I'm just who I am."

The old woman held her gaze. "You'll work it out some way. Love is a funny thing. Sometimes folks that are as different as night and day can still love each other. When that feelin' comes over you, you can't fight against it. It's like a-tryin' to keep the world from turnin'."

Jubilee's heart was too full to speak and she leaned over to hug the old woman who'd worn the same gold wedding band for sixty-five years. "Thank you," she whispered, caressing her grandmother's frail shoulders through the soft cotton nightgown. "After Ma died I felt all hollow and lonely inside, but you took that feeling away. You still do."

Granny's eyes misted up.

Jubilee smoothed back her grandmother's silky hair and fantasized that she and Stephen might be married one day. How wonderful it would be to be Tad's real mother! "I love that little boy like he was my own," she admitted as much to herself as her grandmother.

The old woman chuckled. "He's a darlin', all right. With them big brown eyes of his, he reminds me of a little fawn."

"His mother was a beautiful woman—all regal with shiny black hair. She looked like some kind of queen." Jubilee blinked thoughtfully, analyzing her feelings about Isabelle for the first time. "It's strange, but somehow I'm not jealous of her."

Granny nodded. "That's good, honey. You stay that way. There ain't no sense in a-bein' jealous of a dead woman, none a'tall."

Fatigue lined Granny's face, and Jubilee stood and lovingly arranged the much-washed quilt about her. "You better get some sleep now," she advised, silently asking herself how she could ever get along without her. "It's gettin' later by the minute."

"Jubilee," Granny proposed, a twinkle in her bright eyes, "why don't you ask your feller to that dance over at the Colbys' tomorrow night? He's probably never seen nothin' like that before."

Jubilee bit back a smile, noticing Granny still insisted

on calling Stephen her *feller*. "I don't know if that's a good idea," she answered, the scene at the mill still vivid in her mind. "I imagine seeing a real live Wentworth would scare most of the folks in this hollow plumb stiff— either that or make them mad as fire."

"That's all right," the old woman spoke up, defiance shining in her eyes. "He can't help what his pa done. 'Sides, he don't impress me as a man who'd plow around a stump. I'd say that feller meets his problems head on."

"But, Granny," Jubilee interrupted, clasping her thin arm, "just yesterday the men at the mill didn't take to him, and Jordan McCoy—"

"Jordan McCoy never went to a dance in his life! Reckon he knew no decent woman would look at him." Granny gave a dry chuckle. "Don't worry, honey, he won't be there, and folks will be on their best manners. Just let the women-folks get a gander at Stephen Wentworth. When they see his handsome face and fine manners they'll set all the men-folks straight!"

Jubilee took in the firm set of Granny's little chin and smiled to herself, knowing that in her own way the old lady was as smitten as she. She laughed, then kissed her cheek and blew out the light, filling the darkness with the lingering scent of lamp smoke. "Good night, Granny," she called out, still smiling as she walked to the door.

"Good night, Jubilee. You think on what I told you now."

Jubilee went to her room and started undressing for bed, turning Granny's idea over in her head. She wanted the notion to go away, but it hung there in the darkness, tempting her with its possibilities. If the mountaineers would accept Stephen, he could advise them about the mill and the whole community would benefit. On top of that, it would break down the barrier between him and the men who worked in his logging camps. Yes, the more she thought about asking Stephen to the dance, the more she liked it.

Song of the Lark

So the idea took hold in her mind and rooted itself there like a hearty chickweed plant with long, tough roots.

The next morning Stephen gazed at Jubilee with incredulous eyes. "Did I hear you say you wanted me to go to a dance tonight?"

She clasped his arm as he drove his buggy to the general store so she could buy some staples. She'd been thinking about inviting him for hours, but had just screwed up her courage now. "Yes. Half the hollow will be there."

Stephen frowned and snapped his reins. "That may be true," he said, glancing at her with puzzled eyes, "but I'm not sure it's a good idea to go."

Jubilee sat up a little straighter, trying to pretend she hadn't thought the same thing herself. "Oh, it'll be all right," she returned, nervously adjusting her hat. "Granny said it would be, and I've never known her to be wrong."

"With all respect to Granny," he replied with a laugh, "she could be wrong this time. That little visit to the mill told me how mountain people feel about Wentworths."

Jubilee brushed his words aside, refusing to think of the reception he'd received from her own brother. Why, a blind man could see the decency in Stephen, she thought, stubbornly refusing to believe that anything might happen now that she'd decided she wanted him to attend the social event. "Most of the people in the hollow aren't like Jordan McCoy," she contended, fighting back her own fears. "They're decent folks, and you'll be welcome at the dance."

Stephen gazed at her expectant face, considering her words. Since the visit to the mill, he'd been determined to change the mountain people's view of him. Somehow he had to let them know he wasn't the same man as his father. He'd considered calling a meeting where the men could air their grievances, but guessed most of them wouldn't attend. Perhaps the dance was a godsend in disguise. In fact, the more he thought about it, the more he liked the idea. If he could impress the mountaineers favorably, it might even improve Jubilee's relations with her brother.

"Please come," she begged, her request rough with longing. She held his gaze and refused to release it. *"Just for me."*

Stephen considered the proposition one last time. "Are you sure this is what you want?"

A rosy stain crept over her cheeks. "Yes, of course," she answered, presenting him with her best smile.

Jubilee, her heart pounding a little faster, stared at Stephen's thoughtful face. He said not a word, but when a bemused grin raced over his lips, she knew he would go with her. Obviously he was just indulging her, but she didn't care. She was sure that as soon as the people saw him they would like him, and the thought filled her with joy.

They drove on, and in the distance she pointed out a series of small cascades, glinting with morning light and forming silvery pools, surrounded by blue periwinkle and wild sweet peas. For a while she concentrated on the thud of the horse's hooves and the whir of the buggy wheels; then as Stephen negotiated a sharp turn, she scanned his face.

Something was definitely on his mind besides the dance this evening, she told herself. His thoughts had been elsewhere all day, and, quieter than usual, he'd given simple brief answers to her questions since he'd arrived at the cabin at seven this morning. Struck by his preoccupied expression, she quietly ventured, "Are you thinking about Asheville—about your business there?"

He gazed at her, a glimmer of sadness in his eyes. "No, actually I wasn't. I was thinking of something else."

A long uncomfortable silence stretched between them.

"Well?" she prodded with a smile and a cocked brow.

He laughed and clasped her hand. "I'll tell you tonight," he promised, "I'll tell you after the dance."

They rolled on, but despite the sunny day, Jubilee felt a chill race over her arms. Somewhere deep down inside of her where truths lay she sensed he was simply postponing an announcement she wouldn't like.

After they'd returned from the general store, Stephen went back to the logging camp and Jubilee primped for the dance that evening. In the back of her mind, she was worried how people would receive Stephen, but she was also feminine enough to want to look the best for the man she loved. She laid out a calico gown of sprigged pink flowers on a black background that she'd cut and sewn herself several summers ago. Effie helped her with her hair and Tad handed her a ribbon for it, both telling her how lovely she looked. Jubilee finally gazed into the little scrap of a mirror hanging by the washpan, satisfied with her appearance.

Near dusk, Stephen and Jubilee rounded a bend in the road, and the Colbys' cabin loomed into sight, golden light streaming from its windows. Horses and wagons surrounded a large barn set behind the cabin in a grove of pines whose dark tops stood out in stark relief against a huge orange moon.

Frightened chickens and geese scattered over the clearing as Stephen pulled the buggy to a halt. He jumped from the seat and helped Jubilee to the ground, his dark suit and starched white shirt emphasizing his broad shoulders and setting off his tanned skin. Even before they entered the barn, Jubilee heard strains of fiddle music.

Inside, the building was redolent with the scents of spicy evergreen boughs and ropes of wildflowers which decorated a platform built for the musicians. Glowing lanterns hung from the rafters and illuminated an assembly of people who were dressed in their Sunday best, ladies in calicos and shawls, and men in mismatched jackets and pants. Barefooted children chased each other about the barn, and here and there yawning hounds lay in the shadows.

As soon as the noisy crowd spotted Stephen, a hush fell upon them as if they'd just been doused with ice water. The practicing musicians scraped to a halt and put down their fiddles and banjos, their eyes wide with disbelief. Even the children stopped playing and froze in their tracks. It fact, it was so quiet that Jubilee thought she could hear the sound of her own pounding heart. For once in her life, Granny had given her the wrong advice.

Stephen shot her a comforting look, then strolled toward the musicians' platform and straightened his back. She noticed awed girls whisper to their mothers, who seemed to be as affected by his charm as their daughters. With a confident smile, he obligingly returned each and every feminine glance, apparently knowing just what he was doing. A blush rolled up from Jubilee's bosom. He was more sure of himself with women than any man she'd ever met. The feminine inhabitants of the hollow would be talking about this night for years to come.

Stephen gazed up at an old man who Jubilee had known all her life as Uncle Jesse. "Do you know 'Fire on the Mountain'?" he casually asked the dumbfounded fiddler.

The old-timer pulled his snowy chin whiskers. "I reckon I do," he replied in a high, cracking voice. "I been playin' it since I was eight years old."

"Well, play it now," Stephen ordered, putting a ring of authority into his voice, "and keep the music going." He dragged his gaze over the silent, stony-faced mountaineers, their lank-haired women, their thin, pale-faced children who all gazed at him as if he might be Lucifer himself and said, "I thought we had come to dance, not stand here and stare at each other all night."

The frosty silence persisted.

Then one woman laughed, and finally another, dissolving the tension that hung between Stephen and the inhabitants of the hollow like a clammy fog. When Uncle Jesse struck up the lively tune and the other musicians joined in, the crowd visibly relaxed, and Jubilee felt a welcome rush of relief.

After the opening tune, Stephen took her hand and they danced the Virginia Reel as the lead couple. "You handled that well," she commented as they linked arms and paraded down the lane between the couples and back again.

He stepped into place and saluted her. "I just wagered that a crowd that had gone to this much trouble to get slicked up would rather dance than fight."

Jubilee laughed, beginning to truly enjoy the evening. She let Stephen whirl her about the barn, her skirt belling out like a blossoming flower. The sound of boots pounding against the hard-packed earthen floor resounded in her ears as she compared the dance with the elegant party in Stephen's mansion. At least she didn't have Estell to contend with this time, she thought happily.

When they'd finished the Virginia Reel, she saw Dub Calahan squeezing his way through the boisterous crowd, his heavy brown hair slicked down with macassar oil. A stiffly starched shirt and what passed as a jacket clad his broad chest, while frayed trousers skimmed the tops of boots that had been polished with axle grease.

"Is Miss Effie comin' later?" he asked Jubilee, an eager expression lighting his broad face.

Compassion flowed through her. "No, I'm afraid not." She glanced at the children who ran about the barn playing tag, then back at Dub. "She stayed with Tad," she explained, wishing she'd brought both Effie and the boy. "She should have come."

Dub nodded awkwardly. "I wish she had come, too." He gulped and his big Adam's apple moved up and down. "Would you tell her I remember her from that big revival meetin' two years ago last April? Tell her I recollect her kindly."

Jubilee nodded, too stunned to speak.

"Thank ye, Miss Jubilee," Dub responded, blushing to the roots of his hair. "You're a real thoughty girl." He gazed at Stephen as if he wanted to say something, then seemingly struck dumb, turned and made his way across the barn to a cluster of bachelors who hadn't summoned the nerve to join the dancing.

Jubilee caught Stephen's eye and raised a brow.

"You look surprised," he said.

"Yes—I am. How I wish we'd brought Effie," she murmured sadly. "As far as I know, Dub is the only man who's ever asked about her."

After the next dance, Stephen made his way to a group of dark-clad widows who wore black bonnets and sat in a row like a line of crows on a fence. To Jubilee's surprise, he asked one of them to dance. She covered her toothless mouth with her hand and laughed, but the second granny blushed like a young girl and accepted. After that, he brought them out one by one, letting them enjoy their first dance since their husbands had died.

Jubilee smiled, knowing that these were the women who delivered the babies, nursed the sick, and set the moral tone of the community. If Stephen wanted to make friends within the hollow, he couldn't have made a better choice, for in the mountain hierarchy their place was undisputed and their approval meant everything. Without her advising him, he'd instinctively done the right thing.

After the midnight supper, children lay on piles of hay to sleep and the grannies nodded in their chairs. The music was softer and dreamier now, and Jubilee recognized many of the plaintive English ballads that Micah fiddled out on winter nights before the hearth. When Uncle Jesse began a sweet waltz, Stephen took her in his arms and her heart stroked faster. Every eye in the barn was upon them as the mountaineers watched Hamish Wentworth's son hold her close and she trembled with excitement.

Stephen rested a warm hand on her back and a thrill rushed through her, for in his eyes she read open admiration. He swept her about the barn and her spirit soared with happiness—surely this was bliss. Although she had no idea what the future might bring, tonight there was only warmth, light, and joy in her heart and she could almost pretend that he'd told her he loved her.

Suddenly the music stopped, and a worried murmur ran through the crowd. Stephen released Jubilee and they both turned about to see Jordan McCoy and some of his friends standing just inside the open barn door. Jubilee's heart flopped like a bird in a sack, for McCoy and his bunch looked as if they all had blood in their eyes and hatred in their hearts. Stephen's status at the top of the Asheville social heap wouldn't help him one iota here. Unlettered and profane, these bitter, rage-filled men had come to challenge him, much as one animal challenges another.

McCoy swaggered forward, weaving a little as he walked. "I thought I might find you and that gal here," he ground out, directing his comment at Stephen.

Stephen's first reaction was one of caution rather than fear. A warning sounded within him and his insides grew taut as he counted three men standing behind McCoy. One of them carried a jug of moonshine, which told Stephen that if he could only best their leader, the liquored-up no-accounts would scatter to the four winds.

"Reckon we ain't never had a flatlander at our dance and we don't need one now—'specially a bloodsucker like you," McCoy spat out. He swiped a mean gaze over Jubilee, then let it rest on Stephen, his eyes smouldering cavities in his head. "Why don't you leave now and show this gal how yeller you really are?"

There was a shuffling of feet and some nervous coughs in the background, but Stephen held his ground. "I'm kind of enjoying myself," he said with a lazy grin.

McCoy took another step forward and was so close now that Stephen could smell the scent of liquor wafting from his slack mouth. Then McCoy slipped a glittering knife from his boot. Several of the ladies cried out and one of the children started sobbing. From his side vision, Stephen noticed that Jubilee's face had gone chalk white.

McCoy jutted out his stubbled chin. "Leave now, or I'll cut you open like a hog on butcherin' day!"

"Think I'll stay," Stephen came back evenly, bracing his body for the attack he knew was sure to come. He'd scarcely had time to gather his wits when the bully lunged at him full force. Stephen knew he must finish him off quickly, so he blocked McCoy's swing with his forearm, then caught him on the chin with a hard right. The hillman staggered backward, and taking advantage of his confusion, Stephen twisted his opponent's wrist until the man gasped and dropped his knife.

Stephen swiftly kicked it out of reach so he could face the bully on an equal basis. He sent a blow to McCoy's soft belly, and as the man's knees bent, he rammed a roundhouse to his jaw which broke bone and contorted the lower part of the ruffian's face. McCoy fell on his side like an axed bear and sprawled on the ground, his chest heaving deeply. Seeing their leader down, the trash he'd brought with him hoisted him up on each side and, their eyes frightened, half-dragged and half-carried him from the barn. Seconds later, Stephen heard scrambling feet outside, an exchange of muffled curses, then the sound of galloping horses.

All over the barn there were audible sighs of relief, and Stephen clasped Jubilee's arm, eager for some fresh air. "Let's go outside," he rasped, somewhat surprised that the confrontation was over so quickly.

In that moment, some unspoken emotion passed between them and she nodded and let him escort her outside, her legs none too steady beneath her. As they left, she noted dozens of stunned, surprised eyes all fastened upon Stephen. They strolled outside where the dark sky twinkled with thousands of stars and she trembled with relief. A moist breeze stirred the pines and touched her face as Stephen took her in his arms.

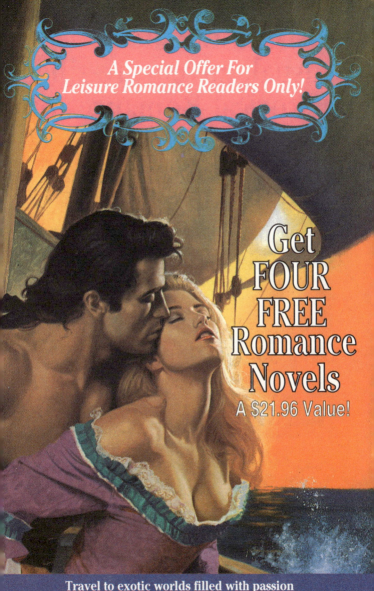

Thrill to the most sensual, adventure-filled Historical Romances on the market today...

FROM LEISURE BOOKS

As a home subscriber to Leisure Romance Book Club, you'll enjoy the best in today's BRAND-NEW Historical Romance fiction. For over twenty-five years, Leisure Books has brought you the award-winning, high-quality authors you know and love to read. Each Leisure Historical Romance will sweep you away to a world of high adventure...and intimate romance. Discover for yourself all the passion and excitement millions of readers thrill to each and every month.

Save $5.00 Each Time You Buy!

Each month, the Leisure Romance Book Club brings you four brand-new titles from Leisure Books, America's foremost publisher of Historical Romances. EACH PACKAGE WILL SAVE YOU $5.00 FROM THE BOOKSTORE PRICE! And you'll never miss a new title with our convenient home delivery service.

Here's how we do it. Each package will carry a FREE 10-DAY EXAMINATION privilege. At the end of that time, if you decide to keep your books, simply pay the low invoice price of $16.96, no shipping or handling charges added. HOME DELIVERY IS ALWAYS FREE. With today's top Historical Romance novels selling for $5.99 and higher, our price SAVES YOU $5.00 with each shipment.

AND YOUR FIRST FOUR-BOOK SHIPMENT IS TOTALLY FREE!
IT'S A BARGAIN YOU CAN'T BEAT! A Super $21.96 Value!

 LEISURE BOOKS   A Division of Dorchester Publishing Co., Inc.

GET YOUR 4 FREE BOOKS NOW — A $21.96 Value!

Mail the Free Book Certificate Today!

Free Books Certificate

4 FREE BOOKS

A $21.96 VALUE

YES! I want to subscribe to the Leisure Romance Book Club. Please send me my 4 FREE BOOKS. Then, each month I'll receive the four newest Leisure Historical Romance selections to Preview FREE for 10 days. If I decide to keep them, I will pay the Special Member's Only discounted price of just $4.24 each, a total of $16.96. This is a SAVINGS OF $5.00 off the bookstore price. There are no shipping, handling, or other charges. There is no minimum number of books I must buy and I may cancel the program at any time. In any case, the 4 FREE BOOKS are mine to keep — A BIG $21.96 Value!

Offer valid only in the U.S.A.

Name _____

Address _____

City _____

State _____ Zip _____

Telephone _____

Signature _____

If under 18, Parent or Guardian must sign. Terms, prices and conditions subject to change. Subscription subject to acceptance. Leisure Books reserves the right to reject any order or cancel any subscription.

A $21.96 VALUE

4 FREE BOOKS

Get Four Books Totally FREE — A $21.96 Value!

▼ Tear Here and Mail Your FREE Book Card Today! ▼

PLEASE RUSH MY FOUR FREE BOOKS TO ME RIGHT AWAY!

Leisure Romance Book Club
P.O. Box 6613
Edison, NJ 08818-6613

AFFIX STAMP HERE

Song of the Lark

"Lordamercy, when I saw that knife I went weak all over," she exclaimed, clutching onto his shoulders. "Just to think that I was the one that brought you here!"

Stephen held her against his hard chest, caressing her back until she stopped trembling. "Actually it wasn't much of a fight," he said against her windblown hair. "That whole pack was so liquored up they could hardly stand."

Jubilee heaved a deep sigh of relief, thanking the Lord the incident was over. She realized that no matter what their condition, Stephen had faced up to the lot of the no-accounts and shown himself a man. He'd accounted for himself well in the mountaineers' eyes, for they valued physical bravery highly, and they'd never forget it. In fact, the inhabitants of the hollow would likely be talking about it all summer.

Calmer now, she stared up at his rugged features now silvered with moonlight. "How about answering that question now—you know, the one you wouldn't answer this morning?"

He smoothed her hair and cupped her face between his big hands, yet still he did not speak.

Then she knew—knew what she'd forced back into the cave of her mind for days now and had refused to accept. "You're leaving tomorrow, aren't you?" she whispered, her voice rough and broken.

With gentle fingers he traced along her jaw and then followed her collarbone. "Yes," he answered simply. "I've been away from Asheville far too long. I'll go in the morning just as soon as I've said good-bye to Tad."

A sick, empty feeling claimed the pit of Jubilee's stomach. "When will you come back?" she asked, only realizing that the statement might seem impertinent after she'd said it.

"Toward the end of the summer," he answered simply, "in time to fetch Tad before school starts."

Aching inside, she stared at his handsome features trying to memorize every inch of his face. Here was everything she desired in a man: his sense of humor, his commanding personality that took control of every situation as tonight, his gentleness—and he was leaving.

"Is there anything I can bring you," he asked, holding her a little closer and moving his hand over the hollows of her back.

The hasty words spilled from her mouth before she could catch them. "No, but there something you can give me now," she answered, surprised at her own boldness. "Just a simple kiss good-bye."

It seemed the giddy sensations his nearness stirred had dried up every drop of her good sense, for all she could think of was kissing him once more before he left. How could she be so besotted with a man who'd made no commitment to her whatsoever? she wondered, realizing that where he was concerned she barely had a smidgen of self-control. Standing on her tiptoes, she looped her arms about his broad shoulders and raised her mouth to his.

For a moment she could see him fighting back his emotions, and she sensed great turmoil within him, and then he whispered, "Yes, a kiss good-bye."

He bent his head, his lips brushing over hers in the slightest breath of a touch. His kiss cherished her soft, responsive lips, then he molded her to his hard-muscled body, and what had started as a languid embrace transformed itself into a tempest of desire.

Familiar sensations unfurled deep inside of Jubilee, blossoming and growing until they consumed all thought. She wanted him in ways she seemed helpless to explain, and she returned the ardent kiss, sharing the same ragged breath, feeling the fire that was coming dangerously close to blazing out of control.

He'd aroused a fierce need in her and she wanted to feel his raw masculine strength overpowering her, consuming her, but she reminded herself that she had no right. They'd made no vows or promises, nor had they any understanding for the future. Truth be told, he hadn't even mentioned taking her back to Asheville when he came for Tad.

Dredging up her smidgen of willpower, she tried to forget the sensations his kiss aroused, and gently eased away from him, realizing it was one of the hardest things she'd ever done. With fluttering lashes, she opened her eyes, her skin still burning from his touch. "It was a fine dance," she remarked in a quavering voice.

His eyes glittered with a hungry intensity, but she could tell he was reining in his passion, exerting a magnificent self-control. "Yes, the best I can ever remember," he replied quietly.

Jubilee tried to erase her love for him, but it seemed he was now a part of her, as inseparable as her own heartbeat. Would he take her back to Asheville with him when he came for Tad, or leave her in the mountains, having no need of her now that the boy was so much better?

She would have to wait until the end of summer to find out. The end of the summer seemed a lifetime away.

Chapter Ten

Jubilee worked feverishly. She planted and picked, hoed and harvested. She pickled and dried every available scrap of food. Having spent many a hungry winter in the mountains, the memory of her deprivation drove her on at a frantic pace. She fetched water, and milked, and cooked, and sewed, and scrubbed, and churned, and washed all the bedding, and put an old setting hen on a nest so she could raise some chicks.

Knowing Tad would be going home soon, she seized every opportunity to teach him something he could take back to the city. She made ink out of pokeberry juice and sharpened turkey feathers to produce quills so he could print the alphabet. More important to her way of thinking, she took him into the woods to teach him things he could never learn at home.

One day as they ambled along a logging trail, enveloped by the pungent scent of pines, he stopped and pointed at some squawking orioles perched on a limb. "Look! There's three birds in that tree." He squinted at the bright yellow and black birds sharply outlined against

Song of the Lark

the green pine needles. "One, two, three," he announced proudly, turning to look at his teacher with a big grin.

"That's right," she praised him. "You can count orioles just like you can count peaches on the table. You're counting better every day."

His bright eyes glistened with curiosity. "Why are the birds howling?" he asked with a puzzled frown.

"They're not howling," she answered, trying to hold back her laughter. "Dogs howl, but birds warble and screech. I'll bet those orioles are squawking about going to the flatlands for the winter," she answered, making up a little story to pacify his curiosity.

He shaded his eyes with his small hand. "But why are they going to the flatlands?" he asked, still watching the birds as they flitted to another tree with a soft purr of their wings. "Don't they like it here?"

Jubilee chuckled at his insistent questions. "Well, it'll soon be too cold for them up here in the mountains. Fall is coming, then winter." She studied his soft face and, trying to prepare him for what lay ahead, added, "You'll be going back to the flatlands soon, too. You'll be starting school this fall.

A sad expression claimed his face. "But I don't want to start school. I want to stay here."

"Oh, you'll love school," she said encouragingly. "It's fun to learn things."

He hung his head. "But I-I can't talk good."

She gently lifted his chin. "That used to be true, but you talk fine now," she insisted, meeting his sad eyes.

Lordamercy, she thought with an inward sigh, the rest of the summer would just fly by and in many ways the boy still needed more confidence. Very well, she told herself. She'd pack every bit of fun and learning into what was left of the season. After all, Stephen hadn't said anything in his letters about her returning, and it might be her last weeks with the boy.

She knelt down and started writing his name in the soft

earth with a stick. "You'll learn to write in school, and the first thing they'll teach you is your name. Look at this," she finished, completing the d in *Tad*. "This is your name. Now you try it."

The boy gazed at the neat letters with amazement and, taking the stick, squatted down and tried to copy what she'd written. She praised his crudely scrawled name lavishly, and they worked for some time scratching letters in the dirt. When he became tired of that, she suggested they finish their walk. She watched him run down the logging trail ahead of her, brimming with pleasure. His once skinny arms and legs were sturdy and tan and there was a bounce in his step. Yes, she'd been right. A summer in the mountains was just the tonic he needed to ease him out of his grief and add some pounds to his slight body.

Presently strange bird calls rippled through the woods, and Tad looked at her with startled eyes. She caught his arm and softly told him that a flock of wild turkey were near. "Let's lay on our bellies in this tall grass," she whispered, "and we can see them."

Soon two or three drab hens came into view, and shortly afterwards several gobblers, their feathers a glossy black, their wattles blood red. The birds leisurely grazed through the little clearing, picking up seeds and pecking at grasshoppers.

"Watch this," she whispered, putting her hands to her lips and making a noise that sounded like a turkey call.

The birds all raised their heads at the same time and stared in her direction. When she warbled out the call again, the gobblers burst out with loud replies.

Tad giggled loudly and, flipping onto his back, covered his mouth with his hands. The turkeys scattered in a wild rush, and, laughing herself, Jubilee rolled over and gazed at her pupil, who was still convulsed with giggles. How wonderful to hear him laugh, she thought, remembering the sad, lost little soul he'd been when she first met him.

An hour later they found a hollow tree that housed a

Song of the Lark

possum and her babies. Jubilee gently lifted the possum from its home with a long stick and showed the boy how the animal would play dead. After Tad had looked at the animal, their discovery prompted a discussion on how mammals nurse and care for their young.

Later yet, they stumbled onto an old bee tree. Taking a rest, they sat on a log and watched the bees buzz in and out of the hole. Jubilee told the boy how she and Micah had once smoked bees out of a tree and stolen their honey. She promised him that when it got dark they would catch lightning bugs in a jar.

One afternoon they looked for arrowheads and Jubilee helped Tad dress up like an Indian brave, marking his face with red clay as a substitute for paint. Two days later, they observed a dragonfly with opalescent wings, then captured tadpoles in a jar and watched them turn into frogs. The same week, they got up at dawn to see spider webs glistening with dew, inspected a huge ant bed, watched butterflies burst from their cocoons, and counted spots on ladybugs.

Jubilee spend two whole days just showing Tad all the trees in the woods and finding herbs and teaching him how they could be used. One sunny afternoon they went fishing, then camped out, and she let the boy help her fry their catch for supper. The next day they sat still as statues as a shy fawn entered a grassy glade and drank from a pool; that same afternoon they spied on a group of beavers building a dam and raccoons washing their catch at the edge of the creek.

The summer wore on and Tad became strong and brown and full of wonder.

At night after he and Granny had gone to sleep, Jubilee sometimes sat cross-legged on her feather mattress, holding the necklace Stephen had given her and marveling at how luminous the pearls were in the lamplight. She couldn't bear the thought of leaving the precious pearls in Asheville, but neither did she want to wear them in front of Effie and appear too proud. So Jubilee put the necklace under her pillow at night and it became a talisman of hope, bringing back the excitement of the day when Stephen had given it to her.

During the quiet evenings she hungrily devoured books she'd brought from his study. They expanded her knowledge, and she glimpsed the vast variety of the lands and peoples of the earth, not only in the present but in the centuries past. What a marvel it all was! How little she really knew, she sadly thought, remembering Stephen's fine education.

By the light of a flickering kerosene lantern she wrote scores of letters, letters to Chambers and Delilah, and Micah too, although he never wrote back. She wrote Stephen about Tad, and in one of his letters to her, he surprised her by mentioning that he would bring her a gift that would change her life—still, he never mentioned his plans for the fall, and sometimes in the wee hours she woke up thinking about him and Estell.

What was happening in Asheville? she wondered with a pang of uneasiness. As it stood now, she had little chance to win Stephen's heart, for Estell was of his class and possessed all the social grace and book learning that she lacked. Was the beautiful blonde weaving her way deeper into his affections while she was in the mountains and knew nothing about it?

Sometimes fear seized her like a sudden spring chill, but she stoutly ignored it. She'd cling to her love for Stephen, and that would see her through the summer. She'd hold steady and do herself proud.

One afternoon when Jubilee and Tad were in the stable, he found a nest of hatching eggs, guarded by a huge red hen. With tiny puffs of yellow fuzz peeping loudly all about him, the boy stared in amazement as one of the eggs started to move. "It's shaking," he whispered to Jubilee in awe. "What makes it move?"

Song of the Lark

"There's a baby chick inside," she answered calmly. "Just watch. In a minute it'll come pecking its way out of the shell."

When the chick split the egg and came out damp and fragile, she scooped it up and settled it in Tad's outstretched hand. He held it gently, his eyes glistening with awe.

"Remember those turkeys we saw? They came into the world the same way." After Tad had held the chick a bit longer she took it from his hand. "We better put it back into the nest," she cautioned, brushing away the quarrelsome hen.

Jubilee could truly say the boy never looked better, and during the last few weeks his confidence had blossomed nicely. As she watched him play with the baby chicks, she suddenly wondered if he'd developed enough spirit to ride again. "Tad," she said, gently caressing his shoulders, "why don't I saddle up General Sherman and we'll ride him down to the creek? You're so light he'd hardly know you're on his back. We could take our poles and do a little fishing before supper."

Tad's face paled. "B-but I-I'd have to get on him to t-to r-ride," he answered, beginning to stutter after he'd been talking fine for weeks.

Jubilee laughed. "Well, yes, but he's a real gentle old mule, and I'd get on right behind you. I'd have my arms around you and you'd be as safe as one of these little baby chicks." She tousled his hair. "Why, you'd hardly know you were riding. It'd feel like sitting in Granny's old rocking chair."

Tad slowly hung his head.

With a pang of concern, she lifted his chin and met his pleading eyes. He desperately wanted to please her, but she saw he was still terrified at the idea of riding. When his lips began trembling, she gently pulled him against her bosom. "That's all right, baby," she soothed, rubbing his little back affectionately. "You don't have to ride. Hush now. Just forget about it."

Filled with regret, Jubilee ran her fingers through his silky hair. Yes, his speech had improved and he looked much better, but dark shadows still lurked in his small heart. Try as she might, she hadn't been able to completely erase the horror of his mother's death. Would he ever be completely well and whole not only in body, but in mind, in spirit? she wondered, still caressing his trembling body.

A month later, Jubilee stood in front of the cabin making hominy. The morning was hot and moist and threatening a cloudburst. As she worked, she listened to the snapping flames under the iron kettle and heard crows flying from one tree to the next, emitting raucous cries.

She poured plump corn kernels into the boiling water, then dumped ash from the chimney hopper into the kettle. She picked up a big wooden paddle and stirred the mixture, watching skin slip from the corn kernels which soon swelled and softened, releasing an aroma that reminded her of baking corn pone. At just the right time she dipped the hominy from the kettle and repeatedly rinsed it in a huge colander to free it of ashes.

She was ladling the clean hominy into crocks for storage in the storm cellar when she heard the faint sound of thudding hooves. Anticipation rose within her and she dried her hands on her apron and walked toward the edge of the clearing, expecting some company for the noon meal. She gazed down the road, and even though she couldn't see the rider yet, her nerves tingled in anticipation.

She shaded her eyes against the noonday sun, and when the rider came around the curve in the road, her pulse raced, for it was a man who sat tall in the saddle. He took off his black felt hat and, revealing his features, waved a greeting before slapping the hat back on his head. Her

Song of the Lark

heart nearly burst from her bosom. It was Stephen.

Within seconds he entered the clearing, slid from the nickering mount, and rushed to meet her, flashing an enticing grin. Dressed in a blue chambray shirt and snug jeans, he looked more casual than in Asheville, and with his inky hair falling on his brow and curling over his collar he was so breathtakingly handsome that she trembled with excitement.

She ran toward him and he clutched her in his arms, pulling her against his hard, warm body. Laughing, he picked her up and swung her about, his eyes twinkling from beneath the shadow of his hat. "Hello, Curly Top!"

He'd finally come, she thought, going weak with joy. As he held her close, the rich aromas of leather and tobacco and bay rum enveloped her, staggering her senses. She was filled with sudden tender memories, and the bliss of the moment poured through her, shattering her composure. "*Stephen*, you're back," she whispered, so overcome she thought she might burst out crying right then and there. "How did you get here so early?"

"I left Miller's Tavern way before daylight to avoid riding in the heat all day."

She brushed back her wild hair and stammered, "I'm making hominy, I-I mean, I made hominy"—she bit her lip and started laughing—"I mean I just finished making hominy!"

Laugh lines wrinkled the corners of his dark eyes. "I know what you mean," he replied, chuckling deep in his throat.

His warm, velvety voice spilled over her, adding heat to her already flushed cheeks. His face was only inches from hers, his eyes gently running over her, his big hand caressing her back. When he lifted his fingers to trace the line of her jaw, her heart fluttered crazily.

She'd thought of this moment every day since he'd left, wondering how he would greet her, and now she knew, for he slid his arms about her waist and pulled her close.

His eyes took on a dreamy glow and his raven head tilted forward as his lips brushed over each of her eyelids and skimmed over her cheeks, leaving a trail of fire in their wake. "How I've missed you," he murmured huskily, easing back just enough for her to see a roguish grin painted on his lips.

The velvety softness of his words made her heart lurch, and she impulsively circled her arms about his wide shoulders and raised her lips to his. His mouth feathered over hers and his hand slid over her ribs to settle at the indentation of her waist. He pulled her closer yet and tunneled his fingers through the long hair and moved his mouth over hers. He smelled of tobacco and pine and the whole outdoors, and her heart pounded against her ribs, making her think she might lose her breath. As the kiss became more insistent, she noticed the warmth of his wandering hands and felt his heart thudding against her bosom. Wild sensations clamored through her and she pressed herself against him, her desire rising by the second. She felt as if she were drowning in the fiery kiss, and she didn't care if she ever came up for air.

Lost in a haze of euphoria, she barely heard a door slam and the sound of running feet. "Papa, Papa, You're here!" Tad cried, scampering from the cabin to meet his father.

Stephen gently set Jubilee from him. He looked at the boy, his eyes sparkling with love, then back at Jubilee and they exchanged a secret smile. "Is there someplace we can really be alone this afternoon?" he asked, a hint of amusement lacing his velvety voice.

From the sound of his words, she guessed that he had more on his mind than sightseeing, and there was a fluttering in the pit of her stomach. "Yes," she answered softly. "I'll have Effie come over to keep Tad and Granny company, and I'll take you to the old Indian caves."

Stephen smiled, then lifted his son and tossed him into the air. He caught the boy with a whoop of laughter, and

Song of the Lark

Jubilee's heart swelled with joy, for she loved them both. Happy as she'd ever been, she joined them, and Stephen put his arm about her as he carried Tad into the cabin.

By the time Jubilee and Stephen arrived at the high clearing where the Indian caves were located, clouds had gathered in the sky and big groves of towering cottonwoods whispered in the moist breeze. Jubilee had always found the caves a source of comfort, but their effect on her was something she couldn't put into words. Here she found an inner quiet she couldn't explain. It was essential to her existence, however, as it had been since she was a child; she wanted to share it with Stephen, the first person she'd ever brought to this place.

The two reined in their horses and dismounted, then loosened the girts on their saddles and let the animals graze on the lush grass. Jubilee glowed with happiness. All the time Stephen had been gone, she'd wondered about Estell, but today as everyone had laughed and talked and enjoyed a noon meal together, he'd only spoken of Chambers, Delilah, and Cleo. Praise the Lord, he'd never even brought up the blonde's name.

The area below the caves proved to be an interesting place. They found crevices on the rocky hill with pockets of moss, ferns, and flowers. Jubilee picked one of the flowering plants and showed it to Stephen. "They call this yellow root," she explained, shaking the clinging earth from its roots. "It's good for treating sore throats."

Pieces of pottery half covered with dirt protruded from the ground, and crude designs reflecting the life of some ancient tribe embellished boulders that studded the steep hill going up to the caves.

Stephen squatted down and, picking up an arrowhead, fingered the jagged flint. "Who do you think they were?" he asked, gazing at Jubilee with a puzzled frown.

"Probably Cherokee or Blackfeet. The old-timers say they had the run of these mountains before the white man came." The wind picked up and Jubilee heard distant thunder and knew a summer rainstorm was about to break. Stephen stood and joined her in staring upward. Since they'd left the cabin, the sky had changed through several colors, and it now became a threatening green covered with angry-looking gray clouds. Soon raindrops pattered down all about them, releasing the scent of moist earth and vegetation.

"We'd better make it up that hill right now," he warned, taking her hand and glancing at the mouths of the dark caves.

They walked upward, their heads and faces bared to the wind that swept up from the small valley below them and broke in torrents over the mountainside. Halfway up the hill a crack of thunder split the air, and within seconds rain drummed on the windswept pines. Big drops plummeted through the heavy air, then fell in sparkling sheets that drenched the climbers.

After they'd ducked into one of the damp, earthy-smelling caves, they relaxed and started laughing, their voices echoing off the cavern walls. Jubilee glanced at Stephen, noticing that his shirt stuck to his muscled torso and moisture streamed from his dark hair. She could see those intriguing crinkles that always fanned from his eyes when he smiled as he did now. His full lips were curved upward, parting slightly, and his strong white teeth shone in the dim light. For a moment they just stood there with the pounding rain outside the cave, then he pulled her close and sparks sizzled across her skin.

"Lord, this summer seemed a year long," he admitted, tenderly brushing back the wet curls from her face.

"Oh, I didn't even think of you at all," she chimed in, running a finger over his high cheekbone and firm jaw, "not more than twenty or thirty times a day." She laughed and clasped his arms. "How long can you stay?"

"About a week. I want to do some fishing with Tad before I take him home."

Song of the Lark

Jubilee's heart dropped. He'd said nothing about her going with him, and she still had no idea if she fit into his plans. She started to bring it up, then bit her tongue, sensing the time wasn't right. She wanted this afternoon to be light and gay—a celebration of his return to the mountains.

She raised a teasing brow. "Where's my special gift," she demanded, "the one that's going to change my life?"

"It should show up tomorrow or the next day."

"*Show up*? You make it sound like it has legs."

"Well, it does," he laughed, "and I hope it will be the best gift you ever received."

They fell silent, and tension hung between them like a thick mist. With a will of their own, her hands clutched his huge shoulders, and feeling their steely muscles flexing under her fingertips, she surrendered to the security of his arms.

"You're the most beautiful woman I've ever set eyes on," he murmured huskily.

The feel of his knuckles brushing against her neck sent a fiery tingle darting down her spine. Passion flared in his eyes as he slowly unbuttoned her sodden shirt, and her heart raced out of control. When he lifted his hand to caress her cheek, then let his fingers trail over her collarbone, she thought her trembling legs might give way beneath her. As he lowered his head and pulled her closer, she closed her eyes; then his demanding tongue flicked teasingly over her lips.

"Open your mouth, little one," he whispered, his breath hot upon her cheek. The sound of his deep voice left her weak, and a sweet warmth already surged between her thighs, forestalling her protests. A rapturous ecstasy swept over her and she complied with his request, shivering with delight.

Stephen, using his tongue expertly, took her mouth in a ravenous kiss that sent fire racing through her veins like quicksilver. An unexpected sweetness welled up within her and she relaxed into his cushioning embrace and wound her fingers in the long wet hair at the nape of his neck.

He tightened his arms about her and excitement swirled in the pit of her stomach. A deep lulling sensation rose up within her and she moaned. At the same time her breasts strained against her wet shirt and her heart pounded crazily. When his tongue entwined with hers and he ran his hand over her buttocks, taking time to explore her curves, a sharp sweetness throbbed between her thighs.

His hand stole into her shirt, pushing the wet material aside, and as he cupped her chilly breast, smoothing his warm palm over its softness, delicious shocks ran through her. He rolled her aching nipple between his fingertips, and ecstasy exploded outward within her, leaving her on the verge of swooning. As he teased and tantalized her with sure strokes, a flame leaped within her, and all the pent-up desire she'd known since setting eyes upon him rushed forward, demanding satisfaction.

Stephen kissed Jubilee with all the passion he'd fought down all summer. Lord, how tempting she'd looked a moment ago when he'd taken her into his arms. With her soft, pouting lips, fresh, creamy skin, and her shirt plastered to her breasts, outlining every luscious curve and displaying her dark nipples through the loosely woven material, no man alive could have resisted her.

How he'd yearned for her the last weeks, often waking at night and thinking of her sweetly curved body and teasing green eyes. The tempting minx remained a great enigma to him. He could find physical pleasure elsewhere. Why had this innocent mountain girl burrowed herself under his skin so thoroughly, even making him wonder if he loved her?

No, he couldn't love her—to think so would be a mistake. It was as he'd always known. The feelings between them were only transitory. He had to take his emotions in hand and focus on the future. After his perspective had cleared, he would realize he wasn't in love with this bewitching child, only in love with the impossible dream she represented.

For a moment she simply stared at him with those incredible green eyes, then a curious frown puckered her smooth brow. She gazed at him through a veil of thick, sooty lashes, a burst of color flushing her cheeks. "Have I—"

"No, it's not you."

"Then, why? You're speaking in riddles?"

Stephen put a finger over her lips. "Let's not talk of it now."

Jubilee gazed at Stephen's face, knowing she must tell him she loved him. During several long sleepless nights she'd anticipated this moment and wondered what she should say. Somewhere deep within her, a voice told her that she should guard her emotions, but it became fainter, and finally vanished altogether. She'd never faced a situation like this, a situation filled with such emotional risk, but she had to take a chance and confess her love, for she needed Stephen the way the wild roses need the sun and the rain. "I have an admission to make," she whispered, trembling with emotion. "I've thought about it all summer, and I must tell you."

His eyes flared with wary surprise. "Yes?"

Suddenly feeling vulnerable and self-conscious, she stammered out, "I l-love you—love you with all my heart and soul," she admitted, still a little unsure of herself. "I've tried fighting it, I know it isn't wise, but I just can't help it. When I first met you, my feelings were so strong for you I didn't think I could love you any more, but I do. I love you more each passing day."

She clutched her arms about him and laid her head on his chest for a moment. "When you're holding me," she said, looking into his eyes, "I feel like nothing else matters. When I'm with you, I know what it's like to feel heaven. I want to spend every day of forever loving you!''

Stephen's face showed awe and he pulled her against him. For a moment, she sensed he was about to speak, but he feathered his hand over her back. She waited for him to make a commitment, and when he didn't, a deep sadness rose within her. She'd made a mistake, she told herself. She'd spoken too soon. She'd spilled out the contents of her heart like a silly schoolgirl and he could only have contempt for her now.

"Those were beautiful words," he finally whispered, "some of the loveliest I've ever heard." He kissed the top of her head. "I'll remember them all my life."

Her heart plunged lower still, but he caressed her face, her throat, and gently moved his lips over hers, easing the sting in her heart. Perhaps he'd confess his love for her one day, too. She had to be patient, to believe, to keep hoping he would, for when all was said and done, he had become her very reason for living.

Stephen gazed down at Jubilee. Her words left him shaken and he wanted to comfort her as he would a lost child. Her confession was almost too much to comprehend, but it made him face up to his deepest motivations.

What a relief he'd caught himself just in time before making a commitment to her a moment ago. Of course, Jubilee was a luscious beauty and she tempted him as she would any living, breathing man. Her brave spirit was another enticement, but no woman would ever set claim on his deepest affections again. Real love was simply too painful, and he must protect his heart at all costs. Shoring up his weakening resolve with newfound discipline, he eased her away and drew in a long, ragged breath.

For a moment the rain pounded down harder as if it would never cease, then it gradually stopped, and the vegetation outside the cave made pleasant dripping sounds. Standing at arm's length from her now, he scanned her perplexed face, reading dozens of questions there. "The storm has passed over. I think we should leave now," he

Song of the Lark

suggested in a broken whisper. His gut tightened with emotion. "If we don't, it'll be dark before we get back."

Her eyes glistened with unspoken queries, but she only nodded her head and replied, "All right." Scarcely disguising the hurt expression on her face, she buttoned her wet shirt with trembling fingers.

After they'd emerged from the cave, they walked down the slippery hill. The scent of spicy mountain flowers sweetened the clean air with a cinnamon-like odor and the birds chattered brightly once again. They gathered up their horses that had taken shelter under a grove of thick oak trees. Stephen stole a glance at Jubilee's lovely face and graceful body as she swung upon her mount, now holding her elegant head proudly. Lord, the child was willingly walking right into a fire and didn't even realize it.

This time he'd managed to tamp down his emotions, but he had no idea how much longer he could keep doing it. There was a storm brewing between them like the one that had just passed over this mountain, a tempest of pent-up desire that swirled nearer with each passing day. Yes, he yearned to tell her that he loved her, but he knew there would be far-reaching consequences for them both. Making love to her would be the height of earthly pleasure, but they just weren't right for each other, no matter how strong the physical attraction between them. He'd struggled with the decision all summer, but her declaration of love demanded that he do the right thing. He couldn't keep toying with her heart. Somehow he had to pull up the courage to tell her he couldn't take her back to Asheville with him.

That evening in preparation for bed, Jubilee opened her window. The night was warm with an occasional breeze from the mountains, and the scent of honeysuckle hung sweet on the rain-washed air. She lay upon her bed, but sleep evaded her and she thought of the afternoon at the Indian caves. She gave thanks that she'd had the courage to tell Stephen she loved him, even if he hadn't responded in kind.

No, he hadn't said he loved her, but she'd seen the promise of love in his eyes and in his face, and she stoutly believed he did love her. The words had almost dropped from his lips, but something had held him back. What it was, she had no idea. She'd just have to be patient and love strong enough for both of them for the time being.

A heaviness centered in her bosom because he'd made no mention of inviting her back to Asheville. She fought back her disappointment. All she could do was hope and pray and wait for him to bring up the subject, for she was too proud to do it herself.

All through the summer—at night after she'd finished work, and on rainy days and Sundays—Jubilee had read the books she'd brought from Asheville. They'd enlarged the horizons of her world, but none of them had told her how to solve her problem—how to make Stephen love her.

Like a threatening ogre, the thought loomed in her mind that within a short week he'd be gone. Would he ask her to return to Asheville with him or would he leave her here alone? She tried to close her mind against the fear rising within her, but again and again a voice within her kept repeating *In a week he'll be gone!*

Had Stephen been hurt so badly that he'd never love again, or could she lead him back to warmth and love—to herself? She only had a few precious days left to find out.

The next day, Jubilee's gift with two legs rode into the clearing in front of Granny's cabin. Laughing, she hastily smoothed down her apron, then hurried outside with Stephen and Tad, who trailed behind, carrying Matilda in his arms. A distinguished-looking middle-aged man with graying hair and a neatly trimmed beard dismounted and nodded a greeting. The stocky gentleman looked to be

Song of the Lark

around fifty years old, and when she and Stephen approached him, doffed his black hat and held it in his hand. Jubilee noticed his kind eyes, and could almost feel a friendly warmth radiating from his lined face.

"This is Dr. Stuart," Stephen explained with a satisfied smile. "He's my personal physician and I persuaded him to make the trip from Asheville to examine your grandmother."

Jubilee gazed at Stephen through a haze of tears, deeply touched by his gesture. Truly, this was the best gift she'd ever received. So shaken with emotion that she could scarcely speak, she finally managed a feeble, "I see."

She put out her hand, and the doctor clasped it in his strong, firm grip. "I'll do my best for your grandmother, Miss Jones. Let's have a look at the lady." He walked back to his horse, and only now did she notice a black satchel hanging from his saddle horn.

With rising excitement, Jubilee preceded everyone else into the cabin, glad it was neat and tidy for the important visitor. She offered the doctor coffee, but he refused, preferring a dipper of cool spring water. Stephen gazed at her, his eyes sending a message of hope. Emotion tightened her chest, and her heart bulged with warmth and gratitude. No, he'd never said he loved her, but didn't this action prove it? He sat down at the table with Tad while she escorted the doctor into Granny's bedroom and introduced him.

The old lady pushed herself up on the pillows and slid a keen gaze over her visitor. "Where'd you get *him*?" she asked abruptly.

Jubilee laughed. "Why, he's ridden all the way from Asheville to look at you, Granny. This is Stephen's doctor and he's come to see if he can make you better."

A stubborn expression settled on Granny's face. "Doc Hall has always been my doctor. He helped me through a bout of scarlet fever and delivered all eight of my livin' children and my stillborn children too."

Jubilee crossed her arms. "What was that you were saying a while back about keeping an open mind until you knew someone?" she asked with a smile.

The old woman frowned like a child whose alibi had just collapsed. "Well, this is different. I don't hold with a-changin' horses in the middle of the stream. It don't show loyalty, or respect either. Us mountain folks stand by our friends."

Dr. Stuart took Granny's thin hand in his. "I've only come to help Dr. Hall, not to replace him. I'd never try to do that." He ran his eyes over her with speculation. "Eight children? What a brave woman you are, and a beautiful one too. I'll bet those blue eyes have melted many a boy's heart." The doctor spoke in a smooth, persuasive voice and flashed his best bedside smile. After some conversation, Jubilee noticed Granny's face softening.

"May I examine you?" the doctor asked kindly.

Tense seconds sped by, then with two pairs of eyes trained upon her the old woman finally huffed, "Well, I reckon there ain't no help for it. Since you come all this way, I reckon I'll let you look at me—but I still like Doc Hall best."

The physician laughed and began opening his satchel. "I hope you'll like me just a little, too."

Jubilee stood by silently, watching the doctor examine her grandmother. It tugged at her heart, for he was so gentle and kind with her, asking her questions about her life and and making small talk about the mountains as he looked her over. He took her pulse and checked her eyes and ears and gently pressed her body with his fingers. When he pulled a stethoscope from his satchel and put it against Granny's thin chest, his eyes deepened with interest. He preformed the procedure several times, then made some calculations on a pad. By now, Jubilee decided that Granny actually liked the doctor, for his charm was hard to resist.

Song of the Lark

When he'd finished the examination, he snapped his black satchel closed. "All right," he said with a congenial smile. "I'm finished. You can rest now."

Jubilee pulled the quilt over the old's lady's frail body and smoothed out her pillow. Soon she could see her grandmother's eyes fluttering together in sleep.

The doctor motioned Jubilee away from the bed and into the sitting room where Stephen was talking to Tad. Upon seeing the older man, Stephen stood, an expectant expression on his face. "Well, how is she, Doctor?"

The physician moved his gaze to Jubilee, then back to Stephen. "Not good. I'd say her poor heart is just about worn out. I'm sure Dr. Hall has diagnosed her condition," the man added, "but simply didn't tell her. There was nothing he could do. Often when you tell a patient that you can't help them, they simply give up."

The appearance of the Asheville doctor had raised Jubilee's hopes, but they now came crashing back to earth in a landslide of despair. "Isn't there *anything* you can do?" she asked, her voice breaking.

A thoughtful look flicked over the doctor's face and he nodded. "Yes, we can give her good care and nutrition," he replied, putting his hand on her shoulder. "That should certainly extend her days." He opened his satchel and took out a small bottle of medicine. "And we can give her this," he went on, placing a bottle filled with white powder in Jubilee's hands.

Jubilee stared at the cool green bottle laying in her palm. "What is this?"

"Nitroglycerine," the doctor answered, raising his brows expressively. "When Stephen said the lady had a bad heart, I suspected she might need this. It's rather a new medicine and, isolated here in the mountains, Dr. Hall wouldn't have access to it."

He took out his pad again and wrote some instructions on it. "Here," he continued, ripping off a sheet of paper and handing it to her. "Give her this when she complains of pain in her chest. It can ward off attacks, and may extend her life by years." A heavy sigh raised his broad chest. "Then again, there are no guarantees."

Jubilee slipped the paper and medicine into her apron pocket and swallowed the despair in her throat. At least the doctor had given her a thread of hope to grasp—and grasp it she would, holding on with all her might. She gave a secret sigh.

If she only had some potion which would win Stephen's heart before the week was out.

Chapter Eleven

Jubilee let Stephen swing her from the buggy, then accompanied him across the loamy ground to the half-finished mill. When he'd suggested going back to the mill site, she'd rattled on for an hour, trying to talk him out of it. But he wouldn't be dissuaded, so here she was, the third day after he'd returned to the hollow, wondering how the mountaineers would receive them.

The sound of ringing hammers echoed through the warm air, but she noticed little progress. True, the men only came to the mill periodically when they had a break from their regular work, but the ineffectual lot didn't even have an organized system to get the logs into place. There was confusion at every turn and they constantly argued and bickered among themselves.

"No, that ain't right," an old-timer stormed at another as they worked on a joist. "Where's that pile of stripped logs for the north wall?" another man yelled. "You mean we ain't got no stripped logs?"

With a jolted heart, Jubilee spotted Jordan McCoy opening a keg of nails with a crowbar. He'd gone downhill since Stephen whipped him at the dance, and she'd never seen a more miserable-looking human being in her life.

The ruffian sent Stephen a hot glare. "You and that gal out here again?" he yelled over the din of noise. His small eyes flared with malice. "You think you can *look* them logs into place? Go on with your business. Get!"

Stephen, his face cool and imperturbable, stared at McCoy while the other hillmen stood idle, assessing the standoff with curious eyes. Jubilee noticed Dub Calahan watching the proceedings with interest, looking as if he wanted to intervene, but holding back.

Stephen approached McCoy with purposeful strides, then paused a few feet away from the man and planted his booted foot on a low stump. He was as taut and powerful as a drawn bow and his dark eyes glistened with intensity. "Look, I can help with this operation if you'll let me," he bluntly told the mountaineer.

A dark flush stole over the hillman's face. "We don't need no help," he replied in a harsh, raw tone.

Jubilee knew he'd be more intractable than ever, and realized that given a chance, he'd kill Stephen for the shaming he'd received at Stephen's hands. She walked close enough to note McCoy's bloodshot eyes and smell moonshine on his breath. "Don't let your pride blind you," she warned, exasperation spilling into her voice. "You and the other men owe it to your families to get his mill done before cold weather sets in."

"You're always stirrin' up a ruckus about somethin', ain't ya, gal?" McCoy snorted, spitting a stream of tobacco juice near her feet. "This is men's business. Keep out of it!"

Jubilee trembled with anger. If she'd possessed a weapon, she'd have been tempted to put a bullet through the no-account on the spot. She wanted to be away from his twisted face, his vengeful personality that tried to dominate everyone about him.

Song of the Lark

One by one, the men stopped working and drifted about Stephen, their faces lit with curiosity. "We can get the fulcrum and pulley over at the logging camp and lift these logs into place," he announced in a reasonable tone.

McCoy scowled and tried to wave the men away. "Don't pay him no mind," he shouted in a gravelly voice. "He's just up to some trick. The Wentworths never did a damn thing for us but work us like mules, and you know that's God's truth. Hamish always paid slave wages, and if a man got hurt on the job or even killed, he never turned a hand to help the family. Micah Jones will be a cripple for the rest of his life, and Wentworth Enterprises never gave him an extra dime!"

Stephen walked among the men, sensing that like McCoy they were riddled with impotent rage. He paused to look at each and every man's puzzled, slightly mistrusting face. "Then maybe it's time we made some changes," he spoke up loudly, not missing Jubilee's look of pleased surprise. "Let me start doing something for you right now. I'll give the whole logging camp some time off. With the equipment and manpower, you can get most of this mill built in two weeks."

A murmur rippled through the crowd. The hillmen pushed back their hats and considered him with keen eyes. A lanky man let out a long whistle. "Two weeks? You'll lose a heap of work," he yelled mockingly. "Far as I've seen, work is all Wentworth Enterprises cares about."

Stephen walked to the logger who'd made the statement and considered his long, lean face. "Yes, but I'll gain too," he replied, knowing the man's words held a grain of truth. "This mill will help the hollow, and in the long run that will help the lumber business."

The sound of rushing water was all that could be heard. Stephen knew he needed a strong ally, but wondered if any of the loggers would have the courage to speak out, when his words would be a direct challenge to McCoy. Then, moving as slowly as molasses in January, Dub Calahan ambled forward. "You ain't foolin'?" the big man asked softly, studying Stephen with narrowed eyes. "You really mean what you're sayin'?"

Dub's emotions showed as readily as a child's and in his expression, Stephen read astonishment, hope, and wary trust. Here in this slow-speaking giant, the mountaineers had a new leader. "Yes, I do," Stephen responded evenly. "I mean every word. I'll give the camp two weeks off, and we'll get that fulcrum and anything else we need to finish this mill."

McCoy lumbered forward like a sullen bear, his fingers wrapped tightly about the crowbar. "The hell, you say," he yelled with flashing eyes. He positioned the heavy bar on his shoulder like a bat.

Instantly alert, Stephen picked up a two-by-four to block the blow, but like a flash of lightning, Dub slammed his fist into McCoy's stomach, knocking the breath from him. The stunned mountaineer staggered backward and dropped the crowbar. His pale face held shock and fear.

"We ain't listenin' to you no more, McCoy," Dub shouted, backing up his stumbling adversary as he talked. His usually peaceful eyes flared in anger as he glanced at the half-built mill, then back at McCoy. "We been listenin' to you since we started buildin' this here mill," he yelled, his face red with disgust, "and we ain't got nothin' but worry and troubles for it. I reckon we been listenin' to you too long about everythin'!"

The others nodded and yelled their approval. The men who'd been browbeaten for so long met McCoy's startled gaze with a new fire in their eyes. The bully rattled off a string of curses, gathered up his things, and stalked toward his wagon, taking his hatred and bruised pride with him. The loggers hooted and waved their hats in contempt while he loaded his gear and drove away, finally disappearing around a bend in the road.

"All right, men," Stephen announced as the mountaineers, new hope shining in their eyes, crowded around him to shake hands. "We'll go to the camp and load the fulcrum, then let the other loggers know they'll be working here for a while."

Now that their task no longer seemed insurmountable, the excited men showed a new spirit. Dub produced a jug of white lightning from his wagon, and the first drink was offered to Stephen. He realized the jug was an offer of acceptance, and knowing what was expected, he hoisted it and took a gulp of raw liquor that flowed down his throat like liquid fire. He coughed and spluttered, playing it broad for his amused audience. "That's the worst liquor I've ever tasted in my life," he gasped, going along with the childish joke.

"Too strong fer you, flatlander?" someone yelled jovially.

Stephen wiped an arm over his mouth. "That stuff would take the hair off a cat," he joked, feeling as if the first layer of skin had just been burned from his throat.

An infectious smile burst over Dub's face, and the others laughed and slapped their legs. "Why, that's been aged three days now," the big man drawled, his eyes dancing with amusement. "I thought it was right meller myself."

In high spirits, the men passed the jug around, while Stephen leaned against a wagon and talked to Dub about setting up an organized work schedule. Gradually, the rowdy group mounted horses or crowded into wagons and started down the road to the logging camp, laughing and giving rebel yells as they went.

Stephen ambled to Jubilee who was talking to an old timer, then casually draped his arm about her waist. By the sound of her surprised laughter, he realized she just couldn't believe what had taken place.

"What you're witnessing," she said in an awed tone, "is a century of mountain pride and suspicion parading right down that road in front of us." She shook her head with amazement. "Lordamercy, I never thought I'd live to see this day!"

Later that week, Stephen and Jubilee drove to a hidden meadow and freed the mare from the buggy shafts so that she could graze over the tender grass. Groves of shimmering cottonwoods towered over them, and in the distance a spring gushed from the mountainside like a lacy veil and fell almost a hundred feet into a blue pool surrounded by boulders. Under the limbs of a mammoth oak, the pair spread a quilt and unpacked a heavy picnic basket, which produced ham, freshly baked bread, and peach tarts crispy with sugar and oozing juice. A stoppered jug provided cool, fresh water.

After they'd eaten, Jubilee put away the food, then looped her arms about her drawn-up legs and stared at the undulating blue ridges, swathed in drifting haze. "You can see forever up here," she remarked dreamily, still moved by the sight of the mountains no matter how many times she'd seen them. "It's so pretty, and I'll bet scarcely another human being has been here since the Indians."

Stephen nodded, but he was silent—too silent, she thought with rising anxiety. With a sudden chill, she guessed he'd chosen this afternoon to tell her good-bye. She sadly realized she'd abolished her own job by doing it so well. Although Tad wasn't completely well, from all outward appearances he no longer needed her, and neither did Stephen. How foolish she felt, having told him that she loved him.

Easing back, she supported herself on her elbows and tried to feign a nonchalance she didn't feel. She scanned the mountains again and decided they had an air of lonely silence about them today. A few moments later, the silence was broken by a flock of raucous blackbirds that alighted in the meadow with a mighty whir of wings, then flew away, cawing noisily.

"The blackbirds are coming in," she observed, trying

to make conversation. "That's a sign that fall is right around the corner. Granny said she could smell colder weather on the way just yesterday."

A smile flashed on Stephen's face. "Smell it?"

She looked into the sparkling eyes she loved so much. "That's right," she laughed, pushing back her hat to emphasize the point. "Some of the old people claim they can smell cold weather coming in—and who knows, maybe they can."

He smiled again, but said nothing.

"Yep, in a month or so, the windowpanes will be all frosty and silver in the mornings and the young'uns will be back in school."

A muscle twitched in Stephen's jaw. "Yes, I know," he responded, giving her a narrowed glance. She sensed his disquiet and she knew she'd been right. He'd asked her here to say good-bye. She could see it in his eyes. He leaned back on his arms and gazed at the mountain. "I wish I could stay here forever," he added pensively. "Everything is so peaceful."

Jubilee tried to put on a brave face. "That's what a lot of flatlanders say. I think outsiders come to the mountains looking for peace. We have a lot of peace up here. Peace and pines and white lightning," she stated thoughtfully. "I reckon that's what the Smokies are famous for."

Stephen tossed her an affectionate grin.

She promised herself she wouldn't cry when he told her good-bye. She had to save her pride. After all, that was all she had now. "But after a while the flatlanders grow tired of the peace and pines"—she smiled tightly—"and even the white lightning." She sighed, her heart aching with misgivings. "A person has to be raised in the mountains to really appreciate them. If they aren't, the hills have a way of being too big and powerful for them."

She studied Stephen's thoughtful face, knowing he had obligations waiting for him in Asheville, a whole life waiting for him in Asheville—a life that didn't include a girl like herself. "I reckon all this quietness forces folks to think about themselves too much," she added, praying her wavering voice wouldn't break while she was speaking. "Most people don't like doing that—thinking about themselves too much. It makes them uncomfortable." His dark eyes never left hers and she wondered if he was composing a farewell this very moment.

Stephen watched the afternoon light filter between the oak leaves and highlight her lovely face. For a few seconds he simply filled his spirit with her, moved by the powerful effect she had on him. A loosely woven shirt and a long tan skirt clad her luscious curves, and her hat was placed far back on her head. The simple clothes revealed her figure to perfection, and the fresh air had put a touch of color in her cheeks, making him want her all the more. What a fetching sight she made with the light breeze swirling her curling locks about her shoulders. How exquisite, but forbidden she was, he thought, his loins prickling with desire.

He moved to her side, took off her hat, and tossed it aside. "You have wonderful hair," he remarked, tunneling his hand through her silky tresses and letting them slide between his fingertips. "It's like burnished copper." Yes, she was infinitely desirable, and there was something fine and proud in her, too. He memorized her green eyes, her straight little nose, her delicate chin, realizing that was all he'd have of her when he left the mountains. "You're so beautiful that sometimes it takes my breath away to look at you," he whispered roughly.

She blushed and glanced downward.

In the distance Stephen heard buzzing bees and the trill of birdsong. To him the mountains had become a beautiful paradise, and even as he trailed his fingers over her creamy neck, his actions had an unreal quality to them as if he were moving in a dream.

He stood and raised her to her feet beside him. He'd brought her to this place to tell her good-bye—that he

Song of the Lark

wouldn't be taking her back to Asheville with him—but at this moment it seemed the hardest thing in the world to do. He needed more time to get his thoughts together, to phrase the words so that they would hurt her the least. "Let's take a walk," he suggested, clasping her hand and glancing at the shimmering pool.

They walked to the pool and the sun brought the color of the oaks on the opposite hillside into play, creating a beautiful contrast against the vivid green of the pines. Hand in hand, they strolled along the water's, edge, and when they were on the far side, Stephen heard a rustling from the woods. On long legs, a small spotted fawn stepped cautiously out of the undergrowth. It nibbled delicately at a stem of goldenrod and picked the tender leaves from a low-hanging limb. Fixing its huge, limpid eyes on them, it stared for a moment, then was off, bounding down the hollow with its white tail bobbing like a small flag.

They explored the rest of the meadow, and Jubilee picked an armful of purple asters that peppered the lush grass in profusion. As they walked, Stephen tried to get his thoughts in order and compose his words. He kept telling himself that Jubilee's job was finished, for Tad was talking well now and had lost most of his shyness. But Tad aside, he still craved her company, her body, the very sight and scent of her. Why couldn't he listen to his head and not his heart? He must tell her good-bye, for their alliance could never work. Being together only made things harder for both of them. Still, just the thought of breaking the news to her sent regret cutting through him like a jagged knife blade.

When they were almost back to the oak, he paused and took her shoulders, knowing he must make a clean break of their relationship, and do it now. He felt her tremble beneath his hands, but he told himself he had to stand firm. An expression of dread rolled over her face, and he suspected she already knew what he was going to say. "I have something to tell you," he began, feeling his insides go taut at the words.

Jubilee's heart fluttered. She'd given him all her love, but she realized it wasn't enough. A sick feeling spread through her stomach as she met his eyes, and then for some unexplainable reason she couldn't understand, she found herself saying, "You once asked me what I'd planned for my life. Now I'm asking you, what are you really searching for?"

His dark brows furrowed thoughtfully. "Happiness, I suppose," he said with a little surprise.

A gentle laugh passed over her lips. "Life is trying to help you find happiness, but you won't listen." She tapped her bosom. "You must risk your heart to find happiness."

He grazed a hand over her cheek, and his brown eyes became warmly languorous, exciting her with their intensity. He leaned close and placed a kiss upon her lips that was as gentle as thistle down. "Yes, I know," he returned with a tender smile. He trailed his fingers over her throat and collarbone, leaving her skin warm and glowing. "I may not have found happiness yet, but I have found a treasure in these mountains."

A thrill ran through Jubilee and she dropped the asters to the ground. Just the sound of his words flushed her with warmth and hope, and their underlying meaning fluttered sweet tremors through her body. She studied his thoughtful face. She could almost hear wheels turning in his head, and she realized a terrible struggle was going on within him. Gradually his expression softened and it seemed as if he'd made an important decision.

Sunlight glinted over his dark hair as he pulled her to him and gathered her in his arms. One of his hands pressed into the small of her back while the other stroked her breast until she glowed with a tender feeling she couldn't put into words. He brushed his lips over her cheeks and throat, making her tremble. A gaze passed between them that left her helpless in his embrace, and in the space of a heartbeat, Stephen lightly flicked his tongue over her lips, filling her with a delicious weakness in her knees.

Addicted to his caresses, she slipped her arms about his neck, burning with pent-up passion. He slanted his mouth over hers, crumbling the barriers between them and sweeping away the last of her inhibitions. He kissed the corner of her mouth, his tongue tracing the contours of her lips. His kisses were gentle at first, then urgent as her lips parted and he explored the moist sweetness within. She trembled with anticipation of the pleasure to come. As his tongue probed deeply, she moaned and drew him closer. Boldly her tongue twined with his without hesitation or coyness, for this was the man she loved body and soul.

With tantalizingly slow movements, Stephen began to unbutton her shirt. She made a feeble attempt to still his hands, but finally stopped resisting. She wanted this, she admitted to herself. This might be their last time together and she couldn't deny herself the opportunity of tasting heaven itself—no matter what the consequences.

He lowered his head to her bosom and inch by inch, as each button was unfastened, he kissed the exposed skin. When the shirt was completely unbuttoned he slipped it from her shoulders and down her arms, then tossed it to the ground. His lips brushed each nipple and the throbbing hollow at her throat. Slowly, so slowly, he now undid the button at her waistband. Her skirt slid down over her hips, followed by her petticoats. His hands cupped her buttocks, caressed them and tenderly kneaded them until she arched to meet him. He slipped off her bloomers and she felt a breath of gentle breeze against her bare skin. At last she stood before him, completely and gloriously naked. Modesty overtook her for a moment, but knowing they were totally isolated, her bothersome conscience surrendered to passion.

Breathless, she fought the hot sensation rising within her as his skillful fingers teased the taut peaks of her breasts and unleashed a pulsing sweetness between her legs. "You're so beautiful," he breathed huskily. "I want to make love to you." He lowered his head a bit and his tongue lazily circled her nipples, first one, then the other, arousing a tormenting ache deep within her. "I must have you now," he whispered huskily, still nuzzling her breasts.

She felt the pressure of his manhood through his trousers pressing against her abdomen, and her heart pounded as if it would burst from her rib cage. At the same time, that nagging inner voice reminded her of the differences in their social stations. *Remember who you are*, it said—*a mountain girl that will never fit into his life*. But she heard herself moan softly, and found herself whispering, "Yes—make love to me."

Stephen stripped off his shirt. Her trembling hands moved to his muscular chest, her fingers twining in the thick, curly hair. Slowly, sensuously, her hand traveled downward to where the hair tapered and narrowed past a flat belly. She unbuckled his belt, then slowly unfastened each trouser button.

He swiftly divested himself of his boots and trousers, then clasped her head in both hands and gently pressed her nakedness to his. She melted into his embrace and warmth radiated through her like sunlight. She noticed his musky male scent, his breath upon her cheek, and as his mouth found her breasts again, she thought she might swoon with delight. Her heart lurched as he swooped her into his arms, carried her to the blanket, and laid her down. He towered over her in naked splendor, and she trembled as she stared at his large aroused maleness that jutted hard and satiny from his shadowed body.

Stephen gazed at Jubilee as she lay waiting for him on the blanket with the artless grace of a child. He sat down beside her and smoothed back her silky hair. Her lashes cast shadows on her cheeks, and her auburn locks fanned out in a riot of glossy curls over the quilt. With her trusting eyes and creamy skin, this girl of the mountains excited him more than any woman he'd ever met. For the past few years it seemed that he'd lived his whole life without really touching another soul, and to find her now seemed fortunate beyond words. A huge emptiness welled within him that needed to be filled, not only by sexual satisfaction, but by something deeper.

He lay beside her and when he brushed his lips over hers, sharp passion made him aggressive when he'd planned to be tender. Afire with desire, he roughly pressed her against the length of his body, finding a warmth and closeness that nourished his soul. The wind rose about them, stirring the scent of the woods, and Stephen totally surrendered to the hot longing within him. He thought of his vow to never become emotionally entangled with a woman again, but pushed it from his mind. All he could think of now was Jubilee and making love to her.

She trembled against him and her heart pounded out of control. Lord, how he wanted this, wanted it more than anything in the world. He was a man driven wild by unbridled passion, and it was pulling him under like a great overpowering tide. How they could blend their totally different ways of life he had no idea, but he knew he must have her—and have her he would.

Jubilee felt Stephen's tongue pierce her lips with a fiery touch, probing them until they opened. Suddenly she became aware of a different kind of fire—one that started in the pit of her stomach and spread like wildfire into her loins. His hot breath traced a path across her cheek, and prickly shivers raced over her sensitive flesh as his lips moved from hers to trail down her throat.

Gently he began to suckle her breast. She felt the fine stubble of his beard and his tongue swirling about her tender flesh, and the gentle scrape of his teeth, and she gasped with pleasure. Aflame with desire, a sharp pulse throbbed between her thighs. Someone moaned and Jubilee was shocked to discover that the sound had come from her own lips. A strange half-frightened, half-thrilling shiver took hold of her as he cupped her other breast and suckled it with loving slowness, tongue swirling, teasing, until queer tingles raced from it in all directions.

When his hand trailed unerringly between her thighs, it seemed she was truly on fire. Never had she been touched this way, physically or emotionally. His long fingers twined into the curls that guarded her womanhood while he darted his tongue in and out of her mouth. She gasped as he slipped a finger into her moist softness to lovingly toy with her bud of desire. Relentlessly he teased her soft hidden places until passion rushed through her in a cresting wave and left her glowing with hunger.

He moved over her and spread her legs. His powerful thighs pressed against her. She tensed against his probing firmness, not from fright but innocence. He allowed his manhood to tease the outer regions of her femininity. His dark eyes glowed with desire as the tip of his maleness penetrated her warm, wet core with a single swift stroke that left her breathless.

"Wrap your legs around my back," he commended urgently. She did as he instructed, and a trembling ran the length of her frame. With a slow twist of his hips he thrust forward and she arched toward him, filled with excitement and eagerness to please him. She experienced an initial sting of pain, but still his body continued with its unerring quest—its ultimate goal total ecstasy.

"Relax, little one," he advised in a soothing voice, smothering her face with kisses.

She caught her breath, the air constricted in her lungs. She could not breathe; she could not move. Her very bones seemed to be melting from his warmth. Suddenly, his lips sought hers, teeth nibbling, tongue gently seeking and probing, then forcefully entering her mouth. Gradually all his maleness filled her, and as he moved deeper within her, she noticed a soothing spreading warmth, a tingling delight—a strange and exciting combination of pain and pleasure. Her skin prickled as the driving force of his passion increased. Gone was the fleeting impulse to resist. In its place was an oddly disquieting, yet pleasurable sense of comfort. Tremors—tingling arrows of fiery sensation—suffused her body. In mounting excitement, she met the urgent probing of his tongue with her own as she responded to the ravishing fullness of his manhood.

Hesitantly at first, then with increasing eagerness, she met his passionate thrusts with unconscious movements of her own. Wild with desire, she arched her buttocks to meet his thrusts, driving him further and further into her until wondrous sensations peaked and engulfed her in waves of pure ecstasy. The tempo of their bodies quickened into an insistent, pulsating rhythm as he plunged deeper and deeper inside her. They both gasped for breath. For a moment her mind fogged and it seemed she had entered another realm. Every inch of her skin tingled with delight and she felt as unfettered as the wind in the trees, as light and dazzling as sunlight sparkling over a mountain pool.

Suddenly Stephen's body shuddered above her. He tensed, groaned, and she surrendered to each rapturous feeling that toppled over her, wanting to cherish the magnificent moment forever. Lights danced in her head as he thrust deeply inside of her—savagely, tenderly, relentlessly. In delirium she clung to him—floating, ascending with him into an ever-expanding, seemingly endless pleasure—then she herself trembled in sweet release. Her heart raced furiously, and she felt as if her emotions had been knocked sideways, buffeted by a mighty wind.

Only as his movements slowed and finally ceased did a semblance of reality return. For a moment Stephen lay quietly, his body still entwined with hers until their ragged breathing ceased. To Jubilee's mind she was now Stephen's woman, and she vowed to be true no matter what the future might hold. It might have simply been the unbridled hunger of their bodies that had given birth to the passionate tryst beneath this ancient oak, but for her, love had transformed the physical act into something sacred.

She looked into Stephen's smoky eyes and he gently traced her cheek. For a moment they said nothing and she was content to let him hold her and remember the exquisite magic between them. She was vividly aware of a serenity that words couldn't express, and for one blessed moment it seemed that they'd conquered all the obstacles between them.

"I feel as if you've bewitched me," Stephen murmured. His hand wandered over her body in an absent caress. "It seemed as if our hearts were beating together, singing as one." His gaze washed over her. "You're so exquisitely lovely my heart aches at the sight of you." He showered kisses over her face as her heart slowed to its regular rhythm. He traced his fingers over her face, following the line of her cheeks. "Do you regret that we made love? Do you—"

"No," Jubilee whispered. "I've never experienced anything like this in my life. Things may have turned out a little differently than we both expected today, but I'm not sorry. I'll never forget today. I'll treasure it in my heart forever."

He gave her a kiss that in its tenderness was more powerful than any forceful embrace. The realization that they'd actually made love was so strong it swept away all her concerns about right and wrong and honor and responsibility. How could she be anything but overjoyed for the magic that had just touched her soul?

Stephen held her, caressing her hair, and then he began speaking in a soft voice. "I have to go back to Asheville soon and we should talk things over."

A familiar dread claimed Jubilee's heart like an icy hand. It seemed that even though they'd made love, she still wasn't good enough for him. Because she was from the backwoods, and uneducated—because she was who she was, they could never have a future together. Her heart thudded against her ribs in anticipation of what he might say. She knew he was considering his words carefully, and a conflicted expression claimed his features. Doubtless it was hard for him to express himself when his heart and mind battled so fiercely.

He brushed a curl from her cheek. "Will you go back to Asheville with me and Tad?" he asked, his dark eyes still shining with desire.

Jubilee drew in her breath, thinking she hadn't heard him right. "What did you say?"

A grin stole over his mouth. "I asked you if you would come back to Asheville with me."

Trembling, she met his searching gaze. "Do you mean it? Do you really want me to?" she whispered, her voice sticking in her throat.

Stephen laughed deeply. "*Want you*? I can't get along without you." He kissed her forehead and ran his fingers through her hair. "And if the truth be told, Tad still needs you, too. He's doing well, but if I separated you from him now, it might set him back."

Now that he'd actually invited Jubilee back to Asheville, conflicting emotions whirled through her. What about her obligations here in the mountains? Could Granny and Effie get along without her, and what would Micah think if he had a change of heart and returned home? She considered the questions, trying to be honest with herself. Granny was holding her own and had actually improved a little with treatment. Besides that, Effie was tired of living alone and wanted to move back to Granny's cabin so she'd have company during the cold months. She thought of her brother with a pang of anguish, knowing that in the final account she must be true to herself.

With a tremendous sense of relief, she realized that

there was nothing to prevent her from going—nothing at all. For one golden moment, she let herself revel in Stephen's invitation, feeling luxuriously satisfied, relaxed, and happy with life. She looked at him through a soft veil of tears. "Yes, if you want, I'll come back with you," she answered throatily.

True, Stephen had made no commitment, nor had he told her he loved her. In fact, he'd cloaked his invitation with concern for Tad, but he'd also said he didn't think he could do without her. And for now that was enough. Some day he would tell her he actually loved her. She knew he would.

The next day was the same as the day before: at five the sun burst over the great Smoky Mountains, bathing the winding valleys in a soft pink glow; the chickens cackled and fluttered about wildly when Jubilee went to gather eggs; and thick bacon sizzled in the skillet as she cooked it, releasing its wonderful scent. The new colt frolicked about the green pasture, trying out his long, wobbly legs, and mockingbirds sang their hearts out, making the woods ring with melody. Everything went on as it had the morning before and the morning before that—and yet, nothing to Jubilee was the same, for Stephen had made love to her, and she was changed forever and eternity.

As Jubilee went about her work, joy flooded through her in a warm tide. Her body tingled with wonderful new sensations. Delightful memories crowded her mind and she tired to recall everything about their lovemaking, having no idea if it would ever happen again. She was now a woman in body and spirit. Over and over again, she repeated to herself the promise she would always honor—no matter how long she lived, she would love Stephen and no other.

Time rushed on quickly now, rushed on like a leaping stream, as she made plans to return to Asheville. She had so many things to do for Granny and Effie before she left;

Song of the Lark

there were so many considerations, so many decisions to make.

The day before she was to go back to Asheville, she woke at dawn. A shaft of pink light wavered its way over the cabin floor and a trill of sweet notes floated into her bedroom with the cool morning breeze. She slipped from bed and pushed away the billowing curtains to see a small lark perched on an old lilac bush just outside the windowsill. The rising sun painted the bird's feathers a rosy hue as it puffed out its small breast, cocked its head, and continued the mesmerizing serenade.

Notes that seemed as sweet as wild honey flowed over Jubilee, offering her comfort, peace, and hope. What was it Granny had said about a person getting their heart's desire when they wished on the lark's song? Was the old custom only something to ease the lives of the impoverished or did it hold real magic? Jubilee's romantic soul chose to passionately believe in its magic, and tears blinded her eyes as she thought of Stephen. She'd given him not only her heart, but her soul as well, and to her a sacred bond now held them together. But from him she'd heard no words of love. She closed her eyes and listened to the lark, tears streaming over her cheeks as she wished from the depth of her being that he would tell her he loved her—just one time. That would be enough.

The next day she packed the last of her clothes, the lark's song still vivid in her mind. Like a buried treasure it was locked deep inside her, and she knew that when she was lonely or afraid she had only to remember that song and the hope it held. The minutes slipped by as quickly as pearls sliding from a cord, and suddenly it was time to go. Stephen had already put her belongings into the buggy along with his and Tad's. Jubilee now went through the cabin, searching for small things she might have forgotten. Her heart brimmed. She and Granny had talked the night before, but it was now time for the final good-bye.

She entered the room, and the old woman, who'd been looking from the window, met her eyes and smiled kindly as she slowly pulled the covers closer about her. Jubilee walked to the bed, unfolded the quilt that lay at its foot, and spread it over her. "Are you cold?" she asked, sadly realizing how painful the parting was for her grandmother.

"A little," Granny replied with a weary sigh. "The summer is just 'bout gone." She wagged her head knowingly. "Change is a-comin' on, all right."

With their double meaning, the words hit Jubilee square in the heart and she nodded, unable to speak.

Granny took her hand and squeezed it. "Oh, don't cry, child. Change is the way of this old world. The seasons change, the woods change, and if the wind blows hard enough and the rain pounds down long enough, even these mountains will change, too."

Jubilee sat by the bed, and Granny reached out to cup her face in her thin hands. Her cornflower blue eyes, still so vital, misted with tears. "But some things never change. You'll always be my Jubilee-girl, I'll always love you, and this old place will always be your home."

Jubilee knew the moment would remain sharp and vivid in her mind for the rest of her life. She gave way to her emotions and tears spilled from her eyes.

"You're a-takin' a big step," Granny added, "but we've all got to take some of them big steps now and them." She wiped the girl's tears from her cheeks with her gnarled fingers. "Now, you go on to Asheville and don't you be a-worryin' about me and Effie none. We'll get along just fine."

Jubilee swallowed the huge lump in her throat, then kissed the old woman's forehead and gave her hand one last reassuring squeeze. "All right," she choked out, the words tearing painfully from her tight throat. She rose, but Granny clung to her hand. "Yes?" Jubilee added, her heart beating a little faster beneath her plain traveling dress.

"If you want to marry up with Stephen Wentworth, you go on and do it," Granny advised, her eyes snapping. "Ain't Micah's business or nobody else's business—just yours!"

Jubilee blinked back her tears.

"You may have to fight for him. You may have to fight the whole town, but if you love him, I reckon it's worth it."

A blush warmed Jubilee's cheeks. How could she tell Granny that Stephen had never even suggested marriage? When all was said and done, she couldn't tell her. She had to leave the old lady with some hope—hope that everything would turn out fine.

"I love you, Granny," she whispered, her voice rough with emotion. She let her hand slip away, then walked to the door, her throat aching with tears. Spurred by an impulse she didn't understand, she hurried back to the bed and hugged her grandmother good-bye, wondering if this would be the last time she'd see her alive. She held Granny as tightly as she dared, then quickly left the room, thinking her aching heart might actually burst apart. Lord-amercy, how the moment hurt—hurt like a knife cutting into her bosom, separating her body and spirit. Outside the bedroom door, she rested and marshaled her courage, pulling in several deep breaths until she felt calmer.

In the front room she saw Effie kneeling beside Tad and joking with him to forestall his threatening tears. "Can I come back and see you, Miss Effie? I think you and Jubilee are the best friends I ever had."

Effie, her face a welter of emotion, squeezed his small body until his bones cracked, then placed Matilda in his arms. "Sure you can, honey. Anytime you want. You take care of that cat, now," she advised, her slow mountain voice quavering. "Don't let her get mixed up with any of them mean town cats."

Stephen drove the buggy in front of the cabin, and, hearing his father, Tad hurriedly kissed Effie's cheek.

Hoisting the huge cat against his chest, he ran outside. When the boy was out the door, Effie rose, walked to the window, and pulled back the cotton curtain. With a trembling hand, she tugged a handkerchief from her apron pocket and blew her nose.

Jubilee watched her standing there dressed in a faded cotton gown, yet clothed in homely dignity. She'd harbored some concern about leaving Granny in her care and imposing on her, but she suddenly realized that this wonderful woman needed an outlet for her abundant love. Effie didn't care about luxuries or comforts—what she cared about was being a member of a loving family. With no husband or children, she needed to be cherished, to be assured of her great worth. If she only had a man or child of her own to care for, how lucky they would be.

Jubilee walked into the room and Effie hastily put away her handkerchief. Jubilee hugged her, feeling her large, soft body, taking in the familiar scent of bacon and biscuits that clung to her clothes.

Effie stood back and ran loving eyes over her. "I made a bite for you all to eat on the way," she said as if revealing a special secret. She picked up a big basket filled with sandwiches, cakes, and a jar of iced lemonade, then put it on the table. She covered it with a clean white dishtowel and offered it to Jubilee with a homy smile.

Tenderness for her cousin welled up in Jubilee's bosom, and she accepted the basket through a blur of tears.

Effie gave a little embarrassed laugh. "Sayin' good-bye sure is hard, ain't it?" she remarked, trying to sound gay.

"It sure is," Jubilee whispered, knowing she didn't need to say anything else. "I'll write, and I'll send money every month."

"I know you will," Effie replied, "and I'll let you know when Dub and the others finish the mill." Her face glowed at the mention of the man's name, and Jubilee

Song of the Lark

suddenly realized she'd been so busy with her own life, she hadn't realized that Effie was in love, too. If only Dub had the courage to come forward and declare himself.

Jubilee put her arm about her cousin's waist and they walked from the cabin. At the threshold, she scanned the scene before her. Stephen's horse was hitched to the buggy, where Tad was already settled on the seat gently stroking Matilda, while General Sherman was tied to the back of the conveyance. Dressed in a fine dark traveling suit worthy of his position, Stephen made the last adjustments to the horse's leather tack. He walked to Effie and gave her his thanks as if she were a fine Southern lady, then took Jubilee's arm and assisted her into the buggy next to Tad.

When he'd taken the reins in his gloved hand, Effie came to the buggy and reached out to hug Jubilee one last time. "It's been a nice summer," the older woman said, tears standing in her eyes.

Jubilee put her hand over her cousin's and forced her trembling lips into a smile. Stephen nodded at Effie, then snapped the reins, and the buggy rolled away.

Jubilee, still overcome with emotion, turned and raised her arm in farewell. She gazed at Effie's teary face and considered her own future. Would she end up like her cousin, a spinster buried in the mountains, or would she live in Asheville as Stephen's wife? Loving a man who'd made no commitments was a risky business, but she'd already given her heart and there was nothing else she could do.

She looked at Stephen's aristocratic profile, and ice crept into her soul. In Asheville, there would be the same disapproving stares and snide comments when people thought her back was turned. But what did she care? What did it matter when she'd be with the man she loved more than the air she breathed?

She grasped the side of the buggy as it jolted over the rough mountain road. Yes, she'd go back to Asheville and face Estell and the whole damn town to boot, she decided, a fire flaring up in her spirit. She'd go back and fight for Stephen's love—and she'd fight like she was fighting for life itself.

Chapter Twelve

Stephen, Jubilee, and Tad arrived back in Asheville on a drowsy September afternoon. They passed a hotel with a veranda running across the front, and several men rose from their rocking chairs and tipped their hats at Stephen. Jubilee straightened her back as the creaking buggy rolled ahead and compared this entry into town with her first. When she'd arrived months ago, she'd been a mountain girl on a mule, the object of ridicule. Now there were polite smiles from passing carriages, and from the pedestrians along the planked sidewalks as well. She was the same person, but now sat beside Stephen and his son. True, people might still be suspicious and wary of her, even talk behind her back, but she was no longer beneath their contempt.

The jiggling buggy wound its way across town, and when it slowed and stopped in front of the mansion, Delilah and Cleo ran out and greeted the travelers profusely. The minute Jubilee's feet touched the ground, she was enveloped in Delilah's warm arms. "Lawsy, I's sure glad to see you, Miz Jubilee," the cook exclaimed, her eyes as bright and welcoming as the summer day. "And Cleo's been so lonesome for Tad he don't know what to do with hisself. Seems like old times now, havin' you two back. Everthin' seems just fine now!" Delilah embraced Stephen, who hugged her right back. "Thank the Lord you's back Mist' Stephen."

Cleo danced about, eager to play with Tad. "How come you stayed up in them woods so long, boy? Come on, let's play some!"

Chambers took the luggage from the buggy, managing a stiff nod at Jubilee. "Nice to have you back, miss," he finally allowed, his face as cold and set as sealing wax.

Once they were all in the mansion, Jubilee noticed the familiar scent of lemon polish, and she was impressed anew with the establishment's gleaming luxury, so different from the world of poverty and hardship she'd left behind in the mountains.

After a huge dinner of fried chicken with all the trimmings, Delilah brought out several of her famous pies. "I knows you gonna be wantin' some of this, Miz Jubilee," she chuckled, serving her a big wedge of apple pie. She patted Tad on the head. "Lawsy, what you done with this chile? I never seen him lookin' so good. He sure put on some weight."

Tad looked at Delilah with dancing eyes. "I met Effie and Granny in the mountains. And I caught fish, and lightning bugs, and a possum—and I learned how to write my name, too!"

"*Ummm*, listen to that child talk!" Delilah laughed. She glanced at Stephen and cocked her head. "Do he run on like this all the time now?"

Stephen sat back and grinned. "I'm afraid so. Isn't it wonderful?"

"It be more than wonderful," she returned, smiling and glancing heavenward, "it be a real miracle."

Cleo sat right beside Tad, gnawing on a drumstick. Tad

Song of the Lark

nudged him in the ribs, then cupped his hands. "Want to hear me do a turkey call?"

"Yeah, let's hear you," Cleo drawled, his eyes dancing with merriment. "Fore you left you could hardly talk a'tall. Now you say you can talk like a turkey."

Tad cupped his hands and gave several loud turkey calls to the amusement of Cleo, who giggled so hard that tears came to his eyes.

After the boisterous dinner, Jubilee met Chambers in the foyer, and decided she'd ask him about the letter she'd sent Stephen's brother before she went to the mountains. "Have you heard anything from Brandon?" she asked softly, thinking Stephen was still in the dining room with Delilah and the boys.

Chambers tightened his lips. "No, and I don't expect to. You shouldn't concern yourself with Mister Brandon. It isn't your affair!"

He paced away, and she gave a little start when Stephen walked into the foyer a few seconds later. His mellow mood had evaporated, and a frown flitted over his brow. "I was on my way to the study and I couldn't help but overhearing Chambers's last statement," he began in a serious tone. "What's all this about my brother?"

Jubilee's pulse raced. She studied his displeased face and wondered how much she should tell him. "I know about Brandon," she confessed in a forthright tone, wanting to have that fact out in the open. "Delilah told me before I went to the mountains, but I made her, so don't be cross."

Stephen scowled, his brows drawn like angry brush strokes. "Chambers is right. Don't expect that anyone in this house will ever hear from Brandon."

Jubilee studied him, realizing that he actually ached to hear from Brandon but wouldn't admit it to himself. "Stephen," she began gently, "don't let this tear your family apart."

His eyes flashed. "Brandon is the one who has torn it

apart. He cut himself off from his family and he won't be making contact with any of us again."

"But—"

"No," he countered, taking her by the shoulders. "Don't say any more about him. The subject is closed. Don't think about him, or worry about him—and under no circumstances try to contact him. It would be utterly useless." His eyes roamed over her, saying he meant what he said, and then he turned and walked toward his study.

Jubilee heaved a huge sigh, thinking Chambers had been right about Stephen's attitude. Before he'd spoken, she'd intended to tell him about the letter, but she was now glad she hadn't. Why upset him further?

She went to the parlor and pulled back the velvety drapes, seeing Tad and Cleo tossing a ball in the ruddy twilight. They laughed and talked, their faces glowing with happiness. How adaptable children are, she thought, thankful that the boys had picked up their friendship again with such ease. And how wise children were, in their innocence, seeming to understand that love and friendship were the very nub of life itself.

She stood at the window a long time, thinking of Stephen, for once wishing he could be more like his son.

"But I don't want to go to school today. *Do I have to?*"

Jubilee scanned Tad as they stood in front of the red brick school building, surrounded by the sounds of shuffling feet and excited children. "Yes, you must," she answered, knowing it would be one of the hardest days of his young life. How she wished that Stephen wasn't busy with an important client and could have been here with them. She knelt down beside the boy and gazed into his glassy eyes, trying to make him understand. "You'll like school because you get to learn things here. Remember how you learned things in the mountains?"

Dressed in a tidy wool jacket and short pants, he gave

a tremulous sigh. "But it was just us there." He eyed the children who streamed past, giggling at his fine clothes. "There are lots of kids here."

Jubilee frowned at a large boy who snickered at Tad's short pants. She'd have to speak to Stephen about the boy's clothes, and Chambers too, who somehow had the idea that the lad should be dressed like a student at an English boarding school. She rose and unbuttoned Tad's collar to make him look more relaxed, then took the cap from his head. "Pretty soon you'll know lots of these children."

The boy blinked his eyes. "Will Cleo be here?" he asked, his face clouding with uneasiness. "I want to sit by him."

Sadness darted through Jubilee's heart. "No, he won't be here," she answered, rising and leading Tad up the walkway.

He gazed at her with troubled eyes. "Why not? Why won't Cleo be here?"

Jubilee wondered how she could explain prejudice and hatred to a six-year-old? How could she reveal the small, mean side of the human spirit when she wanted the boy to believe in hope and magic? "Cleo has his own school," she finally answered. "It's closer to his house."

They were almost at the open school doors and Tad pulled back on her hand. "I want to go to Cleo's school. I want to be with Cleo!"

Tears rose in Jubilee's throat and she knelt by his side again. "No, I'm sorry, baby. You can't go to Cleo's school. Those are the rules." She smoothed her hand over his hair. "Will you try this school for a week? Will you try it just for me?"

He studied her thoughtfully.

"Have I ever lied to you?" she asked kindly.

He shook his head.

"Then try it for me. Believe me, before the week is out, you'll find a new friend."

He surveyed her, weighing her words. "Before the week is out?"

"Yes," she replied, making her fancy promise sign over her heart. She waited expectantly, praying their relationship was strong enough to tempt the boy into the building.

A slow smile broke over his face. "All right," he finally allowed, "but if I don't get a friend by the end of the week, I'm going to be mighty disappointed."

Rising, she clasped his hand and led him through the school building, which was redolent with the scents of paper and glue, floor polish and chalk dust. His teacher's name was Mrs. Rice. A small lady, she sent Tad a friendly smile and took him to his desk. When the woman gave him a new tablet and two shiny yellow pencils, he smiled for the first time that day.

At the doorway, Jubilee raised her hand in good-bye, and Tad slowly raised his own, his eyes still full of doubt and dismay. His clothes were slightly too large for him, and as he gazed about apprehensively, he reminded her of one of the small chicks he'd cradled so lovingly back in the mountains. She threw him a last smile, then turned and walked swiftly down the hall, her eyes stinging with tears.

In the mountains she'd believed him much healthier, but compared to the other first graders how small and tender he was. She thought of the boys who'd thrown clods at her when she'd ridden into town on General Sherman. Would Tad make it though his first day of school or burst into tears when confronted by some bully? Since she'd arrived, she'd always been able to protect and shield him, but this she could no longer do. Today he was on his own, left to his own fragile resources.

Outside the school, a welcoming draft of cool air rushed over her wet face. She realized with the depth of her heart and soul how much she loved Tad, and it almost frightened her. She flicked away a tear, straightened her back, and walked toward the buggy, reminding herself that he wasn't hers to cry over.

All the way back to the mansion, she mulled over the last few weeks that had flown by so swiftly. Since they'd returned from the mountains, Stephen had been attentive, but hadn't made love to her again, or mentioned one word of them having a future together. What a long, winding road her emotions had taken since they'd first met. She'd given her heart unreservedly to him and Tad both, but had no idea if she'd be a permanent part of their lives, or pushed aside. She sighed wearily, for she had no choice but to let things unfold naturally in their own time.

She entered the mansion and found Chambers puttering about the foyer, flipping through some mail. She placed her hands on her hips and told herself this was a day for new beginnings. She'd worn her heart on her sleeve since she'd come to Asheville and she might as well risk rejection to the fullest. "Come on, Chambers, let's go to the kitchen and have a cup of tea. I think I could use one," she commented, lightly brushing past him.

A strange expression settled over his features. "I thought I made myself clear, miss. The tea here is quite inferior and I don't care to indulge. Besides that, I have duties. It would be quite improper—"

She clasped his arm and literally pulled him toward the kitchen. "If I hear you say that again I'll shake your teeth out. If you don't loosen up you're going to fossilize on your feet!"

Sputtering in protest, he entered the kitchen and Jubilee plopped him down in a chair, then proceeded to the pantry and produced a box of tea.

"*But, miss—*"

She slammed the pantry door. "Hush, Chambers. For once in your life shut up and look at what I have in my hand!" She showed him a box of Earl Grey tea she'd had the local grocer import all the way from England.

He rose, took the tea from her hand, and sent her a

glance of utter disbelief. His lips worked in silent amazement. "By Jove, it-it is Earl Grey," he finally stammered, his eyes shining with wonder.

Then a minor miracle happened—in its own way, no less amazing than the parting of the Red Sea.

For the first time since Jubilee had met Chambers he gave her a genuine smile.

Stephen stood and extended his hand to the man across the desk from him. "Thank you for your order, Mr. Phillips. I hope your new home turns out well for you and your wife."

The customer rose and nodded his farewell. "Thank *you*. Everyone knows that Wentworth Enterprises produces the finest lumber in the South. I'm sure we'll be seeing each other again before the house is finished." The man walked to the door, then looked back in afterthought. "Oh, by the way," he commented, a warm smile playing over his mouth, "I wanted to congratulate you on your engagement."

Caught off guard, Stephen stared at the man, momentarily too surprised to speak. Wordlessly, he laid down the papers he held and walked around his desk. "*My engagement?*" he echoed with a laugh of disbelief. "What in the world are you talking about?"

A puzzled look crossed the customer's face. "Well, rumor has it," he replied with a nervous cough, "that you and Miss Pennypacker are going to be wed soon."

Stephen fought down a surge of anger. "I assure you, sir, that rumor has it wrong. I have not asked Miss Pennypacker to marry me, and I have no intention of doing so."

"I-I'm sorry," the man spluttered in a consoling tone. His face turned pink, then scarlet. "It's just that everyone is talking about it"—he glanced down in embarrassment—"so I assumed it was true." Obviously conscious of Stephen's intense scrutiny, he exited the office, silently closing the door behind him.

Stephen picked up the sheaf of papers and smacked them against the desk. Damn, if it wasn't just like Estell to try to pull off something like this. No doubt she had started the rumor while he was in the mountains and the old peahens had spread it all over town. In his mind's eye, he could imagine the blonde now, preening as she gracefully slipped hints into a tea-time conversation.

Since all of Asheville had been waiting for him to choose a bride since Isabelle died, the rumor had doubtless spread like fire over dry kindling. Jubilee popped into his mind and a sick, nauseous feeling claimed his stomach. After what they'd shared in the mountains, if she heard of this it would surely break her heart.

He'd go see Estell immediately and put an end to the rumor, he decided, gathering up his things and leaving the office. It was almost quitting time and several of his departing workers said respectful farewells, but totally preoccupied, he got into his buggy without speaking.

Estell answered the door enveloped in the scent of spicy carnations. She carried a red bloom in her hand. "Why, Stephen," she crooned in a voice as smooth as her pink silken gown, "what a surprise. Do come in. I'm so glad to see you!" A riot of golden ringlets bounced from the back of her head as she extended her free hand to him, looking the picture of innocence and genteel propriety. Her complexion flawless, her powder and lip salve skillfully applied, she strolled into the parlor glancing back over her shoulder flirtatiously. "I've been arranging some flowers for the altar tomorrow. Come and tell me what you think."

Stephen tossed his hat onto a rack and followed her into the dim, overly decorated room, his temperature rising higher by the second. There was no use beating around the bush. How deceiving appearances could be. This angel of light was as conniving as any Memphis trollop and twice as hard-hearted when it came to playing a man for all he was worth. "You might be interested that a customer just congratulated me on our engagement. Now, where in the devil could he have gotten an absurd idea like that?" he asked with exaggerated politeness.

Surprise flew across her face, but she rallied her dignity with surprising swiftness. "Oh, come along, Stephen," she chided as she started working on a bouquet with trembling fingers, "you know how these things get started." She laughed gaily. "There is so much gossip in town, if a person says one word out of place, someone has soon concocted a whole story about it."

"A fact that you know only too well," he said crisply.

She blanched as if he'd slapped her. "Really, Stephen. As Saint Peter writes in his first epistle, a man should refrain his tongue from evil!" She placed a small jeweled hand over her ruffled bodice. "Certainly you're not suggesting that *I* started the rumor. That is just absurd. You know I never gossip."

Stephen led her to a settee and plopped her down none too gently. "*Oh, really*," he came back, sitting down beside her and turning her pouting face toward him. "If not you, who then?"

Her pink lips trembled like a child's. "I would like to feel we are getting closer, and here you are making wild accusations, practically shouting at me. Why, it's the rudest thing I've ever seen!"

Stephen knew she was on the verge of breaking down. "If you didn't start this rumor, who did? I can only believe it was you."

Estell, seeing she was cornered, reverted to her last and best defense. She pulled a lace handkerchief from her pocket and dabbed at her eyes. "I don't understand how you can be so heartless," she sniffed in a breaking voice. "I-I may have hinted that there was some attachment between us, but that was all."

Ignoring the tears he knew she could turn on at will,

Stephen pressed his advantage. "I don't believe you," he announced bluntly.

Estell leaned forward and sobbed profusely. "Oh, you wretch," she wailed, her shoulders rising and falling dramatically. "How could you lead me on like you have—pretending that you cared for me, then play like we didn't have an agreement? Now it seems you're calling me a liar!"

"If the shoe fits—" he began.

"All right, all right!" she sobbed, grabbing his arm and looking him full in the face, to better show her anguished features. "I mentioned to a friend that I was sure you would ask me to marry you—that our engagement was pending." She wiped at her eyes again. "You owe me a proposal, occupying my social calendar the way you have. Trifling with my heart. Why—"

Stephen stood, wondering if she'd gone mad. "Occupying your social calendar?" he interrupted in an incredulous tone. "I've only escorted you to a few functions, all chaperoned by the greater part of Asheville." He narrowed his eyes, realizing what a sharp-clawed little vixen she was. "Did you really think you could coerce me into marriage with social pressure?"

She rose too, tears streaming down her pale face. "You know we have an understanding. You know we do." She stamped her dainty foot. "Don't try to pretend you don't!"

He held her at arm's length, wanting to shake some sense into her empty head. "We have no agreement at all and you know it!"

She pulled from his hands. "That's absurd," she laughed bitterly, gazing at him as if he'd lost his mind. "A rich man such as yourself needs a hostess. You're bound to marry again. Everyone knows you will." She shook back her glossy curls. "You just need someone to help you make up your mind."

Stephen laughed deeply. "Women! I'll never understand them if I live to be a hundred years old," he retorted, his jaw tightening to a rock hard firmness. Surrendering to his fury, he paced about the room, then wheeled and, focusing on her slight form, offered her a satirical bow. "When it comes to wheedling, scheming, and conniving, you win hands down, my dear."

Estell turned, moved to the lace-draped windows, and tightly crossed her arms. She stood there, her bosom heaving. When she whirled about, the helpless feminine guise had fallen from her face like a mask and was replaced by an expression of overwhelming spite. "Yes, I may have started the rumor, but what would you expect me to do, with you enjoying yourself all summer with your little red-haired doxy? I had to see to my own interest," she hotly exclaimed, actually trembling with the intensity of her emotions.

She strolled to him and smoothed her hands over his shoulders. "Do you think I'm so sheltered I don't know what's going on between you two?" Her mouth hardened unbecomingly. "Don't you realize you must marry one of us? Who will it be, Stephen? Me, who has the respect of the whole of Asheville, or that little mountain nobody who is the joke of the town?"

He stood silent, stunned by the vindictiveness glowing on her face.

"Who will it be?" she asked again in a voice that chilled his blood. She favored him with a sweet smile. "The choice is yours."

September rolled into October, and to Jubilee's delight, she discovered that there was a network of wooded roads and bridle paths fringing the outskirts of Asheville. She borrowed Stephen's buggy and regularly took Tad for rides on the weekends, always being scrupulously careful to avoid the spot where his mother had been thrown from her horse. One day Jubilee spied some bright herbs in the shadows, and, her curiosity stirred, she and the boy began exploring the woods on foot.

This Saturday was especially beautiful and she found her spirits rising. The scarlet maples stood out vividly in the afternoon light, and the birches and oaks sported a riot of golden leaves so bright they dazzled the eyes. Surrounded by the soft, pungent scent of the woods, she and Tad spied chirping chickadees, brilliant cardinals, and even a band of blue-winged teal feeding on a partridge vine.

They followed a bridle path and walked farther into the woods where Jubilee picked Solomon's-seal, mullein, and bearberry leaves. Presently she spotted a bed of ginseng. "Oh, there's a patch of 'sang," she told the boy, as thrilled with her discovery as if she'd found a chest of golden coins. She hurried to the five-leafed plants that stood about a foot high. "It's just right for picking, too," she informed him, kneeling down by the bed.

Tad walked to her side and bent down to help.

"Here," she said, guiding his small fingers into the moist earth as he followed her example. "You have to ease it out carefully and not disturb the bed."

He studied a forked root with wonder, then moved his gaze to her. "Why do we have to do that?" he asked, a frown flitting over his smooth brow.

"Sang is real delicate. If you tear up the bed too much, it'll never grow here again," she explained with a smile. "But if you ease the roots out carefully, the bed will soon be as big as ever."

She and the boy gently pulled the ginseng from the earth, and, still glowing from her great find, she dropped the herbs into a leather pouch. Tad worked well for a while, but finally grew tired and turned his attention to a small toad half hidden under a leaf.

Jubilee had just closed her herb sack when she heard a horse's hooves on the soft bridle path. She looked up to see Stephen, mounted on his black stallion, not more than fifteen yards away. Her heart lifted at the sight of him, and Tad ran to his father, calling out that he'd just captured a toad. Stephen dismounted, and she walked to him, laughing as Tad proudly displayed his catch. Stephen smiled and talked to the boy awhile, but when the child ran away to play, he transferred his attention to Jubilee, his face somewhat troubled.

"What are you doing here?" she asked brightly, delighted he'd taken some time off from his work.

"Chambers told me where you'd gone. I found the buggy pulled off the road and followed the path into the woods."

She smiled, truly happy he'd tracked them down. "Yes, Tad and I like to come here and see what we can find." She opened her herb sack and showed him the ginseng. "Look. We found 'sang today!" she announced, wondering why he didn't seem more excited about it. "It's the king of all the herbs. It always fetches a pretty penny, but I won't sell it," she explained, patting the pouch lovingly. "I'll make Tad tea with this. It'll give him lots of energy."

"Do you think it would actually do him good?"

She felt a pang of hurt. "*Of course*. I started giving him spicewood tea early last summer," she retorted defiantly, "and ginseng will give him strength."

Stephen noted her defensive tone and wondered how he could tell her he didn't approve of what she was doing.

"What's wrong?" she finally asked, her voice sharpening a little. "The spicewood tea worked wonders. He's eating everything on his plate and looks better than he ever has." She tilted her brow and smiled. "You can't deny it, because you said so yourself."

Stephen knew she had him there. He had to admit that the boy had indeed gained weight and looked better, but he attributed it to a summer in the mountains and not any particular herb. He turned his disapproval over in his head, searching for the best way to broach the subject.

Song of the Lark

"Don't you want me to give him ginseng?" she asked, regarding him with somber curiosity. "I've been taking herbs all my life and they haven't done me any harm."

"But what if you made a mistake?" Stephen said, knowing this was a good place to make his point. "What if you mistook a harmful herb for a good one?"

She rolled her eyes. "Why, that's impossible," she laughed, trying to make light of the subject. "I know them all. Don't you remember that Pa ran a medicine show? We picked herbs to make the tonic all the time. If we'd poisoned anybody with our tonic, the mountain folks would have put a bullet through us."

"It's just where Tad's health is at stake I can't take any chances," he continued, wishing she could see his viewpoint. Noting her stricken face, he used a softer voice. "Teaching him some mountain song is one thing—but this is another," he explained, caressing her small shoulders to soften his rebuke. "He's still fragile and I don't want him taking something that might harm him."

Her face fell like a wilted flower. "But I—"

"Obviously the spicewood tea last summer did him no harm," he interrupted, "but I want you to promise me that you'll never give him more herbs. Dr. Stuart is nearby, and he can give Tad any medication he might need." He could tell that his demand had crushed her, but he also felt a sense of relief that the tender subject was out in the open.

Tears welled in her eyes. "Why, I'd never give him anything that would hurt him. I—"

Filled with anguish, Jubilee met his serious gaze, her mind going blank as she searched for ways to dispel his concerns.

His face softened and he pulled her to him and kissed the top of her head. "You can take herbs if you wish, but you must promise me you'll never give any more to Tad," he said gently. His eyes deepened with purpose. "I'm asking it as a special favor."

Jubilee felt stunned, hurt, and treated rather unfairly, but what could she do but agree? "All right," she whispered, still aching with the sting of his censure.

"Good," he answered, smile lines splaying from his eyes. He pulled her close and caressed her hair.

Jubilee leaned against his hard chest, biting back her tears. Things had gone well since they'd returned from the mountains and she believed they might have a chance of bridging their social differences, but he'd just proven that whole worlds still stood between them.

"Will you do it, Jubilee? You just have to. I told them you would!" Jubilee glanced at Delilah's amused face, then back at Tad who held her hands and gazed at her with pleading eyes. "Hold on," she laughed, tickled by his excitement. "What are you talking about?"

She'd been sitting in the kitchen when she heard the front door slam and knew that Chambers had just brought Tad back from school. Seconds later, the boy appeared in the kitchen clutching a sheaf of papers, then ran to her, his eyes bright as diamonds.

"They're having a Halloween carnival and they need someone to give a magic show," he answered, managing to slow down enough to explain what he wanted. "I told them you were the best magician in the world and you'd do it."

"A magic show?" Jubilee said, totally surprised at the request.

"Yes, that's right." The boy showed her one of the papers advertising the show. "I told Mrs. Rice that you and your pa and Micah had a wagon and went all over the mountains doing magic and selling the remedy. The parents are supposed to help and I promised her that you would. So you just have to!"

Jubilee thought of the possible negative effect her appearance at the carnival might have. She wasn't Tad's mother, and Stephen might object to her displaying herself

Song of the Lark

in front of the whole town. Weren't the socialites constantly whispering about her strange backwoods ways and herbal cures?

"I don't know, Tad. I think we need to talk to your father about this. You see, I'm not a parent and—"

He tugged on her hand. "But you *are*. You're my new mother because I choose *you*."

Tears pricked her eyes at his passionate declaration.

He hung his head, then looked up again, his eyes moist. "The boys said I don't have a mother, that nobody would come for me—but I told them they were wrong. I told them you'd come."

It was deathly quiet in the kitchen for a moment, and then Delilah looked up from her meal preparations and smiled. "You knows, I think the boy is right," she commented in her mellow voice. "You's the nearest person he's had to a mama since his own went to heaven."

Jubilee remembered the sight Tad had made on the first day she'd left him at school. Due to her, he was dressed normally now and most of the children had accepted him. His confidence had improved, but he was still unsure of himself, and she often noticed the look of dread on his face as he rose and prepared for class. Still, there was Stephen to be considered. Would he approve of her performance or feel that it only underscored her background as nothing more than an itinerant huckster, a seller of snake oil and mountain hokum? Then she realized that he was so busy he probably wouldn't even be able to come to the carnival. If she didn't go, Tad would be left alone again.

"*Please*," the boy begged, his face full of longing that tugged at her heart. "Please come and let them see how good you are."

Delilah cleared her throat. "Oh, go on, Miz Jubilee," she urged with a sharp nod. "It won't do no harm playin' with the children on Halloween. It'll make the boy happy. He's dependin' on you so."

Jubilee ruffled Tad's hair, knowing she just couldn't let him down. "All right," she answered softly. "Tell Mrs. Rice I'll do a magic show."

Jubilee hoisted a scrawled sign reading "Madame Zaranza's Internationally Famous Magic Show" and hung it above her carnival booth. From her place on the stepladder, she looked down at Tad, who was dressed as a pirate, a cardboard sword strapped to his side. "Well, what do you think?" she asked over the noise of the gathering crowd.

His pride apparent, the boy grinned. "It looks wonderful," he replied, lifting up his black eye-patch. "This is the best booth here!"

Tad handed up two Chinese lanterns and she lit them and hung them from the protruding eaves of the booth. Finished, she climbed down and brushed off her skirt, glad she'd found the makings of a gypsy costume in the mansion's attic. A pair of purple satin curtains had become a long skirt, a velvet muffler a sash, and a black-fringed paisley throw a shawl. Delilah's red Sunday-meeting kerchief now held back Jubilee's auburn hair, making her the first red-headed gypsy in the history of North Carolina.

"Those lanterns will attract folks our way when things really get going," she told the boy, her skirt swishing as she moved in front of the booth to compare it to the others.

It was about seven o'clock on Halloween night and the booths had been set up in a circle around a huge bonfire that cast golden light over them. Besides crafts made by the ladies of Asheville, the open-faced cubicles featured popcorn balls, candied apples, and sizzling waffles that pleasantly scented the cool evening air. Already a steady stream of people walked by, leading children dressed as ghosts, goblins, and witches. A platform had been constructed just outside the circle of booths where people could dance, and even now, men placed chairs around the wooden structure, and a string band, spiced with throaty Southern fiddles, was tuning up.

Pleased that her booth was as fine as any, Jubilee moved behind the counter, accidentally stepping on Matilda's tail. The cat wailed and she scooped her up and placed her into Tad's outstretched arms. "Oh, I'm sorry, Matilda," she apologized, smoothing the cat's glossy coat. Wanting to keep her safe until the pet show scheduled for later in the evening, she sent Tad a firm look. "You hang on to that cat now. Don't let her get in the way."

After the boy had calmed down the mewing feline, Jubilee fanned out her magic cards on the counter, then glanced at the growing crowd. People filed past in a thick stream, some of the grown-ups wearing homemade costumes. One man carried his child on his shoulders and had draped a large sheet over them both, making an extremely tall ghost with a pointy head and two sets of eyes.

Jubilee smiled to herself, enjoying the passing spectacle without a trace of guilt. How glad she was that Stephen had approved her taking part in the carnival. What was it she was showing now? Community spirit—that was it, she thought, pleasantly surprised that he'd told her he'd even drop in to see how she and Tad were doing before the evening was over.

"All right, come on up and see the magic show!" she called out to the crowd, itching to get back to her old trade now that she was in the spirit. "Come on up and see the magic show. I, Madam Zaranza, a Romany princess, will reveal the secrets of the East. You will be amazed, thrilled, stunned, impressed, and overwhelmed. The show is only ten cents—only one thin dime," she called, pleased when a crowd that included the tall ghost and two devils started drifting in.

Tad, still clutching Matilda, milled through the murmuring flock, collecting tinkling dimes in an old pickle jar.

To begin the show, Jubilee did several card tricks, then performed her traveling-sugar trick in which she placed four lumps of sugar on the counter, made them jump around, then made them all appear together. People laughed and clapped their hands, and she saw Tad's face glow with pride.

She picked up a spoon, made it appear that she'd bent it, then restored its shape; she made a salt shaker vanish; and she apparently pulled a button off a spectator's vest and caused it to sew itself back on. These were all simple tricks, but she performed them with such style and confidence that the audience oohed and aahed their approval.

A late arrival, a little boy pulling a big bird dog on a leash, worked his way to the front of the crowd. Dressed as a hobo, he peered up from the shade of his oversized hat, his mouth agape at Jubilee's skill.

Hitting her stride, she placed a big bowl covered with a cloth on the counter intending to perform the trick a bit later.

"What's in there?" the lad asked, his eyes dazzling with curiosity.

"That's a magic bowl, young man," she replied, "and I'll show you what's in it in just a moment."

"Go ahead and show me now!" he begged, slapping a dime on the counter.

From the corner of her eye, Jubilee saw Estell and her father in the crowd. The reverend sported a fine coat with a velvet collar and carried a silver-topped walking cane. A smart blue wool ensemble clad Estell's slender body, and pearls looped her neck and hung almost to her waist. Rings flashed on her fingers, and a large-brimmed millinery masterpiece, swathed in black netting, crowned her blonde head, reminding Jubilee of a tea clipper in full sail. Both of the Pennypackers wore sour, bitter expressions that made them stand out in the lighthearted crowd like two lemons in a basket of apples.

Determined that she wouldn't be ruffled, Jubilee continued with her show, all to the consternation of the little boy with the bird dog who kept asking what was in the bowl. He made such a ruckus that the Pennypackers approached the booth, the crowd respectfully parting for them. "Yes, what *is* in that bowl," Estell asked, studying Jubilee with contempt. Her father leaned over the counter and stared at the vessel with wonder.

Jubilee knew she couldn't put off the trick any longer, and with a dramatic gesture, she answered, "*Magic*. The bowl is full of pure magic. I'll show you now!" She snatched away the cloth, revealing a puff of smoke. In her haste, her hand brushed against Reverend Pennypacker's bent head and sent his toupee sailing into the air, to land directly in front of the bird dog.

The crowd gasped, and the reverend clasped his bald head, trying to cover the secret he'd kept from the citizens of Asheville for twenty years. The bird dog lunged from the boy's grasp, pounced on the toupee as if it were a bird, then ran away, shaking the hairpiece wildly. All the blood drained from Estell's face and she fell against the tall ghost, her huge hat wobbling about her head. The hat fell over her eyes, and she slid to the ground in a dead faint.

Ignoring his daughter's distress, the reverend chased after the dog, exciting the animal even more. Matilda chose this moment to jump from Tad's arms and bound after them both, causing more confusion. Soon other dogs and cats, followed by their young masters, joined the melee that became a babble of shouts, growls, hissing and the reverend's piteous calls of "Stop! Stop! Come back with that!"

As the battling animals leaped into one booth and then the next, popcorn balls flew like snow and jars of jams and jellies crashed to the earth, accompanied by the moans of agonized matrons. The animals upset a huge washtub of water that had been set up for bobbing apples and spilled lace doilies into the instant mud. The destruction was total and downright brutal.

With a pounding heart, Jubilee saw Tad streak after Matilda. Without another thought, she leaped over Estell's limp body and chased after him, trying to protect him from the ruckus. In the thick of the mayhem, dogs and cats were covered with jam and jelly and everything was a big gooey mess.

Tad finally caught Matilda, whose coat was pasted with jelly. Breathless, Jubilee pulled the boy to his feet and brushed him off. "I-I've got her!" he proclaimed, a big lump of strawberry jam sliding down his smiling face.

Jubilee heard shouting voices and saw a frantic rescue squad running toward them. "Don't worry," she told Tad with a rush of relief. "You're safe. Everything will be all right now."

Then as she caught sight of Stephen, his brows pulled together and his mouth set in a scowl, she knew that she'd lied. Lordamercy, she thought, her heart skipping a beat. She'd made a spectacle of herself, and from the expression on Stephen's face, she had about as much of a chance of becoming Mrs. Wentworth as the reverend did of finding his toupee.

Chapter Thirteen

"And then there is the matter of the jams and jellies," Stephen announced in an ominous tone. He placed his brandy glass aside and scribbled in his notebook, ticking off yet another item concerning the destruction at the carnival. "The ladies made jelly all summer for this event," he continued with a dark glower, "and hundreds of bottles were destroyed in one fell swoop!"

Jubilee nodded, remembering the taste of the strawberry jam she'd wiped from Tad's face. It was good—not as good as Effie's, but exceptional for town cooking.

Still disheveled from the melee, she sat in Stephen's big leather chair and watched him pace about his study as he lectured her like an angry judge. It had taken an hour to get Tad cleaned up and calmed down, and another to bathe Matilda and anoint her cuts with a slave Jubilee had made herself. By now, the servants were in bed and everything was quiet, except for the occasional sound of a log crumbling upon the fireplace grate.

A glass of brandy sat on the table beside her and she sipped it. At least Stephen had been gracious enough to offer her a shot of liquid courage before he began his interrogation. Lordamercy, to hear him reel off the damage he personally held her responsible for, a person would think she'd destroyed the capitol building instead of a simple Halloween carnival.

"The dogs and cats were a total mess," Stephen droned on in an irritated tone. "Mrs. Miller's dog is now walking with a limp, and Mrs. Snyder's cat, who is a Persian and very sensitive, has gone into some kind of catatonic trance."

Jubilee suppressed a smile as she thought of the Asheville socialites washing jelly from their pets into the wee hours of the night.

Stephen glanced at his notebook again. "Several antique quilts that had been put on display were ripped to bits," he informed her, arching a condemning brow, "and their owner actually fainted."

Jubilee knew that at this point any excuse she could invent would seem totally inadequate. She sighed deeply and poured herself another brandy. "Everything would have been all right if that bird dog hadn't gone berserk and gone after Reverend Pennypacker's toupee." She thought she saw a touch of amusement twist the corner of Stephen's mouth, but she couldn't be sure. "And then Matilda streaked off after the dog like greased lightning—that's when our troubles began."

Stephen passed a sharp glare over her. "That's just it. You and Tad should have had Matilda in a cage!" He continued with her list of crimes, mentioning several prominent ladies who'd lost expensive hats, a tuba player that had fallen backwards into a bass drum when the pack of dogs and cats crossed the dance platform, and a woman who'd experienced the mortification of her false teeth falling into the cider bowl.

"Well, *Madame Zaranza*," Stephen challenged as he tossed the notebook aside, "what do you have to say for yourself?"

Song of the Lark

She rose and stalked to him, noticing that her legs didn't work quite properly. "Now listen here." She tried to tap his chest but missed it and tapped his arm instead. "Tad and Matilda and I didn't cause all that. One thing just led to another."

Lines tensed his brow, but his mouth had started to soften a bit.

She returned to the leather chair, poured herself another brandy and gulped it down, losing track of how many she'd already had. "Why do I make so many mistakes?" she asked, flopping into the soft chair again. "I embarrassed myself at your party, and now I've ruined the whole Halloween Carnival." She bit back her tears and, to her horror, hiccuped, not once but twice.

Stephen observed her sitting there with the brandy bottle clutched to her bosom. Her costume hung in tatters, the red satin scarf dangled from the side of her head, and makeup smeared her face. How like a penitent child she looked, he thought, experiencing a sudden rush of pity for her.

"Go to bed," he ordered with a weary sigh.

She blinked in surprise. "Why?"

"You're sloshed," he announced flatly.

"What did you say?"

He walked to her chair, wanting to snatch the ridiculous scarf from her head. "You're sloshed...pickled... soused...snookered. In simple words, you have a snoutful, and you're on a crying drunk." He took the brandy bottle and placed it on the fireplace mantel.

She walked to him, swaying only a little. "I'm used to moonshine," she laughed in a mocking tone. "This weak town liquor is like drinking water. Why, I've never been drunk in my life!" She hiccuped loudly and covered her mouth.

He caught her shoulders and laughed. "There's a first time for everything, my dear."

She fell silent, seemingly knowing it would do no good

to argue with him. She walked about his desk, then turned, and a faint light twinkled in the depths of her green eyes. "Did Reverend Pennypacker ever find his toupee?" she asked quietly.

Stephen smiled. "Yes—eventually."

"Can he wear it?"

"I'm afraid not. The hair has been pulled out completely in several spots, and what is left is horribly mangled."

She was quiet for a moment, then ventured, "I wonder if he'll have to wear a hat to preach." Amused with the mental picture, Stephen chuckled a bit in spite of himself.

"Did you see Mrs. Colfax's lopsided bustle after she fell down?" Jubilee inquired, her lips twitching in amusement.

Stephen's sense of humor took over and he laughed richly. "Yes, she reminded me of a doodlebug walking sideways across a leaf."

They laughed until tears came to their eyes, and then he moved to her side. "Lord, I can't stay mad at you any longer," he confessed, lifting her chin. "Somehow you, Tad, and Matilda managed to demolish the whole Halloween carnival, but when I recall it all, it was the funniest thing I ever saw."

Jubilee heaved a tremulous sigh. "Oh, I'm so glad. I thought I might have to publicly apologize on the courthouse steps."

She relaxed against him, and as he caressed her hair, a warm feeling welled up within him. "Try to forget about it for now," he suggested, chuckling at the memory of it all. "Everyone will have a much better perspective on things in the morning."

She smiled up at him and he wiped a smudge from her cheek. Her gorgeous face drew his eyes like a magnet and held them mesmerized. Sooty lashes rimmed her sultry eyes and her lips were parted invitingly. The soft lamplight struck fire in her hair, and even with the gypsy scarf

Song of the Lark

dangling from the side of her head, she was so delectable it made his heart ache.

Her heavy lashes swept down, then she glanced up with a penitent expression. "I'm sorry," she apologized, "truly sorry. I—"

"Forget it," Stephen cut in. He took the scarf from her head and flung it aside. With a rush of feeling, he caressed her tangled locks and admitted to himself for the first time since they'd returned from the mountains how much he wanted her.

His mouth brushed hers and there was the taste of brandy on her lips. When she nestled against him, a tingling fire touched his loins and rekindled his pent-up passion. Lord, he thought, gently caressing her back, he just couldn't seem to get enough of her. He gathered her soft body close, drunk not with brandy but a desire to hold her, love her, take her to the highest realms of pleasure.

Surrendering to temptation wasn't wise and he knew it, but he kept remembering the feel of her silky flesh against his fingers as they had made love. Her lush feminine scent invaded his nostrils and excitement flooded over him and made her almost irresistible.

He hadn't planned on this moment, just as he hadn't planned on bringing her from the mountains, but at this point he knew he couldn't forestall it any more than he could stop the sun from rising. In the far recesses of his mind, he felt a prickle of guilt. He had known that situations like this would happen when he'd invited her to come back, but he'd simply put the thought aside, not wanting to deal with it. He did the same now. It was a decision not of wisdom but of deep need.

Jubilee, her mood now serious, circled her arms about his neck and, filled with passionate longing, held his unwavering gaze. Knowing exactly what she was doing, she decided she would cast her pride aside and *make* him love her. After tonight, he would carry her in his mind forever. He wouldn't be able to forget her or ignore her. He would be *forced* into admitting that he loved her. "We haven't made love since the mountains," she murmured, her tone soft and husky. "I was beginning to think you were mad at me," she added, widening her eyes like a child. "Sometimes I wake up in the middle of the night yearning for your touch. *I love you so*. Make love to me now."

Doubt streaked through Stephen's eyes. "You're tipsy," he said, seemingly struggling to regain his composure. "You don't know what you're saying."

"No—I'm not," she retorted, determined to make him believe her. "I've had some liquor, but it's just made me relax and admit to myself what I really want. My mind's never been clearer in my life."

Jubilee trembled inside. Would he think her a loose woman for her bold declaration? Her head told her yes, but a heart brimming with pure love told her that she'd done the right thing, even if he did think she was tipsy. She sensed he was trying to master his feelings, then gradually the tension melted from his face and he held her tightly, sending a thrill down her spine.

He took her mouth almost savagely and she gladly gave way to the overwhelming passion besetting her. Like silken flames, his fingers caressed her breast, and she met his darting tongue with her own. He kissed her deeply and wantonly, unleashing wild, untamed sensations within her soul. Breathless, she finally tore her lips from his. "Yes, this is what I want," she whispered, gazing into his heavy-lidded eyes. "Give me a night to keep me warm all my life."

A muscle worked in Stephen's jaw, then he lowered his head and her heart beat wildly. His steely arms firmly encircled her again, and she felt the buttons on his jacket press into her bosom. He swept a hungry gaze over her face, and when his lips met hers, she clutched his broad shoulders. His lips traveled over her face, searing her cheeks, the throbbing pulse in her throat, her closed lids. Her breasts tingled with a wonderful sensation and her nipples hardened against the corselet she wore under the gypsy blouse.

"It's been too long," he groaned as he moved his strong hand over the hollow of her back.

She leaned her head against his chest, and the rhythm of his thudding heart beneath his smooth starched shirt darted passion through her bloodstream. "Yes, it's been forever," she whispered huskily.

He placed his arms about her, lifting her from the floor. He carried her to the half-open study doors as if she were weightless. She didn't have time to speak or think, just feel, and she yearned for the overwhelming sensations that lay just ahead.

He left the study and carried her up the dim stairs into the cool darkness. Once they were in his softly lit bedroom, she heard the heavy door close behind them. He laid her upon the soft mattress, and a small bedside lamp illuminated his rugged face and sent her senses reeling.

He sat down beside her and trailed his fingers over her face as if he were admiring a work of art. An expression of deep yearning claimed his features and he roughly whispered, "I want you so much it hurts."

His deeply passionate voice made her shiver with anticipation. "I know what to do about that," she murmured, smoothing her hand over his strong jaw.

He kissed the fluttering pulse in her throat and she could feel his warm breath, hear his ragged breathing. Excitement swirled in the pit of her stomach as he rose, took off his shoes, and divested himself of all his clothing but his trousers. His gaze lingering on her face, he slipped off her shoes and cast them onto the carpet, then sank to the bed once more.

Rapture glowed through her as he gathered her against him and slanted his mouth over hers. The kiss became more insistent, and when he eased his tongue into her mouth, she threaded her fingers through his thick black hair, shivering with anticipation. He kissed her deeply, tunneling his fingers through her locks; then he tugged down the gypsy blouse. His lips never leaving hers, he scooped his fingers into the top of her corselet and hefted her breast into his hand to enjoy its silky texture. He teased her aching nipple with tingling strokes and made her gasp with pleasure.

He raised his head, took her hand, and placed it over the long, hot swelling in his trousers. "Feel my passion for you," he told her, his deep, sensual tone igniting her most primal emotions. He placed his moving hand over hers, showing her how to pleasure him, and his male hardness filled her with delicious shock. "Yes, hold me tighter, little one," he urged, his voice a velvet murmur.

A roaring began in her head, and her womanhood felt so hot, so full.

He turned down the top of her corselet and freed both of her satiny breasts. When he slid his palm over them, then gently squeezed her nipples, she felt as if every nerve in her body were aching with sweet fire. She heard a whimpering animal sound of satisfaction, and discovered it came from her own lips.

He kissed her again, refusing to relinquish her breasts from his fondling fingers, and her nipples swelled hard and pebbly against his ministrations. He eased up her skirt and petticoat and ran his fingers over the inside of her quivering thighs. Warmth touched her cheeks as he pushed down her bloomers, nuzzling and suckling her nipple at the same time. His fingers twined in the silky triangle between her legs, teasing and toying with each sensitive curl, and she writhed against the silken counterpane.

He slipped off her bloomers, then her petticoat and skirt, and cast them on the carpet. Resting by her side once more, he slipped a finger into her soft womanhood and teased and caressed it with electrifying touches. She drew in a sharp breath and arched against his hand as the

Song of the Lark

throbbing juncture between her thighs ached for fulfillment.

He placed her hand over the swelling in his trousers once more, and her heart thudded crazily as she freed the fiery shaft and let it rest in her palm. Gingerly, she touched him, shocked and thrilled by the marble hardness of his aroused flesh. The intimacy of the moment sent her world reeling out of control. At last he broke the kiss, to stand and take off his trousers. He towered over her and soft light washed over his huge shoulders, hard chest, and flat stomach. Her gaze inched to his face, and the fire she saw in his eyes shook her heart.

He gently scooped her in his arms, sat her on the side of the bed, then knelt before her. Without explaining his actions, he slanted his lips across hers, untied the cord at the top of her corselet, then stripped it from its eyelets. The tight garment tumbled to the carpet and her flesh was bare to his warm hands. He worshiped her with his fingers, then moved his lips to her sensitive nipples, suckling long and lovingly first one, then the other.

Rocked with emotion, she closed her trembling lids, clutched his broad shoulders, and sighed in ecstasy. When she thought she could endure the delicious torment no longer, he eased her back on the mattress and lay down beside her. He rolled down her garters, then peeled off her stockings and tossed them aside.

She gasped as his fingers tenderly entered her and caressed her until she ached with desire. His dark eyes played over her face for a moment, and then his lips met hers in a kiss that sent fire skittering through her veins.

She dug her fingers into his back and he kissed her more passionately, making her heart skip several beats. His huge frame half covered hers and he nuzzled her throat and her breasts. His fiery lips inched lower, savoring her rib cage and her stomach that was subjected to a rash of moist kisses and light caresses. She groaned as he kissed the inside of her thighs, making her shiver with delight. Now his fingers toyed with her aching nipples while his warm lips invaded the silky triangle between her quivering legs. Incredible sensations rushed through her and she felt as if every nerve in her body had taken wing.

He cherished her damp cleft, then searched through her silky folds with his tongue. His warm mouth at last found the essence of her femininity and as he nibbled at it, she sighed and moaned his name. Her excitement rocketed, but gratification was skillfully kept at bay, making her anticipation that much sweeter. At last surrendering to the rapture he'd elicited, she felt exquisite pleasure tumble through her with the lavishness of a rushing waterfall.

She cried out again and again as her body soared mindlessly, ecstatically, before bursting into a series of brilliant explosions. His fluttering tongue teased her until she shuddered once more with a convulsive passion that nearly took her breath away.

When every fiber in her body sizzled with agonizing pleasure, he positioned his wide-shouldered frame over her and his open mouth descended upon hers. She circled her arms about his neck and returned his branding kiss with all the energy she could muster. He lowered himself so that the moist tip of his shaft grazed against her swollen bud and sweet shock waves rolled down her spine. She arched her hips toward him and he plunged into her and began a slow, tantalizing rhythm.

He moved faster and wild sensations beset her. It started with a warmth from deep inside and spread through every limb. Her heart beat faster and faster. Her flesh tingled; her breathing quickened. His strokes were long and deep and titillating and his hardness rekindled the burning fire that coursed through her veins with every thump of her pulse.

Near wild with desire, she met each of his demanding thrusts. Her nails pressed into his back and flames darted from her womanhood to her belly, her breasts, her arms and legs, taking her to another plane of existence. At last she could contain her excitement no longer and she experienced a crescendo of emotion and passion that exploded within her like a thunderclap. Seconds later, Stephen groaned and shuddered against her, his body relaxing.

Afterwards they clung to each other until their frantic hearts slowed, then he lay beside her and lovingly held her against him. "You were magnificent," he murmured as he fluttered kisses over her face. "I'll never forget this night."

Jubilee looked into his languid, half-closed eyes, praying his statement would be a reality. Wrapped in euphoria, a sweet weariness overcame her, but images from tonight's debacle at the carnival kept nibbling at the back of her mind. Restless, she skimmed her hand over his muscled shoulder, seeking his clemency. "Are you still upset about tonight?" she asked quietly, toying with the hair at the nape of his neck.

He kissed her forehead, then laughed deeply. "No, of course not. It was just what a lot of the people in this stuffy town needed. Maybe they won't take themselves so seriously now." His mouth curved into an unconscious smile. "The good citizens of Asheville will simmer down in a couple of weeks and start laughing, too." He kissed the top of her head. "Go to sleep now, Curly Top. I'll make sure everyone who has a complaint is reimbursed tomorrow."

Jubilee heaved a great sigh, knowing herself forgiven. A tender afterglow shimmered through her flesh, and as Stephen caressed her back, a feeling of deep contentment captured her soaring spirit. She relaxed into the mattress, her body so replete with satisfaction it felt like freshly melted lead.

Yes, everything would be all right now, she thought to herself as sleep closed in about her like a velvet fog. Her blunder wouldn't be counted against her, and after tonight

Stephen could no longer ignore his feelings for her. After what they'd shared, he'd be forced to open his heart and tell her he loved her as she loved him.

Rosy light streaked into the attic room, eliciting a soft moan from Jubilee's lips. Like silken veils, sleep fell away from her lazily, and, exhausted from a night of lovemaking, she burrowed into the mattress and slept a good fifteen minutes longer. At last the scent of cool air sloughing through the open window and the song of a mockingbird forced her to open her eyes and struggle up on her elbows.

She blushed when she saw her clothes lying over the chair; her shoes had been placed neatly beside them. A deep seated happiness swept over her. She'd fallen asleep in Stephen's warm embrace and evidently just before dawn he'd carried her upstairs so that her honor wouldn't be besmirched with the servants.

The sheet was soft against her swollen nipples, and her body tingled with magnificent sensations. She recalled the feel of his moist lips at her breasts, and the sound of his low, husky moan as he poured his hot seed into her. Even now the memory of that moment crested over her like a breaking wave and saturated her senses with pure joy.

She rose and covered her nakedness with a cool satin robe, still thinking about their long hours of passion. Surely by now their relationship had reached a new level. She'd shown Stephen how much he meant to her and had proved that they shared a love no one could deny, not even him.

She'd just put a brush to her hair when she heard the nicker of a horse as the groom walked the animal in front of the stables. The man would soon hitch the mare to a buggy, and a little later it would be time to take Tad to school. She was busy laying out her clothes when a soft knock claimed her attention. She opened the door and saw Tad garbed in pajamas, a stubborn piece of hair sprouting straight up from the back of his head. Clutching Matilda

Song of the Lark

in his arms, he walked into the room as if it belonged to him and held out the huge cat for inspection. "Do you think she'll be all right?" he questioned, his childish voice quavering with concern. "She looks mighty beat up to me."

Jubilee examined the battered cat, knowing her slight wounds would heal just fine. "With more of my magic salve, she'll be like new in a few days. Animals are like that. All she needs is a lot of rest and a lot of love."

Tad reclaimed the cat and cradled her in his arms. "If you think it would be all right to leave her," he suggested, a happy light in his eyes, "let's go to our special spot in the woods today."

"Oh, I don't know," Jubilee answered as she remembered all she had to do. "You don't get home until four and—"

"Not today," he came back quickly. "The teachers are all having a meeting this afternoon because it's the first of the month. We get out at lunch today, so we'll have plenty of time. Can't we please go? I'll work on my printing real hard when we get back."

When Jubilee didn't immediately answer, he clutched her arm and added, "It'll be too cold to pick herbs soon. You know it will!"

He sent Jubilee a pleading gaze that tugged at her heart, and an idea suddenly leapt into her mind. Their "special spot" as he called it was only two miles from the edge of town—an easy distance for someone who was used to walking, like herself. Perhaps they could walk to the woods today and lead his pony. Maybe she could tempt Tad into riding back to the mansion when he became tired as he always did before their long herb-picking expeditions were over.

She stooped down and tweaked his small nose. "All right—you have yourself a deal. We'll walk today and lead your pony. I'll put a saddlebag on her so we can gather lots of herbs."

Tad's face beamed with satisfaction. "Good," he replied, smoothing Matilda's rumpled coat, "we can leave as soon as we've had lunch."

Jubilee ran her fingers through his silky hair. "We'll do just that," she agreed, playfully swatting the seat of his pajamas, "but you'd better get ready for breakfast. Now give me that cat!"

She hoisted Matilda into her arms and watched the boy scoot down the stairs, his glossy curls bouncing appealingly. She petted the purring animal, her mind going over a dozen questions. Would Tad get on his pony? she wondered, recalling the time he'd refused to ride General Sherman in the mountains. Would the boy conquer his fears this afternoon and become completely well?

Jubilee smiled at Tad as she led his saddled pony down the bridle path. It was good to be in the cool, moisture-laden air, and the scents of earth and leather soothed her senses. In the distance, clouds skimmed over the mountains, making the slopes brighten and darken with drifting light and shadows, and closer in, the woods glowed with autumn color.

"Look, Jubilee, there's a patch of yellow dockroot over there!" Tad announced excitedly, pointing at the herb that peeked shyly from beneath an old log. A huge oak drooped over the dockroot, its leaves bright red, contrasting handsomely with the dark evergreens.

"You're right about that," she laughed. She led the pony from the path and walked in that direction. "That weed is mighty good for a person's heart," she added, pleased with the boy's growing knowledge of herbs.

Tad ran ahead of her and tried to push the log out of the way.

Jubilee stooped and began picking the herb. With his sharp eyes, Tad saw more dockroot farther from the path, and they wandered that way, finally losing sight of the trail altogether. The pungent aroma of rotting wood and green foliage touched Jubilee's nostrils as they wound their way deeper and deeper into the woods. With a tinge of guilt she remembered what Stephen had told her about giving Tad herbs, but she reminded herself she wasn't giving him herbs—he was only helping her pick them. While the pony nibbled on the last blades of green grass, she and the boy picked eyebright and goldenseal. Periodically, they tied the herbs into neat bundles and put them into the saddlebag strapped over the pony's rump.

While kneeling, Tad scraped his leg on a sharp rock and looked up at Jubilee with big eyes. "Let's put some slippery elm sap on this scrape," he suggested excitedly. "You told me how good it was for cuts, and I believe you. We could try it out right now."

Jubilee was touched with his belief in her cures, but she dared not go against Stephen's wishes. "I don't think we should. Your father doesn't want me to treat you with herbs," she softly explained.

"But why doesn't he? They're good!"

Jubilee smiled. "You and I believe they are, but he doesn't. We have to do what he thinks is best. We'll put some store-bought medicine on it when we get home."

Disappointment flooded Tad's face, but he nodded in understanding and continued picking goldenseal. They worked solidly for an hour, then sat down on a log and ate some cookies that Jubilee had brought. Busy little chipmunks flitted about them, their bushy tails curled over their backs. Tad flipped them some cookie crumbs and they grabbed them and scurried away, rustling through the dry leaves. He was laughing when distant thunder stirred the heavy, moist air.

Jubilee gazed upward at the patchy forest canopy, seeing bits of gathering clouds through the lattice of tree limbs. The threat of rain had built swiftly, she thought with dismay, guessing that they only had a few minutes before the downpour started. The words were no more than out of her mouth when she felt a speck of moisture on her upturned face. "We'd better go before it starts pouring," she warned, standing and brushing the last of the crumbs from her hands.

Tad untied his pony while she gathered their belongings, and they were on their way. Five minutes later, big drops splashed on her arms. As the wind picked up, rattling small tree limbs, the rain came down faster and faster, and she realized this was no ordinary shower—this was a full-blown storm. "Let's hurry, we need to get home," she said, fighting down her sense of urgency. She took the pony's reins from Tad and walked in the direction of the bridle path.

The trees bent low and the forest floor became soggy beneath their feet. Cold rain pounded down in earnest now, gushing from shiny leaves, plastering Tad's curls to his scalp, and soaking Jubilee's blouse. She stumbled ahead, her skirt hem catching on wet brambles and muck pulling at her heels. She paused to get her breath and glanced back to check on Tad, who lagged behind. After he'd caught up, they plodded ahead, passing a boulder with gurgling rivulets streaming over its sharp edges.

Frightened by a clap of thunder, the pony reared and Jubilee impulsively tugged on her reins. At the same time, her booted foot slipped on a root and her ankle twisted beneath her, making her tumble. On the way down, she put out an arm to break the fall, but twisted her wrist as well. Pain shot up her leg and arm like fire, and unbidden tears stung her eyes.

Tad, his face etched with panic, caught the pony's dangling reins. "A-are you all right? Are you hurt?" he cried, kneeling down beside her.

Jubilee's ankle hurt so badly she thought it might be broken, but she knew she had to remain calm for his sake. "I've twisted my ankle," she groaned, rubbing her good hand over her leg. "I can't put any weight on it."

Tad's eyes grew large and frightened. "I-I'll help you

get up," he stammered. Not thinking, he took her injured wrist and tried to help her up.

She winced in pain. "No, I can't." She attempted to get up using her own power and failed.

The boy put his hands under her torso and tried to pull her to her feet with no success. With trembling fingers, he pushed back the wet curls sticking to her cheeks. "W-what are we going to do?" he asked in a choked voice.

Loradamercy, what *would* they do? she wondered, knowing she had to get him out of the storm. *Think!* she ordered herself, noting that the boy's expression was becoming more frightened by the minute. With a prickle of alarm, she realized he must ride back to the mansion to get his father, who would come and rescue her. She'd wanted the boy to ride, but not like this with him trembling in fear. Still, it was the only answer to the problem.

"Tad," she began, edging her voice with a confidence she didn't feel, "you need to ride your pony home. Tell your father to come and fetch me in his buggy."

The color drained from the boy's terrified face. "I-I can't do that. I can't ride anymore. You know that."

"No," she countered, her voice warm with love, "you *can* ride, you just think you can't."

His eyes dazzled with worry.

"Look," she gently explained, understanding there was a terrible struggle going on within him, "you became a lot stronger in the mountains. Do you remember all those things you learned, the things you did?"

His face tense with anguish, he nodded.

"Well, I think some of that strength of the mountain men has rubbed off on you. You're stronger now. You can do things now that you couldn't before you went to the mountains. If you put your mind to it, you can ride your pony again." She glanced at the pony that whinnied nervously, eager to get out of the storm. "Lead her to that stump. You can stand on it and get a boost onto her back."

Tad's body quaked with fear.

Playing her last card, Jubilee said, "Ride her for me. Ride her back to the house and tell your father what's happened." With her good hand, she touched his face. "Sometimes all of us have to do hard things, but if you face up to your fear it usually melts away." She clutched his hand and tried to channel her strength into him. "I need your help, Tad," she proclaimed passionately. "No one can help me but you—*just you*."

Love shone in the boy's eyes; then, moving as if in a dream, he rose and led the pony to the stump.

Jubilee struggled up on her good elbow and watched him. Rain trickled from his hair, and his shirt stuck to his back and showed his sharp shoulder blades. "That's it. Hoist yourself up."

Awkwardly, he mounted the animal, and when he'd managed to position himself, he looked at her for approval.

"That's good!" Jubilee encouraged him, her heart bursting with pride. "The worst part is over now. Just nudge her in the ribs and she'll take you out of the woods. She's a good, gentle pony, but she's frightened, too. If she breaks into a trot, pull back on the reins and hang on tight!"

Tad managed to turn the pony in the direction she should go. "I-I remember how to hold the reins from when I used to ride. Mama taught me," he cried in a broken voice. The pony moved away and the boy glanced back apprehensively over his shoulder at Jubilee.

"Remember you can do it!"

He trembled, but a spark of confidence lit his eyes.

Jubilee watched him ride away, sending all her prayers and hopes with him. She was confident that he knew his way back to the mansion, but he looked so small, so frail for the responsibility that rested on his slight shoulders.

Now no more than a moving blur, he disappeared in the mist and rain. Fresh tears flooded her eyes, tears of

Song of the Lark

pride and gratitude that the boy had finally faced his deepest fear.

Exhausted, she sank to the spongy earth once more. "Lord, please be with him!" she prayed fervently. "Let him make it home safely."

She could pray no more as sharp pain ripped through her and snatched away her breath.

Chapter Fourteen

Thunder boomed over the mansion, making Stephen push back from his desk and glance at the study windows. He'd been all over town this morning, trying to make retributions for the damage at the Halloween carnival, and he'd stopped by the mansion at about three o'clock to write letters of apology to several ladies. He knew that Jubilee had taken Tad on some outing and supposed they were in town. Still, it bothered him that they might be caught out in the weather, and he left the study to talk to Delilah, hoping she'd know just where they had gone.

"Do you have any idea where Tad and Jubilee are?" he asked the cook as she stirred up a bowl of corn bread.

"I don't rightly know, Mist' Stephen. But one of the maids say they took off together right after the noon meal." She gave him a thoughtful look. "I bet one of them grooms in the stable might know where they went."

"Good idea," he replied, already making his way out of the kitchen.

He thought about sending Chambers to the stable to question the grooms, but this was too important. He

Song of the Lark

wanted to know for himself just where the two were while the worst storm he'd seen in years boomed overhead. He strode through the foyer and opened the mansion's huge front door, thinking to make a dash for the stables. Rain pounded down outside, almost obscuring the lovely grounds, and lightning lit the sky.

Then something caught his eyes that made his heart jump. Through the silvery veil of the rain, he saw Tad riding toward him on his little pony. A tidal wave of emotions burst over Stephen. The terrible day when Isabelle had been killed flooded back, and with it, Tad's refusal to ever ride again. At the same time, pride burned in his heart that the boy had found the courage to face up to his fears.

At a distance he could see that Tad's hair was plastered to his head and water dripped from his sodden clothes. Elation rose in Stephen's heart to see the boy riding, and he ran down the graveled driveway to meet him. But where was Jubilee? He'd expected to see her enter the driveway at any moment, but she wasn't anywhere in sight. Surely she wouldn't let Tad ride by himself in weather like this. His feeling of intense joy quickly changed to sharp concern. Something was terribly wrong.

As he neared Tad, he noticed the boy's eyes were wild and frightened and he clutched the reins so hard that his knuckles were white. Stephen pulled the boy from the pony and held him close; the child's heart was hammering like a locomotive. "What happened, Tad? Where's Jubilee?" Stephen asked, searching the boy's stricken face.

"S-she fell, she hurt herself!" the boy gasped, trembling so much he could scarcely speak.

"*Hurt herself?* Good Lord, what's wrong with her?"

Tad's eyes dilated like those of a small frightened animal. "She can't stand up. I had to ride to get you. We have to save her, Papa."

Worry pounded in Stephen's heart. She could have broken her leg or even worse. "Where is she?"

"O-off the bridle path in the woods. Where you found us picking herbs that one time."

Sickened by the news, Stephen visualized Jubilee lying in terrible pain on the forest floor with the cold rain soaking her to the skin. He took Tad's hand and hurried to the mansion, thinking to turn him over to Delilah before he left to find her. "We've got to get you inside before you catch your death of cold," he told his son. "You can stay with Delilah."

But they'd only taken a few steps when Tad pulled back on his hand. "No, Papa. I want to go with you. *Please let me go*. I can help you find her. I know just where she is!"

Stephen stared at the boy's face, noting a spark of newfound courage. Courage like that, he decided, should be rewarded.

A crack of lightning sizzled into a nearby tree and Jubilee's heart jumped. Ignoring the pounding rain, she used her good arm and leg to inch over the muddy forest floor until she was under a small ledge of rock. There, she was somewhat protected from the storm that was now lashing leaves from the trees in mighty gusts. She examined her fingers but her hand was so swollen she could scarcely move them. Sharp pain shot up her leg, and she could only imagine what her ankle looked like. Had she broken it? she wondered, fretting about how long it would take to heal.

Dusk had settled in. The temperature plunged by the minute, and with the heavy rain, she could only see a few feet from her shelter. She lay muddy and miserable under the little ledge for what seemed like another hour, her ankle now throbbing with a pain that almost took her breath away.

Worry darted through her. With all her heart and soul, she prayed that Tad had made it back to the mansion. Even if he arrived safely, would Stephen be able to find

Song of the Lark

her in the storm? Her spirits had dipped to their lowest when the sound of voices pierced the drumming rain, calling her name.

She eased herself from the ledge and spotted a blur in the downpour—Tad dressed in a yellow slicker. *"Here,"* she rasped, her hopes blossoming once again. When she scooted out a bit farther, the boy ran toward her, a smile on his lips.

"Here she is, Papa. She's over here!" Tad cried as he fell down beside her. Lightning flashed behind him and illuminated his pale face. His eyes shimmered with relief as he brushed back her tangled hair. "I did what you said," he exclaimed in a quavering voice. "I rode my pony home and got Papa."

"Yes, you were wonderful," she praised, squeezing his arm with her good hand. "You've done the work of a full-grown man today."

His mud-speckled face glowed with pride.

Stephen emerged from the gloom, then squelched over the wet ground and knelt beside her, rain dripping from the brim of his hat. The warmth she saw in his concerned eyes touched her spirit and gave her hope that the worst was over.

His heart hammering a crazy tattoo, Stephen anxiously scanned Jubilee. "Are you all right?" he asked, wiping water from her mud-smeared face.

"My hand," she answered, trying to move her fingers. "I think I sprained my wrist, and my ankle is hurting like the very devil."

"I can imagine." He gently examined her swollen hand, and relief poured through him that she wasn't more seriously hurt. "Yes, I'm sure you've sprained your wrist as well as your ankle. But everything is going to be all right," he assured her. After he'd scooped her light body into his arms, he rose to his feet.

She moaned in pain. "Oh, I feel like someone has beaten me with a stick!"

"Just relax. I have you now," he added in a consoling voice. "There's blankets in the gig. It's waiting on the bridle path."

Tad splashed ahead of them as Stephen strode toward the buggy through the mist and rain. The trio were almost at the buggy now and he clutched Jubilee a little tighter. A glow warmed his heart as Tad fetched a blanket and held it out to wrap about her. Stephen knew her ankle throbbed with pain and he gently settled her upon the buggy seat and draped another blanket over her head and shoulders. After the boy had scrambled into place, Stephen swung into the buggy himself and prepared to turn it about.

Never had he felt so happy, so grateful as he did at this blessed moment. Deep in his heart, he knew his son had faced his fear because of his love for Jubilee. Still marveling at Tad's newfound courage, he considered how much the boy must love Jubilee. What a wonderful mother she'd make for him.

Hours later, Stephen entered the bedroom that had once belonged to his mother and closed the door behind him. Carrying a tray with soup and bread, he scanned Jubilee as she slept peacefully in a huge four-poster bed upon silken sheets. Her soft lips were slightly parted, and her bosom slowly rose and fell beneath the pink satin counterpane. Careful not to wake her, he placed the tray on the bedside table, then took a chair by his slumbering patient.

Wind wailed over the mansion's roof and rain pecked against its windows, but flames crackled in the fireplace and made the beautifully decorated room snug and cozy. Stephen's chest tightened as he studied Jubilee's delicately sculpted face and watched light play over her lustrous hair. He smiled to himself. What a flurry of activity there had been when he'd carried her into the mansion. Delilah had given her a sponge bath, then dressed

Song of the Lark

her in a flowing white nightgown while the maids took away her muddy, sodden clothes. Even Cleo had popped his head into the room, only to be shooed away by his mother. Delilah had taken charge of the situation like a mother hen.

Dr. Stuart had diagnosed a severely sprained ankle as well as wrist, then with gentle hands wrapped both injuries in heavy bandages. He'd prescribed laudanum to ease Jubilee's pain, and Stephen knew that at this moment she floated on a cloud of hazy well-being, probably not even aware that anyone was in the room.

He stirred the soup, and hearing the noise of the clinking spoon, she sighed deeply. Gradually her thickly lashed eyes fluttered open, and flushed with sleep, she inched a drowsy gaze over him. "What time is it?" she murmured in a faraway voice.

Stephen leaned back in his chair, knowing how surprised she'd be with his answer. "Ten o'clock."

"That late?"

She tried to sit up, but he stood and eased her against the lace-trimmed pillows. "You've been napping on and off since Dr. Stuart left," he laughed gently. "Delilah made some soup before she went home and I just warmed it up." He reclaimed his seat, then picked up the bowl and leaned toward her. "It'll do you good to eat it."

Jubilee reached for the spoon with her injured hand, but the implement dangled from her limp fingers.

He took the spoon himself. "I don't think that's going to work," he chuckled, leaning toward her. He carefully ladled the warm soup into her mouth, and like an obedient child, she ate half of it and some of the bread.

Letting her rest, he sat back and noted how tired and pale she looked. "How do you feel?" he inquired, taking her slim hand in his own.

"Wonderful," she returned with a crooked grin. "In fact, I feel like I've just had a whole jug of moonshine!"

"I'm not surprised," he laughed. "You have enough laudanum in you."

She met his smile with one of her own and relaxed against the fluffy pillows. "I'm so proud of Tad," she observed, a rasp of excitement in her voice.

Stephen replayed the unforgettable scene in his mind. "Me too," he answered with fatherly pride. "You gave him the courage he needed to ride. You've been giving it to him for months."

A tender expression claimed her face. "Yes, today was his graduation day. I think he'll always be stronger after this."

Stephen took her hand and kissed it. "I have you to thank for that, and I thank you with all my heart."

A soft stain tinted Jubilee's cheeks; then, her eyes moist with tears she whispered, "It was my pleasure. I love him too, you know."

Still a bit groggy, she gazed at Stephen who was garbed in a paisley dressing gown with a red ascot at his neck.

"I'm afraid your ankle is sprained very badly," he said, his look of concern triggering a passionate softness within her. "Dr. Stuart said you should stay off your feet for a month at least."

"But I have to help Tad get ready for school and go over his homework in the afternoons. He's having trouble printing his letters and—"

"That's simple," Stephen cut in, caressing her hand with his long thumb. "A maid can help him in the morning, and after school you two can practice right here."

She nodded, satisfied with the answer. "I'll be glad to see him. I'm sure I'll enjoy his company."

"Tad won't be your only visitor," he said in a velvet-edged voice, filled with promise. His lazy gaze roamed over her, making her pulse flutter. There was a new softness in his eyes, and when he brushed back her hair and smoothed his hand over her shoulder, pleasure radiated through her body like warm sunlight.

Song of the Lark

They talked for a while longer, and then Stephen's features blurred before her. His voice seemed to be coming from a great distance. The laudanum was pulling her under again. She was getting drowsy, so warm and drowsy she could scarcely hold her eyes open.

Stephen watched Jubilee's eyelids become heavier and heavier, then flutter closed. When he was convinced that she was truly asleep, he reached down and brushed a soft tendril from her cheek, letting the shiny hair slip through his fingers.

How concerned he'd been about her! He remembered talking to Dr. Stuart after he'd treated her, and being extremely relieved to know her ankle wasn't broken. Stephen recalled Tad slipping his small hand into his own after they'd walked into the hall and the boy asking, "Will she be all right, Papa? Will she?" He'd pulled his son to him and, with a great tide of feeling, answered in the affirmative.

He traced the curve of her cheek, considering his decision to put her in what had been his mother's room. Why had he done something like that? He'd just acted and not given it a second thought, yet in his heart he knew this was the place she should recover. The accident had forced him to face up to his deepest feelings about her, and in a moment of acuity he realized how vitally important she was to him. Lord Almighty, did that mean that he actually loved her—that he was ready to risk marriage again?

He shuffled through his deepest feelings, finding no answer to his questions. Making love as they had done the evening before was one thing, but giving one's heart unreservedly was another. Eventually all people lost the ones they loved, and having experienced the price once, he feared it was simply too much to bear again.

Still glowing with pride that Tad had acted so bravely, he recalled the boy's actions. Tad had faced his greatest terror and proudly conquered it. Could he ever do the same?

A week later, Jubilee lay in bed staring at the pink silk canopy above her. Bored to tears, she scanned the beautiful room, looking at the pastel carpet and French chairs covered with needlepoint upholstery, and the great marble fireplace with its crackling flames. Everything was so fine. Why had Stephen brought her to his own mother's room to convalesce? she wondered, trying to puzzle out if his actions meant a change in their relationship.

She was mulling over the question when a soft knock sounded on the door and Chambers entered, his face as long as ever. "You have a visitor, miss."

Jubilee spied Estell and wanted to slip under the covers, but knowing that there was no escape, she took a deep breath and girt up her courage. "Yes, thank you, Chambers."

Dressed in a blue wool gown and carrying a white fur muff, the blonde sailed into the room, throwing the butler a look of disgust as he closed the door behind him. "Honestly," she huffed, taking a chair by Jubilee's bed, "I don't know why Stephen keeps that old man about. He's eighty if he's a day, and as sour as a green apple."

Before Jubilee could defend him, Estell pasted a look of concern on her face and started tugging off her kid gloves. "I heard of your unfortunate accident and felt it was my Christian duty to come and call on you." She adjusted her huge hat whose feathers trembled with every movement of her head, then patted Jubilee on the cheek. "Cheer up. You should exult in your tribulation, knowing tribulation brings about great reward."

Jubilee wanted to tell Estell she'd already exulted in about as much tribulation as she could stand, but she couldn't get a word in edgewise, upside down, or even backwards. For five minutes the socialite rattled on about daily events at the parsonage, then she suddenly blurted out, "I do hope your ankle heals before you have to go back to the mountains. It will be so painful for you to travel if it hasn't."

A hard knot formed in Jubilee's stomach. "What do you mean *go back to the mountains?* I'm not planning on going anywhere soon," she returned with escalating anxiety.

A taunting smile swept across Estell's lips. "Don't you understand? After the spectacle you made of yourself at the Halloween carnival the whole town is talking about you. You've become an embarrassment to Stephen. He can't very well dismiss you now, but as soon as you can get around, I'm sure he will. I just wanted to warn you, to prepare you for the inevitable. After all, that's what friends are for—to help each other. *Bear ye each other's burdens* and all that."

Jubilee struggled up on the pillows, a flame of defiance in her bosom. "I'm not planning on ending my employment here until Stephen Wentworth himself tells me I am dismissed—and so far, I haven't heard anything about it," she countered icily.

Estell laughed softly. "You *do* know that Stephen and I are getting very serious about each other, and I expect he will ask me to marry him soon."

Jubilee's heart began a mad racing. *"Marry you?"* she whispered, barely holding on to her composure. She had known that she'd have to fight Estell for Stephen's love when she came back to Asheville, but she'd never expected anything like this.

Estell rose and fluffed out her skirt. "Yes, we'll be setting a date soon," she said with a saccharine sweetness that made Jubilee nauseous. The blonde strolled about the room, picking up a silver-framed photograph of Stephen's mother and examining it with a proprietary air.

Jubilee's initial shock gave way to rage and she wished she could wrench the precious memento from the debutante's lily white hands.

Estell turned, her eyes full of mocking amusement. "You see, when Stephen and I are married, I'll assume the responsibility of raising Tad and we'll have no further need for your services." Frosty contempt underlaid her formal words.

Jubilee shuddered inwardly, for the boy loathed Estell. Under her cold, uncaring reign, he'd retreat into shyness and his blossoming self confidence would wither and die like a tender vine in the scorching sun. Tears stung her eyes, but she held them in check, promising herself she wouldn't lose control of her emotions.

Estell strolled back to the bed, her face wreathed in false solicitude. "I know how hard all this has been on you, dear," she murmured, a shadow of satisfaction creeping over her face. "Trying to fit in where one is helplessly at a loss is always difficult. You will feel much better when you're back among your own kind and can relax."

She turned and adjusted her fluffy hat in the mirror. Bubbling with rage, Jubilee permitted herself a withering stare as Estell glided to the bedroom door, feathers quivering gently.

She opened the decorated panel, then turned, her true emotions masked behind a stiff puppet's smile. "Well, I must be going now, dear," she cooed, settling one of her curls into place. "I have other calls to make, and Father and I are expecting a few guests for tea at five." She waved her hand in farewell. "But don't worry. I'll see you again soon. After all, I'm not one to shirk my duties." She moved into the hall and with a swish of her silken skirts closed the door behind her.

Jubilee fell back against the pillows. How dare Estell come here and taunt her with such a wild tale? Stephen had said nothing of dismissing her or marrying Estell. Obviously the woman had simply taken advantage of her illness to sabotage her self-confidence. She balled her hand, trying to forget everything the debutante had said. None of it was true. It couldn't be!

Then she reviewed all the battles she'd fought in the last six months, having lost them all. Suddenly she felt vulnerable and terribly insecure. She'd alienated herself from Micah, and although she wrote to him regularly, he'd never returned even one of her letters. On top of that, her hopes for Brandon's return had been squashed, and in her heart she knew that although Granny might temporarily rally, she'd eventually be called to glory.

And experiencing the sharpest pain of all, she admitted to herself that Stephen had never even *hinted* about making a commitment to her. She was living on nothing but dreams and false hopes, she thought dejectedly. She went cold with fear and humiliation. At this moment life couldn't seen darker. She clenched her fist a little tighter. If only she weren't trapped here like a caged animal, unable to get out and do something to change her future.

She buried her head in the pillows, her thoughts jumbled together like a nightmare that had no reality or reason. "I won't give in, I won't cry and feel sorry for myself," she whispered as bitter gorge rose in her throat.

But even as she made the promise, hot tears slid from her eyes to be absorbed into the soft linen pillowcase.

Jubilee leaned back in the buggy seat and wrapped her shawl tightly about her. At the top of a hill, Stephen pulled back on the reins and eased the rattling vehicle from the dirt road. A month had passed since she'd been hurt, and now that her ankle was almost healed, he'd taken her on a ride to celebrate the occasion. How wonderful it was to be outside again, she thought, pulling in a breath of cool air. How wonderful to see blue shadows across the painted mountains, to feel the fresh breeze on her cheeks.

Stephen slung his reins about the brake lever, then turned and his eyes caressed her face. "This is Adam's

Point, one of the local sights around Asheville," he declared, his firm mouth curving into a smile. "What do you think of it?"

Jubilee surveyed the little valley below them that was aglow with fall color and decorated with a silvery pond. It was a cloudy, chilly afternoon, and hearing an unmistakable call, she peered upward at a flock of wild geese flying just below the scud of the gray clouds. There were about twenty of them, flying in a long, wavering V, and it thrilled her to hear their wild cry. She let her gaze swing over the valley, then circled it back to him. "It's beautiful," she replied, a touch of awe in her voice. "It reminds me of home."

Stephen nodded. "That's why I brought you here."

His words struck a chord within her and she was keenly aware of his warm leg pressing against hers under the lap robe, firing her sensuality.

She'd desperately longed to ask him about Estell's claims, and during several sleepless nights she'd tried to determine what she should say. But in the end, pride had always stilled her tongue. She'd cast aside her caution on the night of the carnival to gain a place in his heart, and she wouldn't cast it aside again. Surely Estell had only been baiting her, trying to destroy her confidence. Yet, just the memory of her visit brought a chill to her arms that had nothing to do with the cool autumn breeze.

Stephen brushed aside one of her curls. "How is Tad's printing?" he asked, studying her with an approving smile.

"It's getting better," she chuckled, thinking of all the time she'd spent with the boy. "But sometimes he still mixes up his b's and d's, and his m's all have lazy legs."

"Lazy legs?" he laughed. "Well, we can't have that, can we?"

His eyes took on a dreamy glow, and before the giddy sensations he'd aroused smothered out her logic altogether, she searched for a diversion. "Oh, by the way,

Effie writes that the mill is finished, and everyone is mighty proud of it, too." She smiled, recalling the long letter. "She mentioned Dub Calahan four different times. I hope that man gets up the courage to call on her someday."

"Me too," Stephen remarked, his body moving deliberately toward hers and sending her heart racing. The masculine fragrance of his cologne invaded her nostrils and made her more aware of his closeness than ever. He put his arm about her waist and ran his hand up her rib cage. "I imagine he's lonely." Desire flickered in his dark, expressive eyes. "It's not good for a man to be lonely."

With his other hand he traced along her jaw and neck, and passion flared within her like sparks from a wind-whipped ember. "It's been a long time since we were alone—really alone, I mean," he murmured, his breath soft upon her cheek.

Her heart fluttered madly. "Yes—it has."

His face was only inches from Jubilee's. There was nothing forceful in his advances, but they were no less devastating. Her lips parted to accept his kiss, one that subtly lowered her defenses and left her carefully hidden emotions sweeping toward the surface.

His tongue thrust into her mouth, exploring the dark recesses, gradually stripping every ounce of her breath. When she felt him unbutton her blouse, then slip his warm hand into the top of her corselet, she broke the kiss, gasping for breath.

"Your skin is as smooth as a kitten's ear," he whispered, before covering her mouth with his lips.

His velvety voice sent a wave of goose pimples rushing across her skin. Unexplainable sensations erupted deep inside her and made her body tremble. Brazenly, he continued his intimate explorations and rolled her nipple between his fingertips.

His moist lips abandoned hers to glide across the exposed flesh of her breast. Instinctively she threaded her fingers through his dark hair. She held his head against her and allowed him to press enticing kisses wherever it met his whim. A sigh died beneath his kiss when his hand moved to the other throbbing peak.

Now his lips were over hers again. His probing tongue darted into her mouth and fanned her desire to a blazing flame. She marveled at the hypnotic power he seemed to hold over her, the sensations he could create in her. All he had to do was touch her body and it instantly responded. Fire boiled through her bloodstream and she kissed him without reserve, her tongue flicking against his partially opened mouth.

Gradually the kiss melted into a melody of tenderness and he trailed his lips over her cheeks and forehead, the pulse at the base of her throat. Conflicting emotions chased each other across his face, and in his eyes she noted that tormented look she'd seen before he'd made love to her last summer.

What was on his mind; what was he thinking and feeling? And why did he always tamp down his emotions just when it seemed she was getting through to his heart. She needed to speak to him, to unravel this tangle between the two of them and Estell, for some matters just couldn't be postponed. Before she could catch herself, she blurted out, "Estell visited me right after I was hurt. She told me you were going to dismiss me and marry her." Her heart ran away with itself. "Is that the truth?"

Shocked speechless, Stephen met Jubilee's questioning gaze. How dare Estell tell her something like that, he thought with mounting rage. It was bad enough that the snippy socialite had implied to her friends that they were engaged, but ambushing Jubilee while she was laid up was unforgivable.

A heartbreaking expression on her face, Jubilee buttoned her blouse with trembling fingers.

Stephen heaved a long breath and searched for words to comfort her. "No, I'm not going to dismiss you, have

Song of the Lark

no fear of that," he answered, tracing her creamy face with his fingertips. "And I'm not going to marry Estell either." His very tone mocked the idea as ludicrous.

Relief flooded Jubilee's face. "You're not?"

"Lord, no!" he answered, experiencing a fresh wave of disgust. "It's just some wild idea she cooked up while I was in the mountains. She's been going about town hinting that we're engaged, hoping I'll cave in and marry her." He angrily raked through his hair. "The fact that she would lie to you about such a thing makes me want to wring her lily white neck!"

Jubilee's face held a hopeful glow, but his own emotions were tangled in a knot. He supposed that she was waiting for a commitment from him, and in so many ways he actually wanted to give her one. In fact, he had to actually force himself *not* to make a commitment, but in the end his head overrode his impulsive heart.

True, the girl could arouse his primal instincts as no other, and the fact that she didn't discourage his advances made it that much more difficult. But he wouldn't make the mistake of proposing to her in haste and repenting at leisure. He would always provide for her financially, but offering a proposal would amount to the same as saying he loved her—and that he simply couldn't do. Yes, there was something very special between them, but he'd decided that romantic love just didn't exist for him anymore.

The wind swirled Jubilee's hair about her shoulders and chafed her bare crossed arms.

He removed his jacket and draped it about her shoulders, then reached beneath her chin and tipped her exquisite face to him. "You're cold," he remarked softly. "We should start back to the mansion. We'll build a fire and have Tad read for us." The hint of tears in her eyes tore at his heart, but he'd promised himself he wouldn't give in to his emotions, and he kept his promise.

"Very well," she replied in a quavering voice.

He knew his words had left her unsatisfied, but he could

offer no others. While Estell demanded wealth and attention, this sweet child wanted something far more precious. She wanted his very heart, and that was something he couldn't give.

Two weeks later, Jubilee played checkers with Tad in his room after dinner. November rain pattered against the windows and flames whispered in the fireplace as the boy silently studied the board. At last he thoughtfully moved a checker, then looked up at her in anticipation. He'd been quiet and docile all day—too quiet, she thought, deciding he was paler than usual.

"That was a good move," she congratulated him, surrendering one of her pieces.

She waited for Tad to make another move and her mind surged from one thing to another, finally settling on Stephen. The weather had been dreary, but he'd entertained her with stories and presented her with a host of beautiful gowns and shoes as well as little gifts like chocolates and lacy handkerchiefs. Since her ankle was healed, they'd even gone on some short walks, but he'd never brought up the subject of their future, and neither had she for fear of what she might hear.

Every time she thought of their buggy ride, her body stirred with pleasure, but at the same time, her battered pride ached like a deep bruise. On that chilly afternoon, she could have sworn he'd drawn a curtain in his mind to shut her out. Ironically, it seemed that neither she *nor* Estell was to have him. Yes, she could stay on, but what would happen when Tad was too old for a nanny? It would become apparent to everyone in Asheville that she was Stephen's mistress—and with her strong sense of pride, that wasn't something she could abide.

They'd been swept away by passion in the mountains, and after the carnival, she'd initiated their lovemaking so that she could prove that what they shared was mutual. On that evening it had appeared that he'd loved her too,

Song of the Lark

yet he still insisted on maintaining a wall of reserve between them—that same wall she'd felt so strongly at Adam's Point. What did all his extravagant gifts mean when he was already so short of funds? Was he buying things on credit, actually trying to *pay* her for her favors as he would a mistress? What was his guilty conscience trying to make up for—the wedding ring he'd never offered her?

Yes, Stephen desired her, but he didn't love her enough to propose. She believed in marriage, and she had to make plans, plans to live her life without him—otherwise there was nothing ahead for her but sadness. At the same time, the thought of leaving him crushed her heart—the same foolish heart that had got her into this mess in the first place.

Tad coughed, breaking into her deep reverie. The cough was deep and nasty, and she noticed he was sniffling, too. She studied him hunched over the checker board, looking frail and weak. "How do you feel?" she softly inquired, thinking his drawn face reminded her of a small pale mask.

He ignored the checkers he loved so much and pushed back from the table. "I feel tired—and hot too."

A flush colored his cheeks, and he had a strange glitter in his dark eyes, a glitter that nagged at Jubilee's deepest fears. She moved to his side and felt his brow, noting it was hot and sticky. "Come over to the lamp," she suggested, gently taking his arm. "I want to look at your throat."

With drooping shoulders, Tad got up and ambled to the lamp. He opened his mouth and Jubilee discovered that his throat was indeed red.

As she examined him, Stephen entered the room, having just returned from the lumber yard. His face softened at the sight of them, and tenderness blossomed within her. She knew he'd simply come to tell Tad good night, but her heart beat a little faster just the same. How she loved him and wanted to live with him forever! But loving Stephen Wentworth was a thorny problem that involved an uncertain future she was becoming less inclined to bear with each passing day.

His massive shoulders filled the coat he wore, and moving with a powerful grace, he thoughtfully neared the lamp. "What are you two up to?" he inquired, his eyes sparkling with curiosity.

"Tad has a sore throat, and he may have a little fever too," she explained, once more placing her hand on the boy's hot brow.

Stephen laughed deeply. "A fever? Why, yesterday he and Cleo were whooping around like wild Indians."

"No, I think he's really sick," she returned, a trifle miffed by his comment. "This cough just set in tonight."

Stephen examined the boy himself, and a flicker of apprehension crossed his face. "Yes, his throat is red all right," he agreed, placing his palm on Tad's brow, "and he has fever too." He gazed at Jubilee, his eyes clouded with growing concern. "Put him to bed and give him some hot milk. He probably just needs a few days' rest."

He produced a small package from his pocket and gave it to the boy, who unwrapped it to find a toy soldier.

"I picked it up on the way home from work—to add to your collection," Stephen explained, his face alight with fatherly pleasure.

Tad glanced at the costly figure, then laid it on the lamp table. "Thank you, Papa," he murmured, his eyes disturbingly pale and empty. From the carpet before his bed, he picked up Matilda and, without another word, climbed onto the mattress. With a tremulous sigh, he clutched his pet against his chest and closed his eyes as if conceding defeat to his illness.

Stephen regarded Jubilee, a certain tension in his attitude. "Let me know how he's doing tomorrow. If he's worse, I'll send for Dr. Stuart," he promised, his voice marked with growing worry.

Song of the Lark

He looked as if he wanted to say more and his eyes were full of unspoken questions. Whether they pivoted on Tad or herself Jubilee wasn't sure. She wanted to ask him to stay, but silence rose between them like a forbidding mountain, and the invitation stuck in her throat.

After he'd gone to his study where he now worked late every evening, she asked Tad to put on his pajamas. She decided she'd go down and make the hot milk, then bring it up and read him a story. Distressed by the expression on his sad little face, she brushed back his hair and buttoned his night clothes herself.

"I feel achy all over," he sighed, his eyelids half closing.

"That's because you have a cold," she explained, helping him into bed once more. As he slipped under the covers and snuggled Matilda to his side, she thought what he needed was a good dose of goldenseal. It was wonderful for coughs and colds and all sorts of winter ailments. Of course, Stephen had ordered her to not treat Tad with any herbs, but goldenseal had never done anyone any harm and it never would.

She lovingly arranged the covers about the boy and studied his flushed face. She'd fought down her urge to treat him with slippery elm in the woods, but he'd only had a scraped knee then. This malady was much more dangerous. And after all, Stephen didn't need to know everything that went on between her and Tad. Yes, he was a brilliant man and had a fine education, but when it came to herbs, *she* had the knowledge—not he.

Chapter Fifteen

The next afternoon Estell gingerly patted Tad's cheek, then stood back a bit as if she were afraid of catching his illness. "There, there, sweet thing. You'll be right as rain in no time."

With a deep sigh, the boy rolled to his side and pulled Matilda to his chest.

"*Well*," the blonde murmured, batting her eyes in embarrassment, "I suppose he's simply too ill to talk."

Jubilee watched Estell fuss with the bed covers, wishing she'd leave. After the blonde had lied to her about being engaged to Stephen, Jubilee could scarcely stand to be in the same room with her, but she knew the rules of polite society demanded that she accept her visit. How like her to come when she was wanted the least, she thought, realizing she'd only made an appearance to impress Stephen.

Estell spied a box of herbs on the bedside table and poked her fingertip into the container. "Good heavens, what is all of this?" she asked as she picked up the small container and studied it intently. "It looks like a bunch of weeds."

Song of the Lark

Jubilee's stomach churned with irritation and she took the box and returned it to the table. "Those *weeds* are goldenseal," she replied, so focused on helping Tad that she'd forgotten to put them away. "They're wonderful for colds and winter chills. They strengthen the blood and fight infection, too. The mountain folk have used them for hundreds of years."

Estell raised her finely arched brows. "You actually *gave* these filthy things to Tad?"

Jubilee sighed with frustration. "Of course," she answered, trying to keep her temper in check. "They won't hurt him a bit. They'll help him, in fact." Desperate to get the meddlesome woman out of the room so Tad could rest, she infused her voice with a pleasant note and suggested, "Why don't we go downstairs and have some tea? Chambers can brew up a pot of his English blend in a few minutes."

Estell's face brightened up. "English tea?" she echoed, enchanted by the novelty. "Why, that would be nice."

Greatly relieved, Jubilee escorted her from the room. Before she closed the door, she glanced back and noticed that Tad was almost asleep again.

When they reached the parlor, she asked Chambers to make tea while Estell studied her reflection in a mirror, carefully arranging her dangling spit curls. The blonde turned, then started rattling on about her latest ensemble.

"How do you like it, my dear?" she inquired, propping her parasol against a chair. She twirled around, showing off her light green outfit, decorated with swaying tassels. "It's the latest thing, you know," she bragged, her twirling petticoats rustling like swishing tissue paper. "All the ladies' magazines say chartreuse is the rage of Paris now. The French call it Love's Last Sigh. Isn't that poetic?" She sauntered to the mirror again and adjusted her hat that sported both chartreuse and emerald feathers that quivered with every step she took. "This chapeau that I bought on my last trip to Knoxville goes with the gown perfectly, don't you think?''

Jubilee actually thought the ensemble might be pretty if someone else was wearing it. She wondered how Estell could lightly prattle on about fashion when Tad was so sick, and she counted the minutes until the woman left and she could return upstairs to sit by the boy's bed.

Estell walked about the parlor and examined its decorative objects with possessive interest. She nattered on for ten minutes with malicious gossip about her father's congregation, making snide comments about her supposed friends.

Joy rose in Jubilee's bosom when Chambers entered the parlor carrying a tray with a silver tea service and bone china decorated with small roses. He was immaculately groomed as always, but as he placed the heavy tray on a Chippendale tea table, she noticed that he looked pale and tired. At last Estell stopped babbling, took a seat on the parlor sofa, and spread out her skirt dramatically. Jubilee, who planned to rush the woman out after one cup of tea, claimed a nearby chair.

Chambers gazed at her and raised his brows. "Shall I pour for you, miss?"

"Yes, thank you," she replied, realizing by the tone of his voice that he definitely wasn't feeling well.

Estell impatiently extended her cup and saucer, and the butler started pouring tea. His blue-veined hands trembled, and suddenly the ornate teapot slipped from his fingers and poured dark liquid over Estell's skirt.

With a piercing shriek, she bounded to her feet and dropped the cup and saucer on the carpet. Her face scarlet, she brushed at her dress. "You clumsy idiot!" she screamed at Chambers.

Shocked that the woman could be so cruel, Jubilee stood.

How old and broken Chambers seemed as he snatched

up a linen napkin and dabbed at Estell's gown. "I'm terribly sorry, miss."

The blonde knocked away his hand. "Oh, leave it alone, you crotchety old fool! You'll rub in the stain!"

Rage writhed within Jubilee. She recalled the terrible evening Estell had offered her cast-off gowns, minus the flounces, then broken her button necklace. The uppity blonde had never missed a chance to remind her that she was an employee—and now she was humiliating Chambers, who was obviously very ill.

Estell, dabbing at the gown herself, glared at the butler, her eyes blazing. "When I'm mistress of this house your services will no longer be required. It's silly to waste money on a decrepit imbecile like you!"

Bristling with indignation, Jubilee closed in on Estell. "Can't you see the man isn't feeling well?" she snapped, now so close to the virago she could see the well-powdered lines flaring from her hard eyes. "No matter how tight funds are, Stephen would never dismiss Chambers. He's been with this family far too long!"

Estell's eyes sparkled with interest, and Jubilee suddenly realized that in her excitement she'd spoken indiscreetly about Stephen's financial affairs. But it was too late to recall her hasty words now. Suddenly nothing mattered except saying what had been on her heart for so long. "You're always babbling on about your Christian duty," she began, her blood whooshing through her veins so swiftly, it seemed she could actually hear it. "Why, I don't think there's a drop of real charity in your whole wretched soul. And you use the scriptures like a carpenter uses a hammer—to bash things into place the way you want them!"

The blonde's jaw sagged as if the muscles had given way beneath her skin.

Chambers raised a trembling hand at Jubilee, imploring silence, but she couldn't halt the rage tearing through her. She'd always been afraid of making another social mistake, of showing how ignorant she was, but with Tad so sick, she just didn't care anymore. She simply wanted the wearisome girl out of her sight. "Leave this house right now or I'll have a groom throw you out," she ordered in a voice dripping with contempt. "I'll not have you talking to one of Stephen's employees that way!"

Estell widened her eyes. "You won't have it? Well, I never! You're nothing but a jumped-up servant yourself— a little mountain nobody who simply arrived at the right time." Her lips thinned with anger. "Believe me, Stephen will hear of this and you'll both lose your jobs!"

She grabbed her chartreuse parasol and stalked to the parlor entrance.

Jubilee knew she'd made a terrible enemy. Up to this point, Estell had kept up a pretense of civility, but now that she'd taken off her carefully painted mask and revealed the monstrous face beneath it, she would be unbelievably vindictive. But at this moment, all that mattered to Jubilee was having her much belated say. "Wait," she called, raising a halting finger. "If you want to know what I really think about that overdecorated gown of yours, the color reminds me of green pond scum!"

Tears gushed from Estell's eyes and her mouth opened and closed silently, but nothing came out. Her face contorted with hatred and she ran from the room, sobbing. Seconds later, Jubilee heard the front door slam.

The loudest silence Jubilee had ever heard filled the parlor as she and Chambers stared at each other in wonder.

"I'm sorry, miss, it was clumsy of me," he apologized. "I didn't sleep well last night. I—"

"Forget it. You don't need to apologize for an accident."

His face glowed with pride. "By Jove, miss, you certainly let her have it," he remarked, looking younger and even a bit taller. "I thought she might have a stroke when you said her gown was the color of pond scum."

Song of the Lark

Jubilee was amazed that she'd ejected Estell from the mansion, but glad—glad she'd finally done what she should have when the girl came to announce her so-called engagement to Stephen. She felt a smile work its way over her lips. "It was wonderful to see, wasn't it?" she commented, remembering that Estell's face had gone redder than the roses on the teacups.

"More than wonderful—it was sublime!"

She and Chambers started chuckling, then laughing, and Jubilee thought it was the most satisfying laugh she'd ever had.

Chambers bent to pick up the cup and saucer, then scanned Jubilee with new respect. "Jolly good show, miss. Jolly good show!" he repeated his face finally shining with the friendship and approval she'd worked for months to secure.

He held her gaze for a moment, then his expression began to gradually change, and in his face she saw embarrassment, sadness, and even regret. His eyes were full of unspoken words, and realizing he wanted to get something off of his chest, she walked to him and gently took his arm.

"There's something on your mind, isn't there? I can see it in your eyes. Does it have to do with Estell?"

The butler sighed and shook his head. "No, I'm afraid not, miss." He coughed awkwardly. "Actually I-I have a confession to make."

"A confession?" she laughed. "Whatever could you have to confess?"

He hung his head, then gazed up at her with damp eyes. "When you first came here," he began, coloring with unease, "I didn't understand you. I'm afraid I thought myself a little above you." He smiled tightly. "I now realize that was a dreadful mistake."

Jubilee only smiled, remembering his snubs and put-downs with amusement. "Go on, let's hear this confession," she urged, eager to know what he was going to say. "It can't be as bad as all that."

The butler touched his temple as if to blot the memory from his mind. "Yes, I'm afraid it is. Wh-when you gave me the letter you'd written to Master Brandon to mail, I didn't mail it, I-I threw it away."

Jubilee stared at him, feeling as if all the wind had been knocked from her lungs.

"At the time I was sure I knew best," he went on in obvious embarrassment. "You seemed so eager to send it, I only thought to pacify you." He clasped his hand over hers, and she noticed that it was cold and trembled ever so slightly. "You've treated me like a real person. You sent me letters from the mountains, and I'll never forget the way you stood up for me today. It was magnificent. That's why I had to tell you. I'm terribly sorry, miss. I-It was a despicable thing for me to do."

Jubilee had hoped and prayed about the letter for months, and sometimes at night she awakened wondering if she'd touched Brandon with her words. To know that it had never even been sent shook her deeply and left her feeling hollow inside.

"Miss Pennypacker is right," the butler said, blushing fiercely.

"Estell right?" she echoed in stunned surprise. "What in heaven's name do you mean by that?"

Moisture gathered in Chamber's eyes and she realized he was terribly humiliated. "I *am* a crotchety old fool," he said at last.

What an unfortunate mistake he'd made. How tragically it had all came out, yet she admired the courage he'd summoned to make the confession. And how could she condemn him, for in his own misguided way he'd been trying to protect Stephen?

Overcome with emotion, she gathered him in her arms and hugged him tightly against her. He stiffened with embarrassment, but from the corner of her eye she could tell he was pleased by the attention. "It just so happens," she said, patting his back in a friendly gesture, "that I have a real soft spot in my heart for crotchety old fools—and don't you ever forget it."

Jubilee looked down at the tiny figure lying in the bed. Estell had left over an hour ago, and since that time she'd focused her attention on Tad, her spirits plunging by the minute. A flush touched his cheeks and he mumbled incoherently. By now, she realized he had far more than a simple cold or sore throat, and unease steadily built within her. She knew Stephen would be working late again tonight, but an aching hollowness centered in her bosom as she decided he needed to look at the boy right away. After picking up Tad's untouched supper tray, she left the bedroom and quietly closed the door behind her.

She'd only taken a few steps when she heard, "Miz Jubilee, did Tad eat anythin'?"

Surprised, she saw Delilah and Cleo standing at the foot of the carpeted stairs. In answer to the old woman's question, she sadly shook her head.

"I was just comin' up to get the tray," Delilah explained, deep lines streaking over her brow. "Is that poor chile gonna be all right? Is there anythin' us can do for him?"

A somber expression wreathed Cleo's small face. "Is Tad gonna die, Miz Jubilee?" he asked dolefully.

Delilah shot him a harsh glare. "Hush up that silly talk, boy. Nobody's said nothin' about nobody dyin' 'round here!"

Jubilee walked down the stairs, her heart going out to the frightened boy. "No, I'm sure he'll eventually be all right," she answered, giving Delilah the tray, then putting her arm about Cleo's small shoulders. "But he's very sick—as sick as I've ever seen a child be."

Like the sky before a storm, Delilah's eyes clouded with worry. "Poor little thing sufferin' like that, burnin' up with fever—and so sick he can't eat a bite. Lawsy, what is us gonna do, Miz Jubilee?"

Jubilee pulled in a long, steadying breath. Realizing she must act quickly, she met the cook's uneasy gaze. "The first thing we're going to do is get Stephen. Where is Chambers?" she inquired, her concern rising by the second.

"He be in the kitchen, a-piddlin' around, polishin' up some silver trays and such like."

"Well, tell him to take the carriage, go to the lumber yard, and tell Stephen I need him," she ordered crisply. "I'm worried about Tad, just as worried as I can be. His fever isn't coming down a bit and his daddy needs to see him."

Delilah shook her head. "Yes'um, I'll go right now and tell that old man to hurry and fetch Mist' Stephen home!"

Jubilee turned and slowly walked up the stairs, her temples pounding. Once in the bedroom, she noticed that Tad hadn't changed his position, and if possible, he even seemed smaller. He looked so frail, so vulnerable in the huge bed, the sheets tangled about him.

She fluffed up his pillows, rearranged his covers, and, scarcely aware of what she was doing, closed the box of goldenseal and placed it in the bottom drawer of the nightstand. She wrung out a cool cloth and draped it on his brow, then picked up a fan and stirred the air about him, trying to cool him any way she could.

What was wrong with him? she wondered, a sour sickness in the pit of her stomach. She clutched his slender arm and noticed it was almost as hot as his brow. She knew the signs for diphtheria—mountain fever as the hill people called it—but he didn't have that, for his breathing wasn't labored. He coughed occasionally, but neither did he have whooping cough.

For the better part of thirty minutes, she walked about the room with crossed arms, frequently glancing at Tad to see if he'd moved or opened his eyes. Lordamercy,

Song of the Lark

what did the boy have? she wondered frantically. What was gripping his body, burning him up from the inside and sucking the very life from him?

Almost beside herself, she paced restlessly, worrying about Tad and the letter that Chambers had failed to send to Brandon. At last, she heard Stephen's footsteps on the stairs and she gave a prayer of thanks. Seconds later, he entered the bedroom, an uneasy expression on his face. She went to him and clutched his hard-muscled arms, so relieved she almost cried. "I wanted you to see Tad," she rushed out nervously. "He's worse, and so hot I can't believe it!"

At the bed, Stephen took the cloth from Tad's brow and ran his fingers over the boy's flushed face. "You're right, he's burning up with fever."

Jubilee moved to his side. "What do you think is wrong with him?" she asked, her voice drifting to a hushed whisper.

Stephen stared at the boy, his eyes deepening with concern. "I have no idea," he replied, the hurt, perplexed look on his face breaking her heart, "but I've never seen him this sick before."

Aroused by the sound of his father's voice, the boy started mumbling incoherently about his mother. A tear rolled from his closed eyes, and Stephen brushed it away, then frowned, his drawn brows punctuating his concern. A moment later, he wrapped a blanket about his son, scooped him into his arms, and headed for the bedroom door.

A chill of despair ran over Jubilee's arms. "Where are you taking him?" she asked, walking to the door herself.

Stephen paused and stared at her, a taut muscle working in his jaw. "Get your coat and come with me," he commanded in a rough voice. "I'm taking him to the hospital."

* * *

"The morning staff is starting to arrive. I found this downstairs," Stephen explained, handing Jubilee a mug of coffee.

She took the warm mug in her hands and leaned back against the bench outside of Tad's room where she'd been sitting all night. The medicinal-scented hospital ward was chilly and dank and made her more uncomfortable than ever.

New lines etched into his tense face, Stephen sat down beside her with his coffee. How her heart ached for him. She thought of the long night, of the feel of Tad's fevered brow under her hand, of the look of anguish in Stephen's eyes. Dr. Stuart had been with the boy through the wee hours, periodically venturing into the hall to make announcements that were all identical. "His condition is the same, I'm afraid. I'll let you know as soon as there's a change."

Now the night was over and little noises filtered up the stairs. People were beginning to arrive for work; pink light seeped through the window at the end of the hall; soon the sun would break over the Smokies and Asheville would stir with life. Their coffee finished, the pair groped for words as they carried on a halting conversation, trying to comfort each other but finding little to say.

She glanced at Stephen as he bent forward and covered his face with his hands; his broad shoulders sagged with frustration and despair. Jubilee heaved an inward sigh. All night she'd silently prayed for Stephen and Tad, and even Brandon, who tragically had no idea what was going on at home. She considered all the Wentworth males, each with his own problem. How many other tragedies could this beleaguered family endure? How many times could a heart break and keep on beating?

Moments later, Dr. Stuart, garbed in a long white medical coat, emerged from Tad's room, loosening his tie as he walked toward them. Stephen rose to his feet, his eyes gleaming with anticipation. The doctor, his face pale and

Song of the Lark

drawn from a sleepless night, mumbled a morning greeting to Jubilee, then moved his attention to Stephen. "I'd like to call in a colleague," he said in a dull, flat voice.

Alarm flared in Stephen's eyes. "Why? Is there a need for that?"

Dr. Stuart put his hand on Stephen's arm in a gesture of consolation. "I'm afraid this is a complicated case." He took out his notebook, scribbled a name and address, and handed the paper to Stephen. "I'll be the first to admit that I need some help. I'm not completely sure of a diagnosis. This physician is an excellent diagnostician and has an office in Knoxville. I suggest you wire him as soon as the telegraph office is open and ask if he'll come and assist me. Perhaps together we can help the boy."

Stephen took the paper, his gloomy expression lifting a bit. "Yes, thank you. I'll do just that."

The doctor nodded grimly, then, with drooping shoulders, returned to Tad's room.

The news about the Knoxville physician gave Jubilee an initial sense of relief—but was there anything he might do that Dr. Stuart couldn't? Was there anything *anyone* could do to save the boy, who seemed to be drifting away from life as swiftly as a leaf on a stream?

Stephen, his face as stiff as marble, walked past the stairwell and went to the light-filled window. He braced his arm on the sill and golden sunbeams spilled over his tousled hair and tired features. How incredibly weary and spent he looked! Jubilee ached to go to him and comfort him, but there was something in his stance that said he was seeking privacy, that he was looking for a moment of stillness to renew his hope and refresh his spirit.

The noise of footsteps resounded on the bare stairs and Jubilee expected to see a nurse or some other member of the hospital staff. Instead, Estell appeared, sending her heart into a wild gallop. She guessed the girl had intended to catch Stephen before he went to work and let him know she'd been ejected from the mansion.

Apparently not even seeing Jubilee who sat in the shadows, she hurried to Stephen and threw out her arms dramatically. "My darling, I'm so sorry to hear the bad news. I just stopped by to see how Tad was doing and found out he was in the hospital," she exclaimed, clasping her white-gloved hands about Stephen's shoulders. "I came here immediately. I didn't want you to be alone." She searched his face with inquisitive eyes. "How is he? Do they know what he has?"

Stephen untangled the blonde's arms from his neck and started walking back to Jubilee. "No, not yet," he muttered tiredly.

Estell followed, but when she spotted her rival on the bench, she paused, her face twisting with horrified surprise. "What are *you* doing here?" she inquired in scathing tones.

Jubilee rose, intending to answer, but Stephen answered for her.

"I asked her to come. She was kind enough to sit with me last night. When Tad's fever comes down, she'll be the first one he'll want to see."

Estell shot Jubilee a withering glare, then raised her chin. She undoubtedly wanted to say more, but Stephen had spoken with such feeling, she cleverly held her tongue.

Dr. Stuart suddenly emerged from Tad's room, his face set in deep, rigid lines that made him look very old. Three pairs of eyes trained their gaze on him as he ambled toward Stephen shaking his head. "I just don't understand it. I don't know what to think," he muttered dejectedly.

Impatience streaked over Stephen's face. "What do you mean?" he prodded, his burning gaze fixing on the physician. "Has there been any change in his condition?"

The doctor shook his head affirmatively. "Yes, I'm sorry to say there has." He sighed heavily. "I'm afraid the boy has slipped into unconsciousness."

Chapter Sixteen

Stephen had just finished giving the operator his telegraph message when he heard a feminine voice calling his name. He turned about and saw Estell, an excited expression lighting her face. "*Estell*? What on earth are you doing here? I thought you were going home."

"I had to come," she burst out with flashing eyes. "I had to speak to you alone for a moment."

Stephen's heart dipped as she hurried to him. "Has Tad worsened?" he asked, a choking heaviness in his chest.

She seemed annoyed that he would even ask. "No, no, it's not that," she replied in an irritated tone.

He escorted her away from the busy operator to a quiet alcove furnished with a worn leather couch. "Whatever is wrong with you?" he questioned, thinking he'd never seen her so agitated. "Couldn't this wait until later?"

She dug her fingers into his arm "No, it can't wait," she rejoined, tightening her mouth with disgust. "This is important!"

"For God's sake, spit it out then."

She gave him a smug smile. "I know what's wrong with Tad."

Stephen sat down on the old leather couch, pulling her with him. "Really? I wasn't aware that you had medical training," he retorted, outraged that she'd make such a wild statement. "What in heaven's name makes you think *you* know when the doctor doesn't?"

She leaned forward and clapped her hand over his. "Because I know the child has been poisoned!" she announced triumphantly.

All was silent except for the sound of the clicking telegraph key, and Stephen stared at her, wondering if she'd lost her mind. "Poisoned?" he returned, his mind violently rejecting the idea. "I never heard of such an outlandish thing! Who in Asheville would poison the boy?"

Estell's eyes crackled points of fire. Drawing every ounce of drama from the moment, she whispered, "Jubilee, of course. Jubilee poisoned him."

Stephen shot to his feet. A smile had touched the socialite's lips as she imparted the accusation, and at that moment he found her more repulsive than any waterfront harlot he'd ever seen. "That's the most preposterous thing I ever heard. She loves the boy!"

Estell, her expression that of a satisfied cat, rose beside him. "That may be so," she returned, crossing her slender arms and raising her brow, "but she still poisoned him."

Stephen grabbed her shoulders, barely restraining himself from shaking her. "For God's sake, explain all this gibberish. What in the devil are you talking about?"

"I visited Tad, just yesterday afternoon," she simpered, batting her eyes demurely. "I was in his room and saw a box of herbs by his bed. I asked Jubilee if she'd been giving them to him and she admitted it with her own lips!"

The words hit Stephen's gut with the force of a fist. He wanted to believe Estell was lying, but her eyes held the wild excitement of someone in possession of a piece of gossip too delicious to hold back. Besides, the empty-headed chit wouldn't have the wit to invent such a story.

Song of the Lark

The betrayal cut his soul to ribbons, for he never thought Jubilee would deceive him. She was so open, so transparent—but in this, she'd been sly and cunning and played him for the fool. "What type of herb was it?" he rasped, feeling physically sick at the startling news.

"She said it was goldenseal—that it was good for colds and all kinds of winter ailments."

Stephen's mind turned wildly as he searched for an explanation why Jubilee would purposefully ignore his request. "But that still doesn't explain why—"

"Yes, it does," Estell cut in quickly. She clenched his lapels and narrowed her eyes until they were slits. "Don't you see what has happened?" she prodded, coarse, vindictive lines streaking over her face. "She poisoned him *accidentally*. She only thought the dose was goldenseal. She mistook it for some poisonous herb when she picked it!"

Stephen stared at her, weighed down with shock and sorrow. Weary from lack of sleep, he grappled with the idea, not even wanting to consider it.

"That's why she sent Chambers to get you," Estell rushed on, pressing the issue while she had her chance. "She realized what she'd done and was hoping you'd take the boy to the hospital where his life could be saved. It was an accident, but she poisoned him nevertheless." She peered into his eyes as if to send the message directly to his heart. "She poisoned the poor child with her wretched weeds!"

Nausea swirled in the pit of Stephen's stomach. He knew the Carolina woods were full of poisonous nightshade and other deadly plants. True, Jubilee was a skilled herbalist, but even she could make a mistake. He'd given her specific instructions to never give herbs to Tad, and she'd wantonly disobeyed him, going behind his back to dose the boy with God knew what.

His first sense of shock faded to be replaced with white-hot anger. How dare the girl disobey him! How dare she put his son's life in jeopardy with some vile weed!

Shoving Estell aside so abruptly she almost fell, he stormed from the telegraph office, set on having it out with Jubilee.

Jubilee stood by Tad's bed, looking down at him. She placed her hand on his hot brow, savoring this moment of privacy alone with him while Dr. Stuart was elsewhere in the hospital. Why was the boy sinking further and further into sleep, retreating from life as if an invisible hand were pulling him away from earth? She grazed her fingers over the child's pale face as her mind frantically searched for a possible cure.

There were footsteps, and turning she saw Stephen standing at the open door. Obviously something was terribly amiss. His hair was tousled by the wind, his eyes hard, and his whole manner strange and slightly alarming. "What's wrong?" she whispered, her stomach drawing into a knot of apprehension.

A dark, disturbed expression rolled over his features. "Come into the hall. I want to talk to you."

She guessed the Knoxville doctor had refused to come. Thinking she'd never heard his voice sound so cold and empty, she followed him from the room, chills racing down her arms. They faced each other before the window, and the suppressed anger she glimpsed in his face tore at her heart. "What is it? Talk to me," she gently urged, wanting him to unburden himself.

He studied her so intently she could feel the weight of his gaze. Never had she seen him like this. He had disciplined himself to utter control, but she knew that a mighty river of rage coursed through him waiting to surface at any moment. He took her chin in his hand and, with blazing eyes, blurted out, "Did you give Tad herbs after I told you not to? Don't imagine that you can lie to me!"

Jubilee's heart lurched. Taken aback, she wondered

Song of the Lark

how she should reply, for he seemed angry enough to strike her. Despair sank over her like a great weight, but she gathered her courage, knowing she must tell him the truth and face up to the consequences. Surely he would understand that goldenseal had never hurt a living soul. "Yes, I did," she whispered in a scarcely audible voice, "but it was only goldenseal."

He gazed at her with contempt. "You should have asked me about it," he said, firmly clasping her arms. "You shouldn't have taken it upon yourself to dose him, especially after I forbade you not to!"

His words wounded her to the core, all the more because she knew she'd violated his trust. Her head throbbed from lack of sleep and her legs felt like lead. "I couldn't stand by and see him suffering and not try to help him!" she exclaimed, thinking he should be able to understand her reasoning. "And it was only goldenseal," she repeated once more, remembering all the cases she'd healed with the herb.

"You mean you *think* it was goldenseal," Stephen shot back, his accusation piercing her heart like a keen sword.

She pulled away from his hands, hurt and insulted. "What do you mean by that?"

He gripped her arms again. "Just what I said. You gave him an herb thinking it was goldenseal, but it might have been something else—something poisonous."

"Why, that's crazy," she countered, scarcely believing he'd make such an accusation. "I know all the herbs. I know them by name and I can draw their leaves and roots. I know their colors and what months they grow!"

His gaze burned into her, hot and unforgiving. "Have you ever made a mistake?"

She twisted away. "Yes, years ago when I first started gathering herbs," she admitted, backing up a few steps. "But nothing came of it. And I would never make a mistake now. Never!"

Stephen stared at Jubilee's pale, stricken face. She

trembled and tears glistened in her eyes. A sane part of him advised him to pull back, but his life was falling around him. His business was failing; he was mortgaged to the hilt and couldn't borrow another dollar; his brother had abandoned him, and Estell was a constant thorn in his side. It seemed life was nothing but a long, bitter struggle—one unsolvable problem after another. Now his beloved son was about to lose his life. "I can't believe that," he said recklessly, casting his words like stones and not even caring. "All humans make mistakes, even you!"

She came to him, proud, angry, defensive. "Tad would already be dead if he'd been poisoned," she snapped, her eyes bright with indignation.

"That's not necessarily so. Some poisons are slow acting."

"The boy hasn't been poisoned!"

"Can you prove that?"

"N-no, of course not," she stammered, "but accusing me of poisoning him is ridiculous." She went to the window, then turned about, her expression a picture of anger.

Jubilee gazed at Stephen's stormy face, crushed and broken inside. How could he make such a wild accusation when she'd done so much for Tad, when she loved him so much? He was treating her as if she were some ignorant drudge from the backwoods, ignoring that she was a skilled herbalist who'd helped many people. When she'd first arrived in Asheville he'd defended her from those who looked down on her, but now that he was desperate for an explanation for Tad's illness, he'd found one in her supposed ignorance.

Still, she couldn't let all their love and good feelings die in such a horrible way. Somehow she had to make things right. She went to him and clasped his arms, burying her fingers in the soft material of his jacket. "What's happening to us?" she asked, tears burning her eyes. "We've always been able to talk. I thought we had something special—I thought we might have a future."

Song of the Lark

Stephen held her at arm's length, his eyes fixed and icy. "Not really," he said in a harsh tone that left her devastated. Then as if plunging a knife into her heart, he added: "If you haven't guessed it by now, I'm not in the market for a wife."

Crushed, she stepped backwards as if he'd struck her across the face. She stood there, scarcely able to breathe, her heart pounding in her ears. At last she managed to find her tongue and choked out, "I don't understand. What do you mean?"

A tense silence throbbed between them; then, his face heavy and as deeply lined as if it had been chipped out of granite, he said, "When Isabelle was killed I made a vow to myself—a vow that I'd never marry again, and it's a vow I intend to keep." He spoke calmly, but his voice lacked warmth and tenderness. "I don't think I'll ever be able to really emotionally give myself to another woman again."

"Y-you never told me," she muttered, going all cold inside.

"No. I never found the right time."

To Jubilee, the pain was beyond description, beyond sensation even. His rugged face held an expression of finality, and, stunned speechless, she could only stare at him.

"I'm going to talk to Dr. Stuart and tell him about my suspicions," he announced coolly. "There's no need for you to come." With that, he left the hallway, leaving her standing by herself.

When he closed the door behind him, it seemed he'd just closed the door on the rest of Jubilee's life, shutting her off not only from himself but Tad as well. In effect, he'd said that her company and her services were no longer wanted. Scarcely able to stand, she went to the window and clutched the sill, emotions crashing over her like waves.

She gazed at Asheville through a sheen of tears, knowing who had told Stephen about the goldenseal. Estell had claimed her revenge and was no doubt gloating over it at this very moment. The blonde had arrived unexpectedly the day Tad had been so sick, and Jubilee had been so involved with the child she hadn't even tried to hide the herbs. If she'd been more canny—less concerned with her patient and more concerned with preserving her secrecy—none of this would have happened.

She pulled out a handkerchief, reeling with Stephen's second blow. Why had he never told her about the vow of his? she wondered, dabbing at her eyes. Why had he let her assume there might be a slim chance for them to have a future together? Well, now she knew exactly where she stood. She'd been right to run to the attic after Estell had broken her necklace, and right to pack her clothes! She should have just kept on running, but Tad's pleas had softened her heart and her good sense, too, and she'd stayed.

She turned from the window and resisted an urge to rush into the room and tell Stephen how much she loved him. She wouldn't beg and grovel for him to give her the respect and attention she deserved. She gazed at the closed door, tears bluring her vision. She'd lost everything else, but she would keep her pride. She gathered up her skirt and raced down the hospital stairs, her heart bursting with pain.

Chambers let Jubilee into the mansion, then placed his hand on her arm and gazed at her with concern. "Are you all right, miss?" he inquired, obviously too well trained to ask why she'd been crying.

She straightened her back. Upset by Stephen's accusation, she'd walked the two miles from the hospital without giving it a second thought. "Yes, I'm fine." She tried to put some strength in her voice. "Just tired, I suppose."

Apprehension gathered in the shadows of the butler's

face. "How is Master Tad?" he asked, worry flooding his expression.

"Not good," she whispered. "He's slipped into unconsciousness."

Chamber's face went white at the word. *"Unconsciousness?"* he echoed softly. "Oh, I'm sorry, miss. Do you suppose there is anything I can do?"

She managed a smile of thanks. "Just keep things running smoothly like you always do."

Chambers nodded; then his eyes lit with sudden recall and he handed her a letter that lay on the console. "This just came. I was hoping you'd be home soon so that I could give it to you." He patted her arm with an uncharacteristic show of emotion. "Promise me you'll get some sleep, miss."

"Yes, I promise," she returned, but how she would calm her agitated mind enough to sleep, she had no idea.

With a long sigh, she trudged up the stairs to Stephen's mother's room. She sat on the bed and traced her hand over Effie's childlike writing, then, full of misgivings, ripped open the envelope.

She unfolded the single sheet of paper and read: *Dear Jubilee, I hate to tell you this in a letter, but I guess there ain't no other way. The Lord took Granny home a few days ago in her sleep.*

Fresh tears flooded Jubilee's eyes. She had known that Granny's time on earth was almost over, but she didn't expect to hear about her death at a time like this. She hadn't thought her eyes would already be swollen with tears, her head pounding with pain, and her heart aching as it had never ached before.

She picked up the sheet and continued reading, and the awkwardly scrawled lines blurred before her.

She seemed to be doing pretty good, then one morning, I couldn't wake her, Effie wrote. *The bed clothes were smooth as silk and her face was all calm and still. She must have slipped away without any pain at all. She just drifted off to sleep and the Lord took her home in his arms.*

I hated to bury her without you being here, but with bad weather coming in, I couldn't see no other way to do it. We laid her by your grandpa, and marked the grave with a cross that Will Dorset carved. There was a good turnout and the preacher spoke fine words over her—but it don't take the hurt away. It's been awful lonesome here since the Lord took her, and I'm craving to see you in the worst way. Come home soon. Your loving cousin, Effie.

The paper fluttered to the floor and Jubilee fell back against the pillows, tears streaming from her eyes. For the better part of an hour she thought about Granny and the things the old woman had taught her. She thought about the way Granny had sung to her, the way she'd taught her to sew and cook, and preserve food and make a dollar go further than anyone thought possible.

She rose and went to the window. It was snowing lightly, just a few soft flakes lazily whirling down, but in the mountains the snow would be coming down like soft goose feathers, piling up in big drifts. She rested her forehead against the cool windowpane and remembered how Granny had shown her the most beautiful passages in the Bible—passages that would ease an aching heart or mend a broken spirit. She repeated some of them over in her mind, finding comfort in them. The old woman had never been out of the mountains, never seen a play, or a department store, never seen all the things that town folk take for granted. But how wise she had been.

Jubilee's mind drifted to last summer when Granny had told her about the snowy day she'd eloped with Grandpa and the ruckus it had stirred up. And she thought of the advice Granny had given her, to love Stephen even if it meant fighting the whole world. She swallowed the lump in her throat. That advice wouldn't be needed now.

All at once she sobbed deeply, racked with the pain of Granny's death, with Stephen's accusation, with the

Song of the Lark

thought that she had never been anything more to him than a trifling affair. Lordamercy, what a mess she'd made of it all. How foolish she'd been.

She remembered the day Estell had come to visit her, the look on her face when she'd said, "You should go back to the mountains where people understand you, where you feel more at home." She'd hated Estell at that moment, but, hard as it was to accept, there had been a grain of truth in the woman's caustic words. Yes, Estell was right, she decided, suddenly experiencing a sharp pang of homesickness.

People did understand her in the mountains. They understood that she would never mistake a deadly herb for goldenseal, and they understood love, too—much better than folks here who kept their hearts bound in chains and locked away so they wouldn't be hurt. Gradually, she pulled herself together and decided she'd cry no more. She'd slip out of the mansion. She'd go home where she was loved and understood. She'd go home to the hills and see Effie and pay her last respects to Granny.

She'd do all that after she took care of one last commitment of the heart.

Chapter Seventeen

Her hands stiff with cold, Jubilee tied General Sherman to the hitching post in back of the hospital. She felt achy and exhausted and shivered not only with cold, but fatigue and shock. Of course, Tad wouldn't know she'd come to say good-bye, but *she* would, and to her, that fact mattered greatly.

She situated herself in an alley near the hospital and patiently waited for Stephen to leave. The memory of their argument constantly ran through her mind, and she just couldn't bear to meet his accusing gaze again. She knew he'd eventually have to come out to eat, so she chafed her arms to keep warm. Her eyes smarted and her feet tingled with the icy cold, but it was a small price to pay to see Tad one last time.

Half an hour later, she spied Stephen leaving the hospital. She watched his tall form until it disappeared from view. Half frozen, she walked to the front of the building and entered, then hurried to Tad's floor which held the dank, medicinal scent she'd come to know so well. Inside the boy's room, Dr. Stuart, as exhausted as herself, slept deeply in an old armchair. Jubilee neared Tad, her buckskin boots sounding softly on the bare floor. She gazed down at him and took his hand, knowing she'd never forget a single detail of his face. His skin was taut and milky white and there were purple smudges under his eyes. He looked so small and vulnerable in the large bed with its stark white covers, she had to force back her emotions.

"I just came to say good-bye," she murmured, feeling foolish when she knew he couldn't hear her, but needing to make the speech all the same. Her thoughts swirled back to the day she'd met him. "You've graduated, you know," she praised him, squeezing his hand. "You learned to talk and ride again, and do everything I'd hoped for you." A remembered warmth rose within her. "I recall the first day I saw you. You were all hair and scared eyes, and couldn't talk at all. And I remember the first word you said when I started playing your mother's piano." She laughed softly. "What a day that was. Even Chambers got excited!"

She kissed his hand, then placed it in place atop the sheet. "I remember last summer back in the mountains when you saw that flock of wild turkeys," she whispered. "How you laughed when they all burst out gobbling." She gave a weary sigh. "I remember so many things about you, Tad. I started loving you the first day I clapped eyes on you, and I'll keep on loving you until the day I die."

She trailed her fingers over his warm face. "I won't be coming back to town again, but maybe when you're grown, you'll remember me and come to the mountains to visit. I can just see what a fine-looking man you'll be then, all tall and handsome like your daddy." In her heart, she knew that if the boy survived, he'd probably be sent off to fine schools, and soon forget the girl from the mountains who'd taught him to speak again. Perhaps he'd ask Stephen about her one day out of curiosity, and they would talk a little, then change the subject to happier things. She would become nothing but a memory.

Waves of despair engulfed her. She felt drained, and hollow, and sick inside. She had to hurry. The doctor would awaken soon, and Stephen would be returning. Tears stinging her eyes, she hid the bright button Tad loved inside his pillowcase so he'd find it when he got well and he would remember her. It was just a trifle, but he'd claimed such a large part of her heart, she had to leave something of herself with him, if only a small token. She bent to kiss Tad's cheek and felt his moist, uneven breath upon her face. "I love you," she whispered huskily, her nerves throbbing with exhaustion.

His lids fluttered and he sighed deeply.

She prepared to go, then paused, her heart lurching in grief. She'd taken care of him for so long. What if he needed her? No, she'd done all she could, she told herself, finally realizing that her job, like a neatly wrapped package with a tight knot, was all finished. Her simple skills would be of no avail now. A fine doctor was on his way from Knoxville, a doctor who might save the child's life.

If Tad did recover, Hazel Rifkin would produce another woman to look after him in a matter of days. After all, the boy wasn't Jubilee's son—only a child entrusted to her care for a short while. She'd given her heart without reservation, for that was the only way she knew how to live, but she'd paid the price for that decision to the fullest.

She cast a last loving gaze over Tad, then, aching with anguish, walked past the sleeping physician and left the room. She ran down the stairs, her eyes burning with pent-up tears. "Just one more stop," she told herself. Just one more stop and she could set her heart toward the mountains.

Stephen was halfway across the foyer when Chambers met him, his face lined with worry. "Is Master Tad any better, sir?" he asked solicitously.

Song of the Lark

Stephen strode into his study, the butler trailing his steps. "I'm afraid not," he answered, pausing to take off his overcoat and toss it on a chair. "At this point Dr. Stuart isn't sure of a diagnosis. I'm pinning my hopes on the specialist from Knoxville. He'll be in later this afternoon."

Chambers sighed deeply. "Yes . . . I see."

"Where is Jubilee?" Stephen inquired with a twinging conscience. "I need to talk to her."

"Upstairs, sir," the butler answered quickly. "I believe she's sleeping. I spoke with her before she went up and she looked extremely tired."

Stephen nodded. How shocked he'd been when he discovered that Jubilee had left the hospital. Already deeply regretting his actions, he needed to explain himself before the rift between them became too large to mend. "Yes, I'm sure she's exhausted," he agreed, raking a hand over his stubbled jaw and realizing how long they'd both been awake. "I'll let her sleep a few hours before I wake her."

Remembering a business matter, he sat down at his desk. "I have an order I want you to take to my foreman at the lumber yard," he told the servant, riffling through a mass of papers. Not finding it, he opened all his desk drawers, and with a prick of shock found that someone had been through them. The culprit had carefully replaced everything, but he could see that his papers had been tampered with. Experiencing a sudden sense of violation, he met Chamber's perplexed eyes. "Who's been in this study?" he asked, his voice rough with outrage.

The man's face paled. "Certainly not Miss Jubilee. She went straight upstairs to rest."

"Who else has been here?"

A stunned, troubled look gathered in Chambers' eyes. "Only Miss Pennypacker, sir. She said you'd sent her home to fetch Tad some fresh nightshirts. When she informed me of her task, I escorted her to the young master's room and left. She told me she would let herself out."

Stephen clenched his jaw. Damn Estell for the little sneak she was, he thought, furious with the insult she'd dealt him. He'd known her to be vain, shallow, and manipulative, but this new wrinkle in her personality truly surprised him. How sly she'd been, making up an excuse to enter the house, then creeping into his study to reconnoiter! But what would possess someone of her social standing to paw through his personal papers like a thief in the night?

Chambers frowned, horrified. "Sir, surely you don't think that Miss Pennypacker—"

Stephen leaned back in his chair. "Yes, in fact, I do, but that matters little right now. All that matters is Tad getting well." He found the order he'd been searching for and handed it to the butler. "That's all for now," he said as he rose to his feet. "You may go. I'll inform you before I leave."

The man stepped back and bowed his head. "Yes, sir, but if there is anything I can do, you have only to ask." Looking shaken with his master's discovery, he turned and quietly walked away.

Stephen paced about his study, Jubilee's face tugging at his mind. How different she was from Estell, who'd turned out to be nothing more than a common snoop. Where one was warm and intelligent, the other was cold and sly; where one was loving and caring, the other was selfish and self-seeking.

He recalled the smug look on Estell's face as she'd carefully planted the seed in his mind that Jubilee had poisoned Tad. After his talk with Dr. Stuart, he now knew it was impossible. Just as she'd tried to tell him, the doctor had said that a poison would have acted faster.

Estell had dangled the bait in front of him and he'd swallowed it hook, line, and sinker! *Damn it all*, why had he let her influence him at such a critical moment? He

Song of the Lark

should have known better. The gorge rose in his throat. What he'd give to live this day over, he thought, admitting he'd acted rashly simply because Jubilee had disobeyed him and it had stung his pride. Lord, what a hot-headed mistake he'd made of things, he decided, heavily dropping into his chair again.

He pressed both hands over his eyes for they burned with sleeplessness, and then he glanced at the clock and counted the minutes until he could wake Jubilee and apologize.

Stephen knocked on Jubilee's door and waited for a response. He knocked again, but still she didn't answer. At last, he opened the door to be enveloped in her familiar scent that released a warm, tender feeling within him. Expecting to see a shady form upon the mattress, he was a few steps into the dim room before he realized that the bed was empty.

His mind spinning, he lit a lamp. He opened her wardrobe, and with a rush of relief saw that her clothes were there; but after examining them, he discovered that all her mountain clothing was gone. With a sick, empty feeling, he moved to the window and pulled back the velvety drapes to see if he could locate her outside the mansion. There he saw footsteps cut into the mantle of white that covered the vast yard—footsteps that led toward the stables. A dull ache gathered about his heart, and he realized that a search of the those stables would prove that General Sherman was also missing.

Jubilee Jones had left him.

Of course, she might have gone someplace in Asheville, but if he knew anything about this feisty spitfire, she'd gone back to the mountains, snow or no snow. Overcome with concern and dismay, he imagined the icy wind lashing against her as she rode higher into the Smokies. Lord help her, he thought, panicky sickness attacking his churning stomach.

He moved to the dresser and opened a drawer where she kept her money. The empty drawer mitigated his uneasiness a bit. At least she'd had the good sense to take the money she'd earned, and could buy a hot meal and a warm bed tonight.

A soft sheen caught his eyes from atop the bureau, and nearing it, he saw the pearl necklace he'd given her, nestled upon a crocheted doily. With a pang of stabbing regret, he picked up the necklace and held the cool pearls in his palm, knowing this was her way of telling him good-bye. How typical it was of her—one simple gesture that said everything. He let the pearls slide between his fingers and drop onto the bureau, feeling as if part of his heart had just died.

Half stunned, he remembered the day he'd given the pearls to Jubilee, remembered how surprised and pleased she'd been with the gift. He recalled how he'd wanted to take her in his arms that moment, but had refrained because he knew their love would never work. Like a fast-moving kaleidoscope their months together passed before his eyes. He recalled the way the sun struck fire in her curly hair, and the way her laughter sounded like music to his ears. He remembered Halloween night when they'd made love and he'd come within an inch of telling her he loved her—but his common sense had held him back. All the opportunities he'd let pass never to be retrieved again!

Grief settled over him, weighing him down. He'd taken Jubilee's virginity and put her into the position of a kept woman. Was that why he'd given her the expensive gowns when he was already so deeply in debt—because he realized that he had compromised her virtue? And what of the money she needed so much? He'd forced her to leave her only source of income with his despicable rudeness. All this he'd done to her when she'd offered him constant and loving support. His realizations struck through him like a bitter poison and left him profoundly shaken.

Song of the Lark

Already he made plans to go after her. She couldn't be too far down the road by now and—

Bong, bong, bong, the big grandfather clock chimed softly from the floor below, reminding him of his responsibility. It was three o'clock already. In fifteen minutes the train from Knoxville would be in, the train bringing the doctor who might save Tad's life—a train he must meet.

The two doctors stood near Tad's bed in consultation, and all Stephen could do was wait miserably. After what seemed like an eternity, they mumbled something and shook their heads in agreement. At last, the new physician, looking more relaxed than he'd been since he arrived, approached Stephen. "I think we know what is wrong with your son, Mr. Wentworth," he announced, pushing up his spectacles with a bony finger.

"*Yes*," Stephen replied hoarsely, both dreading and anxiously anticipating what he might hear next. "What is his problem?"

"Did your son's illness start with a sore throat?"

"Yes, in fact it did."

The man thoughtfully pressed his lips together, then taking Stephen's arm, escorted him to Tad's bed. "I believe your son has encephalitis," he announced matter-of-factly. "In simple terms, the membranes that cover his brain are inflamed. The disease attacks the old because they are weak, and the young because they haven't built up an immunity against it."

Stephen pulled away, sorrow coiling in his chest like a huge, painful knot. "*Encephalitis*? Isn't that deadly?" he inquired with a sinking heart.

"Not always."

"Please . . . tell me more."

The doctor pulled off his wire-rimmed spectacles. "This type of encephalitis occurs in small epidemics, or more frequently in isolated cases such as this. The symptoms develop rapidly, over a few hours, and are followed by drowsiness and sometimes loss of consciousness."

Stephen swung his gaze to Dr. Stuart. "Do you concur with the diagnosis?"

The older man nodded grimly. "Yes, I do. If fact, I suspected that Tad had encephalitis all along, but I wanted the opinion of a colleague before I gave you the dismal news."

Dozens of thoughts and emotions galloped through Stephen's brain. He transferred his attention to the new physician, trying to understand it all. "Lord, how did he contract something like this?"

"I'm sure it started with a throat infection that went to his sinus cavities, then to his brain," the man answered, hooking his spectacles about his ears again.

Stephen gazed at Tad's pale face, grief weighing him down until he felt leaden. Then something gradually awakened within him. His priorities instantly came into clear focus and he realized that his business problems amounted to less than nothing compared with the threat of losing his son. He gazed at the sad-faced doctors and spoke calmly, trying to ignore his inner pain. "Can you do anything for him?" he murmured in a broken voice.

The new physician rubbed his jaw. "We can treat his symptoms—bathe him in ice water and hope it brings his fever down. If we accomplish that, his body may be strong enough to throw off the infection." The man put a stethoscope to his ears and listened to Tad's heart. "He should reach a critical juncture soon. Tonight, I think," he announced, straightening up and meeting Stephen's gaze with sympathetic eyes. "If he makes it through until morning, he'll gradually recover, although he'll be weak for months."

Dissatisfied, Stephen heaved a heartfelt sigh. He wanted more, wanted some kind of guarantee that his only son would be all right. "Can't you tell me anything else? Can't you—"

Song of the Lark

The doctor shook his head. "I'm sorry—no. Dr. Stuart and I will do what we can, but you must trust the rest to providence." His eyes glistened with empathy. "If I were you, Mr. Wentworth, I'd do lots of praying tonight."

Stephen nodded, and feeling as if he were crumbling inside, silently walked from the room to get some fresh air. He glanced at the bench where Jubilee had sat, wishing desperately that she was here now. She would know what to say during this dark moment; she would know how to give him hope and strength; she would know how to pray.

It was then, during this quiet moment of the soul, that he suddenly realized he might lose both of the people he loved the most.

Chapter Eighteen

Snow had peppered Maple Leaf Hollow since dawn. Now it lay in deep drifts, and where the autumn leaves had not fallen, they made a bright contrast with the white mantle covering the trees. The wind had died down but remained icy cold. Jubilee pulled her coat tighter about her as she and Effie walked toward a little cemetery on the hill, silhouetted against the setting sun.

Jubilee had arrived in the hollow late that afternoon, shivering, half frozen, and tired clean through. All the way home she'd been terribly weary, even a bit light-headed, and she had attributed it all to the shock of Stephen's rejection and Granny's death. But now, she felt downright queer. She mentally stiffened her spine, determined to pay her respects at her grandmother's grave.

There was only the sound of the women's boots crunching through the crisp snow and the trill of a few birds before Effie began talking in a soft, reflective voice, almost as if she were speaking to herself. "I'd been seein' Granny sink lower and lower," she remarked in a sad, resigned voice, "but she wouldn't let me write you. Said you had enough on your mind without worryin' 'bout an old worn-out woman like her."

"Did she suffer any?" Jubilee asked quietly.

A flicker of a weary smile touched her cousin's lips. "No, I don't think so. She was ready to go—almost anxious, like a person a-settin' off on an excitin' trip. The night before she died we sat up and talked awhile, and she got to laughin' 'bout somethin' you'd said one time when you were a little girl. She was asleep when I went to bed, and she just never waked up. The next morning, she looked as still and peaceful as a picture. Seemed like she just stopped breathin' and went to heaven."

They reached the fenced-off cemetery and opened a little gate. Jubilee went on ahead and walked directly to Granny's grave, which she knew would be right beside Grandpa's. She viewed her grandmother's snowy resting place, holding back tears. If only she'd been here. If only she'd known, she thought with regret, wanting to comfort the old lady when comfort was too late. It hurt so much to see the once vibrant woman decline and slip into old age, then death. Why did life go so fast? Why did those you love have to fail and die?

A melodic thrill graced the still air and she noticed a red bird perched on a nearby gravestone. Granny had always told her it was a good omen to see a red bird in the winter, but she now violently rejected the idea. How could it be a good omen when she felt as if her whole world had been turned upside down?

Effie approached the grave and slipped an arm about her waist.

"Tell me about the funeral," Jubilee said, her voice a mere whisper.

Her cousin let out a thoughtful sigh. "After Granny died, the neighbors brought in food and helped out all they could," she answered in her quaint country accent. "Dub Calahan built the coffin and dug the grave. The day she was buried it was snowin' hard, but the preacher gave a fine sermon and there was a big turnout." She glanced down the slope. "Why, there was horses and wagons all the way down that hill. I reckon this area ain't seen such a funeral since your grandpa died."

Jubilee clutched Effie's hand, loving her plain, homy face under a new split bonnet. They were silent, but a great companionable feeling rose between the cousins, and Jubilee found herself saying, "Will you stay a while—just until I get straightened out?"

Effie's voice quavered slightly, but her eyes held even. "Why, you know I will."

Jubilee looked back at Granny's grave, remembering how Grandpa had brought her sprigs of bright red holly berries for a wedding bouquet. Her grandparents had enjoyed almost nothing in material wealth, but still they'd possessed the finest life had to offer, she thought with a rush of comforting relief.

Jubilee walked to a holly bush and twisted off several wiry sprigs. She recalled her grandmother when she'd been bright-eyed and beautiful, laughing at Grandpa's jokes or simply laughing with the happiness of being alive. What wonderful days those had been. "Here, Granny, these are for you," she whispered, placing the sprigs on the snowy mound.

Tears welled in her eyes. The strong smell of wet leaves, soaked ground, and moldy tombstones made her weak and queasy for a moment. She remembered some of the sermons she'd heard about heaven, about the city of jewels and golden streets, and she couldn't imagine her grandmother enjoying such an idle place—not the woman who had thrived on work and tirelessly helping others. But deep inside she was certain she'd find a place in the gilded realm, for if anyone was ever destined for a crown of stars it was Granny.

Jubilee recalled her trip to Asheville, a trip that was prompted by Granny's illness. Oh, Granny, why did it have to end like this? she asked herself, tears burning in

Song of the Lark

her throat. She couldn't help wondering if Stephen had thought of her since she'd left. Had he worried about her making the trip back to the snowy mountains, or had he just been glad to be rid of her? And what about Tad? Had the Knoxville doctor been able to help him? Jubilee's heart ached with anguish, for she'd never know.

She stood beside Effie, trying to gather her emotions, trying to convince herself that life was worth living. Her cousin gave her a comforting hug, and they'd just turned to go back to the cabin when she heard the snap of dry twigs and heavy boots crunching through the snow. Instantly, she scanned the bottom of the hill, wondering if a neighbor had come to pay his respects. A figure emerged from the long, purplish shadows and her heart raced madly.

Micah had come home.

By nine o'clock Effie was in bed and flames crackled in the fireplace, warming the cabin's sitting room nicely. It was then that Jubilee rose from the hearth with a blue and white enameled coffeepot and refilled Micah's cup. After she'd placed the vessel on the grate, she sat across the table from her brother, still amazed that he'd returned to the hollow. "I'm so glad you're here," she began, relishing this private time they had together. "Somehow it makes losing Granny easier."

An understanding smile moved over Micah's lips. "I know. We may have lost Granny, but we'll always have each other."

The simple words made her blink back tears. United in grief, they'd fallen into each other's arms at the graveyard as if there had never been a rift between them. "After our argument, I thought I might never see you again," she confessed, her voice breaking with huskiness.

Micah glanced down, then met his sister's eyes and flushed scarlet. "I know. I'm sorry 'bout those things I said the last time I saw you. I had no call to—"

She reached across the table and his big hand swallowed hers. "Please—you don't have to go on," she whispered hoarsely. "You were upset and just spoke your mind."

He nodded. "I sure did that all right—but there wasn't a day that I didn't regret those words. Lookin' back, I wish I'd cut out my tongue before I said such hateful things."

Jubilee's stomach pitched with emotion, but she remained silent, realizing he needed to unburden his heart.

Micah leaned back and she could tell he was struggling to express himself. "When Effie wrote me that Granny died, I wanted to come home and pay my respects, and I wanted to make things right with you, too." Pain flared in his eyes. "I thought about you all the time, baby sister."

Jubilee forced back tears.

With a troubled expression, her brother stood and restlessly paced about the cabin, occasionally touching the battered furnishings he knew so well. "Effie wrote me through the summer," he confessed, pausing at the fireplace to stare at the flames. His back to her, he stirred the fire with a much used poker. Pine splinters reddened and burst into flame and the pungent aroma of their resin filled the cabin. "She told me how Wentworth had his own doctor come up here to see Granny"—he hung his head—"and she told me how he brought equipment over from the logging camp to help the men build the mill."

So her cousin had played the peacemaker, Jubilee realized, glad that Effie's letters had touched her brother's heart even though her own hadn't. It was Effie's letters and Granny's death that had brought the two of them together again. How ironic that in leaving this world, the old lady had united her family once more, she thought, biting back fresh tears.

Micah turned, regret shining in his eyes. "And she told me how Granny took a likin' to Wentworth." He rubbed his arm across his forehead as he'd always done as a boy when he'd made a mistake. "I ain't ever known Granny to be wrong about a person, have you?

Jubilee shook her head. "No, I haven't. Granny was the best judge of character I ever knew."

Micah nodded in agreement. "That's what started me thinkin'," he went on, his tone threaded with embarrassment. "I figured if Granny liked him, there must be somethin' good in him, even if his name was Wentworth. And Dub Calahan had sided with him, too. Dub ain't fancy, but he's got a level head."

Micah walked behind Jubilee. "I started worryin' 'bout what I'd said to you," he confessed, smoothing his hands over her shoulders. "It near made me sick what I'd done to you. I should have wrote you or Effie, but bein' a man and bein' a dang fool, I didn't."

Jubilee reached up and clutched his hand. How she'd waited and prayed for this reunion, and now her prayers were being answered. She released his hand, then rose and turned about to face him. "Micah, it's over now. You've said enough."

He returned to the fire and thoughtfully paced before it once more. "No, let me have my say—spill it all out while I've still got the courage. Remember when you talked to me last summer about bein' bitter, 'bout how all that hate was gonna eat me up if I didn't get rid of it?"

She nodded, vividly recalling their discussion.

"Well, thinkin' of you every day made me study on your words, and after a while they started makin' sense. I used to believe only folks like us had troubles—that rich people like the Wentworths kept our kind down. Then I got to ponderin' on Tad. The Lord knows his daddy could buy anything for him, but I ain't ever known such a sad little fellow." He chuckled softly. "Granny always said I was hard-headed, but after a while it finally penetrated my skull that everybody has troubles, even the rich folks."

"That's right," Jubilee returned, quietly moving to

him. "Sometimes I think they have the biggest troubles of all."

Her brother cupped her face in his rough hands. "I couldn't see it for a long time, but you were right. Hatin' and feelin' sorry for myself was slowin' me down worse than my crippled leg."

Jubilee wiped a tear from her eye, grateful that Micah had finally accepted what she'd been trying to tell him for years. His hate had burnt off slowly like a heavy fog lifting, but at last it was gone and there was a flicker of hope in his expression.

He gazed down at her, his eyes shining with new prospects. "I scraped together a nest egg in the flatlands, and I've been thinkin' on farmin' this place again. I should have enough to tide me over till the crops start comin' in." He gave her a lopsided grin that warmed her heart. "A man in Raleigh said he could sell all the dulcimers I could make, so I reckon I'll work on them durin' the winters when it's too cold to do anythin' else."

She hugged him tight. "I'm happy for you, so happy my heart is near to bursting."

Micah awkwardly rubbed her back and laughed like a child who has just been forgiven for breaking a piece of crockery. "I reckon I owe Wentworth an apology, too." He eased her to arm's length, reminding her of a huge, penitent child searching for love and affection. "If you two want to get together, I won't stand in your way."

She hugged him again, not having the heart to spoil his moment of joy. How could she explain that his forgiveness had come too late—that she and Stephen had parted forever, and all his good wishes mattered for naught?

After he went to bed, she let the fire die down and carefully covered up the coals to kindle tomorrow's blaze. She braided her unruly hair in two plaits and made ready for bed herself. She hadn't eaten much at supper, but she wasn't hungry and still felt a little queasy.

She made a nest under the warm quilts and tried to go

Song of the Lark

to sleep, but while her body was tired and heavy, her mind wouldn't rest. She felt as tightly wound as a coiled clockspring, ready to burst apart at the slightest tension. She'd felt that way since she'd decided what was wrong with her, since Effie had fried ham for supper and the scent had made her so nauseous she'd almost retched. It was then that the realization had come upon her like a thunderclap. Her swollen breasts, her tiredness, her missed flow; they all pointed to one thing—she was carrying a child.

If only Stephen were here, how wonderful this moment would be, she thought excitedly. Then the ember of joy sputtered out and grew cold. Stephen didn't know about the baby, and with his vow, he certainly wouldn't care. He didn't want a wife, much less a child. The infant would only be a bother and an embarrassment to him, its coming unwelcome news indeed.

But Jubilee welcomed the babe—welcomed it with all her heart and soul. There were herbs she could take that might cause her to lose the child, but the idea of doing such a thing made her shudder. How often she'd wished Tad was hers. To bear Stephen's child was her heart's deepest desire. What she carried within her was blessed, the fruit of her love for the child's father.

Unable to sleep, she lay in the chilly darkness and listened to the rising wind moan through the pines. She marveled at the bit of life growing within her like a sun-warmed seed. She was carrying another human being, a precious soul who bore the mark of Stephen's face, his hair, his eyes. And the child was dearer to her than jewels.

She'd seen several mountain girls bear babies without the benefit of a marriage ring and she knew what lay ahead for her. The child would be called a *brush colt*, but if he was strong enough and brave enough he could get by. Using his mother's last name, he would be accepted and his illegitimacy would be no great handicap. Her case was different. By bearing the child she would be shunned forever—no woman would ever respect her and no man would ever marry her. She'd be an outcast—an object of ridicule, jokes, and speculation.

On that icy night she fastened the center of her life on her unborn child. It would be the cause of all she did, her reason for living, and around its being she would wrap her concern and constant thought.

Days passed, but Jubilee kept her precious secret to herself. She hid her nausea and malaise, and remained cheerful, still awed and shaken that she was going to become the mother of Stephen's child. How could she burden Effie with the news when she'd already shouldered so much, and how could she confide in Micah, who'd just begun to trust Stephen?

Give them some time to heal from Granny's death, let them get a little stronger before you tell them, she advised herself. Still, sooner or later they would have to know, and she constantly wrestled with the problem of how she could tell them without breaking their hearts.

One day after they'd finished their noon meal, Micah sat back to light up a pipe, while Jubilee and Effie rose to clear away the dishes. As Jubilee was bringing a steaming kettle from the hearth to the dishpan, she caught the faint sound of sleigh bells. Surprised, she placed the hot kettle aside and hurried to the window, pushing back the curtains.

There she squeakily rubbed a little circle on the frosted pane and looked out to see a driver slow his team as the horses trotted into the clearing. "Why, that's Dub Calahan!" she exclaimed, noticing he was bundled to the chin and wore a floppy hat pulled low on his head. "I didn't know he had a sleigh." She turned and saw Effie quickly dry her hands and push back her drooping hair.

Dub pulled the team to a halt before the cabin and climbed from the sleigh, his big, darkly clad body a stark contrast against the white clearing. He was soon stamping

Song of the Lark

snow from his boots and knocking on the door.

Micah rose and let him in. "Hello, Dub," he called cheerily, motioning the visitor inside with a wave of his pipe. "Come on in. It's too cold to stay outside."

Dub hung his head, then awkwardly entered the cabin, all gangling legs and bulging arms. Old, mended clothes garbed his huge frame, but his boots were freshly blacked and greased in an attempt to make them look presentable. The red muffler that draped about his neck matched the scarlet flush that slowly rose from his shirt collar and crept toward his hairline.

Micah clasped Dub's big, work-worn hand and pumped it in a handshake. "What brings you to this neck of the woods?" he prodded, trying to draw him out. "Do you have time for a bite of food?"

"No, thank you kindly, I ate before I come."

"Well, how about a cup of coffee, then?"

The mountaineer tugged off his hat to reveal long hair that he'd greased down and parted in the middle. "No— no coffee for me," he mumbled with unease. He glanced at Effie whose eyes danced with excitement. "I brung you this sorghum I cooked up, Miss Effie," he announced as he pulled a large bottle from his pocket and shambled to her.

She accepted the bottle and placed it by the dishpan. "Thank you, Dub," she replied, her eyes shining with pleasure.

The tall man cleared his throat, then blurted out, "I just come over to see if you might like to take a sleigh ride." He nervously rolled his hat in his hands. "I borrowed a sleigh from my cousin over near Hawthorn Creek. The snow bein' so deep, I thought takin' a ride might be right fun." He stared at Effie, anticipation glinting in his eyes. "What about it, Miss Effie, would you go sleigh ridin' with me? I'd be mighty obliged if you did."

The romantic gesture brought tears to Jubilee's eyes and she noticed that Effie blushed like a girl of sixteen.

The older woman's gaze drifted over the pile of dishes on the counter. "I-I don't know. We just started washin' these dishes and—"

Jubilee walked to the dishpan and took her place. "I'll have these dishes washed in no time flat."

"Well," Effie demurred, smoothing back her hair, "I reckon since you ain't got nobody else to ride with you I might go along—just for a little while." Her hands trembled as she took off her apron and dropped it on a chair.

Dub's face glowed with joy. "Better bundle up real good. It's bitter cold out there. I-I wouldn't want you to catch a chill or nothin'."

Effie slipped on her long winter cloak and tied her new bonnet sash. Jubilee ached for her when she got it knotted wrong and had to do it a second time.

"That's sure a pretty bonnet, Miss Effie," Dub observed as he stiffly offered her his arm. "It sets off your eyes real nice."

A dimple played about Effie's mouth as she accepted the awkward compliment. Although her features were far from perfect, when she became excited as now, she radiated a sweetness that made her more than pleasant looking.

"Now, watch the snow around the doorstep," Dub warned gallantly. "There's some slick places out there. Here, let me help you to the sleigh," he said, putting his arm about her waist. "I wouldn't want you to fall or nothin'."

Effie gazed at Jubilee, her face alight with joy. "Well," she said breathlessly, "I reckon I'll be back after a while."

Jubilee nodded, afraid that Effie might insist on washing the dishes if she broke Dub's romantic spell with a long good-bye. Once the door had closed behind the pair, she walked to the window and peered out. Her brother limped across the room and joined her, hurriedly making the wiped-out circle bigger.

Song of the Lark

"Well, if that don't beat all," Micah commented, laughing with soft surprise at the sight before him. "Looks like old Dub came a-courtin'."

Dub helped Effie into the sleigh and gently tucked a quilt about her legs. Once he was aboard, he snapped the reins and they were off, the harness bells jangling merrily. Jubilee noticed they talked excitedly, and before the sleigh disappeared into the woods, Effie tilted back her head with laughter.

"Oh, I'm happy, so happy for her!" Jubilee breathed. "There never was anyone who deserved a little joy more than Effie."

Micah went back to the table and re-lit his pipe, still chuckling softly. "I've been waitin' for someone to do that for years—but I never dreamed it would be Dub Calahan."

Jubilee stood at the window, hope stirring within her that Effie would enjoy the blessing of a real home and motherhood. Then like a bolt of lightning, the fact hit her that their positions had just changed. Everyone always talked about Effie being the old maid of the family. "Poor Effie," they always said, "she'll never catch a man in a hundred years."

Jubilee thought of her time in Asheville that now seemed a million miles away: the things she'd done, the people she'd met, the man she'd loved and lost. It was all over—done and finished. She was home with no prospects. She was now the old maid of the family—an old maid with a fatherless baby on the way.

She took off her button necklace, her once glowing hope and faith shriveling inside of her like a withered rose. Trembling, she walked across the room, opened the top drawer of an old chest, and put the necklace inside. She bit back her tears and slowly shut the drawer, feeling her heart shatter into a thousand pieces.

Chapter Nineteen

A finger of morning light worked its way into the hospital room and moved across Stephen's face, making him nod. Noises floated up from the first floor and he knew the hospital was coming to life—a new day was beginning, a day that would tell if his son lived or died.

After doing all they could, the doctors had gone to get some much needed sleep, leaving Stephen alone with his son. Now full of worried anticipation, he rose and moved to Tad's bed. How young and tender the child looked. His face was pale, his hair tousled, his inky curls a sharp contrast against the white pillowcase. Dark shadows lay under the boy's eyes, and although his chest rose and fell almost imperceptibly, he seemed more fragile than ever.

Stephen laid his hand on Tad's brow, then his face and arms. For the first time in days the boy's skin was cool, and Stephen experienced a relief that left him weak. The tension he'd been carrying inside him for so long slipped away, leaving his mind clear and his muscles relaxed.

During that glorious moment, Stephen knew Tad had passed the crisis, that he'd make it—that the boy would

Song of the Lark

live, and moved with gratitude, he held back tears. It was then that he first started believing in the unexplained everyday magic that Jubilee had once told him about. There *was* magic all about him, from a leaf changing color, to a weedy-looking plant providing medicine, to the healing power stored in a child's mind or a man's heart, he finally decided.

And he'd prayed for the first time last night, prayed with all his heart for a miracle, and it had happened. The realization swiftly organized his priorities. Now he could easily see that love was the most important item on earth. What did it matter if a foreclosure notice for his lumber yard was due any day now? His son was alive, and nothing else mattered.

He leaned over the child and gently caressed his cheek. "Tad," he called softly. "Wake up, son."

The boy's eyelids fluttered open and he stared at his father with confusion. "Papa, it's you," he whispered groggily, blinking his eyes in confusion. "Where am I?"

Stephen laughed low in his throat. "In the hospital. Don't you remember me bringing you here?"

Tad shook his head, his eyes still heavy with sleep. "I'm thirsty, so thirsty," he murmured, pressing his cracked lips together.

Stephen poured water into a glass from a bedside jug, then lifted the boy's head so he could sip it. When the child had drunk his fill, he eased him onto the pillows once more.

Tad restlessly gazed about the room. "Where's Jubilee?" he asked, his tone laced with anticipation. "I want to see her."

About this sensitive subject Stephen couldn't lie to the boy. "I'm sorry. She isn't here. She's gone back to the mountains."

Tears seeped from Tad's eyes. "Gone? She left me?" he asked, his voice breaking with shocked disappointment.

"No," Stephen quickly replied, caressing his arm. "She left *me*, not you."

Puzzlement clung to Tad's small features. "B-but she loves you," he stammered in bewilderment.

Stephen cleared his throat, unable to speak. When he finally regained his voice, he drew in a long steadying breath. "I hurt her badly, I'm afraid," he explained, knowing it would be impossible to deceive the boy even if he wanted to.

Questions blossomed in Tad's dazed eyes. "Hurt her?" he mumbled softly. He tried to form another sentence, but his lips trembled with the effort. Sleep was pulling him under again and he sighed with resignation. Sadness wreathing his face, he closed his eyelids once more.

Stephen rearranged the pillow under his son's head, and as he did so, something slipped from the pillowcase and rattled to the floor. Surprised, he picked up a button—the one Tad had remarked on when they'd all shared dinner that night so long ago. So, *she'd been here*, Stephen told himself, now realizing that Jubilee could never have left Tad without saying good-bye. Obviously she'd left the button in an attempt to tell the boy she loved him. The action was so like her—so filled with love in its simple way.

Stephen inched his gaze over Tad and found that he was already easing into sleep yet again. Mixed emotions stormed within him. A warm glow gathered in his chest that the child would recover, but at the same time, he was riddled with remorse for his actions toward Jubilee. He gazed at the button, then clenched it tightly in his hand, as if to draw strength and comfort from the object.

Lord, what a fool he'd been. He hung his head. They just didn't make them any bigger.

A week later, Stephen walked up the mansion's stairs, carrying his son in his arms. After he reached Tad's room, he gently laid him on the bed. "There you are, young man—back home again."

Tad tried to smile, but Stephen detected a look of profound sadness in his eyes. He took his son's small hand and covered it with his own. "How do you feel this afternoon? Stronger, I hope."

"Tired," the boy breathed; "so tired I could sleep a hundred years, just like that Rip Van Winkle man Jubilee told me about."

Stephen ruffled his hair, thinking of the slow progress he'd been making. After regaining consciousness, the boy had hovered in that dark territory between life and death for days, anchoring Stephen to Asheville. It seemed the child slept most of the time, and it had been days before he could get out of bed and stand on his feet. Even now Stephen doubted that Tad could walk across the room, but at least he was home. He'd come that far.

Tad clutched his father's arm. "Papa, I miss Jubilee so much." A longing settled on his face that pierced Stephen's heart. "I feel all empty inside. It doesn't seem right that she's not here. She *belongs* here."

Stephen nodded, silently agreeing with each of the boy's statements. How he'd counted the days until he could go look for her; how relieved he was that Tad was out of danger and in Delilah's good hands so he could do just that!

The noise of scrambling feet resounded on the stairs, and Stephen gazed at the threshold, seeing Cleo standing there, holding Matilda in his arms. "Hi, boy, you done got well? I been takin' care of this old cat while you was gone, but she ain't no good. She ain't caught one mouse the whole time you was gone!"

Tad's face brightened at his friend's teasing. "She just didn't feel like it. Bring her on over here," he said with a grin.

The boy walked to the bed, and the cat leaped into Tad's outstretched arms.

"Say, what was wrong with you?" Cleo asked, tilting his head to the side. "You stayed in that hospital a powerful long time."

"I had encephalitis."

Cleo widened his eyes. "En-sef-el-eye-tis? Ummm, that sounds bad—*real bad*." He leaned forward to snatch up Matilda and cradle her in his arms. "You better give me that old cat back. She might catch it too."

Tad chuckled. "She can't catch it."

"Well, how'd *you* get it then?" Cleo drawled, his eyes dancing with mirth.

The boys burst out laughing and Stephen laughed with them. It was the first time Tad had laughed since he'd been ill, and Stephen once again felt deep gratitude and satisfaction that the child had survived the crisis and was now home.

Delilah slipped into the room, and when Stephen met her eyes she tilted her head toward the door. He'd seen that look many times as a boy and knew it meant trouble. Her face bearing an expression that hovered between disgust and frustration, she edged toward the door, sending him another sharp look. Groaning inwardly, he followed, knowing there was no help for it. If he didn't talk to her now, she'd keep on pressuring him until he did.

Once they were in the hall, her frown deepened. "Mist' Stephen, what done happened between you and Miss Jubilee? Everybody in this house is disturbed somethin' terrible 'bout it. The maids is disturbed, Chambers is disturbed, and I's disturbed most of all."

Before he could open his mouth, she added, "What ever you done, you better fix it up fast 'cause when I's 'disturbed my cookin' falls off real bad." She pushed out her lip and shook her finger at him. "Why, I's so disturbed I's thinkin' 'bout quittin'!"

Stephen laughed. "That's impossible. You can't quit. You've been working for this family since I was a boy."

Her hands went to her broad hips. "Yes, sir, I can, and

Song of the Lark

fact of bein', I think I will," she proclaimed with a glower that came near to burning his skin.

He threw out his hands. "*But, Delilah—*"

"Now, Mist' Stephen, don't be thinkin' you can 'timidate old Delilah 'cause you's got all that fine learnin' in you head. I's done paddled your bottom when you was a boy"—she narrowed her eyes—"and I's done seen your possible and your impossible too, so's I ain't no more scared of you than I is Cleo!"

She waddled halfway down the stairs, then turned and looked back over her shoulder, her eyes flashing. "Men folks!" she huffed, waggling her head. "Sometimes I think the onliest reason the good Lord put 'em here was for makin' young'uns and choppin' wood. Everybody know most of 'em ain't got no more sense than a blind chicken in a hail storm!" Still mumbling under her breath, she descended the stairs, pausing occasionally to glare up at him.

Stinging from her tongue-lashing, Stephen went down the stairs himself, to seek the sanctuary of his study. He'd almost reached it when he met Chambers, whose face was set in deep lines.

"I say, sir," he began, his voice rising in dismay, "have you heard anything from Miss Jubilee? It was quite distressing for all of us when she left with no word." He cleared his throat. "Speaking for all the servants, I'd like to say—"

"Save it, Chambers," Stephen cut in with a weary sigh. "Delilah has already sung that song, and much better than you, I'm afraid. Your speech is only another verse."

Chambers drew himself up importantly. "Well, if I may be so bold, sir, we are all quite upset, and naturally now that the crisis with Tad is over—"

"I thought you didn't like her," Stephen interjected, smiling at the butler's blank look.

"Not like her, sir? Why, I have no idea what you're talking about."

Stephen felt a prickle of amusement. "Perhaps you don't remember the first day she came here. I recall you said something about her being quiet unsuitable."

Chambers coughed with distress. "Sir, I have no memory of such a conversation," he replied quite seriously. A discomfited expression gathered on his face. "I think that perhaps you are confused."

Stephen walked to his study, thinking how much things had changed in the past ten months. He sat down at his desk and rubbed his hand over his face in frustration. It seemed Jubilee had touched everyone she'd met here. Delilah loved her so much she was threatening to quit, and Jubilee had made a new person out of Chambers—a loving, caring person when only a shell of a man had existed before. He took stock of himself and had to admit that she'd changed him, too—in so many ways it was hard to list them all.

The only person Jubilee hadn't changed was Estell, who was as selfish, manipulative, and conniving as ever. He'd been so busy with Tad he hadn't thought of the blonde in days, and he vaguely wondered what had happened to her. Once again, anger rose within him that she'd rifled through his desk. What mischief was she cooking up now? She was up to no good—that was certain.

Deciding that Estell wasn't worth another moment of thought, he removed Jubilee's button from his pocket and rubbed it between his fingers. What course of action should he use to get her back? She was very sensitive and he had hurt her deeply. Somehow he had to think of a way to show her how truly sorry he was, but at this moment, any words, any action he could imagine seemed totally inadequate.

Yes, he could go to the mountains and offer his apology, but would she accept it? That was the question.

That night, alone in his second-story bedroom, Stephen was packing a few clothes when he heard carriage wheels

Song of the Lark

grinding against his gravel driveway. He walked to the window and saw a man get out of a shabby hack, retrieve his bag, and pay the driver. Even in the shadows, there was something familiar about the figure and his movements, but he couldn't make out the stranger's features.

When the carriage rolled away, Stephen realized it was one of the hired vehicles that ferried people from the railroad station. Seconds later a knock resounded from below, and knowing that Chambers had already gone to bed, he strode downstairs to answer the door before the visitor woke the whole household.

The small lamp that always burned through the night filled the foyer with flickering shadows. After turning the lock, Stephen opened the door, then peered through the darkness. When a younger version of himself stared back at him, he was too startled to speak. With a flash of astonishment, he scanned his late-night visitor wordlessly, then managed to whisper, "*Brandon*—I thought I'd never see you again."

His brother looked much older than the last time he'd seen him; there were bags under his eyes, new lines on his face, and gray hairs sprinkled at his temples. Stylish, expensive clothes garbed his lean frame, but gone was his devil-may-care, boyish expression, having been replaced with an air of weary dissipation. Stephen swallowed back his shock. "What are you doing here?" he managed at last.

Brandon, his expression both apologetic and embarrassed, finally stammered, "M-may I come in?"

Stephen's natural love for his brother and the hurt of his betrayal left him physically shaken. After all Brandon had done, how could he calmly return and ask to enter the mansion as if he'd only been away on a long trip? Nevertheless, Stephen noticed excitement building within him, and his family loyalty came surging back, washing away some of his anger. With great determination, he mastered his emotions and ushered his brother into the mansion.

Brandon, his eyes damp with tears, set down his suitcase and embraced him. Stephen stiffened at first, then found himself returning the gesture, unnamed emotion running wild within him.

"How is Tad?" Brandon asked, his quavering voice rough with concern.

Stephen stared at him with surprise. "He's going to be all right, but how did you know about that?"

Brandon pulled a rumpled telegraph message from the pocket of his cashmere greatcoat, and Stephen scanned the paper, which said Tad was desperately ill and might not live. The signature of the sender made his heart jump, for Jubilee Jones' name stood out in bold letters. Lord, she'd disobeyed him again, going behind his back to get in touch with his brother before she'd left town. Would she never learn to stay out of other people's business? Yet at the same time, he had to admit that when all was said and done, he was happy to see his brother.

"I just have one question," Brandon remarked, his voice thick with emotion. "Who is Jubilee Jones?"

The question reverberated in Stephen's mind, for he'd asked himself the same thing many times. Who *was* Jubilee Jones: a half-illiterate, superstitious mountain girl who would never fit into his world, or the most unique, fascinating woman he'd ever met?

His mind still awhirl, he scanned his brother, knowing that he himself would find inner peace only when he'd answered that question to his own satisfaction.

Brandon sat in a leather chair burying his face in his hands, while Stephen walked about the study, a brandy in his hand. "I had no idea what had happened to you," he told his younger brother, anger seeping back as he remembered what Brandon had put him through. "I didn't know if you were dead or alive."

Song of the Lark

Brandon sighed heavily, then looked up with glassy eyes. The story written on his face was a sad tale of poor judgment and ruin. "I know, I know," he murmured. "It was a selfish thing to do—leaving you here and bailing out like that." He sank back and stared at the ceiling. "Sometimes I wonder how it all happened. How I could have been so foolish?"

"You wanted *your* money," Stephen reminded him, recalling how he'd held out for it with no regard to the damage he might cause. His footsteps took him across the study and back as he tried to tamp down his anger. "Was it worth it?" he asked, pausing at his desk to refresh his drink.

Brandon rose and joined him at the grog tray. After accepting a drink, he bolted it down, then gazed at Stephen with eyes that had seen far too much for their years. "Yes, at first it was. I enjoyed myself thoroughly in New York. I went to all the finest theaters and restaurants." He laughed bitterly. "I had hordes of friends, I'll tell you that." His pale, lined face stamped with repentance, he helped himself to another drink. "Until . . ."

Stephen studied him, revolted that he'd squandered such a great fortune in two years. "*Until—*" he prompted.

Brandon blew out his breath. "Until the money ran out," he answered shamefacedly.

Stephen nodded, pity gradually edging out his anger.

The younger man moistened his lips. "At first it seemed as if I could never spend it all. I stayed in Paris and London for a while, always in the best hotels. And I treated the ladies royally, buying them Worth gowns and diamond trinkets." He paused meaningfully. "But at last it did run out."

"So you're completely without funds?"

Brandon frowned. "Not entirely. My checking account is flat, but I do have some capital. I suppose Papa pounded some sense into my head after all. I bought some stock that has done well. If I can liquidate, I'll have enough to start again."

He let out a sigh of deep regret. "I knew I wasn't a member of the family anymore, that I didn't really have the right to call myself your brother, but I got so homesick I even considered coming back and asking you for a job in the lumber yard."

He crossed the room and flopped into a chair. "But I knew I could never return and face your wrath." He tossed back the whiskey. "I became so homesick for North Carolina I bought some of the Southern papers. One day I read about Isabelle dying. Her family being so old and established, her obituary was in some of the publications." He hunched over and raked back his drooping hair. "I actually bought a rail ticket the day I learned of her death—but in the end, I just couldn't come home," he confessed like a penitent child.

Stephen felt a kick in his guts. What torture Brandon had endured, longing to come home but so full of pride that he couldn't. "Why didn't you write—try to get in touch with us?" he questioned, his voice becoming softer. "Didn't you know I would be worried about you?"

"I-I didn't think you wanted to hear from me," Brandon responded lamely. "After all I did to you, I wouldn't blame you if you did hate me." He slowly stood. "When I got the telegram about Tad, I knew I *had* to come, no matter what. Seeing that telegram changed something within me. I had no idea that Miss Jones was caring for Tad, but I knew she was someone close to the family. Someone here in Asheville had remembered me. Someone had taken the time to contact me—someone felt I was still a member of the family." He hung his head, then looked up again, anguish tightening his features. "Can you ever forgive me? If you can, I'd like to talk to you about the future."

Emotion flared within Stephen, ruining his vow to maintain a strictly objective view of the matter. He remembered Jubilee's words about pride tearing the family apart, and now he knew she was right. Lord, how confused and lost they'd all become in the last few years! He looked at a picture of his father that sat on his desk. The old man had been hard as a Carolina pine knot, and Stephen knew that Brandon's sad tale would have mattered little to him. "He made his bed—let the young fool sleep in it!" he could almost hear the old man storming.

Yet at the same time, he knew his father was wrong, just as he himself had been wrong about so many things. If he kept on carrying the grudge against Brandon, he'd be crushed under its weight. He had to let the past go or forget about any hopeful resolution for the future. He'd struggled to make changes in Wentworth Enterprises and had been successful; now it was time to make changes in his personal life.

He walked to Brandon and put out his hand. The younger man's eyes shone as brightly as if they'd been lit from within. "Welcome home, brother," Stephen said, his deep-timbred voice rasping with emotion. "It's good to have you back."

Early the next morning, Stephen sat down on the side of Tad's bed and, thinking he was looking stronger every day, watched him hold a small picture of his mother in his hands. "You loved her very much, didn't you?" he asked, remembering the day his son was born.

Tad, his eyes full, nodded. "Yes, I just can't forget her."

The words moved Stephen deeply. "That's good. I wouldn't want you to forget her." He caressed the boy's soft hair. "You know you'll never really lose her, don't you?" he asked, thinking how much the child looked like Isabelle. "The best part of her will stay with you forever."

Tad stared at him with glistening eyes. "Jubilee told me something like that once. At first I didn't understand what she meant, but I think I'm beginning to."

Stephen clasped his son's shoulder. "You'll never stop loving your mother, and I won't either, but there's room for other people in our hearts. That's the good thing about love."

Tad widened his eyes. "I know, Papa. Everybody is special. Jubilee told me that, too. And she said that love is the one commodity that grows the more you use it. It's like a big old cake of lye soap that just won't wash away, no matter how hard you rub it."

Stephen smiled, thinking she'd expressed the sentiment perfectly in one colorful statement that would stick in Tad's mind forever.

The boy looked at the photo lovingly one last time, then placed it on the bedside table. He stared at his father with big eyes. "Are you going after Jubilee, Papa?" he questioned, his voice threaded with eagerness. "I think Mama would be happy if you did."

Stephen swallowed hard. In effect, the boy had just given his permission for him to marry again. The child had been able to integrate his allegiance to his mother and his love for Jubilee. He'd been brave enough to love again. Could he say the same for himself? "Yes, I'm going after her. But it may be difficult to get her to come back with me," he admitted, regret cutting through him like a knife. "I hurt her feelings very much."

"I think she'll forgive you. She has a good heart." A thoughtful look came over the boy's face. "Getting her to forgive you won't be the hard thing. The real trouble is that she thinks she's a mountain lion."

Stephen blinked, wondering what on earth he was talking about. "A mountain lion?" he laughed.

Tad sat forward. "That's right. One time she told me she just didn't belong here in Asheville," he added, his eyes shining with intensity. "She said people didn't know what to make of her, and she didn't know how to act. She told me a mountain lion would never be able to live here, but get that critter back in the hills and he'd do just fine."

Feeling poured through Stephen as he considered the depth of her alienation. Somehow he had to make her believe he was proud of her—that she was fine just the way she was. Once she believed that, she would be comfortable living in town. He needed some gesture to show her how special she was and how much he loved her. But, Lord above, what could it be?

He took his son's soft hand, opened it, and dropped the button she'd left in his palm. "Jubilee left this button for you to remember her by," he said, glad the boy was now well enough to appreciate its significance. "Will you do me a favor?" he asked, somewhat surprised at the words he was going to say. "I want you to take care of this button while I'm gone, and put it under your pillow at night. I want you to wish just as hard as you can that I'll be able to bring her back."

Tad smiled and clutched the button tight. "Yes, I will, Papa"—a wide smile shot over his face—"and I like the way you're talking now. You never told me to wish before. You've changed."

A flicker of abashment ran through Stephen. "Well," he mumbled awkwardly, "maybe I have—just a little."

Tad widened his eyes. "Do you think Jubilee is really magic?"

"Well, I—"

"I'm sure she is. She's so special. I've never met anyone so special. Have you?"

"No—definitely not."

A smile shone on the boy's face. "Then I must be right."

His son's words had made him suddenly understand that Jubilee chose to believe in magic not out of backwoods ignorance, but out of faith and joy. It was indeed what made her so special. A moment of deep understanding bloomed in his heart. "Yes," Stephen sighed, "I think you're right."

He obeyed an urge to gather Tad in his arms and embrace him. "Good-bye," he breathed, knowing he must make amends with Jubilee not only for his sake but for the boy's as well. "Delilah and Brandon will see after you while I'm gone." Slowly releasing the boy's soft, warm body, he stood and walked to the door, then turned and surveyed him one last time.

"Don't worry, Papa," Tad piped up cheerfully. "I'll wish as hard as I can."

Stephen, a packed saddlebag slung over his shoulder, jogged down the mansion steps and saw Brandon leading his black stallion from the stable, the mount's tack glinting in the morning sun. His brother was smiling and the wind ruffled his hair, making him look young again and bringing back a floodtide of warm childhood memories. How good it was to have him back, Stephen decided, glad he'd followed his heart instead of turning him away.

After Stephen had strapped the saddlebag in place and mounted, he gazed down at his brother and took the proffered reins from his hand.

"Delilah told me Alice Tallant was still single," Brandon said, a grin playing about his lips. "I think I'll pay her a visit today," he added, looking mightily pleased with life in general.

Stephen smiled to himself. "Good," he offered, knowing that nothing else needed to be said.

Ready to go, he impulsively gazed up at Tad's window. Telling the boy to put the button under his pillow and wish him luck! Lord, was he going soft in the head? If so, he decided it was a rather pleasant feeling that he didn't want to give up.

He glanced at Brandon in farewell, then urged his horse into a slow trot down the driveway. A cool wind meet his face, and excitement sang in his blood at the prospect of seeing Jubilee again. He was almost at the gate when he heard Delilah's excited voice calling after him. He turned his horse and walked the mount toward her, wondering if he'd forgotten something.

Dressed in a Sunday dress with a snowy head rag and shawl, she lifted her calico skirt and hurried past Brandon. Down the driveway she came, waving a piece of paper in her hand. "Mist' Stephen, Mist' Stephen," she called, her shiny face beaming with happiness. "I's got some news for you, sir. You's just got to read this!"

He paced his horse to her, and when they met, she threw a hand over her heart and gasped for breath. "Look here," she cried, shoving a bulletin into his hand. "One of the maids done been to the white church this mornin' and she give me this. Read what it say. There be no way I can make out all them fancy words, but I's got enough sense to know what they be meaning." Her black eyes verily danced with excitement and she stabbed her finger at an announcement set off with flowery scrolls. "Seem to me, this be awful good news!"

Stephen unfolded the bulletin and started reading an announcement edged in ornate scrolls.

Reverend Horace Pennypacker announces the marriage of his beloved daughter Estell to Winston Throg. The couple wed last week in Knoxville and are now on a honeymoon tour of the West.

A deep rumble rose in Stephen's chest and burst from his lips. So, that's what had happened to Estell, he thought with a shaft of joy. "Yes, indeed," he told Delilah, folding the paper and slipping it into his pocket. "That's the best news I've heard in a month of Sundays!"

Chapter Twenty

Jubilee pushed aside the canned food on the cellar shelf and searched for a jar of spiced peaches for supper. Dub and Effie would return from their day visiting relatives with a good appetite, and after several hours of hunting, Micah would be hungry as a wolf. The cellar held a damp earthy scent, and she brushed away a thread of clinging cobwebs, reminding herself that it should be cleaned come spring.

Aided by a sun ray slanting down from the open door, she selected the largest jar of fruit she could find. The glass container shone in the shaft of dust-filled light, its yellow contents reminding her of golden suns studded with cloves. She recalled the day she'd picked the fruit last summer—the very day Stephen first arrived in the mountains. The ache inside of her heart swelled. Oh, if she could only relive the last months; if she could only change the past and make everything all right again.

Suddenly she heard the sound of footsteps crunching through the snow, and her mind leaped to alertness. Pulse racing, she prayed her visitor wasn't a hungry thief scouring the bitterly cold countryside for food.

Song of the Lark

She'd just turned about as a tall man stepped into view, silhouetted against the square of winter light. The glass jar slipped from her fingers and shattered against the hard-packed earthen floor, enveloping her in the scent of spiced peaches. The man was no more than a dark blur against the backlighting and a hat shaded his features, but she identified him immediately. *"Stephen,"* she gasped, her heart slamming against her ribs.

"Hello, Curly Top," he drawled, already making his way down the steps. Lean trousers clung to his legs, and a leather jacket, dusted with snowflakes, covered his wide shoulders. *Lordamercy, he's come*! she thought, her body atingle with joy. She hurried up the steps, desperately wanting to throw her arms about him. Then she caught herself. One look at his handsome face and she would turn all soft inside like a bowl of corn mush. Silly goose! Didn't she have a grain of sense? Hadn't he said he wasn't in the market for a wife? Did she have to make a fool of herself yet again?

"How did you know I was here?" she blurted out, splayed fingers going to her bosom.

He came down the steps and paused above her, his huge form filling the narrow cellar stairwell. "I followed your footprints from the cabin. Don't you have a greeting for me?" he prompted, his eager eyes moving over her.

Jubilee's heart began an uneasy thud. She ached to embrace him, but she dared not give in to the impulse. She had to keep her wits. She glanced down to avoid answering his question. "How is Tad?" she inquired in a quavering voice.

With warm fingers, Stephen lifted her chin. "He'll be fine now, but we almost lost him. He had encephalitis."

Gratitude poured through her, leaving her weak with relief. Still, a worrisome bit of doubt plagued her mind. "S-so my herbs didn't hurt him?"

Stephen had the grace to look shamefaced. "Not a bit. The specialist from Knoxville said they probably *helped* him. They certainly didn't cause him to become sicker."

A great burden slid from her shoulders. At the same time, a sense of righteous indignation seized her spirit. She'd known the herbs wouldn't hurt the boy, but Stephen's disapproval had shaken her confidence and made her devalue her skills.

Gently he clasped her shoulders. "I was wrong," he admitted, looking her in the eyes. "I owe you an apology for what I said."

Her pride simply wouldn't let her consider accepting his apology now. "After what you told me, the apology comes a little late," she challenged, her voice threaded with hurt.

A muscle flicked in Stephen's tense jaw. His eyes deepened with passion as they had the day he first made love to her by the pool. "I realize that," he murmured, his eyes searching her face intently. "But I offer it to you now with all my heart."

How nonchalant he sounded now that he was trying to get back into her good graces, she thought, her tender sensibilities still bruised. Did he think her forgiveness came that easily after she'd worried and fretted herself sick? She backed down a step and removed her body from his hands. "Granny is gone," she whispered, trying to turn the apology aside.

Sadness shone in his eyes. "I'm truly sorry. She was a remarkable woman and I'll miss her." For a moment a heavy silence hung between them, then his expression became warm. "Oh, by the way, your telegram worked. Brandon has returned, poorer but also much wiser. He wants to liquidate his stocks and bonds and put the money into Wentworth Enterprises. With the right contracts, next year at this time we'll be out of the red."

The news made the blood rush strong and joyful to her heart, but still she remained silent. One part of her ached to tell him that she was carrying his child, but in a fresh burst of pride, she decided to keep the precious secret to

Song of the Lark

herself. After learning of his vow, she'd never try to trap him into marriage by making him feel guilty. She'd lose what pride she had left, and when all was said and done, he'd end up hating her.

More nervous by the second, she decided to brush past him and run to the cabin. She scrambled upward, but he was too fast for her. He scooped her into his arms and pressed her against him, and that familiar tingle swirled in the pit of her stomach. She beat against his chest and tried to squirm away, but he held her tight. "Let me go," she demanded. "Go back to Asheville—go back to Estell!"

"That would be impossible," he replied with a dry twist of his lips. "She married Winston Throg."

"Winston Throg?" she echoed, scarcely believing him. "Why, she's crazy in love with *you.*"

"She was crazy in love with my supposed fortune. She snooped around while Tad was sick and discovered I was broke. Throg had always been sweet on her, so she wasted no time in marrying him." Amusement lit Stephen's eyes. "The only thing I can't figure out is why she first suspected that I might be short of funds."

Jubilee could have answered the question, for she vividly recalled the day she'd defended Chambers and revealed that Stephen was having financial difficulties. But none of this mattered now. No doubt Estell would earn ten times over every penny she received from the grouchy, tight-fisted Throg. Sadly, this exciting piece of good news came far too late for Jubilee. She struggled to free herself from Stephen's arms. "What are you doing here? Why did you come?" she demanded, her heart fluttering crazily.

Stephen looked into Jubilee's large, frightened eyes, thinking she was as beautiful as ever. Lord, how he'd missed her, missed her tender face and beloved warmth, her soft voice and silken lips. He gathered her tighter and noticed a pulse throbbing in the hollow of her throat. "I came to do this," he replied, knowing he must tell her only the truth. He nuzzled her cool neck and delicate ear, then brushed his lips over hers, their breaths intermingling. Yes, this was what he'd come for, he thought, now slanting his mouth over hers in a firm kiss. To feel those satiny lips under his, to press her soft breasts against his chest, to know she was safe, enfolded in his arms—this was heaven.

He ran a hand through her cool, silky hair and let a smooth lock slip between his fingers. His heart beating a little faster, he tilted her head backward so he could look into her shimmering eyes. "Lord, how I've missed you. I truly can't find words to tell you how much."

He moved his lips over hers and she trembled in response. When he drew her closer yet, she sighed his name. Now their tongues intertwined in beloved battle and her breath came in rough gasps. His roaming hands moved over her luscious curves and explored the soft body he'd dreamed of since the day she'd left. A low groan reverberated from his throat as he molded her against him. When Jubilee eagerly returned each of his loving caresses, fire ran through his veins and the once tender kiss turned into a white-hot whirlpool of passion.

Then to his dismay, she gradually stiffened in his arms, and a sense of loss and emptiness overcame him. Slowly she moved away, and in the dim light her eyes glittered like two fiery stars. *"No,"* she murmured miserably, "I'm not going to let this happen again!"

He looked down at her, filled with remorse. "Can't you ever forgive me? I'll spend my life trying to make up for those foolish words."

She widened her eyes at his last comment. A tear coursed over her finely sculpted cheek and he flicked it away with his finger. She stared at him silently, but when he lowered his head to kiss her once more, she pulled backward. Their gazes dueled for a moment longer, and then he stepped back to let her pass. He'd never held a

Song of the Lark

woman by force, never kissed one who hadn't wanted to be kissed, and he wasn't going to begin now.

Relief shone in her eyes, and she picked up her skirt and swept past him. Her boot heels clattered as she climbed up the rest of the rocky steps and left the cellar in a swirl of petticoats.

He exited the cellar and saw her run toward the cabin. She disappeared around the side of the structure, and moments later lights bloomed orange in its windows. He was tired, cold, and humiliated as well, for the woman he loved wouldn't let him apologize. He took off his hat and smacked it against his leg.

Snow had started falling again, and a cold wind made him turn up his collar. He sighed heavily and decided this operation might take a little longer than he'd expected. But if this mountain spitfire thought she could get rid of him simply by locking herself away, she had another think coming!

He slapped on his hat, smiled to himself, and started leisurely walking to the cabin.

"No, You can't come in!" Jubilee hollered through the sturdy cabin door. "Go away. I don't want to talk to you anymore."

Stephen had been beating on the door for ten minutes and he balled his fist and banged again, noticing his hand was becoming sore. He searched the vicinity for a large stick, then whacked it against the door, making even more noise. "Don't think I'm going away," he shouted with a ring of determination. "I'll bang till I get in. I'll camp out here all night if I have to!"

"Are you deaf? Go away!"

Stephen pounded for five minutes, then spied Jubilee holding a kerosene lamp to the window and staring out at him. Of course! he laughed to himself. Why hadn't he thought of her precious glass panes before? She'd bragged about them enough, saying Granny's cabin had the finest windows in the hollow, when most of the other cabins only had shutters.

He strode to the window and waved the stick in the air. "You better open up, young lady, or I'll break this pane and crawl in that way!"

A look of horror flooded Jubilee's face. "No, you can't do that! Lordamercy, we had to order these panes from Knoxville. If you break a window, it'll be months before we can get another. We'll freeze to death!"

Stephen chuckled. He'd won his first battle—now for the second. "Let me in, Jubilee Jones, or I'll break out *all* the windowpanes!" he warned, hauling back the huge stick and taking aim at the glass.

Jubilee, her expression fraught with anguish, cried, "No, you wouldn't do that. No one would be mean enough to do that!"

Stephen rotated the stick, ready to swing it, then drew it back over his shoulder. "I wouldn't, huh? Just watch me!" He drew out his actions, then dramatically swung the stick, knowing he would miss the window by mere inches. "Damn," he yelled, stepping a little closer. "I won't miss again!"

When he drew back again, Jubilee placed the kerosene lantern aside and screamed, "No, stop! Wait a minute!"

He heard her scramble to the door, and positioned himself so he could barge in as soon as she threw the latch. It rattled and he stormed into the cabin so quickly that Jubilee staggered backward. Her face a mask of horrified surprise, she clutched at the table to right herself.

Gasping in shock, Jubilee focused on Stephen's grinning face. Loradamercy, the rascal had actually threatened to break all the windowpanes like a rowdy schoolboy just to get his way! Had the suave, sophisticated Stephen Wentworth she knew gone mad? At the same time, she experienced a warm glow that he hadn't let her fob him off by locking herself in the cabin. He slammed the door and walked closer, but she backed away, her temper rising

Song of the Lark

with every step he took. "You must be out of your mind," she rasped in an outraged tone. "You must have gone slap crazy since the last time I saw you!"

Amusement played over his rugged features. "That's right. I *am* crazy—crazy in love with you."

Hot blood stung her cheeks. She stared at him, awestruck. He'd actually said he was in love with her! Her heart leapt in her breast, tears welled in her eyes, and her lips began to quiver. "I-I've never heard you talk like this," she stammered, secretly thrilled at his words.

"Well, get used to it, because starting today, I'm going to tell you I love you every day," he added, trying to take her in his arms.

She twisted away, her heart pounding deeply. He was a man possessed! Could this be the cool, collected owner of Wentworth Enterprises? What would he do next?

He flung his hat upon the table. "I'll bet you're plenty mad at me. I'll bet you're mighty sore." He chuckled a little. "Why, I'll bet you'd like to just haul off and hit me across the face as hard as you can." He smiled, his teeth a striking white in his tanned face. "Well, why don't you? It'd make you feel a lot better."

Jubilee blinked, for she'd nursed that very thought on the cellar steps. Had the man read her mind?

He walked forward, full of wit and good cheer. "Come on," he challenged, tapping his cheek invitingly. "Hit me as hard as you can. Put a wallop into it. Get all the anger out of your system so we can communicate with each other."

Jubilee edged backward, more uncertain than ever. She knew how his hard muscles felt under her fingertips, how his demanding lips felt on hers, but she'd never encountered the strange, unexplainable rush of pleasure he was producing in her now. "D-don't talk crazy," she spluttered, realizing that he'd soon have her cornered.

"I'm not talking crazy. I'm talking damn good sense," he laughed, his cheerful mood wearing down her resentment against him. "Stop edging backward like a scared crayfish and just wallop me good. It doesn't matter—open hand or fist. Put all your weight into it. It'll clear the air and make us both feel better."

Jubilee considered his words. In fact, the more he talked about walloping him, the better she liked the idea. And he made such an irresistible target, standing there tapping his cheek, grinning, inviting her to hit him as hard as she could! "All right," she finally agreed, her heart pounding wildly. She scanned his relaxed body. "Aren't you going to brace yourself?"

"Brace myself?" he hooted with a cocky air. "Brace myself against a little girl like you. Why, I—"

Before he could finish his sentence, she doubled her fist, then swung, putting all her force, all her pent-up anger, all her resentment into the blow. When she connected with his jaw, his eyes shot open in surprise, and to her amazement, he stumbled backward and fell against a flour barrel. Down he went, all arms and legs, landing flat on his back, the barrel tumbling over with him.

Jubilee gasped at the pain in her knuckles not believing her own strength. Her anger and resentment fell away like snow sliding from a steep mountainside and she worried that she'd hurt him. She hurriedly knelt and pushed the barrel aside, then took his head in her arms. "Oh, no! Are you all right? I told you to brace yourself!"

Stephen blinked up at her, his face covered with flour. He moved his jaw with his hand and opened and closed his mouth several times. "Damn, woman! Where did you learn to slug like that?"

He looked so funny, Jubilee chuckled in spite of herself. "Micah taught me," she answered, wiping the flour from his face. "He said he wanted me to know how to protect myself from the peckerwoods."

Stephen struggled to a sitting position. He chuckled as he clasped her hand and kissed each of her knuckles. "All I can say is God help the peckerwoods!"

Song of the Lark

Jubilee was beginning to relax. In fact, she felt better than she had since she'd left Asheville. Suddenly everything seemed better. Tad would live, Brandon and Micah had come home, and since Stephen had confessed his love, it was almost impossible to stay mad at him anymore. When he took her in his arms, they both laughed until tears came to their eyes. "What are we going to talk about?" she asked, ruffling her hands through his hair and dusting flour to the floor.

"I didn't say we were going to talk," he answered, cocking a playful brow. "I said we were going to communicate."

She smiled at him, her emotions all topsy-turvey, her heart melting. "How can we communicate without talking?" she asked, that warm, familiar feeling he always produced stealing over her.

Pulling her with him, he stood, and gathered her in his arms. He reverently trailed his fingers over her face. "I'll show you," he answered, his expression never changing. "It's the best way a man and a woman can ever communicate."

His lips brushed hers, then their mouths welded together in a breathtaking kiss. His hands swept over her, warming her flesh with a tingling passion, and she trembled in his arms. How wonderful it felt, and how she wanted it! They were nearly breathless when he eased her away and gazed down at her with full eyes. "I love you, Jubilee Jones—love you with all my heart and soul."

He'd said it not once, but twice, she thought wildly. She'd felt so lonely and deserted for days that she sobbed deep in her throat. "And I love you, too—even if your name is Wentworth," she confessed in a quaking voice, leaning her head against his shoulder.

He chuckled, then tilted her head so she was looking up at him. "Am I forgiven?" he inquired. "Or do you want to take another swing at me? Warn me if you do, so I can brace myself!"

Jubilee laughed and threaded her fingers into his thick hair, relishing the feel of his thudding heart against her breast. Would it be grace and forgiveness or condemnation and loneliness? The question was easy to answer. Thank God, they'd been given a chance to start over. "I think I've had my fill of retribution for one day," she whispered tenderly. "I forgive you."

He actually groaned with relief, prompting her to study him with a thoughtful sigh. "Somehow you're different. You don't sound like yourself, like Stephen Wentworth."

He beamed down at her. "Funny you should say that. Tad said the same thing recently." His eyes sparkled with deep love. "Where is your button necklace?"

Surprised, she bit her bottom lip. "I put it away for a while."

"Well, go get it, I'd like to see you in it again. I've decided I like it much better than your pearl necklace."

She retrieved the necklace from the chest and gave it to him.

Gently he slipped it over her hair and draped it around her neck. Truth be told, she thought, it did feel right to have the necklace on again. Why, it was like having an important part of herself back again.

His eyes warmly erotic, he stroked her hair. "Will you marry me? Tad needs you desperately but I need you a thousand times more—need you until the day I die."

Jubilee felt as if the ground had vanished beneath her and trembled with emotion. She met his loving eyes, lightheaded with joy. "Y-you want me to marry you?" she asked in a strangled sob. "But what about your vow? I don't understand. I—"

"I've cast that foolish idea aside," Stephen confessed, his eyes growing serious. "I only made it to myself because I was afraid of being hurt again." He kissed her forehead, her cheeks, her eyes. "You taught me that love is the finest thing around. Now I see it's worth risking everything to gain it." His face softened. "I'll no longer be wearing armor on my heart. In fact, it's yours for the taking."

Jubilee throat tightened with emotion. "But you deserve someone more suitable," she breathed, still feeling unworthy of him. "You saw what happened when I lived in Asheville. I made mistakes at every turn, I—"

Stephen laughed and shook her gently. "Oh yes, I forgot about you being a mountain lion. Tad warned me you would bring it up."

Jubilee remembered the day she'd given Tad that particular speech. "But it's true. I don't fit into Asheville society, and you know I don't!"

He cradled the back of her head. "I like my women a bit unpredictable, just like the mountain weather. Besides, don't you know how special you are—how unique and important? You took a little smidgen of a dream and made it into a reality. You showed me a world with no boundaries or rules." His eyes became more tender than she'd ever seen them. "You opened the door to heaven and let me walk in."

"But we're so different."

"Nonsense! We're a man and a woman." He gave her a little kiss, soft as a rose petal. "And we're that close. We may be from different backgrounds, and sometimes have different ways of looking at life, but our values, what we hold dear, are very much the same."

She stared at him, trying to digest all that he'd said.

He cupped her face and kissed her forehead. "Let's have an imagination lesson. Imagine us living back in Asheville."

"I don't think I can. I can't imagine me being Mrs. Stephen Wentworth."

He pulled a horrified face. "Don't tell me that, after preaching to Tad about the most important muscle in the human body, you're going to lose its use." He brushed his fingers over her eyelids and closed them. "Imagine us living in the mansion with Tad and a magic cat named

Matilda. Imagine us eating magic vegetables out of our magic garden—all grown by staying right with the moon, of course. He kissed her eyelids, ruffling her lashes. "And last of all, imagine us producing brothers and sisters for Tad."

She opened her eyes, then slowly placed his hand on her stomach. "No imagination is necessary there. That's already a true fact."

Stephen widened his eyes, then a huge smile broke over his face. "You mean," he stammered, swallowing hard, "that we're—"

"That's right. Are you glad?"

Stephen clasped her waist and swung her about, laughing all the while. "Of course, I'm more than glad—I'm ecstatic," he answered, gently settling her feet on the floor. There was a tender expression on his face that made her heart pound with happiness. "I adore you, Jubilee Jones," he murmured in his deep, silky voice. He clutched her head and planted so many tiny kisses on her upturned face that she burst out laughing. "You're more precious to me than ever. I hope the baby is a girl," he said with dancing eyes. He tilted his head. "If you listen you can hear her and Tad playing right now." He raised a challenging brow. "Now who's the believer?"

She'd never seen him like this, and dumbfounded, she couldn't stop laughing.

He sighed and gazed down at her, his face wreathed in bliss. "I've learned to believe in that everyday magic you were talking about," he confessed in an earnest tone. "I learned to find those everyday miracles and hold them close." He raised her hand and pressed warm lips against her palm. "You showed me how. Now tell me a person like yourself isn't important. Tell me a person like you doesn't deserve to live in the finest mansion in Asheville. And last of all, tell me that you'll marry me."

She looked at him silently, too moved to speak. And now there came a thought so new to her that she was struck with wonder. It didn't matter what anyone else said or thought if Stephen was happy with her. With this wisdom, a strange peace came flowing gently through her veins and stilled her restless heart. All she had to do was open her mouth and accept his proposal. "Yes, I'll marry you—and I'll put it in writing if you want!" she answered, feeling as if the sun were glowing within her heart.

He slipped something from his pocket and laid it in her open palm.

At first she only knew it was hard and cold, then she looked down and spied a button—the most beautiful button she'd ever seen. It was gold and studded with diamonds that glittered like sunlight! She suddenly realized that he'd bought the most beautiful button in Asheville to offer her instead of a wedding ring, and tears rolled down her cheeks. The gesture said everything. It said he not only loved her, but honored and respected her ways. He didn't want to change her, he wanted her just as she was!

Stephen held her close. "I remember what you'd said about saving a sparkly button for your marriage day. I hope this one will do just as well—and I hope you'll wear your button necklace the day we're wed. I want everyone in Asheville to get a good look at it."

She clutched the button in her hand, then stood on her tiptoes and looped her arms about his neck. "Oh, yes. It's the most beautiful button in the world!"

Stephen covered her lips with his, and during that glorious moment, she realized she'd grown into a joy larger than herself, into a bliss beyond words. And she suddenly experienced a transforming strength, a core buried deep within her that would refuse to be daunted by life's storms or trifling problems. Jubilee Jones had followed her heart through both unpredictable weather and fair, and she'd inherited heaven in the process.

That, she told herself, was true magic indeed.

NORAH HESS
Wildfire

Bestselling Author Of *Storm*

"A grand and beautiful love story....Never a dull moment! A masterpiece about the American spirit."
—*Affaire de Coeur*

The Yankees killed her sweetheart, imprisoned her brother, and drove her from her home, but beautiful, golden-haired Serena Bain faces the future boldly as the wagon trains roll out. Ahead lie countless dangers. But all the perils in the world won't change her bitter resentment of the darkly handsome Yankee wagon master, Josh Quade.

Soon, however, her heart betrays her will. Serena cannot resist her own mounting desire for the rough trapper from Michigan. His strong, rippling, buckskin-clad body sets her senses on fire. But pride and fate continue to tear them apart as the wagon trains roll west—until one night, in the soft, secret darkness of a bordello, Serena and Josh unleash their wildest passions and open their souls to the sweetest raptures of love.

_51988-7 $4.99 US/$5.99 CAN

Dorchester Publishing Co., Inc.
P.O. Box 6640
Wayne, PA 19087-8640

Please add $1.75 for shipping and handling for the first book and $.50 for each book thereafter. NY, NYC, and PA residents, please add appropriate sales tax. No cash, stamps, or C.O.D.s. All orders shipped within 6 weeks via postal service book rate. Canadian orders require $2.00 extra postage and must be paid in U.S. dollars through a U.S. banking facility.

Name_____
Address_____
City_____State_____Zip_____
I have enclosed $_____ in payment for the checked book(s).
Payment <u>must</u> accompany all orders. ☐ Please send a free catalog.

Beautiful and spirited Kathleen Haley sets sail from England for the family estate in Savannah. On board ship, she meets the man who will forever haunt her heart, the dashing and domineering Captain Reed Taylor. On the long, perilous voyage, she resists his bold advances—until she wakes from unconsciousness after a storm and hears Reed's shocking confession. She then knows she must marry the rogue.

But their fiery conflict is far from over. Through society balls, raging duels and torrid nights, Kathleen seeks vengeance on Reed's brutal passions and his secret alliance with pirates. At last she is forced to attack the very man who has warmed her icy heart and burned his way into her very soul.

____4303-3 $5.99 US/$6.99 CAN

Dorchester Publishing Co., Inc.
P.O. Box 6640
Wayne, PA 19087-8640

Please add $1.75 for shipping and handling for the first book and $.50 for each book thereafter. NY, NYC, and PA residents, please add appropriate sales tax. No cash, stamps, or C.O.D.s. All orders shipped within 6 weeks via postal service book rate. Canadian orders require $2.00 extra postage and must be paid in U.S. dollars through a U.S. banking facility.

Name_____
Address_____
City_____State_____Zip_____
I have enclosed $_____ in payment for the checked book(s).
Payment <u>must</u> accompany all orders. ❏ Please send a free catalog.

Bestselling Author of *Hand & Heart of a Soldier*

With a name that belies his true nature, Joshua Angell was born for deception. So when sophisticated and proper Ava Moreland first sees the sexy drifter in a desolate Missouri jail, she knows he is the one to save her sister from a ruined reputation and a fatherless child. But she will need Angell to fool New York society into thinking he is the ideal husband—and only Ava can teach him how. But what start as simple lessons in etiquette and speech soon become smoldering lessons in love. And as the beautiful socialite's feelings for Angell deepen, so does her passion—and finally she knows she will never be satisfied until she, and no other, claims him as her very own...untamed angel.

___4274-6 $4.99 US/$5.99 CAN

Dorchester Publishing Co., Inc.
P.O. Box 6640
Wayne, PA 19087-8640

Please add $1.75 for shipping and handling for the first book and $.50 for each book thereafter. NY, NYC, and PA residents, please add appropriate sales tax. No cash, stamps, or C.O.D.s. All orders shipped within 6 weeks via postal service book rate. Canadian orders require $2.00 extra postage and must be paid in U.S. dollars through a U.S. banking facility.

Name_____
Address_____
City_____State_____Zip_____
I have enclosed $_____ in payment for the checked book(s).
Payment <u>must</u> accompany all orders. ❑ Please send a free catalog.

TIMESWEPT TRAVELER
ELAINE FOX

With a thriving business and a stalled personal life, Shelby Manning never figures her life is any worse—or better—than the norm. Then a late-night stroll through a Civil War battlefield park leads her to a most intriguing stranger. Bloody, confused, and dressed in Union blue, he insists he has just come from the Battle of Fredericksburg—more than one hundred years in the past.

Maybe Shelby should dismiss Carter Lindsey as crazy—just another history reenactor taking his game a little too seriously. But there is something compelling in the pull of his eyes, something special in his tender touch. And before she knows it, Shelby finds herself swept into a passion like none she's ever known—and willing to defy time itself to keep Carter at her side.

_52074-5 $4.99 US/$6.99 CAN

Dorchester Publishing Co., Inc.
P.O. Box 6640
Wayne, PA 19087-8640

Please add $1.75 for shipping and handling for the first book and $.50 for each book thereafter. NY, NYC, and PA residents, please add appropriate sales tax. No cash, stamps, or C.O.D.s. All orders shipped within 6 weeks via postal service book rate. Canadian orders require $2.00 extra postage and must be paid in U.S. dollars through a U.S. banking facility.

Name_____
Address_____
City_____State_____Zip_____
I have enclosed $_____ in payment for the checked book(s).
Payment <u>must</u> accompany all orders. ❑ Please send a free catalog.

TERMS OF SURRENDER

SHIRL HENKE

"Historical romance at its best!"
—*Romantic Times*

Devilishly handsome Rhys Davies owns half of Starlight, Colorado, within weeks of riding into town. But there is one "property" he'll give all the rest to possess, because Victoria Laughton—the glacially beautiful daughter of Starlight's first family—detests Rhys's flamboyant arrogance. And she hates her own unladylike response to his compelling masculinity even more. To win the lady, Rhys will have to wager his very life, hoping that the devil does, indeed, look after his own.

_3424-7 $4.99 US/$5.99 CAN

Dorchester Publishing Co., Inc.
P.O. Box 6640
Wayne, PA 19087-8640

Please add $1.75 for shipping and handling for the first book and $.50 for each book thereafter. NY, NYC, and PA residents, please add appropriate sales tax. No cash, stamps, or C.O.D.s. All orders shipped within 6 weeks via postal service book rate. Canadian orders require $2.00 extra postage and must be paid in U.S. dollars through a U.S. banking facility.

Name_____
Address_____
City_____State_____Zip_____
I have enclosed $_____ in payment for the checked book(s).
Payment <u>must</u> accompany all orders. ❏ Please send a free catalog.

KENTUCKY BRIDE

NORAH HESS

Winner of the *Romantic Times* Lifetime Achievement Award

Fleeing her abusive uncle, young D'lise Alexander trusts no man...until she is rescued by virile trapper Kane Devlin. His rugged strength and tender concern convince D'lise she will find a safe haven in his backwoods homestead. There, amid the simple pleasures of cornhuskings and barn raisings, she discovers that Kane has kindled a blaze of desire that burns even hotter than the flames in his rugged stone hearth. Beneath his soul-stirring kisses she is able to forget her fears, forget everything except her longing to become his sweet Kentucky bride.

_4046-8 $5.99 US/$6.99 CAN

Dorchester Publishing Co., Inc.
P.O. Box 6640
Wayne, PA 19087-8640

Please add $1.75 for shipping and handling for the first book and $.50 for each book thereafter. NY, NYC, and PA residents, please add appropriate sales tax. No cash, stamps, or C.O.D.s. All orders shipped within 6 weeks via postal service book rate. Canadian orders require $2.00 extra postage and must be paid in U.S. dollars through a U.S. banking facility.

Name_____
Address_____
City_____State_____Zip_____
I have enclosed $_____ in payment for the checked book(s).
Payment <u>must</u> accompany all orders. ❏ Please send a free catalog.

ATTENTION ROMANCE CUSTOMERS!

SPECIAL TOLL-FREE NUMBER
1-800-481-9191

*Call Monday through Friday
10 a.m. to 9 p.m.
Eastern Time
Get a free catalogue,
join the Romance Book Club,
and order books using your
Visa, MasterCard,
or Discover®*

Leisure Books

Love Spell

GO ONLINE WITH US AT DORCHESTERPUB.COM